"I wish I could remove my stockings," she murmured. "But even this feels heavenly."

Quint swallowed hard and crossed his arms over his chest. The image of her sliding stockings down her bare legs was too erotic to dwell on—not if he didn't want an obvious erection frightening her. "I am not surprised. Traipsing through the mews of Mayfair is exhausting business."

"Indeed it is," she returned cheerfully.

"Why have you returned, Sophie?"

She stared at her toes, moving them back and forth, hesitating. He sensed she was attempting to fabricate a reason because she didn't want to tell him the real one.

"The truth," he said.

"It seemed a nice night for a stroll. You are generally up late, so I thought I'd see if you were still awake."

He snorted. No lady strolled by herself in the middle of the night. "You are aware I live alone. That this is a bachelor's residence?"

"Should I be worried? Are you planning to chain me to your bed and ravish me at your whim?"

He strove not to combine the words "ravish" and "Sophie" in his head; the idea only served to remind him of what he could never have. "Indeed. Merely allow me to remove the other woman there first."

She chuckled. "That's one thing hardly anyone realizes about you: how amusing you are."

Books by Joanna Shupe

The Courtesan Duchess

The Harlot Countess

The Lady Hellion

Published by Kensington Publishing Corporation

The LADY HELLION

JOANNA SHUPE

ZEBRA BOOKS
KENSINGTON PUBLISHING CORP.
http://www.kensingtonbooks.com

ZEBRA BOOKS are published by

Kensington Publishing Corp.
119 West 40th Street
New York, NY 10018

Copyright © 2015 by Joanna Shupe

All rights reserved. No part of this book may be reproduced in any
form or by any means without the prior written consent of the Publisher, excepting brief quotes used in reviews.

To the extent that the image or images on the cover of this book
depict a person or persons, such person or persons are merely
models, and are not intended to portray any character or characters
featured in the book.

If you purchased this book without a cover you should be aware
that this book is stolen property. It was reported as "unsold and
destroyed" to the Publisher and neither the Author nor the Publisher
has received any payment for this "stripped book."

All Kensington titles, imprints, and distributed lines are available
at special quantity discounts for bulk purchases for sales promo-
tion, premiums, fund-raising, educational, or institutional use.

Special book excerpts or customized printings can also be created
to fit specific needs. For details, write or phone the office of the
Kensington Sales Manager: Attn.: Sales Department. Kensington
Publishing Corp., 119 West 40th Street, New York, NY 10018.
Phone: 1-800-221-2647.

Zebra and the Z logo Reg. U.S. Pat. & TM Off.

First Printing: June 2015
ISBN-13: 978-1-4201-3556-5
ISBN-10: 1-4201-3556-2

eISBN-13: 978-1-4201-3557-2
eISBN-10: 1-4201-3557-0

10 9 8 7 6 5 4 3 2 1

Printed in the United States of America

To my parents,
who first showed me what happily ever after looked like.

And to Rich,
who gave me my very own.

Acknowledgments

Many people were instrumental in shaping the Wicked Deceptions series. Thank you to the countless friends and acquaintances who patiently answered my questions about titles, pistols, science, and everything else I struggled with.

I am so grateful for the New Jersey Romance Writers, as well as my own critique group, The Violet Femmes. To Janet, Michele, Maria, Tina, Diana, Julie, RoseAnn: Thank you for all of the advice, the last-minute reads, the toasts, and the friendship.

Thank you to Laura Bradford for her guidance and for believing in me. I am so grateful to have her in my corner. Also thank you to Peter Senftleben for loving this series as much as I do and giving it life. I love when my writing makes him laugh.

Grateful does not begin to describe how I feel about Diana Quincy, Michele Mannon, and JB Schroeder. These ladies are my rocks. And a giant thank-you to my plot maven, Lin Gavin, who reads everything first and (usually) insists I can do better. She is my harshest critic, my biggest fan, and my first line of defense.

Thank you to my sister, Denise, who started me on this crazy journey. And to my mom, who first introduced me to romance books, thank you for believing in me. You're a tireless champion, and I hope I made you proud.

To my two little girls, I hope you both grow up to be strong, smart, kind, and kick ass women. Thank you for understanding when Mommy sneaks away with her laptop for an hour or two every day.

I need to thank my amazing husband, who has always supported my dream to write. He goes above and beyond, smoothing the way for me to pursue this career, and I appreciate him more than I can say. I am one lucky lady.

To the readers, bloggers, reviewers, writers, and fans, thank you for supporting romance, most especially historical romance. You make this the greatest job in the world.

Chapter One

February 1820

Padding the crotch of one's trousers required a surprising amount of skill. Too big of a bulge drew attention. Too small and you risked the thing slipping down your leg.

Fortunately, Lady Sophia Barnes had enough experience to achieve the perfect balance. No one looking at her now would believe her a lady of twenty-seven, the daughter of a wealthy and powerful marquess—not dressed as she was, in gentleman's finery from head to toe.

Just as no one would believe her spare time was spent investigating matters for a class of women most Londoners did not even want to think about.

The evening, though chilly and unpleasant, had been moderately productive. As Sophie approached the hackney, the driver jumped down to open the door. Her maid, Alice, sat inside, huddled under blankets. Alice waited until the door closed before she spoke. "Well, my lady?"

Sophie knocked on the roof to signal the driver.

Then she pulled a folded paper out of the pocket of her greatcoat. "No trace of Natalia, but I did find this." Beth, the girl who'd hired Sophie, was worried that ill had befallen her friend. Though Beth had now found herself a protector, Natalia still worked in a tavern near the docks, where extra coins meant taking a customer to the second-floor rooms. The two girls corresponded every week without fail, and Natalia hadn't sent word for almost a month.

Tonight, Sophie had gained access to Natalia's room and searched it. The only letter she'd found was in Russian.

Sophie stretched her unencumbered legs in the small space as the carriage rumbled forth into the night. Breeches really were a spectacular invention. "I wish I knew what it said. Beth only speaks English."

"We'd need to find someone who can speak Russian, my lady."

A name came to mind. A name she tried not to think of more than five—or ten—times a day. She often failed even at that. "I do know someone who speaks Russian. Lord Quint. He gave a short lecture during a gathering at the Russian Embassy three years ago." Sophie had attended, standing in the rear of the room. She hadn't understood a word, but oh, he'd been glorious. Speaking on some recent scientific discovery, he'd commanded the attention of everyone present, even making the dour-faced Russians laugh at several points.

Alice clucked her tongue. "La, his lordship won't be speaking it for long, that's for certain."

"Whatever do you mean?"

Her sharp tone caught Alice's attention. "I thought your ladyship knew. He's near death's door, that one. I saw one of his lordship's kitchen maids three—no, maybe four days ago. Fever's set in. His lordship won't let any of the staff tend to him and won't allow a physician in."

Sophie's stomach plummeted through the carriage floor and onto the dirty Southwark streets. No doubt Alice told the truth. The maid's network of servants would put any foreign spy service to shame. *Quint . . .* near death's door. Oh, God. She knew a bullet had grazed him that night at Maggie's house, right before the fire had swept in. But she'd assumed he'd recovered. Everyone had said the injury wasn't serious. Damn, if only she hadn't been so wrapped up in her own life—

Her fist banged the roof. The driver opened the small partition and Sophie barked in her low register, "Stop at the southwest corner of Berkeley Square instead." Quint lived just down the square from her father's town house so she would get out and let Alice continue on.

"What are you going to do, my lady?"

Was it not obvious? "I'm going to save him."

Alice gasped. "You cannot very well show up at his front door"—her hand waved at Sophie's attire— "dressed like that."

"Why not?"

"They'll not let a stranger inside to see him, even one dressed as a gent. And besides—"

"Do not even start lecturing me on propriety. We bid farewell to that ship eons ago, Alice. Not to worry, I'll manage a way into his house."

By the time she arrived at the servants' door of Quint's town house, Sophie had conjured a plausible story. A bleary-eyed older woman in a nightcap opened the door, a frown on her wrinkled face. "Yes?"

"I am here"—Sophie deepened her voice—"at the

behest of His Grace the Duke of Colton to attend to his lordship."

The woman held up her light, looked Sophie up and down. "You're a surgeon?"

"A valet, though I do have extensive medical knowledge."

"From a duke, you say?"

Sophie lifted her chin. "Indeed. And I do not think His Grace would appreciate you leaving me on the stoop to freeze."

The woman stood aside to allow Sophie to enter. They went into the kitchens, where Sophie removed her hat and greatcoat. "Where may I find his lordship?"

"His chambers. Won't let anyone in, not even a doctor. Most of the staff's already left. Figure every one of us will be out on the street in a day or two."

Without another word, the woman turned and shuffled to the corridor. *Must be his cook*, Sophie thought, and followed. "Stairs," the woman mumbled, handed Sophie her lamp, and continued on.

A few wrong turns, but Sophie finally found the master apartments. Inside, the air was cold and stale, the fire left untended. Moonlight trickled in from the windows, enough to allow her to see a large shape, motionless, under the coverlet. Quint. *Please God, let him be alive.*

She rushed over, and then nearly gasped. *Dear heavens.* His condition was worse than she'd feared. His skin was waxen, his lips cracked and swollen. His eyes were closed, with blue-black smudges underneath them. She shot her hand out to feel the side of his throat not covered with a bandage. Though his skin burned to the touch, she exhaled in relief. A pulse. Weak, but there.

She set her light on the table beside him. "Oh, Damien," she whispered, unable to resist gently smoothing the damp hair off his fevered brow. "This is what you get for eschewing a valet, you stupid man."

A strangled, pained sound came out of his throat when she checked the wound. Now red and ugly, the hole oozed when she gently poked it. He made another noise and weakly tried to shift away. At least he'd shown signs of life. Striding to the bell pull, she began a mental list of all the items she required.

Had she arrived in time, or was it too late? Ignoring the worry in her gut, she vowed not to fail. He would not die.

"Hear that, Quint?" she said loudly. "You. Will. Not. Die."

After ten minutes and many tugs on the bell, a weary, rumpled footman finally arrived. He'd clearly been asleep, but she felt absolutely no sympathy for the servants. They'd abandoned their master, which, whether he'd asked for it or not, was unacceptable as far as she was concerned. And Quint deserved better.

"Rouse every servant. Tell the cook to boil hot water. I need fresh bed linens and clean towels. Bring every medical supply in the house. And send for a physician."

"But—"

"No arguments. His lordship is near death and I mean to save him, so do what I say. Now, go!"

Chapter Two

"You have a visitor, my lord."

Damien Beecham, Viscount Quint, did not bother looking up at his new butler, his attention instead focused on the rows of letters in front of him. He had to get this idea down. Now—before it was too late. "Pass on the usual response, Turner."

The butler cleared his throat. "I beg your lordship's pardon, but the name is Taylor."

Quint grimaced. He could hardly be faulted for forgetting the lad's name, could he? Taylor had only been on the job for a few days. Or was this further proof of Quint's worst fear becoming a reality?

Nearly three months since the shooting. Three months and he was no better. Oh, the wound had closed, the fever abated, yet everything else that followed had only worsened.

He exhaled and dipped his pen in the ink pot. The invocation he'd adopted these past weeks went through his head: *Remain occupied. Engage your mind while you can. Prepare for the worst.* He looked back down at his cipher. "Apologies, Taylor. No visitors. Ever. Until further notice, I am not receiving callers."

"She said your lordship might say no, and if so, I was to tell you her name—the Lady Sophia Barnes. I was also to mention she planned on coming in whether your lordship allowed it or not."

Quint felt himself frown. Sophie, here? Why? Displeasure was quickly replaced by an uncomfortable weight on his chest. He could not face anyone, most especially *her*. "No. Definitely not. Tell her—"

Before he finished his sentence, Sophie charged into the room. Smothering a curse, Quint threw down his pen, came to his feet, and snatched his topcoat off the chair back. He pulled on the garment as he bowed. "Lady Sophia."

He'd known her for years—five and three-quarters, to be precise—and each time he saw her, he experienced a jolt of heady awareness. There'd never been a more remarkably remarkable woman. She had short honey-brown hair that gleamed with hints of gold in the lamplight. Tall for a female, she had long, lean limbs that moved with purpose, with confidence. Her nose and upper cheeks were dusted with freckles that shifted when she laughed—which was often. People fell under the spell of that laugh, himself included.

"Lord Quint, thank you for seeing me." Holding her bonnet, she bobbed a curtsy in an attempt to give the impression of a proper young lady. No one who knew this particular daughter of a marquess would ever believe it, however. She and Julia Seaton, the Duchess of Colton, were close friends, and the two of them had landed in one absurd scrape after another over the years. Last he'd heard, the two had required rescuing from a gaming hell after a brawl erupted.

"As if I'd had a choice," he said dryly.

She laughed, not offended in the least, and Quint noticed Taylor, mouth agape, hovering near the threshold, eyes trained on Sophie. Good God. Not that Quint hadn't experienced the same reaction in Sophie's presence a time or two. "That'll be all, Taylor. Leave the door ajar, will you?"

The butler nodded and retreated, cracking the heavy door for propriety. Ridiculous, really, when the entire visit was already deuced improper. "I hope you at least brought a maid, Sophie."

"Of course I did. She's in the entryway, likely planning to flirt with that baby you call a butler." Her lips twisted into a familiar impish half-smile. Once, she had given him that smile, leaned into him, and parted her lips . . . right before he'd kissed her.

The memory nearly distracted him from the fact that he didn't want anyone in the house. Bad enough he had to keep the staff. "I am not receiving callers," he told her. "And this is not going to help your reputation."

She waved her hand. "No one worries over a spinster nearing thirty years of age. Now, shall we sit?"

He happened to know she was only twenty-seven, but no use quibbling with her. He glanced about. Books, papers, and various mechanical parts littered every surface. Not to mention there were the three heavy medical volumes on his desk—all on mental deficiencies. With rapid flicks of his wrist, he closed each one and moved the stack to the floor behind his desk. He then came around and cleared a chair for Sophie.

"Thank you." She lowered gracefully into the seat and arranged herself, bonnet in her lap. "I apologize for barging in. Your butler did try to turn me away, but I haven't been able to locate you elsewhere. You've become something of a recluse."

Better to be a recluse than take a trip to an asylum. He sat in his desk chair and said, "I have been occupied."

A tawny eyebrow rose. "So occupied you missed the opening lecture at the Royal Society last Tuesday?"

"I had a conflict," he offered, lamely.

"A conflict? With what? You've never missed one of the opening lectures before. Not in recent memory, at least."

He tried not to react, though he wanted to grit his teeth. "I did not realize my schedule was your concern."

She sighed. "Oh, dear. I've upset you already—and I haven't even arrived at the purpose of my visit."

"Meaning that learning the purpose will only upset me further?"

"Yes, I daresay you shall not approve, but I've nowhere else to turn."

"Why do I feel a pressing need to close the door before you speak?"

She shot to her feet, so Quint started to rise as well. "No," she said, "please, stay seated. I think more clearly when I am standing."

Reluctantly, Quint lowered. He had no idea what she wanted, but with Sophie it could be nearly anything.

Whatever her troubles, Quint did not care. Could not care. A healthy distance between himself and others must be maintained, especially with anyone who'd known him before the accident. Therefore, he'd hear her out and then show her to the door.

He waited as she traveled the study floor, slapping her bonnet against her thigh. Nervous, clearly. Her dress was both expensive and flattering, yet her boots were worn. No jewels. A practical woman underneath the trappings of a lady.

Interesting.

And he hated that he still found her interesting, even after she'd so thoroughly rebuffed him more than three years ago.

"What in God's name is *that*?" She pointed to an abandoned teacup on the desk.

He shot up and grabbed the forgotten porcelain container, which held a greenish-brown gelatinous mixture comprised of various herbs and spices. It looked every bit as terrible as it had tasted. He set the cup inside his desk drawer.

"Why are you here, Sophie?"

She folded her arms over her chest, a motion that called attention to her small, enticing breasts. He forced his eyes away as she spoke. "I would normally approach Colton or Lord Winchester with this request, but as you know, they are both unavailable. You are the only person I can ask."

"Your flattery overwhelms, madam."

She stopped and pinned him with a hard stare. "I did not mean to offend you, as you well know. Stop being obdurate."

"Fine. I readily acknowledge I am to serve as the last resort. Pray, get it out, Sophie."

She straightened her shoulders, lifted her chin. "I need you to serve as my second."

Lord Quint never sputtered. He did not fluster or ever forget himself. Logical, reasonable, and maddeningly unflappable, she knew the viscount could be counted on to keep a level head. It was one of the things Sophie liked best about him.

So when his jaw dropped, she braced herself.

"Your *second*?" Quint's brows flattened. "You need me to serve as your second? For a *duel*? As in, ten paces in a field at dawn?"

"Yes. Precisely that."

"And with whom in the name of Heracles would you be dueling?"

She nibbled her lip. What were the chances she could avoid explaining it before he agreed? "Does it matter?"

He traveled around the bulk of the desk and stopped in front of her. Though she was on the tall side, he was a few inches taller. She liked that he didn't loom over her. It allowed her to better see his face, and he had an interesting face. Astute brown eyes with golden flecks. A strong, angular jaw. High, sharp cheekbones that set off a nose too masculine to ever be called pretty.

His hair was shaggy, his clothes rumpled and appallingly ill-matched. No, he did not inspire swoons in the ballroom, but perfection had never interested Sophie.

And there was the root of the problem.

The man was intelligent in ways most people couldn't even comprehend. They thought him odd. Unsocial. Aloof. He never danced or paid afternoon calls. But those opinions, if he even paused to hear them, didn't affect him as far as Sophie could tell. He exuded confidence, unshakable beliefs that were based on well-researched facts. His ability to recall the smallest detail he'd read fifteen years ago fascinated her.

Quint folded his arms across his chest. "Yes, it very much matters. And it's not as if you can hide the other party's identity, if I'm to serve as your second—unless you plan to blindfold me. But all of that is irrelevant as I cannot, in good conscience, allow you to go through with a duel."

Without a cravat, the strong column of his throat shifted and rippled as he talked, and she was reminded that she'd once had the opportunity to experience the power in his lithe frame. Had once shivered as he'd clutched her so tight she could hardly breathe.

But that was long ago, years now, all before he'd fallen in love with someone else. A lump formed in her throat, regret nearly choking her, but she forced it down. "And I cannot see how you can possibly prevent it. I do not need your approval."

Cocking his head, he studied her with shrewd scrutiny. "What happens if I say no?"

She lifted a shoulder. "I shall muddle through somehow."

"If you do, your reputation will suffer."

"My reputation has already suffered—which is why I have accepted the challenge. To *repair* it."

He huffed a seemingly exasperated laugh. "That is ridiculous."

"Oh, because I'm a woman I cannot have honor?"

"I never said that. Women can duel if they so choose, as far as I'm concerned. Stupidity is not ascribed to gender. What's ridiculous is thinking no one will learn of it. Nigh on impossible to keep a duel private these days."

"Yes, but you won't tell anyone. Neither will I, for that matter."

"Your opponent might, as could the surgeon who

is taxed with removing a ball from your chest. But it hardly matters because I cannot serve as your second."

"Cannot—or will not?"

A flush stole over his cheekbones. Was he embarrassed? She'd never, ever seen him blush. "Cannot," he said. "And you'd better not go through with it."

Intolerable, high-handed males. Sophie had suffered them her whole life. Between idiotic rules and unrealistic expectations, an English woman's life was more constricting than stays after a five-course meal. "I must. And will you tell me why?"

"No. Will you tell me why you need to duel?"

She shook her head. "No. I cannot."

He shifted, coming close enough to send her pulse racing. She could see the rise and fall of his chest, the shadow of tomorrow's beard on his jaw. Strong, wide shoulders, lean waist. Heat radiated off his body to warm her in all the places ladies never mentioned—places that Sophie happened to like quite a bit. He was such a complicated specimen of brains and brawn, a combination she happened to find particularly appealing.

Not to mention he had full, strong lips that she knew firsthand were quite adept at turning a woman's insides to jelly. Well, hers, at least.

"Cannot, or will not?" he asked, refocusing her attention.

She hated having her words turned around on her, so she ignored the question altogether and sidled away. "Will you at least teach me how it's done?" She peered at the stack of books on the floor behind his desk, the ones he'd hidden when she entered. They were all medical journals on . . . diseases of the brain.

Every single one. Now why hadn't he wanted her to see those?

"Dueling? You want to learn how to stand on a field and shoot at another person?"

She glanced up at him. "Yes. I've never even fired a pistol before."

"Firing is not the hard part. Hitting something is the trick."

"I thought the point of a duel was to miss."

"Deloping is considered ungentlemanly. Have you not even read the *Code Duello*? The point of a duel is to restore your honor while not getting yourself killed. And to place your bullet where it will do the least damage."

"See how little I know? You can teach me."

"No. I cannot involve myself in this. You should merely apologize to whichever lady you've slighted and end it."

"It is impossible to apologize. And why can you not be involved?"

He placed his hands on his hips. "Many reasons. Six, to be precise. Would you like them in alphabetic order or order of importance?"

She sighed. This was going badly. She had no one else to ask, no one with a chance of keeping her secret. And she and Quint were friends . . . of a sort. Based on their previous history, she'd thought he'd agree. That he would, at the very least, want to protect her. What could she do to convince him?

"Fine. I shall ask someone else."

He quirked an eyebrow, his expression too knowing, drat him. "And whom shall you enlist in this tutelage?"

She rapidly searched her brain for a name, for any

bits of gossip she'd overheard. "Lord MacLean has been rumored in a number of duels. He must know the way of it."

"And he's a rake. Burned through the entire lot of Edinburgh innocents and had to come to London just to ravish more. Your reputation would never survive it."

"That hardly signifies." In more ways than one. "I merely want the ins and outs of the thing. And if you will not show me, I will find someone who can."

His jaw hardened, but his eyes burned into her, churning with an emotion she'd never seen before. Was it . . . doubt? It gave her pause. Quint moved about the world with ease, with no need to question himself because he was rarely wrong. Any criticisms he encountered were for matters he cared little for, such as the unfashionable length of his hair or his appalling sartorial sense.

But this was new. He looked . . . uncertain.

"Then you must do whatever you feel necessary," he finally said, reaching to knead his temples with his fingertips. "I apologize I am unable to fulfill your request. Taylor will see you out." He bowed and then headed for the door.

She watched him go, stunned at both his rudeness and the expression on his face.

"Quint," she called to his back. He stopped but did not turn. "Are you all right?"

"Never better," he answered and disappeared into the corridor.

"No," she whispered into the empty room. "Somehow I think not."

* * *

"Well, that did not take long," Alice said once they were on the walk back to the Barnes town house. "Did his lordship agree, my lady?"

"No."

A pair of older ladies strolled near in the rare spring sunshine, and Sophie smiled politely as they passed. The streets of Mayfair were busy once again, with horses and carriages each way you turned—a sign that another Season was nigh.

The familiar heaviness settled in Sophie's chest. She dreaded the next few months. More dress fittings. More inane chatter. Dancing with the men her step-mama foisted on her. Pretending to ignore the pitying, curious glances.

She had no one to blame but herself. Some mistakes could not be undone.

Alice came alongside. "What shall you do now?"

"I'll figure something out. Do not worry on it, Alice."

Her maid made a dismissive noise. "A dangerous game your ladyship is playing."

"So you've said on more than one occasion."

"I wish your father had not let you sit in on some of those cases, my lady. It was not proper for a young girl at such an impressionable age to hear sordid tales of criminal behavior."

Sophie hid her smile. Oh, she had loved every minute. Instead of ignoring her after her mother died, her father had kept her even closer. Wherever the marquess went, so did his little girl. The quarter sessions he would oftentimes attend were her favorite.

When she was nine, she'd told him she wanted to be a magistrate when she grew up.

He'd laughed. *My dear, girls cannot be magistrates,*

*though you'd make a fine one. But you're to marry and have
your own family. That is what proper young ladies do.*

Sophie didn't like to be told no, especially because
"that is what proper young ladies do." Hang propriety.

Turning to Alice, she asked, "Did you learn anything from Lord Quint's staff?"

"Superstitious fools, the lot of them," Alice snorted.
"All but the butler, who seems entirely loyal to his
employer. The rest of them believe his lordship to be
the devil himself."

"The devil? Ridiculous." Quint was far from evil. He
was intelligent and kind, a man most of London did
not understand for his eccentricities. But the devil?
"Why would they believe such a thing?"

"Say his lordship stays locked in his study for hours,
never sleeps nor eats. Never leaves. No visitors. Rooms
off limits to the staff."

"Never leaves?" She'd suspected something was off.
He hadn't missed an opening of the Royal Society in
recent years, a fact she could attest to because she
always attended as well. Quint routinely gave a speech,
and Sophie could listen to him lecture for hours. He
had a deep, clear voice that rang with knowledge and
purpose, his ideas elucidated logically. His talks were
heartfelt and passionate, and Sophie felt the depth of
that passion down in her soul. It was the closest she
allowed herself to get to him.

Instead, he'd shut himself up in his house to study
books about diseases of the brain. Odd—though perhaps she'd never known him as well as she'd thought.
Merely because a man kissed you as if his next breath
depended on it didn't mean you were of a like mind.

Especially when that man proposed to another
woman within three weeks of said kiss.

Sophie forced that thought away. *You rejected him. What did you think he'd do?*

"It does seem strange," Alice said. "But as your ladyship knows, it hardly matters if it's true. Servants love to gossip."

This felt like more than gossip. Something was wrong. Yet Sophie couldn't very well explain her intuition to her maid. How did one describe that gnawing, slightly nauseated sensation in one's belly that was more suspicion than fact? But Sophie trusted her gut—it had led her away from trouble more often than not.

Besides, were she and Quint not friends after all this time? She'd saved his life two months ago, though he didn't know it. For nearly a week she—along with a physician—had cared for him, bringing him back from the edge of death. Once he'd begun to recover, however, she'd instructed his staff on what to do and stayed away.

She recalled a few minutes earlier, the uncertain expression that had appeared on his face. A hopeless, confused sort of look, as if he'd lost his way in the world. If he had a problem, she might be able to help. If not, then perhaps she could pick up tips on dueling.

"Alice, I believe I'll return there tonight."

Her maid clucked her tongue. "I cannot see how that's wise, if you don't mind my saying. Not when his lordship has already refused."

"Perhaps I can help him to see reason."

"Heaven help his lordship then, my lady."

Sophie nearly rolled her eyes. "Would you rather I attended the duel without learning how to do it properly, then?"

"I'd rather your ladyship did not attend a duel at all."

Unfortunately, that might not be a choice, but she refrained from saying so to her maid.

Barnes House, the London residence of the Marquess of Ardington, stood on the northwest side of Berkeley Square, not far from Quint. While not as big as Lansdowne House at the other end of the square, Barnes House was an impressive stone structure with massive columns, portico, and rows of windows. Sophie never wanted to live anywhere else.

When she and Alice crossed the street, a soft voice reached her ears. "My lady."

Sophie slowed as a cloaked woman emerged from around a waiting hackney. Her hood was pulled low to obscure her face. Alice was suddenly by Sophie's side. "Here now," Alice said. "Who are you and what do you want with the lady?"

The woman shied away, reconsidering her approach in the face of Alice's protectiveness. "It's all right, Alice," Sophie said, stepping closer. "Were you searching for me?"

The woman revealed the slightest bit of her face. "I apologize for searching your ladyship out on the street."

Sophie relaxed. "Lily! How nice to see you again."

She offered a curtsy. "I know your ladyship said no payment was necessary, but I wanted you to have this." She held out a parcel. "It's nothing much, just some fancy soap I had a boy pick up in a shop."

Sophie tried to refuse, but Lily was determined. "Please, my lady. To find my sister after all these years, and happily settled at that, I cannot tell your ladyship what it means to me."

Sophie did not want to hurt the other woman's feelings, so she accepted the box. "Thank you, then. I am honored to accept it."

This is why Sophie enjoyed helping people, especially women who seldom found a champion. Magistrates ignored them—or offered aid in exchange for physical favors. Runners were expensive and generally more interested in a higher class of clientele. To whom should these women turn, then, when in need?

Sophie gave them hope. An ear to listen. Answers.

She reached to squeeze Lily's hand. "All my best to you and your sister."

"Thank you, my lady." Lily curtsied and withdrew, disappearing around the side of the hack.

Alice sniffed as they neared the stoop of the Barnes town house. "A lightskirt approaching a lady on the streets of Mayfair in broad daylight. I do not know what this world is coming to, my lady."

"Oh, Alice. She'd likely been standing there for hours. The very least we could do was speak with her. And she brought me a gift. I think it's sweet."

"Some days I regret starting your ladyship on this path."

That was a partial truth. There was one event, from ages ago, long before Alice came to work for her, when a kitchen maid had been accused of theft.

Jenny had been her name, and Sophie had liked her. She'd often snuck eleven-year-old Sophie currant buns and sugar paste when no one was looking. So Sophie hadn't instantly believed the upper house-maid's tale that Jenny had stolen money from the housemaid's room—especially since Sophie had observed a footman flirting with both girls. The two maids had argued only the week before, making it clear they didn't care for each other. Wasn't that reason enough to doubt the allegation?

Unfortunately, Jenny had had no proof she hadn't taken the money and no one had believed her denials. Then, when ten pounds was located under her mattress, she had been tossed out without a reference. Sophie tried to get her father to intervene, to help Jenny, but he refused, saying the housekeeper would take care of the matter. The servants were not Sophie's concern.

When Sophie saw the housemaid's smug smile over the next few days, she was positive the girl had lied. No one listened to her, however, and the matter was firmly dropped. Sophie had been heartbroken to learn that Jenny had died in a cholera epidemic shortly after leaving their service.

The tragic tale left a lasting mark on Sophie's brain, one never forgotten. The truth mattered, regardless of what class one was born into.

"Do not be ridiculous," she told Alice. "I enjoy these cases and I am good at it. Yes, this officially started when your sister was accused of stealing her employer's silver, but if not for her, it would've been someone else. I feel as though I was born to do this."

"Well, my sister is ever so grateful your ladyship stepped in and found the real culprit. To think, one of the grooms sneaking in the house and pilfering the forks and knives."

Sophie snickered. "One would have assumed him smart enough to wipe the liniment off his hands first."

"As we've seen, your ladyship, most criminals are not at all bright."

"And thank heavens for that."

Chapter Three

Quint put his hands on his hips and stared down at the perfectly matched set of ivory-handled Manton dueling pistols. Should he give her these or the newer tube-lock pistols he'd purchased in January?

Pistols.

A *duel.*

Antimony, why would a woman of such intelligence and wit participate in this primitive ritual? The level-headed thing to do would be to parley with the aggrieved party, discuss the slight, and come to some sort of resolution satisfactory to both sides. To risk one's life over something so trivial was absurd, in Quint's opinion.

Reservations and common sense aside, however, he'd asked Taylor to retrieve the pistols. Quint planned to have them wrapped and delivered to her. If he could not teach her himself, at least she would be well armed. God knew he'd never need the deuced things again.

All day, he'd considered writing to the Marquess of Ardington. The marquess was a powerful man, involved at the highest levels of government, and Quint actually liked him quite well. Shouldn't the marquess be warned of the danger his daughter faced? At best, her reputation would be shredded in a duel. At worst, she could be killed. Each time he'd picked up a pen to dash off a note, however, he'd set the pen back in the tray. He couldn't do it. With anyone else, he would wash his hands of the whole business. But Sophie . . .

Though he was loath to admit it, there was another reason he hadn't written to her father. After more than three years, he still had a soft spot for her—which merely proved his idiocy. After all that had happened between them, he could not deliberately hurt her.

His entire life, Quint had been considered odd. Different from other men in his pursuits and interests. From the first moment he'd met Sophie, however, he'd felt a deeper understanding in her sharp gaze, that she was a woman unlike any other. Another misfit. And he had hoped.

They'd begun a casual flirtation at events over many months, and she had seemed to enjoy teasing him. He'd often found her staring at him from under her long brown lashes, an occurrence guaranteed to send a bolt of lust to his groin. During one particularly dull ball, he'd wandered away, as he frequently did, to the host's library, knowing the books would be far more interesting than the small talk, and Sophie, surprisingly, had followed.

A noise behind him caught his attention. Sophie stood there, breathtakingly beautiful in a cream-colored gown that shimmered as she moved. She shut the door, locked it, and Quint's pulse leapt. "You should be in the ballroom, Sophie."

The edge of her mouth kicked up as she drew near. "Are you ever going to kiss me, Quint?"

"Do you want me to?"

"I followed you in here, did I not?"

"You answered a question with another question, Sophie."

"As did you."

He smiled, unable to resist her, and stepped forward. Without asking permission, he placed one hand on her hip and another around her neck, thinking she'd back away. Instead, she leaned in to his touch, welcoming it, her skin soft and warm. Her chestnut eyes grew dark, fathomless pools of invitation, and he was lost. "Yes, then. I should very much like to kiss you," he admitted. "But I should not."

"Life would hardly be worth living if we were to obey all the rules." Her hands reached up to tangle in his hair as he bent and sealed his mouth to hers.

That one kiss had been monumental. Life altering. She'd been willing and pliant, and he'd lost all sense of himself, forgetting they were mere yards away from a crowded soirée. And he'd been so sure, so certain at the time, that his feelings were reciprocated.

Only, he'd miscalculated. With the subtlety of a sledgehammer, she'd broken his heart into millions of molecules and scattered them like pebbles. He would be unwelcome as a suitor, she'd said, the encounter nothing but a momentary fancy.

Under normal circumstances, serving as a beautiful woman's "momentary fancy" would not be a hardship. But with Sophie . . . it had mattered. A lot.

Ended up a fortunate turn of events for her, however. Quint would not wish himself on any woman, considering what his future held in store.

As a boy, he had witnessed his father's mental decline

and the toll it had taken on his mother. She had cried all the time, hardly eaten, and had consulted with countless apothecaries, physicians, and scientists about a potential cure. All for naught. She had exhausted herself and ignored her son, and the viscount had never recovered.

Quint had vowed never to let that happen to him. He would never succumb to the madness that had overtaken his father. He would be smarter. Sharper. Work harder at his focus, memory, and stamina. No matter the cost, he'd avoid his father's fate.

And it had worked until a bullet had grazed his neck last February, nearly robbing him of his life.

A brisk knock on his study door interrupted his thoughts. Taylor appeared, a cloaked figure behind him. "My lord, a visitor."

Every cell in Quint's body came to attention. He recognized that shrouded form. Why had she returned? "See that we're not disturbed, Taylor." His butler started to turn away and Quint added, "And remind me to review my visitation policy with you later."

Taylor nodded and left, after which Sophie drew down the hood of her cloak. She wore no bonnet or cap, her brown hair twisted in a simple knot at her nape. The yellow glint of candlelight reflected in her dark eyes. Her mouth quirked. "Do not blame Taylor. I was already in the house, coming up the servants' stairs, when he found me. He couldn't very well kick me out then."

"Why have you come back, Sophie?"

"What have you there?" She came closer and peered at the box on his desk. "Are those pistols?"

He sighed. May as well deal with her now. Then he could get back to his cipher. "Yes. This pair was crafted by Manton, who produces the best dueling pistols in the world."

"What makes them superior?"

He tried not to notice her nearness, how shifting an inch or two would bring their shoulders together. He cleared his throat. "Manton discovered weighting the barrel allowed for a steadier shot. Less recoil in the forearm when the charge is fired. They are remarkably accurate at the right distance. I have others, but this is likely the easier set for you to use."

"Hmm." Her fingertip slid down the ivory handle. "Why did you have them out, if you do not plan to help me?"

"Because it is important to have the very best equipment for whatever task you undertake. Since I had no way of knowing what pistols you intended to use, I planned to send these to you. I will not need them."

"Have they been loaded?"

"Absolutely not. The barrels are empty." Less chance of someone—him, most likely—getting shot.

"But how can I practice if they are empty?"

"You need to build up your arm strength in order to hold them steady for a prolonged period of time. Women have a lower percentage of muscle mass in their upper body and torso, so you need more practice than pulling the trigger if you want an accurate shot."

"See, that is exceedingly helpful. I cannot trust anyone else to tell me these things."

A sharp and unexpected sense of satisfaction coursed through him, followed quickly by resentment. She was clever, using flattery to get what she wanted. He preferred facts, however. "You are aware, of course, that duels are illegal. And that most result in death or serious injury."

She tilted her head up to find his eyes. "Some, but not most. And I question the validity of such a statement. No actual data can be gathered as most duels are private and unreported, especially those with no injuries."

Heat suffused his body. Christ, when she used words such as "validity" and "data," Quint wanted to do unspeakably improper things to her. Dragging a hand through his hair, he put some distance between them. "There's little use in debating the point. In case you've forgotten, you've asked for my assistance and I have refused it."

"Which I refuse to accept. Not only are you the most clever man I know, you're a friend. Who else is in a better position to help me than you?"

Now he would appear churlish to refuse. Smart.

He flexed his fingers, thinking. While he did not appreciate being manipulated, he did not want to see her hurt. And if he showed her how to operate the damn things, would she go away and leave him in peace?

"If I give you your hour, do you promise not to return?"

"Yes," she answered quickly, enthusiasm lighting up her face.

"And what if you show no aptitude for firearms? Will you abandon this silliness?"

"Of course. I do not have a desire to die." She removed her cloak and threw the heavy garment over a chair. "I'll suggest swords instead."

"If that is your idea of a jest, I am not laughing."

Sophie bit her lip. No, Quint's face did not show any hint of amusement. With his eyes narrowed and mouth curved into a frown, he looked quite dour—even for a man who tended toward the serious. All the more reason she sensed something was off with him.

She forced herself back to the conversation. "Of course I am jesting." *Not in the least.* "Now, let us begin. I need to return before daybreak."

That did not appear to make him any happier. "Just how did you escape, by the way? And how did you sneak into my house without any of my staff stopping you?"

She dared not tell him of her abilities. Only Alice had an inkling of the talents Sophie possessed, and no one else need know. "My maid is covering for me. She's entirely trustworthy and discreet. And your kitchen door was unlocked. I assume your cook forgot to lock it on her way to bed."

He pulled at his full bottom lip with his thumb and forefinger, clearly contemplating something. The action brought attention to his mouth, and her skin began to tingle with the memory of what it had felt like to have those lips on hers. He was a remarkable kisser, with a single-minded focus and thoroughness to make a courtesan blush.

That was the thing about Quint: Whatever he chose to do, he did well. His viscountess would be a lucky lady, indeed.

Too bad it would not be Sophie.

She glanced away and took a deep breath. These reactions to him would not do, not if she planned on paying attention.

"Let's examine the weapons," he said, dropping his arm. "Pick one up, if you please."

Sophie reached into the velvet-lined box and lifted

one of the pistols. The ivory handle was cool against her palm. "It's heavier than I assumed."

"That is why you need to practice holding it, as I said, to build up your arm strength. The steadier you keep it, the more accurate your shot. And if you cannot hold it steady, then do not go through with a duel."

"Understood." She peered down the barrel, pointed it at the floor. "Will you show me how to load it?"

"No. The seconds oversee the loading of the pistols. All you need to be concerned with is not dying."

"But how shall I practice properly if I cannot load it?"

She expected him to argue, but he surprised her by sticking to the practicalities. "You are aware you'll need to drive out into the country in order to shoot, I hope."

"You needn't treat me like a child, Quint. I plan to spend a few days in Sussex. I daresay there's enough space on Papa's estate to discharge a cannon and not be overheard."

He held up his hands. "Fine." Reaching into the case, he withdrew various bits and pieces, which he lined up on the desk. His thorough explanation covered both the construction of the pistol and firing mechanism, as well as the function of the other items originally contained in the box. He showed her the paper cartridges, how they were used. In all his diligence, however, he never touched the pistol once.

She began to shift impatiently, ready to actually *do* something.

"Are you listening to me?" he asked sharply. When she nodded, he lifted a skeptical brow. "What can cause the pistol to misfire, then?"

"A dull flint, soft frizzen, weak springs, over-primed

pan, clogged touch-hole," she recited none too smugly. "Anything else?"

"Let's see you load it," he said by way of answer.

She did so quickly, efficiently, and then looked to him for confirmation. He nodded in approval and she grinned, inordinately pleased with herself. "Are we finally ready to practice?" she asked.

"Anxious, are you?"

"Well, I must return home before someone notices I'm missing. Otherwise, you'll be putting these pistols to use when my father requests your presence at dawn."

"Fair enough. Switch yours for the empty one." He strode to the center of the room.

She didn't bother switching pistols. It wasn't as if she would shoot him. "Wait. Should you not take one as well?"

"No. I'll pretend," he said, flexing his fingers. She'd noticed him doing that motion a few times, especially since she'd started handling the guns. A nervous habit?

"Your challenger decides the distance," he explained. "Ten paces is common, though I've heard of six or eight. The seconds will mark it off. Take your position."

She stepped off ten paces then turned to face him. "Here?"

"Good. Once you're both ready, you'll be given a signal after which you'll have three seconds to fire."

"And I should aim for . . . ?"

"The extremities. Shoulder. Arm. You do not want a death on your hands or your conscience."

Hard to argue there. "What happens if both parties miss?"

"Then your challenger must decide if his honor is satisfied or not."

She examined the pistol in her hand. It really was quite pretty, with its gold accents and pearl handle. The wood was smooth and polished. "Have you ever engaged in a duel?"

He made a sound. "Absolutely not. It's barbarism. I bought those to examine how they work, to see how Manton improved upon the design."

"But you've attended a duel, surely?"

"Two. Both Colton's, when he was still too young and stubborn to see reason. Sort of like someone else I know."

She ignored that. "What room is directly below us?"

Quint's brow lowered as he considered the question. "The wine cellar, as I recall. But—"

Sophie squeezed the trigger as he'd taught her, the barrel pointed at the floor. The flint swung down, struck the frizzen, sparked, and the pistol went off with a loud crack. A puff of acrid smoke encircled her and she wobbled from the surprising kick of the shot. Exhilaration coursed through her, a heady mix of relief, power, and awe. "Gads, that was fun!"

Using her free hand, she batted the smoke. "May I—Quint, whatever is wrong?"

He stood frozen, his pallor gone the color of fresh snow. His chest heaved as he stared at the pistol in her hand. "Quint?" She came closer and noticed his hands were shaking. "I apologize for firing. I could not resist—"

"Get out."

She blinked. Had he said—?

"Now, Sophie. Get out of my house and do not come back. *Go!*" The last word was nearly a roar, a shocking tenor of voice from a normally soft-spoken man.

Stunned into obeying, she hurriedly replaced the pistol in its case and found her cloak. He now faced the wall, away from her, his head clasped tightly in his hands as if he was in pain. She started to apologize once more, but thought better of agitating him further.

"*Leave!*" he rasped, and she bolted into the corridor, closing the door softly behind her.

Instead of leaving, however, curiosity and concern had her pressing her ear to the wood. A fast, rhythmic huffing sounded from inside the study. Was he wheezing? Heavens, perhaps he was ill. After ensuring no servants hovered nearby, she ever so slowly turned the latch and cracked the door.

He hadn't moved, except to reach out and brace himself on a chair back. She could only see his profile, but his lids were screwed shut, and it appeared he could not draw enough breath into his lungs. He gasped again and again, weaving on his feet, and her stomach clenched at the sight of his misery. What was happening? Was his heart giving out?

Mesmerized, she debated whether to rush in and offer assistance or stay in the corridor. If he was anything like her father and younger brother, he would not appreciate a witness to his weakness. Men were remarkably prickly about illness. But what if Quint was in grave danger?

"My lady."

Sophie straightened and leapt away from the door. The butler's expression etched with disapproval, he marched forward and quietly closed the partition to the study.

"Is he ill?" she whispered.

"I really could not say, my lady. However, perhaps it is best if your ladyship returned to your own home."

"But should we not call a physician? Or at least wait to ensure he recovers?"

"His lordship has asked that no physician be admitted to the house. Ever. And I do not believe he would appreciate one being sprung on him." The butler did not seem overly concerned about the health of his employer. Was this not the first time Quint had fallen ill?

He gestured toward the front door. "Now, I must insist, your ladyship, as I'd like to retain my post."

She clenched her fists, anxious to check on Quint but not wanting to get the staff in trouble. "I'd best go out the service door, Taylor." With the cloak on her shoulders, she pulled the hood low over her face. They traveled silently through the house and down to the kitchens.

Taylor opened the door. "Would you prefer a footman to see you home, my lady?"

"No, that won't be necessary." She moved onto the stoop. "You'll see to him, won't you?"

"Of course, my lady. However—" He closed his mouth abruptly, obviously thinking better of what he'd been about to say. Which would never do, of course.

"Go on," she prodded.

He glanced over his shoulder, dropped his voice. "If you should care to return, simply send word and I shall ensure your ladyship need not pick the lock again."

By the time Quint recovered, Sophie had long departed.

Good. He didn't know how he could face her after

tonight. Bad enough the staff remained in the house, that they were witness to the embarrassment of Quint's failings. He kept removed from them as best he could but suspected Taylor had drawn his own conclusions after the last episode.

He swiped perspiration off his brow. Began reciting Locke's *An Essay Concerning Human Understanding*. It was one of his favorite passages, on how all human knowledge comes only from experience. Fine and good for Locke, of course, since he'd retained his sanity. What rational understanding could be deduced from these debilitating attacks of pure terror? Even the brightest of enlightenment thinkers would likely be baffled by Quint's condition.

After another moment, his respiration restored itself to its usual rate.

He struggled up out of the chair, weaker than he wanted to admit. The fits, when they came, left him exhausted and with a blistering headache. Opening a window, he welcomed in the fresh air to remove the smell of gunpowder.

She'd actually fired a pistol in his house. He rubbed his temples. Only Sophie would dare do something so reckless. It was part of what he admired about her. But that sound and smell had set off a waking nightmare for him, one he could never admit to her. One he could never admit to anyone.

"My lord," Taylor called through the partition. "Was a pistol fired?"

"Yes, and you might as well come in, Taylor."

The door opened and the young butler appeared. Quint could read nothing in the lad's placid expression, no disapproval or worry, which was something of a relief. "Is there anything I might bring you, my lord? Tea?"

"Yes, that would be much appreciated. Also"—he gestured to the pistols—"take these below and have them wrapped up. I want them delivered tomorrow to Lady Sophia, the daughter of the Marquess of Ardington."

"Very good, sir. Shall I also request a carpenter to come and repair the hole in the floor?"

Quint glanced down. A small, round hole now marred the floor by the leg of his desk. He did not want workmen in the house. He did not want anyone in the house, really. And that hole would serve as a reason why. "No. Not just yet."

"I thought you should like to know that her ladyship left through the service door, my lord. I instructed a groom to follow her at a discreet distance."

"Good thinking, Taylor." He dropped into his desk chair, ready to distract himself with work. "The mews are not always as safe as Lady Sophia clearly believes them to be."

"Indeed, your lordship, that is sadly true. Though the lady is certainly brave. Not what one expects."

An understatement. And Quint was not sure if she was brave or just reckless. The distinction hardly mattered, though. She was, however, distracting—and Quint could not afford distractions.

But it was the fondness in Taylor's voice that made Quint frown. She'd gained herself another admirer, it seemed. "Yes, she is precisely that. She is also persuasive. Remember who pays your wages. No visitors, Taylor."

Taylor lifted the box containing the pistols, then bowed. "As you wish, my lord. I will send up some tea."

Now alone, Quint removed a small key from his waistcoat and unlocked the top desk drawer. Withdrew a ledger he never let anyone see. He flipped to the last entry and reached for his pen. In clear handwriting, he wrote the date. Then he catalogued the circumstances preceding the fit, as well as the symptoms he'd experienced during the episode. Every detail, written down for later examination. He would cross-reference this one against the others, looking for patterns. Similarities.

Answers.

It's all in your mind, he told himself. *There is nothing physically wrong with you.*

While he knew it to be true, it was as if his body believed something else altogether. The fits were debilitating. Humiliating. Like nothing he'd ever experienced before in his thirty-three years. And if it happened in public with witnesses, he knew what they would believe. Knew what would happen then.

The same thing that had happened to his father.

Bed straps. Bloodletting. Freezing-cold baths. Emetics.

Quint shuddered. No, he preferred death to a lengthy stay at a hospital—or worse, a madhouse. Nor would he permit unqualified surgeons or physicians to poke and prod at him. He would happily swim in the swirling pits of insanity rather than subject himself to a charlatan.

How much time did he have left? His father had been thirty-eight when the fits started and had lived only four more years after that. Quint was already thirty-three. Did that mean he would not live to see forty?

The thought depressed him.

He often stared at his father's painting in the gallery, looking for signs. What had the viscount been thinking? Had he noticed anything strange with his health? Had there been any clues to the madness in his future?

Will I turn out to be just like you?

The current medical texts and journals believed the answer to be yes. That madness, fits, and anxiety— the sort his father had suffered—traveled in the bloodlines. And there was no known cure. Quint refused to believe it, however. He would heal himself, if given enough time. The answer was in the evidence contained in the journal, the tests he'd conducted over the past three months.

So far, he'd experimented with spices as well as hot water baths, both to unpleasant conclusions. He'd brewed flavored teas, which tasted nice but hadn't helped. Then there were the various herbs and plants that also failed to produce results and tasted terrible. He was loath to try an opiate derivative. A poppy extract would dull his senses significantly, a feeling he routinely avoided at all costs. Precisely the same reason he never drank spirits. He needed to retain the clarity, yet reduce the fear and anxiety.

He wanted to get better—and he would get better, if he could remain focused on the problem. Continue his research. Avoid distractions.

Which meant no more Sophie.

Chapter Four

Sophie slid the small door open, the rusted hinges protesting loudly in the silence. The soft golden glow coming from inside the unused garden shed meant her maid was already here.

"Oh, thank heavens," Alice said when Sophie came through. "I swear I don't know how much longer I could have stood it. Something crawled across my foot a few minutes ago."

"Probably just a mouse." Sophie threw off her cloak and turned her back to Alice. Her maid began unlacing her gown.

"It still gives me the shivers, my lady."

"Get me changed, then, and you can return to the house." Within minutes, her gown, petticoats, chemise, lacy drawers, and stays had been removed. Sophie unbuckled the strap on her thigh where a shiny, sharp knife rested in a leather holster. Shivering, she stepped into the plain smalls Alice handed her. Next came the binding.

This was Sophie's least favorite part, though it wasn't as if she had large enough breasts to worry over. In fact, Sophie's long and lean body had never been precisely "womanly." Her whole life, she'd longed for curves. A blessing her prayers had gone unanswered, yet even still, her male clothing had required extensive tailoring.

She turned in slow circles while Alice wrapped the cloth tightly about her torso. Next came stockings, trousers, a fine shirt, braces, and a waistcoat. Alice tied a cravat neatly around a high collar that would aid in hiding the lack of an Adam's apple or whiskered jaw. A pin in the neckcloth finished the look.

"There. Now let's fix your hair," Alice said and reached for a jar of pomade. Sophie removed the silver combs in her short curls and sat in the small wooden chair. Her maid rubbed the mixture through her fingers and then straightened, pulled, and swirled Sophie's hair into a fashionable, foppish style. By the time Alice was done, Sophie would look like one of the poets women swooned over—if one did not look too closely.

When Alice stepped back, Sophie rose and slipped her feet into her male dress shoes. Finding footwear in Sophie's size had proven difficult, so she'd taken a pair belonging to her younger brother and stuffed the toes with cloth. They were not comfortable, exactly, but would do. The topcoat slid over her shoulders easily, the garment having been heavily padded to give her more of a man's broad shape. One greatcoat, walking stick, and hat later, she'd been transformed.

She turned to leave, but Alice's voice stopped her. "Wait, my lady! The spectacles."

Once they were in place, Sophie struck a manly pose. "How do I look?"

"Like the prettiest dandy in London."

She smiled. "Then we've got it right."

"And just where is your ladyship off to, so that I may inform the search party later on?"

"Very funny. I'm merely visiting Madame Hartley."

"Another missing girl?" Alice asked.

Sophie slipped on her gloves. "Indeed. And since I never found Natalia, I intend to devote all my efforts to finding this one."

"Be safe, my lady."

"Always, Alice," Sophie said and slipped into the gardens.

Twenty minutes later, she alighted from a hackney, taking care not to trip in her oversized footwear, and tossed the coachman a few coins.

"Thank you, m'lord," the man returned with a tip of his hat.

She ignored him—most gentlemen treated the lower classes with a healthy dose of disdain—and sauntered up to the familiar dark red door. A sharp bang with the head of her walking stick and the partition swung open. "Sir Stephen," the big guard, Mulrooney, said in a heavy Irish accent. "Welcome. Madame Hartley will be anxious t' see you."

Sophie relinquished her greatcoat, hat, and stick, and then pitched her voice deep. "A drink first, I think, Mulrooney."

"Excellent. I'll tell the mistress you've arrived, sir."

Crowded tonight, Sophie thought as she strolled into the closest side room, where the stench of smoke and sweat nearly choked her. A footman arrived with a heavily watered whisky, Sir Stephen's preferred spirit, and she grabbed at it gratefully as she covertly observed the men lounging around card tables. Women assumed brothels were all about fornication—and they were—but the amount of time gentlemen spent here was surprising. They chatted, gamed, and drank at all hours. With the number of recognizable titles around the tables, this might as well be White's or Brooks's.

She affected a bored expression when a few looks came her way. As predicted, none lingered. People saw what they wanted; no one assumed she was anything other than a green lad out for a bit of evening sport. And if she kept a slight distance, she could carry it off without question.

The whisky, smooth and woodsy, helped calm her nerves. Sir Stephen had made a few enemies recently, and Sophie dearly hoped not to encounter any of them this evening.

"Sir Stephen." She turned at the sound of the feminine drawl and found Madame Hartley at her side. "How lovely to see you again so soon. I know Joselle will be happy you're here."

Madame Hartley ran the most exclusive brothel in London, but they both knew Sophie was not here to enjoy the girls. "Then it would be a shame to disappoint her," Sophie returned.

The abbess murmured, "Joselle is in the blue room at the end of the hall."

Sophie took the carpeted stairs to the second floor. Doors flanked the upper corridor, and the sounds coming from behind them were both mysterious and erotic, a hint of the world forbidden to ladies. Grunts, moans, sighs . . . a slap followed by a giggle. Ropes creaked and snapped under mattresses. What limited experience Sophie did have fueled her imagination and the sense of longing inside her. She wanted to feel that passion, so much so that she now ached in all the places that made her a woman.

Or could the tingling under her skin be a result of seeing Quint?

She'd wanted to kiss him earlier tonight. Badly.

Why would he bother kissing you again? He wouldn't, not after she'd told him their one and only kiss meant nothing—a sentiment he must've agreed with because he'd gone and fallen in love with the "Perfect Pepperton" chit. Blonde, demure, ideal in every way, she had put all the other marriageable girls to shame. When his betrothal had been announced, Sophie had died a thousand times inside.

While she cringed at the humiliating way his betrothal had ended—his future bride dashing off to Gretna Green with a groom—she could not say she was sorry for it. That silly girl had not deserved Quint. No one did, really. No one was good enough for a man so unique, so intelligent.

Certainly not Sophie.

Ladies aren't supposed to enjoy it so much. And they certainly aren't supposed to tell the man what to do.

Lord Robert's voice, even years later, rang in her ears, the humiliation still sharp. So foolish she'd been. So innocent. She'd loved him and he'd used her and thrown her away like a pile of refuse.

Now, at the end of the corridor, Sophie knocked and entered. A young, pretty blonde girl came to her feet. "Oh, thank you for coming, my lady," Joselle said, and then clapped a hand over her mouth. "I mean, sir."

Sophie smiled as she locked the door. She'd never bothered trying to fool the girls. If anyone knew a man's body from ten paces, it was a woman who made her living on her back. "That's all right, Joselle. We are alone now. I trust you've been well."

"I am worried sick. Did your ladyship have a chance to visit The Pretty Kitty?"

"I did. I spoke with your sister's friend, Mary. She

hasn't heard from Rose in a fortnight either and they already cleared Rose's room out. The man who looks after the girls told me she was busy with a customer."

Joselle wrung her hands. "They've done something terrible with her, I just know it. She was getting out. Had a protector, she said. She wouldn't need to work at The Kitty. She was so happy . . ." Her face crumpled, and Sophie rushed to awkwardly pat her shoulder.

"We will find her. I swear, I will do whatever I can, Joselle."

"I know you will, my lady." Joselle dragged in a deep breath. "I never wanted her working in one of O'Shea's places. He don't look after his girls. Treats 'em like garbage."

Sophie knew of James O'Shea, rookery legend and owner of The Pretty Kitty. Rumors abounded of his violence and cruelty. O'Shea may or may not have been involved in Rose's disappearance, but this was now the second girl gone missing from The Kitty since October. "And you are sure Rose has not gone with this man, the one she said was going to take care of her?"

"I'm sure. She would have written to me. Even if she was living somewhere else, Rose would have sent me word."

"Do you know anything about this man, the one who made the promises to her?"

Joselle shook her head. "All I know is he was a gent. I am worried she'll be one of those girls who've been washing up along the river."

As was Sophie. Three dismembered bodies thus far, each a young prostitute. "I plan to return and see Mary once more. Perhaps she knows more about this mystery gentleman. Certainly he would have been one of Rose's regulars."

Joselle nodded grimly. "Thank you, my lady. We are so grateful for all that you do."

Sophie gave her a small smile. "I shall return after my next visit to The Kitty, I promise. Now I best return downstairs before I cost you any more money this evening."

"Well, let's give 'em a show, my lady." Joselle leaned over the bed and gripped the bed frame. Using her hands, she began banging the wood against the wall. "Oh!" she yelled. "Fuck me harder! Harder!" She moved faster, an intense rhythmic slapping against the plaster. "Yes, oh God, yes!" A few more noises then she rattled to a stop.

Sophie bit her lip to keep from giggling. "Who would've guessed Sir Stephen had it in him?" she said quietly.

The girl playfully cocked her hip and tossed her long blond hair. "I'm so good I can make a dead man see stars, my lady."

When Sophie finished with Joselle, she returned to the main floor. She wanted to speak with Madame Hartley before she left.

A footman presented her with a crystal glass. Sophie took the drink and swaggered over to a banquette along the wall. She sprawled on the velvet cushions, taking up space as men do with arms bent and legs spread, trying to appear as if she'd been recently satisfied. Of course, she had very little experience to draw on; but the trick, one assumed, was to look inordinately pleased with oneself.

"Sir Stephen." Madame Hartley approached. "I trust you enjoyed Joselle?"

"Indeed, I did," Sophie answered with a wink.

"Excellent. Might I have a private word, sir?"

"Of course." Sophie rose and trailed the abbess to the back part of the house. When they reached Madame's office, the proprietress gestured to a chair. "Let us both sit for a moment, my lady."

Once they were seated, the abbess retrieved a note out of her desk. "This is from Pearl." Sophie accepted the paper, which likely contained any hints of gossip the courtesan had overheard. "Joselle has been quite upset," Madame noted. "Do you believe you can help her?"

"I will certainly try. One of the boys at The Kitty watches out for me in exchange for coins. He'll keep an eye out for anything related to Rose."

"Excellent. I am grateful for your ladyship's help. To assist women who would otherwise be helpless is truly a gift, my lady"

Warmth flooded Sophie at the praise. She loved what she did, and receiving recognition for her small achievements was flattering. "Joselle is worried her sister may be the next girl pulled from the Thames," she said, referring to the prostitutes recently found mutilated and tossed into the water.

"I certainly hope not. It is a terrible business, not one that any girl deserves, no matter how she makes her living. Whatever small part I can play, your ladyship only need ask."

"Thank you." Sophie slapped her knees and stood. "I believe Sir Stephen must get back home."

"Be careful, your ladyship."

While Sophie waited on Mulrooney to collect her belongings, the front door opened and a group of men poured in. A short, blond man caught her attention and her stomach sank. Lord Tolbert. *For heaven's sake.* The very last person Sir Stephen needed to run into.

She held her breath. There would be no avoiding the hot-tempered earl in the small entryway. Tolbert took off his greatcoat and looked up, dark eyes narrowing as they landed on Sir Stephen. Sophie straightened; as a rule, she refused to cower.

Sophie had met him in polite circles before, of course, though his overexuberant attentions made her skin crawl. Since his gaming debts were legendary, she suspected his interest in Lady Sophia had far more to do with her dowry than any affection.

Last week, in a considerably less reputable establishment than Madame Hartley's, Sir Stephen had made the mistake of drawing away a girl Tolbert had secured for the night. She'd needed to speak with the prostitute and hadn't known of Tolbert's dealings. None of that mattered to Tolbert, however, and the ensuing argument had devolved into a challenge.

A challenge she'd not formally acknowledged, since there wasn't anyone reliably discreet enough to act as her second. Part of her had hoped Tolbert would forget about the supposed slight. Judging from the expression on the man's face now, however, that hope was unfounded.

"Sir Stephen," Tolbert drawled, tossing his greatcoat and hat to one of his unfortunate friends. "So the coward finally emerges from under his rock. I've been looking into you."

Sophie swallowed. "Have you?"

"Why is it," Tolbert sneered, "no one knows where to find you? I must've asked every chap I know; yet none knew where one Sir Stephen, that's you, could be found. And something even more interesting . . ."

He paused for dramatic effect. "There is no Sir Stephen Radcliff in my copy of Debrett's."

"Perhaps you are using an outdated version," Sophie replied in her haughtiest man-voice.

"No, indeed, I am not. You know what I think." He took a step closer and whispered, "I think you are a fake, Sir Stephen. You are in disguise, posing as a member of our elite little world. And I mean to find you out."

Perspiration gathered under her arms. If only Tolbert knew how close to the truth he was . . .

She lifted her chin as she tried to put a little distance between them. "You're half-cracked. I've been in London for nearly a year." God save her for telling this lie. "I'm cousin to the Viscount Quint."

"That lunatic?" Tolbert laughed derisively. "Everyone knows he's mad."

It wasn't anything she hadn't heard said about him countless times over the years. In the *ton*, anything beyond the normal routine was thought lunacy—and Quint was anything but normal, thank heavens. Though she wanted to leap to Quint's defense, she lifted a shoulder. "He seems perfectly fit to me."

"And you are lodging there, with Quint?"

She forced a nod. Thank heavens Quint never allowed visitors. All she needed to do was get Taylor to tell a small fib if anyone called for Sir Stephen.

"Good," he continued, dark brown gaze glittering in triumph. "Then I shall pass that information along to my second. You will be hearing from him." He moved forward and Sophie retreated until her back hit the wall. Tolbert poked her shoulder. "There still is the matter of my honor."

"Will you accept an apology?"

"No. I will not. As a matter of fact"—he grabbed

her arm roughly—"I think I should keep an eye on you until morning, when we can settle this as gentlemen."

Panic froze her insides. Stay with Tolbert until morning? He'd discover her lie in a ridiculously short amount of time, long before the sun came up.

"Here, now." A beefy hand reached between them and pushed Tolbert back a few paces. Sophie glanced up and found Lord MacLean there, his normally jovial expression gone hard as he stared at Tolbert. "The gent has tried to apologize for whatever transgression you've suffered. Now you're to accept his apology and forgive the slight, Tolbert. Do you not even ken how it's done?"

Tolbert's face twisted in anger. "This is between gentlemen, MacLean. *English* gentlemen. So you may run along now, *laddie*." Sophie heard the snickering of Tolbert's companions.

MacLean rocked back on his heels. "Jesus, you're even stupider than your mountain of debt suggests. Are you gonna apologize, man?"

Tolbert glanced over his shoulders at his friends, who were all avidly observing the exchange, then turned back to MacLean. "I never apologize."

MacLean just grinned and scratched his jaw. "I suppose I've been itchin' for another early morning. You'll hear from my second, Tolbert."

Sophie saw Tolbert's throat work, though he tried to put a brave face on it. "And just whom might serve as your second?"

MacLean slapped Sir Stephen on the back, which nearly caused Sophie to pitch facedown on the carpet. "This *laddie* here will do it. What do you say?"

Both men turned their attention on her. "O-of course," Sophie sputtered in her deepest voice. "I'd be honored."

* * *

Quint finished the instructions to his steward, folded the paper, and sealed it. The one positive light on his illness: The viscountcy had never been in better shape. His investments were flourishing, accounts perfectly balanced, all correspondence answered. When Quint finally did succumb to madness, whoever assumed guardianship of the estate would have an easy time of it.

Taylor appeared after a brisk knock. "My lord, if you'll pardon the interruption."

"What is it, Taylor?"

"Your presence is requested in the ballroom."

The ballroom? The butler had to be mistaken. "The ballroom has been closed up for years. Who would—?" His jaw snapped shut. He didn't need to ask because he already knew. Unbelievable. Once more she'd gained access to the house—and after he'd explicitly told her not to return two nights ago.

His eyes narrowed on Taylor. "Well, did she pick the lock or did we leave the door open?"

"Neither, your lordship."

Quint rose and came around the desk. "Let her in, did you?"

Taylor had the grace to appear sheepish, his ears turning crimson. "Her ladyship was quite persuasive."

She always was, he thought, as he took the stairs. Quint knew better than to lay blame at his butler's feet. Indeed, he was keenly aware of precisely whom to take to task.

The ballroom door stood ajar, light spilling into the corridor. Taylor must've instructed one of the maids to set the candles. Quint wasn't sure how to feel about his staff rushing to do Sophie's bidding. Though, to be fair, his staff likely relished any activity to fight the tedium of the Beecham household.

He entered, ready to give her what for, and stopped short at the sight that greeted him. Long legs—long, *shapely* legs—encased in buckskin breeches. Tall, black boots. A short military-style jacket that women favored for riding. All the breath left his chest and his cock twitched, instinct swiftly taking over. Sweet, merciful cadmium . . .

When he recovered enough to speak, he noticed her amused half-smile. A hundred questions leapt to mind—starting with *why?*—but what came out of his mouth was, "Did Taylor see you like this?"

"No, I kept my cloak on until he left. Though I hardly see why that matters."

The idea of anyone witnessing her so . . . so *revealed* did not sit well. The outline of her lithe body clearly visible, it was a sight to make any man lose his mind with lust. And Quint realized, gut churning with possessiveness, that he didn't want any man to see her. Any man save him, of course.

"Why are you here?"

She pulled her arms from behind her back to reveal two foils. "I thought you might like some exercise."

Fear replaced the stirrings of desire. Since the shooting, he hadn't intentionally raised the rate of his heart for worry of another fit. What if exercise worsened his condition? Granted, each fit had been triggered by a specific event or thought, like an attempt to go outside or the sound of gunfire. He doubted fencing would hurt, but how could he be sure?

"I don't think—"

"You are not allowed to refuse." She executed a

single feint with her right arm. "It will do you some good, in my opinion."

He rubbed the back of his neck and contemplated his research. If it was hereditary, as he suspected, then nothing would prevent the impending madness. Not to mention, if he fell ill, he could leave or order her from the room.

You just want to ogle her arse in those breeches.

Without dwelling on that last thought, he closed the distance between them, held out his hand. "Where did you get these swords?"

"I borrowed them," she said with a lift of her shoulder and handed him a foil.

"And what about those clothes? Did you borrow them as well?"

She glanced down at herself. "No, they are mine. The breeches are unbelievably comfortable. Dresses are impractical garments, especially for fencing."

"A duel, scuttling about the mews after dark, not to mention all the excursions with Julia over the years . . . I swear, you court danger at every turn. Has anyone the vaguest idea what you're about?"

She sauntered away, hips swinging, providing him with the precise view he wanted—and he froze. *Saint's teeth,* his imagination had not done justice to the perfect, high roundness of her buttocks.

"I do not require a keeper, if that is what you are implying. Now, shall we?" She spun and lifted her arm into correct position, weapon pointed at him with her front foot forward.

"Have you fenced before?"

"I've taken a few lessons at Angelo's academy. You'll not have an easy time besting me."

"Is that so?" He hefted the foil, tested the weight in his hand to get a feel for it. "Fencing is a thinking man's—or woman's—sport. You need to plan ahead. Not react rashly." Lifting his arms, he stretched out his back and shoulders. "Can you keep a level head, I wonder?"

"We may never know if you cannot cease stalling."

"*Allez!*" he growled and lunged at her.

She defended his parry, and returned with a thrust of her own. He soon realized she had skill. What she lacked in strength she made up for with speed, her movements precise and quick. She obviously had not lied about the lessons, and he suspected she'd taken more than just a few. Despite his resolve to go gently with her, he soon found himself perspiring and breathing hard from the exertion. It felt . . . exhilarating.

"You're smiling," she said, her breath equally labored.

"Am I? It must be because this is so terribly easy."

Her eyes flashed and she began attacking him with renewed vigor. He nearly laughed. She was utterly predictable.

"Is that the best you can do, Lady Sophia?" He led a charge of his own, driving her backward as she defended herself with the blade.

"You've been holding back," she accused, the flush on her cheeks deepening as her movements faltered.

This time, he did laugh. "Is your shoulder burning yet?"

"Like the fires of Hades!" she snapped, then flicked her wrist and slid his blade out from between their bodies. She stepped in close, so close he could see the beads of sweat on his brow, the damp tendrils at her temple curling so enticingly—

Her foot shot out behind his ankle, pulling, while at the same time her free hand pushed on his shoulder.

Even distracted, Quint saw her intention. Subtlety had never been Sophie's strength. With a smirk, he shifted his weight to counterbalance her effort, which caused her to lose her equilibrium. He wrapped an arm around her waist to keep her from tumbling to the ground.

"A nice effort—for a woman," he taunted, attempting to infuriate her.

He failed miserably. Something sparked in her eyes—but it was not anger. Instead, it was hot and wicked, and her gaze dropped to his mouth.

She was thinking of kissing him. He had no doubt. With her lips parted, the rate of her breathing significantly increased, and her stare locked on his mouth, she had one thing on her mind.

And he wanted nothing more than to oblige her.

They were close, hips aligned, with their legs melded together in a tangle. His body stirred, a purely physical reaction he could not hide, and he itched to touch her. To taste her. The problem was, he didn't want to be a "momentary fancy" this time. If he kissed her, she could still say she hadn't wanted it. He needed her to be sure. Needed her to kiss him of her own free will.

It was the same reason he'd never had a mistress. Yes, most every man he knew kept a woman tucked away in a small house somewhere convenient, but Quint could not see the logic in it. He did not want a woman to pretend, to allow his advances only because she coveted his coin. Not that he hadn't ever paid for a tumble in his youth, but honest passion, true desire between two willing people, was a hundredfold more satisfying.

He wanted Sophie willing.

But what then? A mad husband was a terrible burden for a wife.

Suddenly, she used her free palm to push his chest. He dropped his arm to release her. Springing forward, she wasted no time advancing, her blade high and fast as it slashed toward him, and he convinced himself he'd been mistaken about the interest in her eyes. Perhaps a result of the fencing? She attacked him logically, precisely, and he countered with a combination she did not expect. Her muscles shook from the effort, exhaustion on her face. He could nearly taste the victory.

"Wait!" she cried. "There is something in my boot."

Panting, Quint lowered his foil and watched as she turned, presenting him with her backside. She bent over, slowly, and he could not tear his eyes away from those lush, gentle swells encased in tight fabric, not even if the ghost of Newton himself suddenly sprung up from the floor.

They were perfect. Each just the right size for a man's hand. He swallowed, his groin tightening. Breasts drew some men, legs others. Quint had always loved a woman's buttocks. Soft, plush, and ideal for cushioning a man's hips. And right now, Sophie's were poised high as she played with her boot, positioned exactly as if a man might take her from behind.

His cock filled, blood rushing at the mental picture. It would take little effort to free himself, lower her breeches, and bury deep—

In a blur, she pivoted, blade up and ready. Before he could blink, the tip landed square on his chest.

He glanced down, frowned, and tried to shake the lust from his brain.

"You *lose*." She grinned and straightened. "Not bad—for a woman."

Chapter Five

"You tricked me," he accused.

"Yes, that's true," Sophie readily admitted, bouncing on her toes. The thrill of the victory coursed through her veins.

"I thought you had something in your boot," he said unhappily, like a petulant child.

"Unlike you, I am not bound by any gentleman's code. I may fight as unfairly as I wish. And you lost." She couldn't help but grin. "You cannot think I'll apologize for it."

His gaze narrowed. "You are quite determined when you want something. Do you let anything stop you once you've decided on a course?"

"No, not if I can help it. And admit it, you are surly merely because you did not foresee my brilliant plan."

"Brilliant plan?" he scoffed. "A rock in your boot?"

"It worked, did it not?"

An annoyed huff served as his answer.

Sophie laughed as she started for her abandoned cloak. Time to return home before her absence was noted. She was also having trouble concentrating with Quint in such a sweaty and disheveled state. The opening on his shirt had widened, showing a patch of chest lightly covered in dark, springy hair, now damp from exertion. It was deliciously improper and intimate, and every part of her tingled at the sight.

He'd almost kissed her. For a moment, with his arm around her, she'd felt something powerful between the two of them. And it scared her how much she'd wanted it.

She picked up her cloak, turned to him, and cleared her throat. "Quint, I wanted to apologize for the other evening, with the pistols. I should not have fired without warning, or at least asking first."

He grimaced. "I overreacted, and for that I beg your pardon. I haven't heard a pistol fired since that night and it . . ." He trailed off.

"It what?"

"Nothing. Got a bit rattled, is all."

She'd seen him through the door. Rattled? He'd been nearly apoplectic. "You did a very brave thing that night," she said, "trying to stop Maggie's attacker."

"It was stupid of me. I didn't think it through. If I had, I would have grabbed a weapon, at least."

"You couldn't have known—"

Quint held up a hand, cocked his head. When he did not speak, Sophie asked, "What is it?"

He turned to her, intensely serious. Heavens, those beautiful, full lips. She could not help but stare. "Did you hear that?" he asked, quietly.

"No. What should I have heard?"

He frowned. "I heard glass breaking. A window, perhaps." He beckoned her with his hand. "Come. I need to see what's happened."

She held up her palms, as if to ward him off. "What

if someone sees me? I believe it prudent that I remain here."

He sighed. "First, I know you shall scamper away the second my back is turned, and since there may well be a threat on the property, I should like to keep an eye on you. Second, if there is a threat, it is best you are with me instead of here by yourself."

"Nonsense. More than likely it's a mouse."

"I do not have mice, at least not ones large enough to break glass." He lifted his foil and removed the cap covering the tip for safety. "And you are being illogical, Sophie. Do as I say now, or we waste precious time in an argument I will undoubtedly win regardless."

She'd seen Quint in a debate and he was very, very good. And they both knew it was not a mouse. Reluctantly, she lifted the other weapon. Quint was already to the door, so she had to hurry to catch up. He stopped abruptly and she nearly slammed into his back. "Quiet," he said over his shoulder.

He crept into the hall and Sophie followed, staying close. Silence echoed throughout the house, and the carpet muffled their footsteps as they traveled toward the stairs. Quint's home tended toward the austere, she'd noticed. The furnishings and carpets were all in excellent condition, but the space held no life. There were no flowers to brighten it up. No family portraits or other artwork she'd seen, and his study seemed the only room he actually used. Heavy covers concealed the furniture, as if the lodgings were temporary and he planned to move at any moment.

At the bottom of the stairs, he paused to listen. She waited on the first step, feeling ridiculous. The odds that a person had gained entry to his house—

A floorboard creaked somewhere near the back of

the house, and Sophie held her breath. Perhaps one of the servants was not abed yet. Foil raised, Quint started in the direction of the sound. Before they'd taken a dozen steps, a shadow slipped out of Quint's study and into the corridor. A man. He was wrapped in a brown cloak pulled low over his forehead. The shadow glanced their way and froze, and Sophie saw he was wearing a black mask, like some sort of high-wayman.

"Do not move," Quint ordered the man and took a step toward the study.

In an instant, the intruder bolted. He ran toward the dining room, which Sophie knew would lead to the terrace. Quint sprinted after him, Sophie right behind. He was faster, though she did her best to keep up. In the dining room, she saw the figure throw open the French door and disappear outside. Quint skidded to a halt at the threshold, and she heard him utter a curse.

"Why are you stopping?" she shouted. "Go after him!"

When she came alongside, he was standing there, still as a statue, his face contorted in anger and misery.

"What is wrong? Are you ill?"

"No," he snapped.

"You are letting him get away?"

He said nothing, his lips pressed tightly together.

Confused but determined, she ran out onto the terrace. "Then I shall get him myself!"

Quint stared, mouth agape, as Sophie streaked across his terrace like some sort of avenging Valkyrie. He hadn't thought for a moment that she would give chase, alone. Had she no sense at all? Whoever that man was, he would not want to risk discovery, which meant he'd hurt Sophie without remorse. Christ, she could be hurt. Killed.

For God's sake, man, he told himself. *Just go.* She should not be forced to risk herself because he was too bloody afraid. What kind of a man was too scared to leave the house? *Do it,* his brain shouted.

He took a deep breath and placed his foot on the stone beyond the dining room. Before he could take another step, his heart tripped and cold perspiration broke out all over his body. No, not now. He swayed, determined not to give up, and gripped the frame. Brought another step forward. *Focus on the logic. You've done this a thousand times before.* A breeze fanned his skin, an unwelcome reminder that he was partway out of the house, and his vision sparkled. The sense of panic intensified a thousandfold and, with a desperate lurch, he threw himself backward into the safety of the house.

Bent at the waist, he placed his hands on his knees and struggled to draw air. Shame and guilt washed over him. He could not do it, could not go out there, no matter how much he needed to. Was this to be the rest of his life, then? Ruled by unfounded fear and uncontrollable physical reactions? Perhaps he should go ahead and put a ball in his brain now.

Anger rose in his blood, sharp and fierce. At himself, at Sophie, at the person who'd dared to break into his home. And where was his damned staff? He stomped to the bell pull and nearly yanked it off the wall.

He was waiting at the terrace door when a slightly winded footman appeared. "You rang, my lord?"

"An intruder has gained access to the house. He ran into the gardens, most likely headed to the alley. Take this sword"—he pointed to the foil on the ground—"and make sure he has gone. Take care not to engage him in a fight, however. It's not worth your life." He turned to add over his shoulder, "When you're done, see that Lady Sophia returns home safely. Then report to me in the study."

"Very good, your lordship," the boy said, taking up the weapon.

Quint retreated to the study. The one room in the house that he enjoyed. The one room in which he spent most of his time. And the one room just invaded by a footpad. So what had the intruder been searching for?

The study sat at one end of the library, the stacks of old, familiar tomes more precious to him than a lover. He'd read all of them, most more than once, and had discovered a passion for learning in this very space. Even though his parents had hired the best tutors, Quint had preferred to teach himself. Reading at the age of two and fluent in four languages by the time he'd turned eight, he'd studied alone for long hours.

His father had died when Quint was six. Quint had begged his mother not to send him away to school, to let him stay with her, and for a few years she had allowed it. But when Quint turned ten, she would hear no more arguments and he was shipped off to Eton.

School had been excruciating, especially the first few years. The absurdly facile lessons had frustrated him, and the other students had mocked him for the questions he asked during instruction. The boys had been merciless, both in and out of class, though Quint had tried his best to ignore them. Kept to himself. He was there to learn, after all, not make friends. And though he was physically capable of fighting back, why on earth would he lower himself to such a base display of unenlightened behavior?

Everything changed the day four older students locked him outside in his smalls. Mid-January, the weather was near freezing and his bare feet had begun turning blue when two boys from a neighboring house took pity on him. They brought him inside, warmed him up, and gave him clothes and tea. When he recovered, his two saviors marched over to Quint's hall, busted down the door, and proceeded to beat the stuffing out of the boys responsible. It was the most fearsome and humbling sight Quint had ever witnessed in his eleven years.

And a lifelong friendship had been born.

Nick Seaton, then just a duke's forgotten second son, and Simon Barrett, the prized future Earl of Winchester, soon taught Quint everything one could not learn in books. How to throw a proper punch. How to cheat at cards. How to sneak out without getting caught. Quint, on the other hand, helped both boys with their studies. The three of them were inseparable, and school grew tolerable.

Fate had thrown them together, and Quint remained grateful for the two men who'd saved him on more than one occasion. Now, however, he thanked providence that both of his childhood friends were in absentia, that they would not bear witness to his humiliation. He still felt like the eleven-year-old boy out in the unforgiving cold, trying to comprehend what made him so different, so *broken*. And he'd rather no one saw his failing struggle, his desperate attempts to remain sane.

Sighing, he brought his attention to the present. On the far wall stood a glass curio case, which he kept locked. Inside were various bits and mementos he'd picked up in his travels over the years. Nothing particularly valuable, but the intruder must've thought otherwise because he'd broken the thing open. So that was the crashing sound Quint had heard earlier.

He was inspecting the shelves for missing items when Sophie's voice shattered the silence. "Well, I lost him in the mews," she panted. "Dratted man was fast. He turned up Charles Street and disappeared on me."

Quint could not look at her. Could not withstand the questions or the pity. He stared intently at a small refracting telescope from Rome. "Regardless, I thank you for your effort. John will see you home."

Silence descended, and he sensed her waiting. What in the hell did she want him to say? He had no explanation, no answers. And he absolutely did *not* want to have a damned conversation about it. Everything inside him wanted to howl, to scream, in anger and frustration as misery boiled inside him, rising like a tide he struggled to contain. One crack and the levee would burst . . . and no telling what would happen then.

"Are you dismissing me?"

Her dismay caused more emotion to leech out, a sliver in the wall of his composure. He straightened and crossed his arms. "Hard to believe I would dare to speak rudely to such a paragon, the perfect daughter of a marquess out running amuck in men's clothing. But dare I shall. Consider yourself dismissed, Sophie," he snapped. "The lessons are over. The advice, the exercise, the everything . . . it is over. Leave and *do not come back*."

"You stubborn man," she said, her eyes narrowed to slits. "I have done nothing but try to help you. Why are you so unwilling to accept it?"

Fury and embarrassment roiled inside his gut, and he clenched his hands to keep from throwing something. "I do not need your help. I do not need anyone's help."

"Is that so? Because this *paragon* noticed how you fell apart at the report from a pistol. How you refused to give chase—"

"*Enough!*" he roared and snatched the first thing within reach—the crystal ink pot from his desk—and hurled it against the wall. Dark blue spattered on every surface, gruesome evidence of a bestial violence he'd never displayed before. Chest heaving, he closed his eyes against the sight. God, he was no better than an animal. He pressed the heels of his hands to his eyelids. It was getting worse. *She* was making it decidedly worse.

"Quint," she said quietly. "Let me help you. Whatever is wrong, it can be fixed."

He shook his head. So optimistic, his Sophie. She'd been indulged and pampered her whole life, her father allowing her to do as she pleased without consequence. He was beyond redemption, however. How could he make her understand?

"This—I—cannot be fixed. The sooner you believe me, the sooner you will cease interfering in my life and leave me alone."

"Is that what you think I've been doing, interfering?"

He hated the way her face fell, how her shoulders slumped. Most of all, he hated himself for the disease rotting his brain. He needed to drive her away, when what he really wanted was to pull her into his arms and never let her go. But this was how it had to be.

"My lord." Taylor knocked on the open door and

peered in. "I thought I heard a crash. Is anything amiss?"

Quint swallowed and dug for composure. "Everything is fine. See that Lady Sophia gets home, will you, Taylor? I am going to bed." Without a backward glance, he strode out of the study and toward the stairs. One thing he knew, sleep would be a long time coming.

Noises pulled Sophie up from the depths of sleep. She fought it, snuggling in deeper, until light spilled into the room. "Go away," she mumbled and flipped the bolster over her head.

"My lady," Alice said, "his lordship is requesting your presence in his study when you've dressed."

Her father wanted to see her—and so early? That jolted her awake. "What time is it?"

"Nearly one."

Sophie blinked. "It is? I cannot believe I slept so late."

"That is what happens when you stay out all night," Alice muttered.

"I was not out all night. I returned at a fairly reasonable hour." Only, then, she hadn't been able to fall asleep. The evening's events with Quint kept turning around and around in her head.

She rolled over and then groaned. There wasn't a part of her that did not ache. Even the tops of her toes hurt. "Do I have time for a bath?"

"His lordship is with his man of affairs. I suppose he won't notice if you're a few more minutes." Alice went to the door and poked her head into the corridor.

Sophie struggled to sit up when Alice returned. "Do you think this is about The Talk?" Sophie'd heard it so many times that she could recite it. *You need a husband, Sophia. I won't always be around to look after you. This year, I expect you to choose one.* And while she loved her father dearly, she had no intention of following his orders. Her failure would disappoint him, which she regretted, but there was no hope for it. Marriage was impossible.

Her maid went to the wardrobe. "It's about that time, I'm thinking."

Sophie sighed heavily as she swung her legs over the side of the mattress.

"His lordship only wants to see you settled and happy with children of your own, my lady. All fathers do."

Guilt pressed down on her. She would be married now, if only she hadn't been so stupid. She'd actually believed Lord Robert would offer for her. *Many betrothed couples anticipate the wedding night, Sophia. And we'll be betrothed as soon as I can speak with your father.*

Only, he hadn't approached her father afterwards. She'd waited and waited, hope fading each day, until she'd finally cornered him a week later at a soirée.

"Robert," she said once they were alone. "I thought you planned to speak with my—"

He looked at her coldly, his face nearly unrecognizable in its unfriendliness. "Then you misunderstood," he said. "My wife will be pure when she comes to the marriage bed."

Sophie gasped. "I—I was pure."

"Then where was the blood?" he sneered.

"I do not know. I'm told not all women bleed the first time."

"They do. And you were far too . . . enthusiastic for a virgin. To marry you now would dishonor my family."

The memory made her cringe. *Dishonor.* She'd seen the truth in his eyes, that Robert would never believe her. That something was *wrong* with her. To that point, Robert had married another girl not long after and they had moved to his family's estate in Wales. And Sophie had vowed never to allow anyone to humiliate her ever again.

She would not inflict her shame on another man.

By the time she'd bathed, dressed, dried her hair, and entered her father's study, it was near three. "Good afternoon, Papa."

Her father glanced up from his desk. His secretary was there, pen scratching madly over parchment as the marquess dictated directions. Papa was an important member of Liverpool's inner circle, and he spent his days on both government duties and estate matters. Though he was busy, however, he always made time for her.

Her father's face softened as he rose. "Sophia! There's the beautiful smile to brighten up my dreary day. Come here, my dear."

She warmed under his affection, as she always did. Her father was demonstrative and loving, never afraid to show how he felt about his family. He was still handsome at fifty-eight, tall and fit, with graying brown hair and sideburns. When she drew close, he reached for her and kissed her cheek. "I hope I haven't interrupted your busy day. Yates, would you mind giving us a moment?"

"Of course, my lord." The secretary gathered his things and quit the room.

When the door closed, he said, "Let's sit, shall we? I have something I need to discuss with you."

She folded into the chair across from his desk, clasped her hands. Readied herself.

"My dear," he said, resuming his seat. "I know what it is to be young and enjoy one's self—believe me, I got into my fair share of scrapes in the day—but you are a lady and the rules are different. Each year I give you the same lecture, and each year you ignore it. So I fear drastic measures must now be taken."

Sophie blinked. This was not The Talk. Drastic measures . . . whatever did he mean? "Papa, I know you wish me to marry. I will find someone this Season, I promise."

"That has been your answer every year since your debut. Yet you remain unmarried. You discourage suitors so handily it could be considered an art. I know I am partly to blame because I've indulged you all these years. But after your mother . . ." He took a deep breath and her heart squeezed painfully, both for his loss of a wife and her loss of a mother. He continued, "This Season will be different. I already have someone in mind for you. Therefore, should you not make your own choice, I will be making it for you."

Her stomach dropped as her jaw fell open. "No! You cannot mean it."

"I do."

"Why?"

"Sophie, I am nearing sixty. I should like to see you settled. Perhaps hold a grandchild or two before I go."

The idea would've knocked her off her feet had she not been sitting. She'd never considered . . . Of course, she knew he would die someday, but that day always seemed so far in the future. He was all she had. Yes, she had a stepmama and a half brother, but it wasn't the same. This was the man who'd rocked her back to sleep each time she'd had a nightmare . . . the man who had let her slide down the banister in her nightclothes . . . the man who let her keep a pet piglet in the house.

"And the closer you get to thirty," he continued, "the harder it will be to form a good match."

Her mind reeling, she wheezed, "Who . . . who is he?"

Her father shook his head. "I shan't say for fear you'll come up with a way to scare him off, but this gentleman meets all my requirements in a husband for my only daughter. Just know that you will be married this year, whether you choose him or I choose him for you." He shuffled a few papers on his desk, unable to meet her eyes, and she realized how uncomfortable he seemed.

She did not believe him. Her father would never marry her off to someone she did not want. She just needed to give him time. Put forth a reasonable effort at this year's parties. Go for a few drives in the park. Then he would relent, she was sure of it.

But a small amount of doubt stayed with her the rest of the day.

Chapter Six

The next afternoon, Quint's mood was blacker than obsidian. The broken glass and ink spots in his study had been dealt with, but he was no closer to determining the person responsible for the break-in or what he had been looking for. From what Quint could tell, everything was in its rightful place. Nothing of value taken. His work was safely tucked away in a location no one save him would ever find.

In addition, guilt compounded his other worries. He'd lost control in front of Sophie. Acted like a child, shouting and throwing things. How could he ever face her again?

A timid knock on the study door interrupted his concentration. "Yes?" he snapped.

One of the maids—Elizabeth? Eliza?—appeared. "My lord, there's a man at the door asking for a Sir Stephen. He seems quite adamant that the gentleman lives here. What should I tell him?"

"Where is Taylor?"

"He is downstairs, my lord. I was dusting and heard the knocker."

"Who did he ask for—a Sir Stephen? No one by that name lives here. Tell him he has the wrong house."

"That's just it, sir. He says he does have the right house, that it's one of your lordship's guests."

Guests? Quint rubbed his forehead. "Who is the caller?"

"Lord MacLean, your lordship."

That gave him pause. He'd seen MacLean over the winter in the clubs and various social events, but the two of them hadn't exchanged even ten words. Why would a Scottish earl—one he and Sophie had discussed recently—be on Quint's stoop asking for a nonexistent houseguest? "Show him to the front drawing room, will you?"

She bobbed a curtsey and shut the door. Quint rose and lifted his coat off the chair back, shoving his arms into the sleeves. Could this have something to do with Sophie's duel? He started around his desk and wondered if she had gone to MacLean after all.

Cursing himself a fool, he buttoned his coat and continued to the drawing room. Sophie *should* go to MacLean. Hadn't Quint told her never to come back? He'd been purposely cruel last evening in the hopes of keeping her away. So relief should be the prevailing emotion, not this burn blossoming in his chest—a burn he suspected might be jealousy.

Lord MacLean stood when Quint entered. "Apologies for disrupting you, Quint. I was inquiring after your houseguest, Sir Stephen."

Quint motioned for the man to sit as he lowered into a chair. "I fear someone's bamming you, MacLean. I have no houseguest."

The ox-sized Scotsman frowned, appearing genuinely perplexed. "I heard him say it with my own ears. Why would your cousin lie?"

"My cousin?"

"Ran into him at Madame Hartley's two evenings past, in an argument with Lord Tolbert. Apparently Tolbert challenged the pup to a duel, wouldn't accept an apology instead. I had to step in, and Tolbert took offense to a Scotsman involving himself in a dispute between *English* gentlemen."

Quint's eyebrows lifted, and MacLean nodded. "Indeed. I could not let that stand, you ken. Tolbert's to meet me on a field of honor and Sir Stephen's agreed to be my second."

Familiar pieces of information slid around in Quint's brain: Duel. Buckskin breeches. MacLean. Young pup. Cousin to the Viscount Quint—and then they fell into place. Good God.

She had truly gone too far this time.

His fingers curled around the edges of the armrests. It was all he could do to stay seated, not to jump up and . . . what? Shake his fist in impotent anger? Pen a strongly worded note? It wasn't as if he could charge through Mayfair, demanding answers. Christ, hc was pathetic. "What does Sir Stephen look like?" he forced himself to ask.

"Young. Scarcely out of the schoolroom, if you want to know the truth. A bit short, but then everyone seems short to me. Brown hair. Spectacles. Thin."

Hiding her eyes. Smart. No, *not* smart, he corrected. Nothing about her scheme showed intelligence. Did she have any idea of how utterly ruined she would be if discovered? A litany of questions peppered his brain, but no answers emerged. He could not imagine a single reason why she would be out and about in London Society dressed as a man. At a *brothel*, no less.

Pending a tower with an impenetrable lock, there would be no stopping her—and he could do nothing. He'd never regretted his condition more than at this moment. To think of her out in London, at night, unchaperoned, dressed as a man . . . any number of unfortunate things could happen. She needed a keeper—only her keeper would *not* be London's biggest rake. The last man Quint wanted in Sophie's proximity was the one before him now.

MacLean watched him closely, awaiting a response. On occasion, a reputation as a madman could definitely serve as a benefit.

Quint snapped his fingers. "Of course, my *cousin*. How could I forget the lad? I mostly keep to my study and cannot keep track of his comings and goings."

"So he does live here?"

"Yes, he has been known to knock about the place. But keep your distance from him."

"Why's that?"

"He's unpredictable. Raves like a lunatic some nights. Other days he cannot get out of bed." He tapped his temple. "*Non compos mentis.*"

MacLean lifted a brow. "Well, I wanted to speak with him about Tolbert. He was supposed to call on me yesterday, yet he never showed."

Understandable. To pass herself off as a man would be infinitely easier at night than during the day. At least she employed some restraint. "And as the boy's appointed guardian, I am afraid I cannot allow that. His mental status would make him an unreliable second. He might suffer a fit and shoot you instead." MacLean frowned but nodded, and Quint asked, "Do you happen to know why Tolbert challenged Sir Stephen?"

MacLean pushed his large frame out of the chair and grinned. "I dinna ken the whole story, but I heard it was over a woman at The Pretty Kitty."

Quint choked, which he quickly covered with a cough. "Is that so? I'll be sure and ask the lad next time I see him. So take care, for your own sake, to give Sir Stephen a wide berth. I would not even approach him, were I you." He stood up and held MacLean's stare. "Stay far, far away from Sir Stephen."

MacLean held up his hands, his brows raised. "Not a problem. But he might get into less trouble if you can fatten him up. Lad's skinnier than a fence post."

A large carriage waited in the alley behind the tea shop. The driver jumped down at Sophie's approach. "Greetings, my lady."

"Good day, Biggins." He flung the door open for her and set the step. "Thank you." She climbed up and inside, the well-sprung vehicle creaking slightly in protest. The curtains were drawn and a lamp had been lit in the interior. Biggins closed the door behind her.

"I apologize for being late," Sophie told the two women waiting inside as she settled on the seat.

"Not a problem, my lady," Pearl Kelly said, smiling. "Mary and I have just been comparing tricks of the trade, as it were." Carefully positioned chestnut curls framed Pearl's delicate face, the style both youthful and flattering. Though it was early in the day, her jewels glittered in the dim interior. Sophie had never seen Pearl without something sparkling on her fingers and ears.

"I am indeed sorry to have missed that conversation. Perhaps—"

"No, you know that I cannot." Pearl wagged a finger at Sophie. "Lady Winchester and the duchess both would have my hide. Not until your ladyship is married."

Sophie bit off the retort, that she would never be married, because what was the point? No one believed her anyhow. She turned to the thin, black-haired girl next to Pearl. "Mary, thank you for agreeing to meet with me. I would have come to you at The Kitty, if it were possible, but I am afraid Sir Stephen must remain out of sight for a few days."

Sir Stephen may have extricated himself from his dawn appointment with Tolbert, thanks to Lord MacLean's intervention, but now he was involved in another, also thanks to Lord MacLean. Who knew the men of the *ton* were such a hotheaded bunch behind closed doors?

Mary shrugged. "No problem, milady. It's not every day I gets a chance to chat with Pearl Kelly and the daughter of a marquess."

"And sneaking out won't cause any problems for you?"

"No, milady. My friend Tibby will cover for me."

"Still, it's best not to keep you. I wondered if you could tell me about Rose's fancy gent, the one she believed would set her up in a house."

"Set her up? Rose never said anythin' to me about gettin' a protector, your ladyship."

"She told her sister, apparently. I thought she might have shared the news with you as well."

"I'm afraid not, milady. She did have some regular

customers, but I never heard that one of them was sweet on her."

Sophie exchanged a quick glance with Pearl. "So these recent regulars," Pearl said. "Any idea of their identities?"

Mary cocked her head and contemplated the question. "Well, let's see. I only knows 'em by what she called 'em, er, their pet names. . . ." She raised her eyebrows.

"Yes, I understand." Then Pearl said to Sophie, "They give them names based on the gentleman's performance or preferences in the bedroom."

"Ah," Sophie said. "And so?"

"Let's see. One of O'Shea's men. She called him Sweaty. Another gent, called him *La Gauche.*" Mary put her hand in her lap, extended one finger, and swung it to the left. Pearl sniggered and Sophie blurted, "They can do that?" which caused Mary and Pearl to dissolve into a fit of giggles.

"Very well," Sophie drawled to get back to the issue at hand. "Anyone else?"

"There was the Watcher. Never wanted to touch her, just watch her . . . you know." Mary shifted on the seat. "One of 'em she called King George because he seemed not right in the head, God rest His Majesty's soul."

"Not right in the head, how?" Sophie asked, sharply.

"Erratic, I think. Not violent, just . . . strange. Talked all sorts of nonsense. But I don't think he would have hurt her, milady. Rose had a good head on her shoulders."

"I do not doubt it, but evil does not always show itself outright. Others you can think of?"

"Oh, there was a man who stammered when he got

excited. Tangle tongue, she called him. That's all I can remember, your ladyship."

"Thank you, Mary. Will you send word if you encounter any of these men? I'd like to see if I can learn their identities."

"I will, milady. More 'n likely they'll start seeing other girls at The Kitty."

Sophie dug in her reticule, pulled out a few coins, and handed them to Mary. "Hide these and use them for yourself."

"Thank you, milady. I will."

"You shall escort her back?" Sophie asked Pearl.

"Indeed, my lady. Be safe."

"And you as well."

A second visitor arrived not long after MacLean departed, one Quint could not turn away—no matter how much he wanted to.

"Quint, thank you for seeing me." Lord David Hudson strode into Quint's study, leaning slightly on the walking stick in his left hand. "Although you will need to explain why you refuse to come to me, illness or no."

Hudson had served as Quint's contact at the Home Office for seven years. Razor-sharp and charismatic, Hudson was undoubtedly one of the most important men in the British government, though what he actually *did* was a bit vague. He'd recruited Quint for service during the Napoleonic conflict, and Quint had enjoyed his years of developing complicated codes the French could not break. The two kept in loose contact these days. Hudson knew Quint was working on something but did not know the particulars. Quint preferred to keep his work to himself until it was completed.

"This could've been handled in correspondence," Quint said. "There was no need to come all the way to Mayfair."

"Yes, your man did attempt to turn me away at the door. And suffice it to say I did not come for the hospitality." He glanced around for a place to sit.

Quint reluctantly cleared a chair of its contents. "What if I had contracted something contagious?"

Hudson strode to the chair, flipped up the tails of his topcoat with a flourish, and sat. He propped his walking stick against the desk. "But you have not contracted anything. You are perfectly well."

Better not to argue, Quint thought. He had no intention of explaining precisely how *unwell* he was. "Now that you are here, perhaps you can explain why you wanted to see me."

Hudson rested his elbows on the armrests and steepled his fingers. "How much do you know about the current political status of Greece?"

Quint cocked his head and sifted through the pieces of information inside his brain. "I know that revolution has been brewing there for a number of years, and that the Filiki Eteria has begun massive initiations with the plans of launching a liberation campaign against the Ottomans. The Greeks have the support of Alexander I, who is presumably hoping to colonize after the bloodshed, and England would rather Russia not get a foothold so close to our shores."

"Very good. Castlereagh has maintained the need for status quo on the face of it, to preserve the peace of Europe as long as we can. But I am orchestrating things quietly to make sure, whenever it begins, this skirmish goes the way we want."

"Ah."

"Yes, you can see where I am headed, I suppose. I know the work you did against Bonny, and I also know your penchant for solving the unsolvable puzzle. I suspect you are attempting to crack Vigenère's cipher during your self-appointed incarceration. I do not need to tell you how valuable that solution would be to the British government when every other government in Europe uses it. We could read and decipher every coded message ever sent. So the question becomes, who else knows of this work?"

Scary how much Hudson knew. "Absolutely no one."

"I understand you had an intruder last evening. Why would someone bother doing that, do you suppose, unless you were close to cracking it?"

Quint stilled, hardly able to breathe. How had Hudson learned of last evening? "I haven't the faintest idea."

"Because there *is* no other reason. Are you certain you have not told anyone about your work? Lady Sophia, perhaps?"

Goddammit. Quint searched the other man's face, but Hudson gave nothing away. There was no clue as to how he knew of Quint and Sophie's . . . friendship. The man had ice in his veins; little wonder he'd risen so high in His Majesty's service. "No, Lady Sophia is a friend. Nothing more."

A small twitch of his lips was Hudson's only discernible reaction. "I assume whoever broke in did not find anything. Is whatever you are working on in a safe place?"

"Yes."

"Any chance you will tell me where you keep it?"

"None."

Hudson tapped his fingers together in a slight show of irritation. "Quint, Castlereagh is . . . unpopular. People are unhappy with his policies, Peterloo, the Six Acts, and the like. And this discord is affecting his mind. Public opinion can be quite harsh when it turns against you."

Quint tried not to react. He knew how the game was played. Hudson did not care to be thwarted, so now he'd loaded up his quiver with well-appointed arrows. Quint watched and waited.

"Doubtful he'll last much longer," Hudson continued, "and so we must begin to think about the future of England."

"And you hope to succeed him?"

Hudson grimaced. "Heavens, no. Much too high profile for me. I prefer to remain in the shadows, where the real power resides. But there is someone already in mind, someone who will listen to reason when it becomes necessary. Like if, for example, a peer of the realm needed our protection."

The skin on the back of Quint's neck prickled. God, he hated politics. Why intelligent men did not instead put their time and efforts to more worthwhile pursuits, such as science and philosophy, boggled his brain. Disease and famine might well be eradicated if not for politicians. And agents of the British government.

"I cannot produce what I do not yet have, Hudson. The work is under way but not finished. When it is ready, you will have it—and not a moment sooner."

The man smiled amiably, though his eyes remained as hard as flint. "Of course. Just as long as I am the one to receive it."

Meaning Quint might sell the cipher solution to a

rival empire. "Whyever would you not be?" he countered coolly.

"I cannot imagine. But we find ourselves in strange circumstances these days, do we not?"

As Quint stared at Hudson, he quickly catalogued the man's appearance. Shorn dark hair, the kind one used to see under wigs, receded off his forehead to form a point in front. Nails clean and short. Elegantly appointed with expensive tailoring. Same limp, from an injury he'd suffered fighting with Wellington in Portugal before landing in government service. No stain, smudge, or speck of dirt to mar the presentation. Why men wasted so much time on their appearance never failed to perplex Quint.

Nothing seemed out of place, yet there was something off, something he should be noticing. He knew it instinctually. The same walking stick Hudson always carried, the inside no doubt hiding a long, sharp blade. A small chunk of wood was missing from the handle, near the knob.

None of that should make Quint uneasy, however. So why did part of his brain insist on searching where nothing existed? There was only one answer: His mind had clearly deteriorated even further than he'd originally thought. The idea depressed the hell out of him.

Hudson snatched up his walking stick and levered out of the chair. Quint rose as well, disconcerted. "I shall leave you to it, then," Hudson said as he started for the door. "Good day, Quint."

When Hudson departed a few moments later, Quint called Taylor to the study. "Yes, my lord?"

"Taylor, the members of the staff, what are we up to now? Ten?"

"Nine, your lordship. The upper house maid quit earlier today."

Quint searched his desk for a clean piece of paper. "Assign one of the other maids, or hire a new one. It matters not to me. Thank you, Taylor. That is all."

"Pardon me asking, but has your lordship ever given thought to acquiring a valet?"

Pen paused over the ink pot, he said, "No. Why?" He did not want a valet. Hadn't had one since he was twenty. They disapproved of his odd hours and his tendency to dress himself. They were worse than nursemaids, and Quint did not need to be cared for like a child. Like an imbecile. Oh, hell . . .

"The maids, my lord, are responsible for many tasks in a household this size. The additional requirements of your lordship's wardrobe—the mending, the polishing, the pressing—are quite outside the scope of what they normally do for a master of the house. It's a valet's job. I believe we would have more success in retaining maids if there were a valet about."

Quint's face must have shown his horror, because Taylor quickly added, "We could keep him below stairs, my lord, if you'd rather. Your lordship need never see him. But he can tend to the clothing, relieving the maids."

It made sense, damn it. Quint never cared for convention, but perhaps it was unfair to ask the maids to do more than their share. "Fine. Find one, but keep him out of my sight."

"Thank you, my lord." Taylor retreated, leaving Quint alone to contemplate his exchange with Hudson.

Just how was Hudson coming by the information? It had to be someone inside Quint's house, someone observing and passing notes along to the Home Office.

And then there was the intruder. While the layout of Beecham House was not complicated, the man had known precisely where to find the most expeditious escape. That suggested familiarity with the house. As well as someone who was aware that he and Sophie were otherwise engaged in the ballroom. So who was it?

The Beecham household attracted a hodgepodge lot, mainly due to Quint's reputation as a difficult employer, and the fact that he never bothered with references. Anyone on his staff may not be whom they claimed. No employment agency would work with him any longer, so anyone he hired came off the street. Not that it mattered; whatever an employment agency could tell him would be far less than Quint could observe himself.

Taylor's interview a few weeks back, for example. Fresh-faced lad, borrowed shoes, too thin, a fading, round burn mark on the inside of his right wrist. Too young to have ever served as a butler but desperate for any position he could find. Quint had hired him on the spot. Regardless, he knew nothing about the lad's background.

Glancing around the walls of his study, he frowned. This house was his last remaining solace, the only place to which he could retreat. He'd grown up here . . . buried his parents here . . . come into the title in this very room. It was the one place in the world he'd felt safe.

Until now.

Chapter Seven

Quint stared at the basket on his stoop. A red woolen blanket covered the top, and there was a large paper pinned to the thick fabric that read: *For his lordship.* "Whom did you say delivered this, Taylor?"

"It's unclear, my lord. The person departed before Cook answered the knock."

Quint scratched his jaw, thinking. With the break-in a few nights prior, he supposed any number of things could spring out. "Better step back, Taylor," he said.

The butler moved away and Quint lifted the edge of the blanket. He saw . . . brown fur. And legs.

He flipped the blanket off and found a sleeping dog. A puppy, to be precise. Light brown body with black fur surrounding its nose. A fat scarlet ribbon had been tied in a bow around its neck.

"Why, it's a little dog," Cook said, she and Taylor now peering over Quint's shoulder. "And ain't she a cute one."

Quint grimaced. "Dogs are not cute. Dogs are messy, dirty, and exceedingly dumb. They demand attention and eat . . ." He drifted off as the creature began to stir, its legs twitching in awareness. It blinked a few times and rolled on its back to stretch.

"A boy dog, I be thinkin'," Cook laughed and then quickly sobered. "Beggin' your pardon, your lordship."

"No need to apologize for drawing the obvious anatomical conclusion," Quint said, rising. "The question is, what are we to do with it? We cannot keep it. Perhaps the boys in the stable—"

Cook gasped. "But, my lord, that dog is for you. Someone wanted your lordship to have him."

The dog twisted to his stomach and stood up. His ears flopped over, they were so large, and he put his oversize paws on the edge of the basket and tried to climb out. "Yes, but I do not know the first thing about domesticated animals. How to care for it, what to feed it."

"Why, it's not hard, my lord. Once you get them trained properly, that is."

Quint dragged a hand down his face. Christ, the animal would urinate—and worse—all over his house.

Taylor cleared his throat. "If I may say, my lord, I believe the dog would be a welcome addition to the household. The staff would appreciate the opportunity to care for it."

"Oh, yes," Cook added in a rush. "I agree, my lord."

Now Quint looked an ogre if he tried to get rid of the thing. "Dogs need exercise. Who is going to take it for walks?"

"I'll have a footman do it."

"And I suppose," Quint said to Cook, "you are going to tell me you shall feed the thing."

"Indeed, my lord. We've got more than enough scraps for him."

The puppy was still struggling to get out of the

basket, though the wicker sides were higher than its head. Quint bent down and tilted the basket until the creature was able to tumble out. Tail wagging madly, the puppy bounded down the steps and began sniffing the earth.

Quint knew who'd delivered the puppy. She could not keep from interfering, despite the harsh words he'd leveled at her. Why was she so determined to poke and prod him? The dueling practice, the fencing . . . and now a dog. He did not have time for an animal. Every bit of his concentration needed to be in research and experimentation, in finding a way to return to his previous self. The man before the accident.

He still hadn't decided what to do about her other identity, Sir Stephen. The whole thing would be amusing if it weren't so incredibly reckless. Was there a purpose to her sojourns as a gentleman, or was she bored? And how had no one discovered her secret before now? Quint would recognize her no matter the costume, convincing or not.

The dog dashed up the steps and rose to stand on its hind legs, oversized front paws resting on Quint's boots. The creature looked absurdly happy—his big, round eyes sparkling and vacant—and Quint wondered what a creature so stupid as a canine had to be so bloody jolly about. It seemed to want something from him, but Quint had no idea what he was supposed to do.

"He wants your lordship to pet him," Cook said, gently. "Go on, then. Give him a scratch behind the ears, my lord."

Feeling ridiculous with both Cook and Taylor watching him, Quint reached to stroke the puppy's head with one finger. Soft. He'd never touched a dog before. His mother hadn't allowed pets. He had studied animals out in the country and ridden horses, of course, but he'd never petted a dog. The creature seemed to like what he was doing, though, if the tail wagging was any indication.

Without warning, the puppy licked Quint's palm. Quint snatched his hand back and straightened, then shook his head at his own ridiculousness. Licking was instinctual to animals in the Canidae family, both as a method of grooming and to show appeasement. Still, he wiped his hand on his trousers.

"What breed of dog is it, do you think?" Cook asked.

"A mastiff, I think," Taylor answered. "And judging by the size of his paws already, a large one at some point in the future."

"How much do you know about dogs?" Quint asked his butler.

Color rose on the young man's cheeks. "I grew up in the country, my lord, and my family had animals of all kinds."

"Excellent. Consider the dog your responsibility, then."

The puppy scampered down into the yard once more, ears bobbing, and Quint wondered at this bizarre gift. A dog. What had she been thinking?

"I am pleased to care for him," Taylor said, "but the honor of bestowing a name should be your lordship's."

"A name? By which to call it, you mean?" What did one name such a creature? Giving it an identity made him uncomfortable, as if he was treating an animal as a human being. And naming the dog would make it more difficult to rid himself of the thing.

Of course, if he gave it away, there was every chance Sophie would merely gift him another one. He sighed.

Probably less trouble to keep the cursed thing at this point. "*Canis horribilis.*"

"My lord?"

"His name. *Canis horribilis.*" Quint pointed to the puppy, now digging under a bush. "Fitting, I think."

Taylor's mouth flattened, but he said, "An excellent choice by your lordship."

Quint grinned. "I am glad you approve, Taylor. Now he's all yours." He spun and started for the kitchens. He'd taken one step when something thumped against his ankle. The puppy waited at his heels. "Go with Taylor, Canis." Tongue hanging from the side of its mouth, the dog sat on the ground and blinked at him. Quint pointed at the butler, scowled at the dog. "Go, Canis."

Nothing. The animal stared at Quint patiently.

Quint dragged a hand through his hair. If he knew Sophie, she was nearby, someplace close, to observe his reaction. So he certainly hoped she was enjoying this. Stepping forward, he brushed by Taylor and returned to the threshold. "Do not expect my gratitude," he shouted into the dying light.

He swore he heard giggling before he disappeared into the house.

The distinctive odor of the Thames filled the carriage and Sophie turned toward the window. In the daylight, the docks bustled with rough-hewn dockworkers and sailors unloading cargo as well as efficient-looking customs officials on patrol. At night, however, the area had an eerie stillness to it. The revenue officers barred people from the docks in order to protect cargo against theft, so the men moved inland to the brothels and bars.

At last, the wheels slowed to a stop. Sophie threw open the door and climbed out. The driver jumped down and she experienced a moment of surprise at the man's size. He hadn't appeared so large up on the seat. She fished in her pocket for a few coins, handed them over, and started to leave. "I'll be waitin' for you over there, sir," the driver said with a tip of his hat.

She paused. While she appreciated the gesture, it struck her as odd that he assumed her errand a quick one. "No telling how long I might be."

"No worries, sir. I am happy to wait."

Hmm. This was the first driver she'd hired who had not departed the second he'd been paid. Nevertheless, it would be foolish to argue.

Located at 259 Wapping Street, the Thames Police Office was an unassuming three-story structure on the riverbank. Having been established here some twenty-odd years earlier, the police surveyors were charged with seizing and detaining any offenders detected in the act of criminality in and directly around the Thames. While this may have started as a way to guard against piracy and thievery, the men's responsibilities also included handling any bodies found in the river, the very reason Sophie was now here.

She knocked on the door. After several minutes, a man arrived, unlocked it, and allowed her in. He was short and wore spectacles. She guessed him to be in his late thirties.

"Good evening," she told him, stepping inside on the rough wood floor. "I am Sir Stephen Radcliff. I should like to speak with someone regarding the unfortunate discovery day before yesterday."

He peered over his spectacles. "I beg your pardon, sir, but we have many unfortunate discoveries here. To which one are you referring?"

"The girl. The one missing a hand." She held up her right arm to demonstrate. "I fear she may be someone I know. I should like to see her, if possible."

"Surgeon's got her downstairs," he said as he strode toward a large desk against the wall, "but there's not much in the way to recognize her by now. Have you ever seen a body pulled from the water, sir?"

Sophie stood a bit taller. Or tried to, at least. "I have not, but I shall not be turned away. The girl may very well be my valet's sister, and I mean to set the man's mind at ease." She slid a few coins across the surface of the desk.

The clerk wasted no time in pocketing the silver. "Of course, sir. Follow me."

He came around the desk once more, a large ring of keys in his hand. There was a lamp on the corner, which he picked up as well. Sophie followed him to the door, which the clerk unlocked to reveal a set of steps. They descended, the soft light throwing shadows on the plain, dirty walls. Doors fitted with heavy locks stood on both sides of the corridor. They continued on to the far end, where the man used another key to open a thick, wooden door. "We keep it locked at night," he explained and gestured for Sophie to enter.

This room was brighter than she expected, with multiple lamps positioned around the large space. Instruments covered every surface, a macabre silver reflecting in the glow. There were three long tables, two of which were covered with cloths. A young, bearded man with blood on his clothing—the surgeon, she assumed—leaned against the empty third examination table, a lit cheroot in his fingers. There were dark smudges under his eyes, as if he hadn't slept in a very long time.

"This gentleman wants to see the girl pulled out day before yesterday, the one missing a hand," the first officer said.

The surgeon tiredly lifted his cheroot and asked, "Do you mind? Might keep your eyes from watering if you're not used to the other smell."

She nodded, grateful. The underlying scent was already quite strong—a rank, noxious odor of decaying flesh. He gestured to a long table where a sheet-covered lump rested. "Right here." He walked over and flipped the cloth with a flick of his wrist to reveal a bloated, pale naked form with an incision down the center of her body. Sophie had to dig her nails into her palms to keep from reacting. She'd never seen a dead body, let alone one pulled from the water. The skin was gray and loose, torn in places, the stomach distended. Her hair had been cut short, a rough, haphazard effort. Pity constricted Sophie's chest as she forced herself closer.

"Couple of surveyors found her yesterday around noontime. Some boys were throwing rocks at something floating in the water near Horsleydown and the surveyors went to investigate. Pulled her out and brought her here."

Sophie swallowed hard. "Do you know what killed her?"

He pointed to purple marks around her throat. "Strangled."

"And her hand was severed."

"Yes, very neatly, too."

She walked all around, studying the body from various angles. The smell grew stronger and she fought the urge to gag. She took a handkerchief from her coat and held it over her nose. "That mark there, on her leg. Is that a tattoo?"

"Yes. It's a small playing card, the queen of spades. Likely a mark from whatever house in which she worked. It's not a common practice, but there are a few who do it."

So not Rose, who had been employed at The Pretty Kitty. Sophie experienced a small measure of relief until she realized this meant *another* girl had been murdered. This made a total of four found in the last six months—and that still left Rose unaccounted for. She thought of Natalia, the tavern worker that had disappeared a few months back. Could she have been another victim as well?

"Anything else you can tell me about her, or any idea when she was killed?"

He blew a long, thin stream of smoke from his lips. "Generally takes at least two days in the water until they float to the surface, depending on the tempera-tures. Dead before she went in the water. Appears as if she was raped as well."

Sophie closed her eyes briefly. A tragic end for anyone, prostitute or lady. "Thank you. I think that is all I need. May I leave money for a proper burial?"

That seemed to surprise him. "Leave it with the clerk, sir. I think she'd appreciate that."

The door closed behind the young man, and the officer, who'd eavesdropped the best he could, stroked his beard. Sir Stephen, he'd said. No good reason for a fresh-faced gent to visit the Thames police in the dead of night. Came to see the girl, the latest victim in what the papers were calling the River Murders. He'd asked too many questions, in the officer's opin-ion. Seemed he wanted to know more than just the girl's identity.

Sir Stephen had asked the surgeon about the other victims as well. Why? His initial curiosity had been for the most recent girl—not all the others. So why had he lied?

One person in particular paid the officer good money to keep an eye on things on Wapping Street. Secret, weekly reports of the investigations and activities in the office, which the officer wrote without fail and delivered to the requested address. It was the main reason he preferred working the desk at night. With the constant stream of surveyors, watermen, and constables in and out of the office during the day, it was nigh impossible to piss without someone watching over your shoulder.

At night, however, the officer could do as he pleased. The surgeon might work late if a fresh body awaited, but he stayed on the lower floor. So there was no one to stop the officer as he picked up his pen and found a fresh sheet of parchment.

Quint stood just inside the terrace doors and watched as Canis gamboled away into the dark gardens, the puppy's big ears flopping wildly. Two days since Canis had joined his household and Quint had to admit the invasion hadn't been as bad as he feared. The animal hardly ever left his side and Quint found it . . . strangely comforting.

Not that he would admit it.

Taylor had the right of it; the staff had instantly taken to the animal, eager to participate in frequent walks and feedings. But Canis always returned to Quint's side. The beast had attached himself to Quint, and there wasn't a damned thing to be done about it.

How had she known?

Canis began barking happily. It was the same unrelenting sound when he wanted Quint to pay him attention. Someone was out in the gardens—and it did not take a genius to deduce who might be out there. This was beginning to be a habit with her.

"You may as well show yourself," he called. "He'll not let up until you do." Tenacious did not even begin to describe the beast when he wanted something.

The yapping ceased and soon Sophie appeared, looking adorably sheepish, with Canis cradled in her arms. "I had not planned on disturbing you. I merely wanted to make sure you had not given him away." She climbed the steps to the terrace, set Canis on the ground, and then drew closer. She wore a black cloak and bonnet, which he assumed were her skulking clothes.

"I ought to, but the staff have grown attached to the curst thing."

"Just the staff?"

He did not care for the smug set to her lips. "I named him, did I not? What more do you want from me?"

"Does it feel better with your shoes off?"

He glanced down at his bare feet. Hard to say when it had started, this preference for the cold marble floor beneath his naked feet, but it helped him feel *alive*. A true gentleman would never be seen without shoes, yet Quint wasn't about to put them back on. If she found it offensive, she was welcome to scuttle home. "It feels . . . bracing. As if the cold roots your legs to the floor. You should try it one day."

She lifted her plain skirts to reveal brown half boots with black laces. Bending, she pulled the laces loose, then stood and started toeing off her shoes. Quint watched this with a mixture of fascination and horror. Was the woman truly going to remove her footwear? Propriety had never concerned him, but even *he* knew this was beyond the pale.

Two soft thuds and her stocking feet made an appearance. His heart kicked hard in his chest, and this time it had nothing to do with fear. Encased in thin stockings, her feet were small and delicate. She wriggled her toes and sighed, a sound that caused heat to unfurl in his groin.

Tools of bipedal locomotion, he told himself and snapped his gaze to the gardens. *Nothing more.* They were functional appendages that should in no way be tempting. He should not be thinking of running his tongue along the smooth instep . . . or wondering how the soft underside would feel as it slid along the backs of his thighs—

"I wish I could remove my stockings," she murmured. "But even this feels heavenly."

Quint swallowed hard and crossed his arms over his chest. The image of her sliding stockings down her bare legs was too erotic to dwell on—not if he didn't want an obvious erection frightening her. "I am not surprised. Traipsing through the mews of Mayfair is exhausting business."

"Indeed it is," she returned cheerfully.

"Why have you returned, Sophie?"

She stared at her toes, moving them back and forth, clearly hesitating. No doubt attempting to fabricate a reason because she didn't want to tell him the real one.

"The truth," he said.

"It seemed a nice night for a stroll. You are generally up late, so I thought I'd see if you were still awake."

He snorted. No lady strolled by herself in the middle of the night. "You are aware I live alone. That this is a bachelor's residence?"

"Should I be worried? Are you planning to chain me to your bed and ravish me at your whim?"

He strove not to combine the words "ravish" and "Sophie" in his head; the idea only served to remind him of what he could never have. "Indeed. Merely allow me to remove the other woman there first."

She chuckled. "That's one thing hardly anyone realizes about you: how amusing you are."

Only she would believe that. Amusing was not a word anyone had ever used to describe him. Odd, strange, and aloof were far more likely. "Not everyone appreciates my humor."

"Admit you are fond of the dog, Quint."

Never. "Did you know the Romans sent mastiffs into battle wearing armor in order to attack the enemy?"

She sighed, irritated with his evasion, and he hid a smile. "As always," she said, dryly, "you are a wealth of information."

"Actually, I find myself quite in the dark these days."

Her eyebrow rose. "Oh? About what?"

"I cannot think of a single reason you should be sallying about London in the dead of night, dressed as a man, even if to visit the Thames Police Office. Would you care to enlighten me?"

"How . . ." She crossed her arms and thrust up her chin. "Are you having me followed?"

"Yes. And you should hardly be surprised. If any woman in the history of England ever needed constant supervision, you are she."

"The driver. I should have known." She rubbed her

forehead. "I cannot fathom your audacity. You have no right to oversee my activities, and furthermore I am doing quite fine on my own."

"Only because no one gets a good enough look at you. How anyone could mistake you for a man is beyond comprehension. You are a hairsbreadth away from the scandal of the decade, Sophie."

"And you are wasting your time if you think to stop me."

"I never said I wanted to stop you. If I did, I would write to your father and inform him of what I know." He held up a hand as panic clouded her face. "I will not do so unless I feel you are in immediate danger. But that does not mean it's wise for you to do this. Therefore, I've hired someone to drive you about and ensure your continued safety—no matter what you are wearing. But what I do not understand is *why* you are posing as Sir Stephen in the first place."

He didn't think she'd answer, the silence stretched so long. "You'll laugh," she said quietly.

"I sincerely doubt it. Tell me, Sophie."

"I've fallen into a bit of a . . . diversion," she explained with a wave of her hand. "I investigate things. For people—women—with no other resort. Prostitutes, servants, and the like. It started when my maid, Alice, her sister was accused of stealing the flatware in the house in which she worked. After I figured that one out, someone else came to ask for help and it kept going from there. We found I had an easier time dressed as a man, not to mention people took me more seriously."

Though he wished such treatment were not the case, he did not doubt her. Women were not afforded the same accessibility as men in any culture. Still, this hardly set his mind at ease.

"Investigating. And here I thought you were not in immediate danger. It's even worse than I feared."

"It is not!" She stamped her foot. "I'm helping people. And I am careful."

"Yes," he scoffed. "Duels. Standing in as MacLean's second. Visits to gaming hells."

She pinned him with a hard look. "You are surprisingly well informed for a man who never leaves his house."

"Shocking, is it not? Yet I remain current on all your antics. What do you think that means?"

"I could not begin to guess."

"It means," he said with all due seriousness, "that if I could learn of it, others could learn as well. Which is why I hired someone to protect you. God, Sophie. Do you know what could happen to you in a brothel? You could be dragged into any nook or empty room and be forced to do unspeakable things. Things a woman like you should never know about."

"A woman like *me*." She let out a brittle laugh, and he could see the flush of anger on her cheeks. "You have no idea what sort of a woman I am, what I know or do not know. And I do not require a guard. You are not my father, Quint, nor my husband."

A well-placed blow, and he felt it keenly, his body tensing. He gave her a stiff nod. "Indeed, I am not. But that does not mean, as a friend, I do not feel responsible for your welfare."

"Why?"

"Because if your repeated visits to my house are any indication, you seem to care for mine."

Chapter Eight

A strange disappointment filled Sophie's chest, eradicating any anger at his high-handedness, and she had to look away. Right. He cared about her—in a *friendly* way, of course. Just as she cared about him. As a friend. Indeed.

So why, then, did she wish he'd said something more? Something different. *Because you're feeling something more, nitwit.*

"And what if I refuse?" she asked, getting back to the conversation at hand.

"If you refuse or attempt to evade the guard I've hired, then I *will* write to your father."

She studied him, but his expression gave nothing away. If it was a lie, she could not tell. But she recognized the deliberate set of his chin, the hard, unrelenting lines of his jaw. "Fine."

The puppy trotted up, sniffed Sophie's toes, then continued on to Quint. He sat on the ground by the viscount's naked feet. Very masculine, naked feet. Just staring at them started a quiver deep in her belly. Did his skin look like that all over, slightly pale and dusted with brown hair?

"And," Quint continued, "you must promise to stay out of places such as The Pretty Kitty."

That got her attention. She gasped. "Absolutely not! I must have the freedom to go wherever is necessary for the information I seek. Sir Stephen affords me that freedom. I am perfectly safe there."

"Safe!" He tilted his head back, a mirthless laugh erupting from his throat. "You are anything but safe, even dressed as a man. Sir Stephen does not possess the strength to stop a brawl or evade a footpad. That part of town is more dangerous than most, Sophie. And what happens if a man who prefers to bed young, feminine-looking lads takes a fancy to Sir Stephen?"

A fancy . . . to Sir Stephen? Good heavens. She could only blink at him.

"I see the idea never occurred to you, my lovely innocent. It is one thing to visit Madame Hartley's, where gentlemen act in a fairly civilized manner. A house such as The Pretty Kitty is another matter entirely. It is far more unpredictable. There are no rules there."

"I am hardly innocent. And I am not completely daft. I know what happens inside bawdy houses. You'll be pleased to know that I always carry a weapon to protect myself."

He quirked a brow. "What sort of weapon? I know it is not a pistol."

"A knife. I carry it wherever I go."

"Wherever you go? Even now?"

She nodded, eager to prove she wasn't a total ninny. "Of course."

He turned and closed the short distance between them. She caught the calculating gleam in his brown eyes. It had her taking a cautious step back.

He advanced, his large frame crowding her, and

she held up her hands to ward him off. "Quint, what are you—"

"What if I can find it?"

"Find what?"

"The knife. If I can locate it and disarm you, will you abandon this silliness after I prove how inadequately prepared you are?"

Her spine met the edge of the doorframe, yet he kept coming, effectively trapping her with his body. He wore only a waistcoat atop a fine lawn shirt that hadn't seen the good side of a pressing since Michaelmas, with the laces partially open to reveal the hard angles of his collarbone. Awareness prickled under her skin. "I am not inadequately prepared." Why did her voice sound so strange?

He didn't look as if he believed her. "Let us conduct an experiment, shall we?"

He reached into the folds of her cloak, clasped her hands, then raised and pinned them above her head, securing them with one of his own. With her cloak thrown open, the taut planes of his chest brushed the tips of her breasts, which began to tingle in appreciation.

His free hand settled on her hip. "If I can relieve you of said weapon, then no more visits to bawdy houses and gaming hells."

"That is unfair!" She struggled in his grasp. "You're holding me captive. At least let me have use of my hands."

His eyebrows shot up. "You think some drunken, randy rogue or cutthroat will fight fair? This is not Gentleman Jack's or Angelo's. An assailant will restrain you as quick as you can blink—and you are not strong enough to get free."

At that, she gave a renewed effort to break his

grip. He held fast, however, and let her flail for a few moments. When she stilled, she panted, "Devil take you, Quint. I am not amused. Let me go."

"I am not amused either. And you, you stubborn woman . . . you need to be taught a lesson about safety."

"Safety? Need I remind you just who bested whom in your ballroom during our fencing exercise? I can take care of myself."

He did not comment as the fingers of his free hand began traveling up her rib cage, over layers of clothing . . . and ripples of sensation coursed through her body. She shivered when his palm slid over her stomach, his thumb coming to rest between her breasts. The pounding rhythm of her heart echoed in her ears. "Hmm. Not here," he said, the deep, husky sound like warm honey as he nearly cupped her breast. "Where else might it be?"

When his fingers started south, Sophie shook herself. She could not let him win so easily—even if his touch did turn her knees to jelly—so she twisted her body once more, this time with everything she had. Surprise flashed on his face before he tightened his hold. She continued to struggle, jerking on her arms and shoulders to free herself, but he would not budge. His palm glanced over her hip and then her upper thigh, and she began to use her legs, kicking, though her skirts and his proximity prevented her from doing serious damage. "Getting closer, am I?" he said, his eyes glittering in the light of a nearby sconce.

The smug set of his beautiful mouth annoyed her. He presumed victory, and Sophie did not care to be dismissed so easily. She raised her knee and aimed for the one spot where men felt it most keenly—but Quint shifted and she connected with his inner thigh instead. "Curse you," she ground out, chest heaving with exertion.

A flash of teeth emerged in a rare grin. "I fully expected that move first. You almost caught me off guard."

"You are enjoying this entirely too much."

"Indeed, this is the most fun I've had in ages." Curling his fingers, he began gathering up her skirts and lifting them. Cool air brushed over her ankles. "Besides, how could I not enjoy having a beautiful woman at my mercy?"

The words irritated her further. "I am hardly at your mercy."

He chuckled, still collecting fabric in his hand. "Give over, Soph. You are seconds away from losing."

The edge of her skirts fluttered against her knee, and anger at her helplessness built like a thunderstorm in her chest. Clearly she would not best him physically, so she needed to employ a bit of strategy. Only one idea came to mind, however. So, rising up on her toes, she sealed her mouth to his.

He stiffened in shock, but only for an instant. His lips came alive and then, heavens, he was kissing her—really *kissing* her. Intently, as if he'd been waiting a lifetime to do it—which wasn't true, of course, since he'd fallen in love with the Perfect Pepperton. But Sophie no longer cared if he loved someone else. Nothing mattered but this very *non*-friendly kiss. Her breasts swelled inside her stays until she could hardly breathe, his hand cupping her jaw to keep her still as he kissed her with exquisite precision.

Finally, after what felt like hours, he slid his tongue along the seam of her lips, and she opened eagerly to let him in. He invaded, overwhelming her senses with a delicacy and skill that would have buckled her knees had he not pressed her into the wall.

His tongue twined with hers and Sophie matched his movements, determined to affect him every bit as much as he affected her. And he growled, a deep rumble of male desire that thrilled her. She never wanted this to end. It felt reckless and yet completely *right*, as if this was the one thing that had been missing from the last three years of her life.

Suddenly her hands were free and she immediately threaded her fingers through his thick hair to hold him closer. He responded by tilting her head and deepening the kiss into something more urgent, far less gentle. His tongue continued to probe, to explore. An answering ache built within, centered between her legs, and she began an exploration of her own, her palms moving up his arms to clutch his wide shoulders, marveling at the feel of him under her fingertips. So much strength there, and the heat that radiated off his big body seeped into her bloodstream, igniting her from the inside.

His mouth broke off and he dipped to kiss her jaw, her throat, the evening bristle on his face gently teasing her skin. She shuddered as hot, open-mouthed kisses rained across her skin. "Oh, God, Quint."

She should stop him. Run from his house as quickly as her feet would take her. Go home, undress, crawl under the covers, and ease this burning craving at her own hand. Safely. And alone.

But she didn't. No way did she want this to end. Instead, she pushed on his shoulder to reverse their positions and dragged his mouth back to hers. He approved, kissing her with renewed vigor. His palm covered her buttock, bringing her pelvis in line with his, whereby he rocked his hips at the precise spot she ached the most. She moaned into his mouth.

The sound of barking gradually registered through the fog in her brain. Quint must have heard it, too, because he broke off to rest his forehead to hers. Sophie clung to him, gasping for air, more shaken than she expected. It was as if he'd reached within her and turned everything inside out.

The puppy barked once more, and Quint released her with a sigh. "Canis, quiet."

"What did you name him?"

"Canis horribilis."

"'Horrible dog'? I should have known you would not choose anything as simple as Spot or Blackie."

Quint lifted a shoulder. "It suits him. Though I am unsure why you believed I needed a dog."

"Because I live to torture you."

"Does that also explain why you just kissed me stupid?"

No, that was more to torture myself. It only served as a reminder of the things she'd never have. Things she didn't deserve.

Sophie stepped away and pulled the edges of her cloak tighter, wrapping up all those dark desires and wicked yearnings. She kept her voice even. "I was attempting to win your silly game. And now that I have, I must return home." Spinning on her heel, she strode across the terrace and headed for the gardens.

"Sophie," he called just as she reached the stairs.

When she turned, she saw the glint of metal in his hand. *Her knife.* "How . . . ?" Somehow he'd removed it while they were kissing. Unbelievable.

His eyes glittered. "You *lose.*"

She thrust her chin up, forced a light tone. "You

may keep it. I have others at home." She started down the steps, and then stopped. "Oh, and Quint?"

"Yes?" He was watching her intently, his expression annoyingly smug.

"Look down."

Quint's head dropped. Immediately, his body stilled as if he were caught on a frozen pond threatening to crack below him at any moment.

Beneath his feet lay the terrace. Quint was outside.

Quint stared at the smooth white surface of the terrace. He could do this. He *had* done this, not even ten minutes ago with Sophie here. He'd been outside and the world had not crumbled around him.

Of course, he'd leapt indoors the instant he'd realized, but for a few moments he had been *normal*—not a near-cripple unable to leave his house.

He took a deep breath, held it, and slid his toes onto the stone. His pulse jumped, so he closed his eyes and hurried to shift his other foot in line. The surface of his skin turned cold as perspiration broke out on his brow, and his lungs constricted. *Do not think about it,* he repeated, but it did not help. He gasped, desperate for air, and his heart nearly slammed out of his chest.

Damnation. Irrational fear crashed over him, a wave of immense failure that had him retreating into the house. He could not do it. Safely inside, he bent over and rested his hands on his knees, drawing in great gulps of air.

He'd researched anxiety, this "deluded imagination" as it was called. *The dread of something worse than the present.* And while he yearned for a solution, the rational side of him knew there likely would not be.

As Byron said, *There is an order of mortals on the earth, who do become old in their youth, and die ere middle age; Some perishing—of study, And some insanity.*

Sighing, he straightened. Disappointment weighted him down. Each day, he expected to be better, yet each day ended in defeat. Except for tonight when kissing Sophie. Too bad he could not kiss her each time he wanted to leave the house.

And why had she kissed him? To distract him, certainly. Had there been another reason as well, or was that wishful thinking on his part? He would like to imagine she'd been overcome with passion, desperate for him . . . but he dealt in realities. Practicalities. Why would she want him now—a broken, cowardly excuse for a man—when she'd rebuffed a perfectly healthy version years ago?

She wouldn't, he told himself. Sophie could choose any man, and she'd made it clear long ago Quint was not under consideration.

He stared out at the darkness, wondering if perhaps he should give up hope—on Sophie, on going outside, on ever being *normal.* "'Do not spoil what you have by desiring what you have not,'" he said aloud, a quote from one of his favorite Greek philosophers, Epicurus. He should ask one of the maids to embroider the saying on pillows and litter the house with them.

He needed to return to more important matters, such as discerning the identity of the intruder. His list of observations regarding the staff was near complete. Yet even so, he couldn't point to one servant as having an obvious motive for breaking into the study. Theft, yes. But if any of them were of a mind to steal, there were plenty of smaller items and even paintings that would fetch a fair penny if fenced. And while he may be oblivious to much in his household, he was fairly certain the staff weren't robbing him blind.

"My lord."

He turned to find Taylor striding toward him, a note in hand. "Yes?"

"This was just delivered." Taylor offered the paper from his own fingers, which no proper butler would ever do. A proper butler would have the paper on a salver and present it with great flourish. Though Quint had to admit, he definitely preferred the non-flourish method. Another reason he liked Taylor.

Quint slid his thumb under a seal he recognized and then noticed Taylor hovering. "Yes?"

"It has been some time since your lordship has eaten, so I had Cook prepare something. It is waiting in the study, my lord."

Quint was not particularly hungry and he hated to be needled, but he supposed he should eat. "Fine."

He glanced at the parchment. A note from Colton. Julia had given birth to a boy. An heir. God help the ladies of the *ton* in twenty years, Quint thought with a grin. Along with reporting on the mother's health and the baby's exemplary constitution, Colton invited Quint to visit Seaton Hall. Quint hated the idea of disappointing his two friends, but traveling anywhere was out of the question.

He'd best concoct a plausible excuse, however, or Colton might very well show up on his doorstep.

Activity buzzed inside The Black Queen late on a Friday evening. Hazard tables, croupiers, roulette wheels . . . the frenzy kept the guests hopeful while they emptied their pockets. Sophie, decked out in

Sir Stephen's finery, strolled to the nearest table and placed a few bets while searching the room.

A far cry from where she'd been earlier tonight, at one of the Season's first events, dressed in a ball gown and pretending to enjoy herself. Sophie did so much of that lately—pretending—that it was becoming difficult to remember the real woman.

When one of the house girls drew near, Sophie gave a nod to attract her attention, and the lightskirt soon arrived at her side.

"Wanna buy some time, luv?" She smelled of gin and sweat, her clothes threadbare.

Sophie shook her head. "I am looking for Molly."

Pearl had sent a note earlier—through Alice, of course—with the name of a girl to see tonight in hopes of getting some answers. With any luck, Pearl's connection would be free. Sophie did not care to be at The Black Queen any longer than necessary. It was another of O'Shea's establishments, and not in a reputable area of town.

"That's her, over there." The girl pointed to the back, where a brown-haired girl was bent over, whispering in a gentleman's ear. Sophie slipped the girl a coin, then headed for Molly. When she drew near, Molly glanced up and gave Sophie a once-over. Her lips twitched before she put her mouth near the man's ear once more. Whatever she said made him laugh and pat her backside, and Molly straightened to face Sophie.

"Were you wantin' go somewhere private, sir?"

"Yes, I do. Where?"

Molly grinned. "Follow me." She brushed past Sophie and continued to a door by the faro tables. A large, rough-looking man with a forbidding expression opened the door and Molly sailed through, Sophie following behind.

At the landing, they nearly ran over a girl on her knees. A man leaned against the wall, his trousers undone, pushed to the tops of his white thighs, while the girl worked his male member with her mouth. The act was not unheard of, certainly, but it was the first time Sophie had ever seen it in person. Head bobbing, the girl pulled her lips over the taut, glistening flesh, wet sucking sounds filling the cramped space. Sophie stood motionless, unable to look away. The scene was strangely titillating. The man's lids were closed, his face slackened in pleasure, and he didn't even notice the interruption. But the girl's eyes landed on Sophie—and she winked.

A hand on Sophie's elbow pulled her farther down the corridor. "In here," Molly said, throwing open one of the doors. She crossed to sit on the small bed and her hands went to the laces on the front of her shabby gown. "What might your lordship be lookin' for tonight?"

"Nothing of that sort." Sophie held up her hand. "I just need to talk."

"Oh, you like to watch? We get plenty of those, too." She reached for the hem of her gown, lifting.

"No," Sophie said quickly. "Pearl Kelly said you might be able to help me with some information."

"Pearl Kelly." Molly grinned. "Well. I haven't seen her in years. Known her forever, since before we even had tits. She's got quite a life for herself now. So what did she send you here for?"

"Have you heard about the bodies being pulled from the river? The girls?"

Molly shook her head. "No. Why?"

"One of the girls who died, found a few days ago,

she had a marking near her ankle. A small playing card, a black queen. The surgeon said it was a tattoo, most likely from whatever house she worked."

Molly nodded. "O'Shea makes all of us get 'em." She lifted her leg, pointed to her stocking-clad ankle. Sophie could just make out a black smudge under the wool. "He says it's to remind us of where we belong." She rolled her eyes. "As if we could forget."

The barbaric practice of permanently marking women like cattle caused bile to rise in Sophie's throat. "Have any of the girls gone missing recently? I am trying to find someone, a girl from The Pretty Kitty. The Thames police think she might've been pulled from the water two weeks ago. If I can find a man who knew both of these dead women—a customer, perhaps—then I might find whoever was responsible."

Molly shook her head, her gaze sliding away. "I can't think of anyone who's gone missin'."

An obvious lie, and Sophie had no intention of letting it drop. "Are you sure? This girl, the one found mutilated two days ago, obviously worked here at some point. Brown hair. She had blue eyes with a small scar—"

Molly made a choking sound, then covered her mouth with her hand. Sophie could see the emotion on the other woman's face from across the room. "Tell me, Molly. It's plain you knew her. Tell me who she was."

Molly drew in a ragged breath. "I can't," she whispered, and Sophie noticed something new in Molly's eyes. Fear.

"Of course you can." Sophie frowned and stepped closer. "You can help me find whoever did this to her. Please, just tell me what you know."

A tear slipped down Molly's cheek and she quickly

brushed it away. "I can't," she repeated in the same hushed tone. "If I do, he'll kill me, too."

"Who?" Sophie pressed. "Who will kill you? You must tell me, Molly."

Molly shot to her feet. "Forgive me for sayin', but I don't have to tell you a thing, my lady." Sophie jerked at the form of address, but Molly continued, her voice quiet and determined. "This is a lark to you, to come down here and ask questions, nosin' around. Then you get in your fancy carriage and go back to your nice house on the other side of town." She placed her hand on her chest. "I got no choice but to stay here. And if they find out I been talkin' about things I shouldn't, I'll be breathin' my last."

The words hurt, as true as they were, but Sophie did not let them deter her. "He rapes them, Molly." Molly closed her eyes, and Sophie continued, "He forces her and then he strangles her. And then he cuts off her right hand before throwing her into the river like refuse. If you know who would do such a horrible thing, then you have to say it before anyone else is killed."

"No, I don't. I feel poorly for those girls, but they ain't me." She lifted her chin. "And sometimes there are fates far worse than being killed. O'Shea don't like his girls talkin' and causin' trouble. I can't help you. Now I need to get back to the floor." She started for the door.

Disappointment rolled through Sophie. There was no way to force the girl to tell what she knew, and Sophie could not protect Molly should O'Shea find out. "What if I pay you?" That got Molly's attention, so Sophie said, "I have some money saved. What if I can pay you for the information? You could use the money to leave London, go far away where O'Shea cannot find you."

Molly's lips turned into a sad, resigned smile. "There's nowhere O'Shea can't find us, if he has a mind to. You best leave it alone, miss—else you're likely to find yourself a Thames trout, too."

As Molly reached for the latch, Sophie blurted, "How did you know I wasn't a man?"

The girl gestured to Sophie's crotch. "Your bollocks. Men carry 'em around like the most precious things on earth. You walk like you've nothin' hangin' between your legs."

Sophie was still pondering that piece of information as she stood downstairs, preparing to leave. As she shrugged on her coat, she noticed an errand boy accept a note from one of the floor bosses. The boy waited for instructions, nodded, and raced out the front door. Sophie hurried to follow him outside. When the boy started off down the street, Sophie chased him, calling for him to stop. She cursed her shoes, which prevented her from catching him.

The boy glanced over his shoulder, his wild red hair sticking every which way, and slowed to a stop. "Wot is it, guv?"

"You work here, running messages and the like?"

His expression turned wary. "So wot if I do?"

"I bet you know everything that happens inside."

He puffed up, as only a young boy could. "I know my fair share."

Sophie took out a coin from her coat and presented it to him. "This is yours if you'll answer a question." Then she described the missing girl. "Do you know her?"

He shook his head. "Girls, they keep to themselves, mostly. O'Shea don't care for 'em talkin' when they should be tuppin'." Two fingers reached out and snatched the coin.

"Wait," she said before he could dash away. "What's your name?"

"Red." He pointed to his head.

"Well, Red, there's plenty more coins where that came from. Would you like to earn them? All you would need to do is be willing to keep me informed."

Chapter Nine

After securing Red's promise of help, Sophie continued down the street and glanced about. No hacks anywhere in sight. With no choice, she began to walk in order to find one, her hat pulled low as her mind turned over the conversation with Molly.

Molly had known the girl's identity. Fear had prevented her from saying. Fear of O'Shea, certainly, but had there been fear of someone else? Did Molly know the killer? If so, the prudent thing would be to tell someone so the man could be caught and hanged. Though Sophie could hardly blame her hesitancy; women like Molly held little faith in law and justice, since they saw so little of it in their own lives.

Perhaps Sophie should return on another night and question a different girl, one who might be willing to share information. She shuddered to think of what O'Shea did to the girls under his control to frighten them. If rape, mutilation, and strangulation paled in comparison . . .

The night was fairly quiet despite the early hour. Two cats fought nearby in a tangle of screeches and hisses, and the faint revelry from a nearby tavern spilled out into the street. Both served as a comforting reminder that she was not completely alone in this deserted stretch.

A noise caught Sophie's attention. A boot scraped on stone—a sound out of place considering the desolation on the street. The hairs on the back of her neck stood up. Was someone following her?

She glanced around, checking. Nothing moved, not even the wind. Her trepidation rising, she transferred her walking stick to her left side, slid her right hand into an inside pocket, and clasped the comforting weight of her knife. She increased her pace. Bishop's Gate was not far, and there should be enough activity there to lose whoever might be behind her.

Her heart pumping, she regretted evading Quint's man earlier. If she hadn't, she could be on her way home by now. Another sound, this time closer.

It all happened in a flash. She spun to find a large shape nearly upon her but did not have time to focus on his face before the glint of a blade caught her eye. A knife streaked toward her chest. Holding up her right arm, she tried to block the attack while shifting her body. The weight of the blow landed on her forearm, dislodging the knife in her hand. It clattered to the ground, and there was a sharp sting near her shoulder. She had no time to examine it, however, because the man slashed once more, this time near her belly.

Sophie jumped back and raised her walking stick to defend herself. The ineffectual adornment bounced off the man's shoulders, not affecting him in the least. A sneer twisted his lips as he advanced. She hadn't ever seen him before. Crooked nose and large, rough features. He was missing two teeth from the top of his mouth, but otherwise seemed fit. Even if the heavy greatcoat were not hampering her legs, she could not outrun him.

He moved quickly, aiming for her stomach again, and she reacted on instinct. Using all her weight, she bent low and threw herself into him. It put him off balance, just enough that she could slide her boot behind his foot and trip him. He fell backward—but did not release her. Instead, he pulled her down as well and she landed with a jarring thump on the ground. The side of her head slammed against the walk and pain exploded behind her eyes, the impact dazing her.

"Fucking cunt," she heard the man grunt before he rolled to slash the knife across Sophie's thigh. Sophie kicked as hard as she could, her boot catching him on the knee. Struggling for breath, she knew she had to get to her feet. On the ground, she was as good as dead. But everything hurt and she felt dizzy. Dear God, was she going to die on the street?

What felt like a large tree trunk rammed into her stomach, knocking all the air from her lungs. Sophie gasped, closed her eyes, and curled into a ball to protect herself. Then the sharp crack of a pistol erupted, and she tensed, expecting to feel a searing pain rip through some part of her body. None came, however, and the last thing she saw before the blackness rose up to engulf her was Quint's guard standing over the attacker, a smoking pistol in his hand.

Quint heard the commotion before the study door even opened. Loud voices were uncommon in the house, generally heralding an unwanted visitor.

He was halfway around the desk by the time Taylor

threw open the door. "My lord, he just arrived," Taylor said, standing aside as Jenkins entered, a limp form cradled in his arms. Quint's insides went cold. Christ almighty, it was *Sophie*. Dressed in man's garments. And . . . dead?

"I didn't know what else to do, my lord," Jenkins blurted as Quint rushed forward. "Figured you'd want me to bring him 'ere. He's lost quite a bit of blood."

With a desperate lurch, Quint reached for her, the need to touch her overwhelming him. Thankfully, Jenkins did not question it, just placed the body in Quint's outstretched arms. She was tall but thin, and stirred as Quint held her close. "I am fine," she murmured against his shoulder. "Just need to rest a few moments."

His chest seized painfully, this time from panic of a different sort. How badly was she hurt? He sucked in a breath and said to Jenkins, "Follow and tell me what happened."

He pushed by both men and strode quickly for the stairs, taking them two at a time. He went to the chamber adjoining his and kicked the door open. Striding inside, he placed her on the bed. "Taylor!" he shouted.

"Yes, my lord," Taylor said from directly behind him.

Quint began unbuttoning Sophie's outer garments. "Send a footman to Barnes House for Lady Sophia's lady's maid, Alice. Then bring every medical supply we have in the house. Fresh cloths. Boiled water. *Now!*"

"Shall I send for a physician as well, my lord?"

"No," Quint replied emphatically. "Absolutely not. I'll tend to her—him—myself." He slid the greatcoat off her arms, and she groaned at the movement. The slash in the fabric near her right shoulder caught his attention. Blood stained the fabric. *Goddammit.*

"What happened, Jenkins?" he barked, tossing the

coat on the ground. He went for her boots next and noticed another slice in her trousers. Wet, dark crimson spread over her thigh. That laceration would need to be treated first. On the unused washstand, he found a clean linen towel. "Here, press this against the wound on his thigh."

Jenkins came forward and did as instructed, which earned a groan from Sophie. "Apologies, my lord," Jenkins mumbled and then continued his report. "He did exactly as your lordship said he would. Tried to give me the slip in the mews, but I was ready for him. Followed him to The Black Queen over in—"

A large, darker-skinned man burst in, a stack of clean towels in his arms. Quint blinked, paused in the process of removing Sophie's boot. "*Who the devil are you?*"

The man drew himself up. "I am Vander, your lordship's new valet. I have brought you fresh linens."

His manner of dress was English, but the voice revealed his eastern heritage—India, specifically. Quint's eyes narrowed on the interloper, helpfulness notwithstanding. "And you were to remain below stairs, where we would never cross paths with one another."

Visibly shaken, the valet nodded and placed the linens on the bed. He hurried from the room, not saying another word.

"Quint," Sophie gasped, regaining his attention.

New valet forgotten, he slipped off her boot. "Continue, Jenkins."

"So The Black Queen. Do you know it?"

"Yes," Quint gritted out. Had she completely lost her mind? A gaming hell in that part of town was no place to go alone, lady or no.

"Weren't there even an hour before he came out

and started toward the corner. I followed at a distance so he wouldn't scent me. Then this big fellow come out from an alley and pulled a knife. Lad put up a good fight, but the fellow got in a couple good swipes before I came alongside."

Quint removed her second boot and hurried to slide her arms out of the topcoat. "And where is this fellow now?"

"Dead, more 'n likely. I put a ball in his head, picked up the lad, and came straight here." Jenkins chuckled. "The lad knocked that big ox off his feet. Never seen anything like it. Swiped his boots right out from underneath him. That's a brave one right there, my lord."

"Yes, very brave," Quint muttered from behind clenched teeth. "I'll take over now. That will be all, Jenkins. And thank you."

"Happy to help, my lord." Jenkins stepped back and Quint pressed on Sophie's thigh to staunch the flow of blood. Quiet footfalls were muffled by carpet as Jenkins departed; then the door closed.

"Please do not be cross with me," Sophie whispered, her voice quivering with pain.

"Cross does not begin to characterize what I am experiencing right now." White-hot boiling rage. Paralyzing, debilitating fear. Frustration at his worthless inability to protect her. Regret he had not informed her father of these outings. So much emotion bubbled up inside him he thought he might choke.

"I am not seriously injured, Quint. A few nicks. I bumped my head on the ground when I fell, and it made me a bit dizzy."

"Oh, is that all?" he drawled.

A heavy sigh escaped her lips. "I am relying on your

levelheaded reasonableness. Do not get upset over something so trivial."

He was not feeling particularly levelheaded or reasonable at the moment. "You are bleeding all over the coverlet. I would not call that trivial." Using one hand, he loosened her cravat to make her more comfortable. "I shall wait for your maid to remove the rest of your clothing."

"Not necessary." She yawned, likely an aftermath of the energy expenditure as well as the concussion. "Do what you must. I need to return home before I am discovered missing."

He stared at her, studied the dirt and smudges marring creamy skin. Exhaustion etched her fine features, while the bedclothes turned crimson with her lifeblood. Someone had tried to *kill* her. Quint had known the risks, yet allowed her to carry on regardless. This was every bit as much his fault as hers. "Aiding you in this deception has lost its appeal, considering what happened this evening. Perhaps if you are discovered missing, it will prevent future acts of harebrained recklessness."

Her lids snapped open, the brown irises cloudy with pain. "You would not dare. If I were found here—"

Taylor knocked and entered, thankfully cutting off Sophie's objections. Whatever her argument, Quint did not want to hear it. Taylor set a large tray down on the bedside table, and a maid came in to light the fire. After asking the girl to hold the towel on Sophie's thigh, Quint busied himself by taking stock of the strips of linen, salves, and herbs. The butler had wisely included a bottle of brandy. "Bring me a knife, Taylor."

Quint strode to his chambers and thoroughly

scrubbed his hands with soap and fresh water. When he returned, he found Sophie's lady's maid by the bed, pressing the cloth on Sophie's wound. Sophie's lids were closed, her skin pale. He knew she was in pain, yet she was admirably determined not to show it, her body clenched to bear the agony. A fire now blazed in the long-forgotten hearth to bring some warmth to the musty space. A small knife had been placed on the stack of linens.

He uncorked the brandy and splashed a large amount in a glass. Selecting a vial, he sprinkled some powder into the liquid, stirred it, and handed the glass to the maid. "See that she drinks it."

The maid sniffed it. "What is it?"

"Peruvian bark." Knife now in hand, he moved to Sophie's side.

"Pardon me for asking, my lord, but shouldn't we give her laudanum instead?"

"With a head injury, I'd rather not. The opiate will slow her responses. And we'll accomplish more in a shorter amount of time if you follow my instructions without questioning them."

"It's fine, Alice," Sophie rasped. "I'll drink it. I trust his lordship." The maid helped Sophie raise her head enough to throw back the brandy in one mouthful. Quint would have wondered over Sophie's familiarity with spirits if he weren't so petrified about her bleeding out on the bed.

He put the blade to her trousers, preparing to rend them.

"No!" Sophie said. "Do not cut my clothing. Pull it off instead."

"Which will be infinitely more painful for you. Do

not be ridiculous, Sophie." He raised the knife to the wool once more.

She made a feeble attempt to clutch at his arm. "Quint, stop. I need my clothing to wear home."

His gaze locked with hers. Stubborn, maddening female. He was of half a mind to let her stumble home dishabille. It would serve her right for embarking on the mad scheme in the first place. "Please," she whispered.

"Remove her clothing," Quint ordered the maid and moved to the far side of the room.

He stood with his back turned, listening to fabric rustle and Sophie's gasps of pain each time she was forced to move. With anyone but her, Quint would have felt vindicated by those tiny expressions of abject misery. But the sounds she made twisted his insides, the idea that she'd been attacked strangling him.

A thump followed a grunt. He heard the maid move the bedclothes. "There, my lord."

Spinning, he found the injured side of her body exposed, while bedding covered the rest of her. Skin gone the color of flour, Sophie's eyes were screwed shut. She panted in obvious torment. The wound on her shoulder had started bleeding again, while a steady stream of blood dripped from the cut on her thigh.

"Was it worth it?" He picked up a fresh cloth and pressed it to her leg.

"Yes," she gasped, turning even paler.

"Liar."

Working efficiently, Quint cleaned the wound thoroughly. Then he stitched it neatly, Sophie gritting her teeth with each pull of the needle. When he finished, he bound the leg tightly. Thankfully, the cut on her shoulder was shallow and did not require stitches, merely cleaning and bandaging.

He handed the jar of salve to her maid. "Use this on the wounds when you change the dressings, but you absolutely must wash your hands each time. Do not touch her unless you've done so."

The maid's mouth tightened. "My hands are clean, my lord."

"Not clean enough. Wash them. Soap and fresh water. Every time."

"She will, Quint," Sophie rasped. "Won't you, Alice?"

"Yes, of course, my lady," Alice said, still frowning at Quint.

"Alice, would you mind waiting in the corridor a moment? I'd like to speak to his lordship."

Alice looked as if she wanted to argue, but, after a warning glare in Quint's direction, she left the room.

"I don't believe your maid likes me," he remarked when they were alone and was pleased to see a small smile twist Sophie's lips.

"Do not take it to heart. She is not accustomed to having anyone else fussing over me."

He reached for the bedclothes and started to pull them over the injured side of her body. It was the first time he'd allowed himself to really look at her. All creamy, soft skin. Tight linen encircled her chest to flatten her breasts. A pity, that. But it was what she wore over her hips that did him in. A plain pair of men's smalls—without doubt the most erotic sight he'd ever beheld. Her maid had pushed the thin fabric up Sophie's leg to expose the injury and left the garment on for modesty. It had the opposite result on

Quint, however; heat suffused his body, his shaft coming to life.

He'd never seen a woman dressed in men's clothing before, and it was strangely arousing. And when had he lowered himself to lechery? For God's sake, she was injured and all he could do was ogle her. He dropped the bed linens as if they were hot, covering her.

Her lids fluttered open. "Thank you for your assistance. But I cannot stay. As much as I dread the walk home, I must go."

The idea of letting her out of his sight had him gritting his teeth. But he had no way to keep her here, short of tying her down. He scrubbed a hand through his hair. "What time do the servants rouse?"

Her eyes fell shut once more, as if the lids were too heavy to lift. "Shortly before five."

He pulled out his pocket watch to check the time. "It's half past twelve. Sleep for three hours. I'll have my coachman take you home before four."

She did not respond and he stood there, feeling ten thousand times a fool. How could he have allowed her to carry on in this ridiculous game, a lark that could very well get her killed? Whatever investigation she was pursuing was not worth her life.

"I can hear you frowning," she said, her eyes still closed. "Come and sit with me. Stop thinking for five minutes, Quint."

He brought a chair over and placed it at the side of the bed. He sat and focused on her beautiful face, the long, brown lashes fanning her cheeks. The luscious lips that had kissed him so passionately only a few nights ago. She was lovely, normally so full of vibrant energy and intelligence. He'd never seen her this quiet before. "You'll have to tell me, you know."

Her mouth hitched. "Only if you promise to help me—not try and stop me."

"Sophie, you cannot think to continue. Not after tonight. Whatever you've stumbled upon is too dangerous."

"I'll do what I must. And if you are worried about my safety, then come with me."

He stiffened, his muscles protesting at the mere suggestion of going outdoors. "You know I cannot."

"I know no such thing." She yawned. "I think nearly dying after the shooting affected you, but you can recover." Her words were slurring together, a sign of her exhaustion.

But something she said caught his attention. "Wait—how did you know I almost died?"

She did not answer, however. Her breathing had evened out. She'd fallen asleep.

Chapter Ten

Last night could only be categorized as a disaster, Sophie thought the next morning. If she were making a list of things never to repeat, getting knifed— twice—in the streets of East London would be at the top. Who had attacked her? A random footpad?

And the journey had been for naught because Molly hadn't wanted to help. Sophie would need to write Pearl, see if the courtesan knew of any other girls who might speak with Sir Stephen.

Alice entered just then. "Good morning, my lady. Would you care for breakfast?"

The thought of food turned Sophie's stomach. "No, not yet. I would like your help getting up, how-ever."

Her maid nodded and helped Sophie get out of bed. Each step on her injured leg sent sharp pain throughout her lower body. By the time she relieved herself and returned to the mattress, she was gasping, wet with perspiration.

"You best stay in today, my lady. You're not fit—"

A knock sounded before the Marchioness of Ar-dington, Sophie's stepmama, peeked in. "Oh, good.

You are awake." She entered, closed the door behind her, and approached the bed. "You've had two deliveries this morning, Sophie. I knew last night's ball would be a success."

"Deliveries?"

"It's exciting, isn't it?" Her stepmama beamed, clearly hopeful this would be the year Sophie would find a husband. "A huge bouquet of flowers arrived. Here's a card. Along with another note delivered for you this morning." She held out two pieces of paper.

Sophie took them both, frowning. The only person who would send her anything would be Quint. But the idea of him sending flowers was laughable. Quint was not the hearts and romance type. She would sooner expect him to fly to the moon than ever write a sonnet to her eyes.

"Well, open the note from the flowers. Let's see who they're from," her stepmama urged.

Sophie tore the seal and read the short note. *I very much enjoyed our dance last evening. Your servant, Lord MacLean.* Before she thought better of it, she smiled.

"You're smiling. That must be a good sign. I'm dying to know who sent them."

"Lord MacLean. We danced last evening." The last dancing she'd do for a while, considering her leg.

Her stepmama's face fell. "Oh, Sophie. I am not certain he's the right man for you. I know he's well titled and fairly handsome, but really, his reputation is less than desirable."

"You needn't worry. I have no intention of marrying Lord MacLean." But that reminded her of something. "All anyone could talk about last night was how Papa has picked my husband. In fact, I hear the betting books are full of wagers as to who the unfortunate man might be."

"He's of the mind you do not believe him. He thinks by making it public, it'll convince you."

Well played, Papa, Sophie thought. She hadn't expected that. "Why is he so eager to get rid of me? Can I not just live here a few more years?" Like until death.

"Darling." Her stepmama came forward and clasped Sophie's hand. "Marriage is not so terrible, as you seem to think. Your father and I have great affection for one another. We both want you to have it as well, but you cannot wait forever. And do you not want children of your own?"

A flash of rumpled, brown-haired boys with telescopes and test tubes went through her mind. Sophie was surprised by how much the image appealed to her. But then she thought of explaining her stupidity to the one man who valued intelligence above all else . . . and the pleasant warmth in her veins turned to a chill. He deserved better than a woman so corkbrained as she.

"Now, shall we do some shopping today? I was thinking we could go to the milliner first and then—"

"I cannot," Sophie blurted. "I am unwell."

"Oh, dear." Her stepmama's forehead lowered in concern. "You do appear flushed. Have you a fever?"

"No, nothing so serious. It's my monthly courses." She felt bad for the lie, but she *had* been bleeding after all. From her leg, of course, but still. And this way, no one would question her staying in bed all day.

Understanding lit her stepmama's face. "Of course. I'll have Alice prepare a posset for you. You rest and feel better." She smoothed a hand over Sophie's brow and stepped back. "I'll check on you later."

Now alone, Sophie started to roll over and then realized she still held the unopened note. Pulling it apart, she saw neat lines of random letters in rows down the page. It was . . . a code. She huffed a laugh. No doubt who had sent it. Only Quint would fashion her a note in the form of a cipher.

Smiling, she reached to ring for Alice, who had discreetly retreated earlier. When the maid arrived, Sophie requested her writing supplies. Quint hadn't provided any sort of key or clue to the puzzle, so an answer might take some time. Soon, she was propped up in bed with her traveling desk, studying the patterns of letters to arrive at a solution.

It took a quarter of an hour. When she finally decoded the message, it said:

AN EXPLANATION IS EXPECTED. NO LATER THAN TOMORROW. THE USUAL TIME AND SETTING. A REFUSAL RESULTS IN CONSEQUENCES. Q.

She read it again, then sighed. No question what "the usual time and setting" meant. He wanted her to come to his terrace after dark. But what sort of consequences? He had threatened to tell her father once. Would he dare?

Sitting through a lecture outlining her idiocy and recklessness, which Quint would surely relay posthaste, held little appeal. And Quint would most definitely try to prevent any more excursions by Sir Stephen. Sophie had no intention of giving up, however. She'd found something worthwhile, something she was *good* at doing. And if she could help people, was that not worth a few bumps and bruises?

And there was little Quint or anyone else could do to stop her.

* * *

She made him wait two days.

Quint nearly peeled the paper from the walls in his impatience and frustration. He had no recourse other than to send her another note—and she knew it. In those interminable hours, he imagined her dressed in man's clothing and carousing in every gaming hell, opium den, and brothel in London. It nearly drove him mad.

Correction, *madder*.

His mood was decidedly dark by the time she appeared in his gardens shortly before midnight on the second day. He stood at the threshold, waiting for Canis to finish digging in the dirt, when a cloaked figure with a slight limp emerged from the gloom. The dog bounced happily around her feet, his tail wagging furiously, and she awkwardly bent to scratch behind the dog's ears.

Quint's own reception would not be as friendly. He was still furious with her. Furious for the stupid risks and idiotic chances she took with her person. He wished he didn't care, that he could leave her to her own devices. Wash his hands of her, like any rational man would have done long ago. But he was incapable of letting her go.

She straightened and lowered the hood of her cloak. Moonlight illuminated the fine arches of her cheekbones, the curve of her upper lip, the gentle slope of her nose—and Quint momentarily forgot his anger. Tenderness and longing filled him, along with a heat more elemental in nature.

He thought of their kiss, the one from the other night in this very spot. How she'd clung to him and whimpered in his mouth. Would she claim it a momentary fancy this time as well?

"I see you solved the puzzle I sent. Did it take you two days?"

Her mouth hitched as she drew closer. "Indeed not. It took less than an hour. You must be slipping, Quint."

"Of course I am slipping. I am mostly mad. Have you not figured that out yet?"

"You are no madder than I."

He snorted. "Oh, that is reassuring. The woman skipping about town in men's clothing." And smalls. Damn it.

"I hardly skip. Though I have been told I need to improve my walk."

"What?"

She waved her hand. "Never mind. Well, I am here for the lecture. You may commence at any time."

Of course he wanted to lecture her. To rail and argue with her until she saw reason. But Sophie would only bristle, and the exercise would accomplish nothing. He had to understand why first, and then he could wage logical arguments to convince her of dropping the matter. "Why do you want to do this?"

"I must. Why should I not try and help others when I can?"

"Not good enough, Sophie. If it were benevolence, you would find another way to be charitable. Countless ladies perform altruistic deeds, but none put their lives at risk. Why have you chosen to dress as a man and mix with the lowest scum London has to offer?"

"Because these women have no one else. They cannot afford a Runner and the magistrates rarely bother. Should they not have someone to turn to with their problems?"

"Of course they should. I am uncertain why that

person has to be *you*. Why not give them the funds to hire a Runner, if that is your concern?"

She crossed her arms and pressed her lips together, remaining coolly silent.

"It's obvious to me that you enjoy the danger and duplicity. The risk is the reward, isn't it?"

"No, the solution is the reward. As fond as you are of puzzles, certainly you can understand."

"Yes, but my life is hardly in jeopardy when I am working on puzzles in my home, at my desk."

She sighed, her eyes sliding away. "Then you obviously do not truly understand."

"And just what would I not understand? How it feels to be trapped? How it feels to be unhappy with your prescribed lot in life?"

Her gaze snapped back to his. "How did you . . . ?"

"Because I know you. And a person who readily pretends over and over to be someone else, who eagerly courts danger without thought to the consequences, is unhappy with her present circumstances." She blinked rapidly, and he knew he'd hit the mark. "So tell me, why are you so unhappy, Sophie?"

She took her time in answering. "I merely need something of my own. Something worthwhile that I can be proud of. And I am good at it. Maggie has her art and her efforts to better the lives of these women, should they choose to pursue another livelihood. And Julia has her children to care for—"

"Including Colton, who is every bit a child himself."

Sophie flashed a brief smile. "But I have nothing. I cannot draw to save myself and I will never have children or a husband. So why not this?"

"What do you mean, you will never have children or a husband? You could've married ten times over. In fact, Lord Yardley offered for you only two Seasons ago. Someday, you'll choose a suitor—"

"Or my father will choose one for me."

The resentment in her voice set him back on his heels. That did not sound hypothetical. "Has he settled on someone, then?"

"Yes, he has a man in mind. He said if I do not choose a husband myself by the end of the Season, he will approve a marriage without my consent."

Quint hadn't expected it. Hadn't thought the marquess would finally draw a line in the marital sand. He swallowed. This . . . this feeling in his chest— a sharp, crushing pain, as if he would crack apart at any second—was nothing he'd experienced before. Not with the fits. Not when his betrothal ended. Not even when Sophie'd broken his heart.

He struggled to draw in a breath. "Who?" he rasped. Who would be the man so fortunate as to spend each night wrapped around her long, willowy frame?

"He will not tell me. He fears I will scare the man off if I learn his identity."

"Your father is a wise man," Quint noted.

"Perhaps, but I still believe I can change his mind."

"Why?" He honestly did not know why she avoided marriage more earnestly than a well-seasoned libertine. What was she so afraid of? The propagation of the human race was instinctual in both males and females: men to spread their seed as far and wide as possible, and women to nurture and protect the young. It was elemental and necessary. So what did Sophie hope to gain by resisting?

"I have always convinced him in the past. Though he did go one step further this time by making the edict public knowledge. That was new."

The marquess would only announce it if he was serious. Sophie had to know that. "No, I mean why do you want to change his mind? Why not just marry and be done with it?"

She grimaced. "Because I would rather not. And my reasons are my own."

Sophie's leg screamed in protest as she bent to pet Canis, yet she welcomed the pain as a distraction. Quint's perceptiveness was, at times, especially grating. Such as now, for example. It should come as no surprise that he would uncover what she was about. He'd always understood her as no one else did.

"Let us get back to the matter of these investigations."

She straightened, fighting a grimace at the pinch in her thigh. "We've been round and round on this, Quint. You cannot force me to give up."

"Then what if I offered to help you?"

"Then I would ask why you would make such an offer. Because if it is an attempt to control me or my methods, like preventing me from visiting brothels or gaming hells, I would politely decline."

He lifted his hands, all innocence. "I only want to keep you safe. Perhaps if we work together, I won't need to suture your leg again any time soon. Or worse."

She stared at him. Was he telling the truth? Would he truly help, without trying to manipulate her? The offer was tempting. She could use someone to talk with, someone capable of drawing inferences and conclusions . . . and no one did that better than Quint. "What would that mean, working together? You'll escort me on these errands?"

A muscle jumped in his slightly whiskered jaw. "No."

"Why not?"

"If I were able, I would. Believe me."

No, she refused to believe it. She wanted to know more, to learn about this illness that had convinced him he could not go outside. If she did, then maybe *she* could help *him*.

She recalled their kiss, the one in this very spot. He'd ended up outside and, though it had surprised him, it hadn't killed him. And it had been a very nice kiss. An *amazing* kiss. She wanted more. More kisses, more touching. More everything. After all, it wasn't as if she'd ever have a husband to do these things with.

And who knew how much longer Quint would tolerate her visits? He'd told her on multiple occasions not to return. One of these days, he might truly *mean* it. She needed to enjoy these stolen moments with him while she still could.

Her gaze flicked to his mouth as an idea occurred. "So I would come here at night, discuss any developments with you?"

"Yes, precisely. But no more recklessness. We decide *together* on how you proceed."

"I'll only agree on one condition."

His brows lowered. "And what is that?"

"You kiss me whenever I want."

Surprise registered on his face before he let out a startled, choked sound. "Kiss you?"

"Yes."

"Sophie, you cannot ask me to kiss you. It's . . . absurdly improper."

"You've already kissed me—twice—so I fail to see why it is such a bad idea."

"One of those times *you* kissed *me*, and we should

not be kissing at all. You should not be kissing anyone until you're married."

Which would never happen. "Loosen up, Quint. You seem to enjoy kissing me and I know I like it as well. Where is the harm?"

Ladies are not supposed to enjoy it so much.

Sophie beat back Lord Robert's voice. Quint hadn't seemed to mind her enthusiasm; still, it would do her well to remember not to get too carried away.

"Oh, God," he muttered under his breath, dragging a hand down his face. "You are unbelievable."

"True. And you know how determined I can be when there is something I want." Suffering through his amazing kisses while helping him conquer his fear at the same time? Oh, she wanted that. Badly.

"And I also know how you never stop to reason anything through. You are too innocent to realize, of course, but kissing generally leads to other more intimate things."

Heat sizzled through Sophie's veins at the idea of "other more intimate things" with Quint, and warmth settled low in her belly. She swallowed and said, "That is what I have you for, to retain a level head." After all, he didn't feel anything for her other than friendship. Remaining calm should be easy, at least for him.

"I should refuse," he said. "But I'm at a rather large disadvantage, since you may just decide to leave and never return. There would be little I could do to force you to come back. I shudder to think what would happen to you then."

Nerves and excitement bubbled up in her chest. "That is true. Does this mean you agree?"

"Newton help me, but yes. I'll kiss you and I'll assist your investigations."

And I'll find a way to fix you, she thought. "Excellent.

I knew you would see things my way. Shall we start now?"

He slanted her a glance. "With the investigation, you mean?"

She shook her head. "With the kissing."

Arms folded across his chest, he lifted an eyebrow. "Oh, so that's what you think, that you can crook your finger at me and I'll do your bidding? I may be cracked in the head, Sophie, but all the other parts work just fine. Which means I'm still a man. And *this* man kisses a woman when he wants to, like when she makes him laugh. Or when her smile knocks him back ten paces. Or when she's so beautiful he can't breathe. Not when it's an obligation."

Sophie blinked. Words would not come, her mouth gone dry at the heady declaration. It was a wonder she could stand upright, what with her bones rapidly turning to jelly. "All right," she finally managed.

His gaze darkened. "Of course that look happens to work as well," he said quietly, advancing on her.

"What look?" She instinctively took a step back, then winced as a stab of pain radiated through her injured leg.

He froze, concern pinching his brow. Without a word, Quint bent, picked her up, and carried her deeper into the house. "Wait, where are we going?" she asked.

"To the study. To sit down. It's obvious your leg is paining you."

Sophie wrapped her arms around his neck, enjoying the shift and play of muscles beneath his clothing. When they reached his study, he did not set her on her feet. Instead, he crossed to an armchair by the fire and lowered into it, setting her on his lap.

"Let me see the sutures," he said gently. "I want to ensure the wound isn't infected."

"It's fine," Sophie said. She was not shy, but sitting on Quint's lap in the middle of the night for a businesslike examination of her wound had her squirming.

"Be still. I want to see for myself." He lifted the gauzy layers of skirts and petticoat. The leg of her drawers was wide enough that he could push it up to see the wound on her thigh. "Excellent. The skin is healthy. Alice must be keeping her hands clean."

She expected him to adjust her clothing to cover her—but he didn't. Instead his large hand smoothed over her exposed leg, eyes raking her skin, while her heart fluttered behind her ribs.

"Sophie, I need to tell you—you expect me to retain a level head, but you should not rely on me. I'm not exactly in control of my faculties these days. Seeing you like this doesn't help, either." His hand indicated her lower half. "And I do not want to hurt you. I beg of you, rethink your request."

If she'd had any concerns about his state of mind, his speech eliminated them. Would a madman really give fair warning? But there could be another reason for his hesitation, one far more humiliating. "You would not hurt me. And I think you are stalling. If you don't want to kiss me—"

He closed the distance between them in a blink, pressing his mouth to hers, his tongue immediately pushing inside. He kissed her hard, desperately, his mouth rough and smooth at the same time, and she loved every second. She held nothing back, using her tongue and her hands to explore while his lips slanted over hers again and again.

The warmth in her belly spread until her breasts were heavy, aching. Moisture gathered in her cleft, the beat of her heart evident there in a rhythmic pulse. She became aware of Quint's hardness beneath her backside—a thrilling, heady proof of his desire for her. For Sophie, not the Perfect Pepperton or any other woman. He wanted her, and she gloried in the knowledge. It was all she could do not to rub against his erection.

And then she did rub against it.

He groaned into her mouth, a pained-yet-excited sound she'd never heard from him before. Lust raced down Sophie's spine. Her fingers trailed over his broad shoulders, reveled in the heat pouring off his frame. The opening in his shirt was just wide enough for her to slip a hand inside, testing the smooth, taut skin of his chest. His heart thumped under her palm, while the soft hair tickled her fingers. She ran her hand over his chest, enjoying the feel and the taste of him, and the tip of her finger brushed over his nipple.

He gave a quick intake of breath and then drew back to murmur, "Sophie, you're killing me. We should stop before this goes any further."

All she heard was "stop"—and so she rose up to kiss him once more.

Chapter Eleven

One kiss, he'd promised himself.

Kiss her quickly—yet long enough to ensure she did not complain. That had been the plan. But he hadn't expected her to be so enthusiastic. A virgin, even one of twenty-seven, should not have him so flustered with mere kisses. The probability of such an occurrence had seemed incredibly low when this exercise began.

He should have known Sophie would defy logic.

Quint's control unraveled the second her mouth found his once more, with any thoughts of ending this long forgotten. She kissed as she did everything else: with exuberance and passion, a reckless disregard for anything but the moment at hand. He could not stop from giving it back to her in kind.

With one hand cupping her head and the other on her leg, he clutched her tight. Licked at her mouth. Nipped at her lips. Tasted her until she gave a needy whimper in her throat. The sound wound its way through his groin to sharpen his arousal. God's blood, how he craved her. He'd frigged himself so often in the last few days thinking of her, it was a wonder he hadn't chaffed.

He could barely think, barely breathe, and the animal instinct—the desire to give and receive pleasure—took over. And with this particular woman on his lap, it was impossible to resist. It had been a long time since he'd felt this heady rush of lust drag him under the surface of rationality—and he welcomed the sweet oblivion.

His mouth left hers to trail across her jaw. He sucked the lobe of her ear between his lips, scraped it with his teeth. A gasp escaped just before she pressed her lips together tightly, as if to stop the noise. Which would never do. "I want to hear you, Sophie," he whispered in her ear. "Every sound. Every sigh. Do not hold back on me."

Next, he worked his way down the silky-soft skin of her throat. She threw her head back, giving him better access, of which Quint took full advantage. He felt drunk on her, out of his mind with this craving for her. A small part of his still-functioning brain could not believe she was allowing these liberties with him. The man whose suit she had refused. Yet here she lay, on his lap, soft and pliant, and offering up no protest. Pulling him closer. Kissing him. And he was not yet insane enough as to pass on such a rare gift.

Two fingers dipped inside the layers of her bodice and lifted a pale and perfect breast over the cloth, revealing it. "So pretty," he murmured before drawing the rosy tip inside his mouth. He alternated between sharp pulls and laving the taut nipple with the flat of his tongue, determined to drive her mad.

Her fingers threaded his hair, holding him close. "Quint," she sighed, the sound barely above a whisper. The more he sucked, the more restless she became.

"Don't stop," she said. "God, Quint, I am burning alive."

His hand returned to her thigh, where he brought it up to cup her mons. Heat scorched his skin and she rocked her hips against his palm. "Yes," she groaned, and the friction against his aching cock nearly had his eyes rolling back. A few more of those and he'd spill in his trousers for certain.

Releasing her breast, he lowered her against the armrest until she was nearly flat across his lap. Her eyes, half-lidded and sultry, watched him, while her chest rose and fell rapidly. "Remain still," he told her. "Let me feel you."

With her skirts already gathered around her waist, he only had to find the part in her drawers. He spread her open and then her glistening vulva lay bare before him—the downy brown hair covering her mons and the pink, dewy lips of her labia externa and interna. He swallowed. Perfection. Utter perfection.

Without thinking, he swiped a finger through the moisture gathered at the entrance to her vagina and brought the digit to his mouth. He closed his eyes and savored the sharp tang of her arousal on his tongue. Sweet. Saint's teeth, what he wouldn't give to have his face between her thighs. But he didn't want to frighten her.

"Please," she panted, as if sensing his hesitation. "Don't stop." Her glittering gaze implored him to keep going and the desire in his groin grew heavier.

Further proof of his madness, no doubt, but he had no intention of stopping.

He slowly traced the folds of her labia with his thumb and explored every bit of her before pushing one finger inside her vagina. Her lids fell on a moan as her hips pushed up, bringing him deeper. The walls were hot and slick. And tight. He shuddered, imagining that wet, warm tissue clasping his erection.

Keeping his own raging need in check, he began a teasing slide in and out of her channel. Coaxing a response from her. Then he added a finger, stretching her further.

"Oh, yes," he heard her say. He watched her body take his fingers deep inside. Felt her tremble. Then he curled his fingers, searching for the one spongy, sensitive spot—

She shouted and thrashed atop his lap. "Quint, oh God."

He knew she was close. Her clitoris, the distended vascular bundle of cells at the top of her cleft, was swollen and taut, so he applied his thumb to it with relentless intensity. "Feel it, Sophie. Let it happen."

Sophie clawed at him, the armrest, the fabric of the chair, anything she could reach. "Oh, God. Yes," she whimpered. "Right there."

Her thighs shook and her walls clamped down on his fingers. She clenched and then cried out, orgasm overtaking her. It was beautiful. The kind of image a man remembered to his grave. Her head thrown back, eyes closed, lips rosy from his kisses, shivering in ecstasy. He held on as best he could, prolonging the experience, until she twisted away with a shiver.

He dropped his head against the back of the chair, released her, and struggled to catch his breath. It took some effort to calm himself. Sophie seemed similarly undone as she lay boneless in his lap, a hand pressed to her chest, eyes shut tight. The study clock continued its usual tick, as if the world hadn't just turned upside down.

Everlasting hell, what had he done?

Shame and loathing rolled through Quint. He'd . . . defiled her. She was a virgin. The daughter of a marquess. That she'd asked for it did not matter. He should know better—hell, he *did* know better. He just hadn't been able to refuse her.

Hadn't been able to stop himself.

Which stood as more proof of his imminent decline. His father had talked incessantly of copulation during his fits—dirty, filthy words—and had masturbated until they'd tied his arms down. That Quint had inflicted this utterly inappropriate act on a gently bred lady only verified what he already knew of his future.

He was not fit to be around others.

And his stupid cock was not listening. It lay hard and heavy in his trousers. Ready to mate at any second.

God, he hated himself in that moment. He adjusted her skirts to cover her.

"I am . . . I had no idea," she murmured. Satisfaction and wonder laced her tone.

"And I beg your pardon for it. I should not have taken things so far."

A crease formed between her brows. "Why not? Granted, it was a bit more than a kiss, but I'd hardly complain." She struggled to sit up, so he helped to right her. "I daresay I'll never look at your hands in quite—"

"*Sophie.*" He set her on the floor.

She laughed. "Quint, there is no need to be so serious. This was my idea and any regrets may be placed squarely at my feet. Not that I regret it, mind you."

"You should."

"Why? Because we are not married?"

"That, yes, but there is an even greater reason."

"What?"

"Because I am nearly insane."

The next evening, Quint scratched his pen furiously over the paper, the idea bursting forth from his mind. He must get the thought down in its entirety—before it was forgotten and gone. What if he split the coded message into parts and then performed a frequency analysis on each letter by section?

The hour well past midnight, he'd dismissed the staff some time ago. The coals had long faded, the temperature in the room decidedly chilly. Still, he wrote. When he finished, he placed his pen on the tray and sanded his paper. "Did you enjoy your ride with Lord MacLean?"

A gasp carried the length of the room. "You knew I was here?"

Only the instant she'd entered. He was attuned to her, down to the subcutaneous membranes under the layers of his skin. "Of course. And you did not answer my question."

She lifted her chin stubbornly, a look he happened to adore. "A waste of time to ask, then, how you are aware of my perfectly innocent ride with MacLean this morning." She stood and put her hands on her hips. "I do not like that you are having me followed. Especially during the day. It is unnecessary."

He disagreed—and with MacLean around, Quint had all the more reason to keep her under watch. The Scot was a practiced reprobate, Sophie a reckless innocent. A clear recipe for disaster if ever there was one.

"I believe it necessary," he told her, "considering

your nocturnal activities. Criminals and footpads do not disappear in the daylight."

"I am aware of that. But I am fairly certain MacLean could fight off any ruffian who dared approach."

Quint clenched his jaw. Yes, no doubt MacLean could protect her. The sane Scottish lord could leave his house. Take her for rides in the park. Could likely club any attacker using a full-grown oak tree, if needed. But who would protect Sophie from MacLean?

"That may be so, but your kilt-wearing hero does not know what I know—and he may be caught unaware. And you are wasting your time by arguing."

"You are exceedingly stubborn."

"In that, we are well matched. All you need do is give up your ventures as Sir Stephen and I will happily dismiss Jenkins."

She snorted in response. "You said you would help me, not try to stop me."

Yes, he had—but he'd never expected the bargain she suggested. A bargain that had him hard and straining inside his trousers all damned day. It was all he could do not to pounce on her and lift her skirts.

Nevertheless, he would not allow it to happen again.

And not because of the antiquated belief that women should wait to find pleasure in the marriage bed. No, his resolve had to do with *him*. For whatever reason, she had wanted to dally with him. He didn't pretend to understand it and had foolishly allowed his feelings for her to momentarily cloud his better judgment.

But she deserved better than a coward, a madman afraid to leave his house. The perfect and beautiful daughter of a marquess, she was braver and more intelligent than half the men in Europe. And he was . . . broken. Still that eleven-year-old boy standing in the freezing cold, knowing there was something wrong with him. He had no right to force himself on this woman, to touch her in any manner.

So despite the powerful, burning desire for her, he had to refrain from any further physical contact. Even kisses.

"I said I would help you, and I shall. Come with me." He reached for his piece of foolscap and stood.

"Where are we going?"

He stood close enough to see the pulse leaping at the base of her throat. *Ignore it*, he told himself. "I need to lock this away." He held up the paper. "And we may talk privately there."

"And we are not private here?" She glanced about the obviously empty room.

"Perhaps, but one never knows." Especially when a member of his staff was likely passing information along to the Home Office.

Without waiting for further arguments, he led her to the rows of books at the far end of the study. On a high shelf, he plucked the edge of Hobbes's *Leviathan* and the latch sprung. Sophie gasped as the bookcase opened. "You have a secret passage!"

"Which will not remain a secret if you do not lower your voice."

He took her hand and stepped into the tiny corridor, closing the hidden door behind them. Darkness descended. He never brought a light when using the passage, as he didn't need it. The trip was one he made often, sometimes out of need and other times out of weariness.

Sophie clasped his hand tightly, her breath coming faster. "Should we not have a lamp?"

"No." He led her along the cramped space. It was not wide enough for them to travel side by side; rather, she pressed herself nearly flush against his back. "Just do not let go of me. Otherwise you may miss a turn and fall into the pit of crocodiles."

A hand smacked his shoulder. Quint smiled.

"Here are stairs," he told her. He guided her up the first step. Counted the eighteen. Then at the top, he found the latch and pulled it to open the door. Flickering light from the fading fire illuminated his bedchamber. He let go of Sophie's hand, set his paper on the bed, and crossed to add more coal. "Push that closed, will you?"

Sophie shut the passage door while he tended to the fire, then he went to the bed. He'd designed the rosewood frame with squat, square posts, and without a canopy. Each of the posts had a small, decorative cap on top. Quint lifted and twisted the cap on the lower right post to reveal the wooden box hidden within. He withdrew the box, which was about the size of his forearm, and placed it on the coverlet.

"What on earth . . ." she breathed over his shoulder. "How positively clever! What do you keep in there?"

He slid the lid back, revealing the inner compartment. "This and that." Rolling his progress on the code, he tucked the pages inside, around some other drawings. Just let Hudson try and find that.

"Are you working on something important?" She was close—so close her skirts brushed his leg, unnerving him.

"Possibly. Won't know until I get it right."

"You think this may have something to do with the break-in." A statement, not a question.

"Yes. In the past, the Home Office has sought my help with various code problems. There is one cipher that is thought to be unbreakable, oftentimes called *le chiffre indéchiffrable*. If I can find a way to crack the cipher without the necessary key code, it would draw the attention of quite a few governments, including our own. It would be like having the only master key to every locked door in the world." The box now closed, he slid it back into the post.

"I . . . had no idea you did this sort of work for our government."

He glanced at her sharply. She wore an odd expression. "Why would you? No one knows, except the man I work for. And I trust you won't tell anyone." Sophie shook her head. "Good. Now, shall we discuss your investigation?"

"Oh, of course," she said quickly, reaching into the pocket of her dress to produce a folded piece of paper. "I wrote everything down, as you asked."

"Excellent." He unfolded the parchment and read ⸺er very neat handwriting.

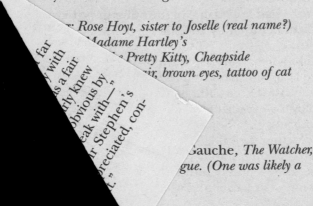

: *Rose Hoyt, sister to Joselle (real name?)*
⸺*Madame Hartley's*
⸺ *Pretty Kitty, Cheapside*
⸺*ir, brown eyes, tattoo of cat*

⸺ far
⸺y with
⸺s a fair
⸺ly knew
⸺bvious by
⸺eak with—"
⸺r Stephen's
⸺eciated, con-
⸺"

⸺Gauche, *The Watcher,*
⸺gue. *(One was likely a*

"*La Gauche?*" he asked. "Because he favored his left hand?"

Sophie's face turned crimson and she pressed her lips together. "N-not exactly," she stammered. "It has to do with his . . . his . . ." She gestured vaguely in the direction of her waist.

He chuckled. "I understand. This has been quite an education for you, has it not?"

He resumed his perusal:

Missing: Unknown woman
Employment: The Black Queen, East London
Description: Brown hair, blue eyes, queen of spades
    tattoo above ankle
Last Seen: ??
Death: River police pulled her from the water on
    16 April, 1820
Body: Missing right hand, raped and strangled
Regular Visitors: ??

"This was the reason for your visit to The Black Queen? To see if you could draw a correlation between the two women?"

"Yes. I had hoped one of the other girls there would confirm her identity and her regulars."

"And?"

"They were too frightened—fearing O'She more than our hand-collecting murderer." Likel good cause. O'Shea did not have a reputation employer—especially to women. "But one cle the missing girl," Sophie continued. "It was her reaction. I could go back and try to sp

"No," Quint stated emphatically. "S esence was noted and clearly not ap ering what happened when you le

She stretched her shoulders, and the flickering light danced across the nape of her neck. He tried not to notice. "Not necessarily," she said. "That could have been a random occurrence."

"Unlikely. The chance of a random attack is very low, especially when you factor in your visit to the Thames police. There very well may've been a corrupt officer or two who would not appreciate someone asking questions. I believe you attracted the wrong kind of attention with both visits."

"I fail to see how you can be certain."

"I am not certain. No one can be certain. But I've weighed the various factors mathematically using Bayes' rule and believe there is a high probability that the attempt on your life was intentional."

He could tell that news upset her. She worried her bottom lip with her teeth. "Why would anyone want to kill me?"

Quint held up the paper with her notes. "The answer lies somewhere in this."

Chapter Twelve

Sophie was in trouble—not nearly as much trouble as someone trying to kill her on a street in Whitechapel, of course. But a different sort of trouble, and one no less disconcerting to her well-being.

Fact: She was alone with Quint in his bedchamber.

Fact: He was talking of theorems, secret messages, and mathematical probability.

Fact: She was incredibly, distractingly aroused.

The warmth in her belly slid south, a sharp tingle that resulted in a distinctive throb between her legs. How she could be so attracted to one man and not melt into a puddle at his feet was a testament to her sheer strength of will.

She cleared her throat. "So how do we find the ˙swer?"

'By looking for patterns, which you have already ˑn by visiting The Black Queen. We need to carry further. What do we know about the four girls ˑom the river, other than they were each miss- hand?"

"They were all suspected prostitutes. Each fairly young."

"Estimated to be between nineteen and twenty-two," he elaborated. "Which is not significant in itself. Most women in prostitution are young." He sat on the edge of the bed and folded his arms. "What else?" he asked, waving his hand as if to hurry her along.

Sophie shut her eyes for a moment, concentrating on the bits she'd heard. "Each girl washed up along different spots on the river—"

"Unsurprising, considering the unpredictable currents. Variations in weather and detritus in the water would also factor as to how far a floating body may travel. And?"

"Um, mudlarks discovered the first. Dockworkers numbers two and three. River police found the fourth."

"So we discount method of discovery. What about the bodies?"

"Each was missing her right hand. Why is that, do you suppose?"

"Hard to say." Quint stroked his jaw. "Is it the sense of touch he's trying to prevent? As most people favor their right hands, is it symbolic of robbing her strength? Also, it's a unit of measurement; is the murderer using them to 'measure' the crimes figurative? Or, does he make them use that particular har some perverse physical act, and retain it as sake?"

"I can see you've given it some thoug astonished.

"There is little else to do when tr own home." He shrugged. "H the other two girls pulled fror worked and anyone who might be able to identify them?"

"No, not yet. They were badly decomposed by the time the surgeon saw them. He could not tell me much."

He cocked his head. "Any other girls missing from The Kitty or The Queen?"

"One from The Kitty. Her sister is the one who originally hired me. I haven't been able to find out what happened to her. She disappeared without a trace, so I strongly suspect she's another victim."

"Careful," Quint warned. "You may be right in your assumption. But when you look for coincidences, you're bound to find them. You must stick with facts."

"Makes perfect sense to me. Two girls, both prostitutes for O'Shea, and both go missing in such a short period of time. Is that not a strong indicator?"

"There is no causal relationship with coincidence. Meaning there is no cause and effect. Just because two brothers die on the exact same day ten years apart does not mean there is anything sinister afoot. Merely because this other woman disappeared does not mean she's been killed by the same man—or even killed. She may be visiting her aunt in Shropshire."

She sighed unhappily, and Quint chuckled. "No said this would be easy."

ight be for you, if you were willing to leave e."

ed. "It's not a matter of being willing. I eave. I am *unable* to leave."

athy streaked through her.

that look," he snapped, getting to finger at her. "Do not *pity* me. nything but that."

"I do not pity you, Damien," she said. "I believe you are being stubborn and childish."

His lip curled. "Is that so? Was my father being stubborn and childish when he started pulling his own hair out of his head in giant clumps? Raving and shouting at all hours? Knocking his head into the wall?"

How terrible it must have been for him, a small boy, to witness such madness in a loved one. But she did not see how it mattered. "And you believe your fate to soon be the same?"

He jerked his chin, avoided her eyes, and remained silent.

So, yes. That was what he believed. It was beginning to all make sense.

"Were you not just lecturing me on drawing inferences where causal relationships may not exist? Yes, your father might have been insane. But it doesn't guarantee that you will follow the same, precise path."

"Perhaps. Yet prevailing medical theory certainly favors that exact outcome."

"Yes, but—"

"Do you not think I've turned this over in my mind countless times? That I haven't looked for even the faintest glimmer of hope that this is a physical ailment rather than one of mental acuity? Spent hours and hours searching for a cure? I've tried tens of remedies, I've experimented with nearly everything I've thought—"

He snapped his jaw shut and spun away. After a few seconds, he dragged a shaking hand through his unruly brown hair. Her heart constricted. To Quint, this must be absolutely terrifying, and she hadn't meant to upset him.

"I am sorry," she said after a long moment. "I should not have pushed."

"No, you did nothing wrong. I am . . ." He blew out a long breath and placed his hands on his hips. "I find myself at my worst around you."

She drew near and saw the emotion in his golden-brown depths, a reflection of the hurt and confusion inside him. "Your worst is still better than my best. Probably better than most anyone in London, in fact."

He shook his head. "You are only flattering me because I know your secret."

He was wrong, but she did not correct him. "Your experiments, have any of them helped? Or at least shown progress?"

"Only that one time, on the terrace. With you. When we were kissing."

"Well, good thing you still owe me payment this evening. Come with me."

Quint stared outside, then cut his gaze to Sophie. "This is a terrible idea."

"I think it's a perfectly sound idea." They had now returned down to the ground floor. She stepped out of the open terrace door and turned to face him. "You kiss me and at some point, I'll lead you outside. As long as you keep your eyes closed and allow me to do all the work, you'll be fine."

"But how does that solve the problem? It's a temporary fix, based on my remaining oblivious."

"It's a start, Quint. Perhaps if we do it often enough, you won't worry about doing it on your own."

"Sophie—"

"What is the worst that could happen?"

"You called me Damien," he blurted.

She blinked up at him, her impish smile reflected in the soft light coming from the room behind him. "Did I?"

He nodded. "Yes. In my chamber. I've never heard you say it before."

Even in the dim surroundings, he saw the flush steal over her cheekbones. "I'm sorry. I shouldn't have assumed—"

"No, I liked it. I haven't been called by that name for a very long time." Lifting his hand, he brushed the backs of his knuckles over her cheek. Then he tucked a short brown wisp of hair behind her ear. "And to answer your question, the worst that could happen is that I have another fit."

"Which I've already seen," she said matter-of-factly. "So you have nothing to fear."

Merely because she'd seen one did not mean he relished repeating the experience. And that was not his only concern. "Lest you forget, our kiss last evening got a bit out of hand." An understatement. He'd rushed her out of his house, fearing what he might do if she stayed. He'd wanted to take her hard and fast, bury himself inside her until they both exploded. "For the sake of your innocence, I think it best if we skip tonight's venture."

"Allow me to worry about my innocence. And I hardly think you're going to ravish me on the terrace, for heaven's sake."

He was not so sure—not with Sophie involved. Each time he touched her, he forgot what little reason he still possessed.

She placed her hand on his chest, stepped closer. His heart pounded beneath her palm while his mind warred with itself. On one side of his brain, logic was standing on a chair, waving its arms to get his attention. On the other side, lust and yearning rubbed their hands together in unholy anticipation.

When she tilted her head to meet his eyes, the determination and desire in her glittering gaze had him admitting defeat.

Bending, he took her mouth. Her lips were soft and ready, and they responded to him eagerly. He clasped her tight, so tight he could feel every curve pressed against him. The night wove a dark, protective cocoon around them and he soon forgot about everything else but Sophie's lips and tongue.

Her arms wound around his neck, breasts flattened to his chest. Taller than most women he'd known, she fit him perfectly, their hips nearly aligned. Therefore, he didn't have to reach far in order to place his hands on her deliciously round backside.

He deepened the kiss, demanding more. She did not disappoint, her tongue twining with his. Blood rushed in his veins and pooled in his groin, his penis rapidly engorging. Everything in him begged for friction, for the ability to drive and thrust. To root and mark. To devour and conquer.

He rolled his hips into her pelvic bone, and Sophie whimpered, her nails digging into his scalp. He loved her responses. She held nothing back, a woman completely without artifice when it came to her desire. A rarity among ladies, especially unmarried ones.

"Quint, please," she breathed when he broke off to kiss the slim column of her throat.

"Who?" He slid a hand to her breast, plumped it, and found the nipple through the thin layers of cloth. Pinched it.

"Damien," she gasped. "Oh, God. Don't stop."

"What do you want, *delicia*?" His lips trailed the bare skin along the edge of her bodice.

"Is that . . . Italian?"

"Latin. But I shall use Italian, if you prefer, *cara mia*."

She shivered. "What about Greek or Russian?"

"*Psihi mou.*" *My soul.*

Her breath hitched.

He kissed the plump mounds of her décolletage. "*Lyubov moya.*" *My love.*

Another kiss.

"Or German. *Ohne dich kann ich nicht leben.*" *I cannot live without you.*

She was panting now. She must not understand what he was saying, or she'd have run screaming. And he meant every word, he suddenly realized.

Grabbing his head in her hands, she dragged him back for a frantic, scorching kiss. He rapidly lost the ability to speak—in any language.

Damnation, he wanted . . . he needed . . . a *wall*. There was a wall behind her. Never breaking from her mouth, he backed her up until her spine met the surface. He clutched fistfuls of her skirts and hitched them to her waist. He cupped her mons through her drawers. So hot. And the cloth was wet.

"Yes," she hissed. "Oh, yes. More."

His fingers parted the cloth. Touched her slick crease. He groaned. If there was a heaven, it would feel like this. He slipped one finger into that tight sheath. Only, it wasn't enough this time. He needed to taste her.

He dropped to his knees. "Hold these up for me," he said, shoving up the various skirts.

Her eyes, glazed with lust, stared down at him in

the near darkness as she gathered the cloth in her hands. "Why? What—"

"Throw your left leg over my shoulder."

Without waiting, he positioned her leg where he wanted. Then he slid his hands up her thighs, parted her drawers, and licked her. His erection throbbed, but he ignored it. Nothing mattered but Sophie. The way she trembled. The way she gasped when his tongue flicked her clitoris. The mewling noises when he applied gentle suction with his mouth. The moans when he speared the opening to her vagina with his tongue.

And when she peaked—her body tightening and then convulsing—he held on, riding her through it. Finally she stopped shaking and he released her. He tried to regain his composure by taking a few deep breaths, his forehead resting on her thigh. His own body was aroused to the point of mind-numbing pain.

Knees aching, he placed his hands on the floor to push up. The hard stone under his palms caught his attention and his eyes flew open. He was out on the terrace. Outside.

He'd just lifted Sophie's skirts and pleasured her with his mouth *outside*. Against a wall. Where anyone might happen to see. Granted the terrace was mostly dark and the hedges near the mews were taller than he. And it was the middle of the night. But . . . still. Sophie did not deserve to be treated like a two-penny tart on payday.

Bloody hell, he'd done it again.

She had trusted him not to ravish her on the terrace, and that's precisely what he'd done. He'd have to apologize. Again.

Sighing, he rose to find her slouched against the wall, breathing hard. She clutched his shoulder.

"That was . . ." Wonder broke out on her face. "Unlike anything I'd ever imagined. And did you see? You're outside." She grinned. "I told you we could do it."

His chest ached, but location had little to do with it. "Sophie," he started and then licked his lips. The tantalizing taste of her was still on his skin, taunting him with his loss of self-control. "I must apolog—"

"Do not dare." She put her hands on her hips. "Do not apologize, Quint."

So they were back to Quint. He shook his head. "I must. This is entirely improper and highly disrespectful. I should not be touching you in such a manner. Even if you do not push me away, I should have more restraint. It's just that . . ."

"What?"

"I completely lose myself when I am around you."

Her expression softened. "That is the sweetest thing you could ever say."

"You should not be flattered," he told her sharply. "You should be *terrified*. God only knows what I will do next."

"I am not scared of you. Do you think I go around kissing any man I can find? I promise you, I don't. I *trust* you, Quint."

"That is a mistake. You should not trust me. I am—" He pinched the bridge of his nose. "You should leave here and never come back. Now, while your reputation is still intact."

"Hang my reputation."

"You do not mean that."

She looked like she wanted to say something, her intent stare never leaving his. He could sense an inner struggle, which he could only assume was about what had just happened on the terrace. "You are saner than you realize. I understand the fits, Quint, but I believe your situation is manageable." She swept a hand around them. "See?"

"Manageable?" A dry, brittle laugh escaped. "So do I have your permission to lift your skirts any time I need to leave the house?"

"Would it help?"

He threw up his hands. "Christ, Sophie!" He turned and stalked toward the house.

"Wait!" she called. "Did you not want to enjoy being outside for once?"

"Trust me," he said over his shoulder, "I enjoyed it. And do not move. I am rousing a footman to see you home."

Late the next morning, Sophie found herself sitting in Madame Hartley's office, taking notes. Not even an hour ago, the brothel owner had sent word through Alice:

> *One of my girls has gone missing. Please, come quickly.*
>
> —*M.H.*

Sophie had rushed through her toilette and dashed out to catch a hackney. With the light drizzle falling, it had taken longer than usual to find a free conveyance. Finally, she arrived at Madame's back entrance, heavily cloaked, as she had no choice in daylight but to dress as a woman. Madame had quickly ushered her inside.

The proprietress was beside herself. She took great pride in her establishment, which was reflected in the treatment of the girls in her care. They were provided with medical care, days off, higher-than-usual wages.

She also did not overwork them. But one of her newer girls, Pamela, had gone missing in the night. It was as if she disappeared into thin air.

First Sophie spoke with Annabeth, one of Pamela's roommates. She'd asked Madame to give them privacy, in case Annabeth found it easier to speak away from her employer. Only, Annabeth hadn't stopped crying long enough to give Sophie any information.

"Annabeth, I know it's terrible. But you have to talk to me. Whatever I can learn will help us find her."

The girl wiped her eyes and nodded. "I beg your pardon, your ladyship. I just can't seem to stop crying."

Sophie tried to think like Quint. Don't make assumptions. Discover the facts. After all, Pamela had only been working as a prostitute for two months. Perhaps she'd realized it was not a life she wanted. "Did she seem happy here? Any complaints?"

Annabeth's red-rimmed eyes went wide. "No, my lady. She liked it here. Said it was better 'n her last job, and she was sendin' the money back to her parents in Dublin. We was friends. She would've told me if she was unhappy."

"Did she have plans to return to Dublin?"

Annabeth shook her head. "There was an uncle she wanted to get away from. He'd been taking liberties since she turned ten and she swore she'd never go back."

"Did she have any regulars? Any men who asked for her, any she talked about?"

"I'm not sure, my lady. Madame can give you their names, most likely."

"I will ask her, but I wondered if anyone sticks out in your mind? A man she favored? Or one she dreaded servicing?"

Annabeth thought for a moment. "A couple of the gents were real nice to her. I remember her talking about a big Scotsman."

MacLean?

"A duke asked for her a couple of times. She tried to get along with everyone. Sweet as treacle, Pammy was."

"Well, what about the not-so-nice ones?"

"Recently there was a gent who tried to get a bit rough. But Madame installed bells in our rooms after what happened earlier this year." Sophie nodded, recalling the girl who'd been beaten and slashed with a knife. "So Pammy rings the bell and they come runnin'. Pulled him off her something quick."

Sophie wrote down everything. "Do you know who it was, or have any description of him?"

"No. Pammy didn't like talking about it."

"Did she have any jewelry on her, anything that might help identify her?"

"Didn't have nothing of value, if that's what your ladyship's asking. Nothing nobody would'a robbed her for. But she did have a ring she wore. Looked fancy, but it was paste. Belonged to her mum, and she said she wouldn't ever part with it. I never saw her take it off."

"What did the ring look like?"

"Silver, with small green stones. Looked like one of them clovers, you know, from Ireland."

"Yes, I know what they look like. Thank you, Annabeth. I believe I have enough to go by. If you think of anything else, please let Madame know."

Annabeth left and Madame came back in. Sophie got right to the point. "Who was the man who roughed Pamela up, the one pulled off her?"

Madame lifted her elegant chin as she sat in the

chair opposite. "I do not like discussing my customers, even to you, my lady. One man's preferences may seem distasteful to another. We try to accommodate all our patrons, regardless of their proclivities."

"Yes, I understand that. But wouldn't a girl like Pamela know the difference between playful rough and scary rough? If she rang for help, I'd think that was scary rough."

"Pamela did not like any kind of rough play. There were events in her background that made her a poor companion for this particular man. At the time, I warned her and she decided to proceed anyway. I think she thought the money would make up for the discomfort. But this man did not hurt her, if that's what your ladyship is thinking."

"How do you know?"

"Because he is a regular patron, my lady, and I've never had any problems with him before. I think he and Pamela were not a good match."

"Who were her regulars?"

"She did not have any regular customers, my lady. In truth, she hadn't been here long enough."

"Well, can you tell me about last evening? Whom did she see?"

"I beg your ladyship's pardon, but I would prefer that remain confidential."

"Madame," Sophie said sharply, "I realize this is awkward for you, but in order to find out what happened, I need to piece together her last few hours here. I promise not to question the men directly about Pamela. But I need a place to start."

Madame pressed her lips together. "She came down about nine. Went up with her last customer around one. There were three men last night. Comte de Saxe, Lord Weston, and Lord Tolbert."

"Tolbert was the last man to see her?"

Madame nodded. "Yes. But Mulrooney saw him leave a little after two. Pamela was not with him."

"When was she noticed missing?"

"Not until after eight this morning. Her bed was not slept in."

Sophie wrote all of this down to discuss with Quint later. "And these three men, all regular patrons? Any problems with them in the past?"

"The *comte* only visits us when he travels to London once or twice a year. The other two are regulars, yes, my lady."

"Any problems with Weston or Tolbert?"

"None that seem relevant. Would your ladyship care to speak with Mulrooney?"

Sophie eyed the proprietress carefully. Was Madame trying to put Sophie off from asking her more questions? "Yes," she said after a moment, "I would."

Chapter Thirteen

When it finally happened, Quint knew he had no one to blame but himself.

The afternoon sunshine warmed his face and shoulders while he stood on the terrace, enjoying the open air. Since the incident with Sophie, he'd returned to the small open area a few times, if only to remind himself that he could. It was liberating, not to mention exhilarating. He didn't dare go farther than the terrace. But it was a start.

He wished Sophie could see him.

"Here you are."

Quint turned and his stomach plummeted to the ground. *Bollocks.*

The Duke of Colton was now striding toward Quint. He looked healthy and happy, his black hair gleaming like pitch in the sun.

And it hit Quint that he'd never responded to his friend's invitation to come to Norfolk. *Hellfire and damnation.*

"Your butler said I could find you out here. He told me you aren't home to callers, which I assume is just because you're in the midst of one of your all-consuming projects."

Best not to deny it, Quint reasoned. "And yet you got past him."

"My never-ending charm, no doubt. How have you been?" Colton slapped Quint on the back. "I was a bit surprised not to hear back from you. But I suppose you've been busy."

"I have. And congratulations, by the way."

Colton grinned. "Thank you. Julia did most the work, of course. But he's a fine-looking lad. Just like his papa."

Quint nearly rolled his eyes. "Enjoy it now. I shudder to think of the trouble he'll give you in twenty years."

"He won't be able to get anything past me. The disadvantage of having a reformed degenerate for a father."

"So why did you leave Norfolk? I would think you'd want to stay near Julia and Olivia." Olivia was the duke's two-year-old daughter. "Not gallivant about Town."

"Julia sent me. She is worried about Lady Sophia. I guess her letters have been vague and impersonal, and she refused to come to Seaton Hall to visit the future duke. Julia is concerned, and when my wife is concerned, I get no sleep." He folded his arms across his chest. "You haven't seen Sophia about, have you?"

Only nearly every luscious inch of her. When he closed his eyes, he could still see her glistening vulva bared before him like a banquet. "No," he croaked. "But then I haven't really been out and about."

Colton's gray gaze assessed him. "Why not? Season's started up. Don't you have lectures and assemblies and debates to attend?"

"I'm working on a few things that have been taking up most of my time," he answered vaguely.

"Well, now that I'm here, you can take a break for some fun. Winchester's back in Town. Why don't we head to White's and meet him for a bit to eat?"

"You hate White's. You said the members are crustier than the bread."

"Then let's go to Brooks's. Or Boodles. Hell, a gaming hell. I don't care. Let's go anywhere."

Quint swallowed. This was the moment he'd feared for nearly four months. "I cannot. Not today. But I could ask Cook to whip up something for us. This one's been here awhile. She's pretty good."

Colton cocked his head. Frowned. "Quint, you're a terrible liar. It's one of the reasons Winchester and I never let you play cards, even though you can memorize a deck. What aren't you telling me?"

"Nothing. But not everyone can jump to do your bidding the second you arrive in Town."

It came out harsher than he'd intended, and Colton's eyebrows jumped. "I didn't realize my friendship was so taxing on you. I was not asking for your hand in marriage, Quint. Merely to share a meal."

"I apologize. I didn't mean it like that. I'm busy, is all."

Colton stared, not saying anything, for a long minute. "Fine. Then I'll leave you to it."

Quint relaxed, relieved. No chance Colton would let the matter drop, but at least Quint would gain a reprieve during which to craft a better lie for the next visit.

"But there was something I needed to ask you first."

Quint braced himself. "And what is that?"

"As you know, we asked Winchester to be Olivia's godfather." He shifted on his feet a bit, and Quint realized Colton was nervous. "Well, we'd like you to be Harry's godfather."

"You named him Harry, after your brother?"

Colton nodded. "We did. Will you do it? It would mean a lot to Julia and to me."

Emotion clogged Quint's throat. He wanted to refuse, to tell Colton he'd likely be mad in a matter of years. But he couldn't refuse. Not to Colton, the man to whom Quint owed so much. "Of course. I would be honored."

"Excellent." Another slap on the back. "It won't be for another few months, but you'll come to Seaton Hall. I'll let you know when, of course."

"Of course," Quint mumbled. "I'll be there."

God, how would he ever manage it?

"What is *that?*"

Canis came bounding up the stairs. "That is my dog."

"A dog." Colton spun to face him. "*You* have a dog? You, who never even brush your own horse?"

"Horses are different. And Canis was a gift I could not return."

Colton's expression turned shrewd as he searched Quint's face. "A gift from whom?"

Quint pressed his lips together, kept his eyes on the gardens. Colton would spot the lie anyway.

"Good God. A woman?"

"Don't be ridiculous," Quint scoffed, though it sounded lame to his own ears.

"I cannot think of another single reason you would not produce a name. Which explains why you did not give the creature away."

He really needed to find less intelligent friends. "Were you not just leaving?"

Colton's mouth quirked. "You know, I believe I will take you up on that offer of food."

Sophie let herself into Quint's gardens. Strange to be doing this during the day, she thought with a half-smile. But she could not possibly wait until this evening, not when she had so much to discuss with him.

The rain had abated, for now anyway, and the sun was making a valiant effort to break through the thick layer of clouds. She decided to go to the terrace instead of the servants' door. Quicker to Quint's study that way.

Canis appeared, loping toward her as his tail wagged furiously. "Hullo, boy." She bent and scooped him up. He seemed to be growing at an alarming rate. Quint's staff must be taking good care of the dog, she thought as Canis licked her face.

Laughing, she climbed the terrace steps, went to the door, and threw it open. She stepped inside . . . and drew up short.

Three pairs of astonished eyes were now focused on her.

Sophie did not often use crude words, but this seemed a completely appropriate circumstance in which to do so.

Oh . . . damn.

The Earl of Winchester, the Duke of Colton, and Quint all shot to their feet. Canis wriggled in her arms, begging to be let go, so she bent to place him on the floor. She swallowed, rose, and, with as much dignity as she could muster, gave a deep curtsy. "Gentlemen."

Colton was the first to speak. "Lady Sophia. What a . . . surprise." His gaze cut to Quint, then slid back to her. "We had no idea you planned to join us for lunch."

"Yes," said the earl, motioning to the footman for another place setting. "Thank you for joining our little gathering to celebrate my return as well as Colton's son. Because why else would you come to Quint's—"

"—unchaperoned—" the duke broke in.

"—in the middle of the day—" the earl said.

"—through the gardens," the duke finished.

"Colton. Winchester." Quint glared at both his friends, his voice low and serious. "Behave yourselves." He started for the inner door. "Lady Sophia, a word, if you please."

"Of course," she mumbled and trailed him into the corridor. He held the door open and shut it behind her. Instead of speaking there, however, he continued on to his study. When he shut them inside, he reached to cup her cheek. "I'm sorry. I had no idea they would—"

"No, it's my own fault for coming in the middle of the day, thinking you'd be alone."

"A reasonable assumption on any other day, but not this one, apparently. What would you like to do?"

"I think I must stay for lunch, no?"

Quint nodded, appearing equally unhappy about this development. "Yes, it's probably best. Be prepared, though. They'll not let you off easily. Stand your ground. And don't be afraid—"

"I can handle them, Quint." It was sweet, this concern of his. But she'd known Winchester for ages, and Colton was a lamb now that he'd become a father. Moreover, she counted both their wives as very good friends. And if there were ever two men who did not want to anger their wives . . .

"They won't tell anyone, you know. They'll just—"

"Demand answers from you the second I'm out of earshot."

He grimaced, handsome in his rumpled annoyance, and she stepped in, placed a hand on his chest, and rose up on her toes to press her lips to his. It was deep yet gentle, and it ended much too soon.

"And I apologize. I know this is the last thing you needed right now."

He bent to steal another kiss, longer this time. "It could be worse," he finally said against her mouth. "Their wives could be here as well."

Sophie knew Julia and Maggie would be informed the instant the group disbanded after lunch. No help for it now. "At least if they are questioning me, they won't be focused on *you*."

"Doubtful. But tell me, why did you come?"

"Oh." She stepped back and removed the paper from the pocket of her cloak. "Another girl has gone missing. One of Madame Hartley's. I went earlier today to question the staff." She handed him the paper. "I thought we might discuss what I learned."

"Tonight," he promised, taking the paper to his desk drawer, where he safely stowed it. "Let us return, before they barge in."

He took her elbow and led her back to the dining room. Colton and Winchester had given up all pretense of eating, both staring avidly at the door, mouths twitching in amusement.

Sophie tried to ignore them as she handed her cloak to a footman. Quint held out a chair for her. "Thank you." With shaking hands, she settled her napkin in her lap. "Now, Colton, why don't you tell us all about your son?"

It was the longest meal of Quint's life—and he'd once attended a thirty-two-course state banquet in Constantinople.

Sophie showed grace under pressure, he had to admit, directing the conversation toward safe topics. Colton's son. Julia's recovery. Simon's wedding trip. Maggie's latest art exhibit. With her brilliant smile and heartfelt laugh, Quint could hardly tear his gaze away from her. And her lips . . . she'd kissed him in the study. Kissed him as if it had been the easiest, most natural thing in the world. He'd liked it. Really liked it, in fact.

He was used to having her around. As much as he knew he was bad for her, he still had enough sanity left to see that *she* was good for *him*. The experiment on the terrace had proved that. But he should not take advantage of her any longer.

He just wasn't sure he could stop himself.

"Did you hear what I said, Quint?"

Quint blinked at Winchester. "You asked if I planned to attend Maggie's opening, which takes place in three weeks."

Colton chuckled. "I'd love to know how you do that. Keep one ear on the conversation while your mind's elsewhere."

"A skill I could most definitely use in Parliament," Winchester quipped. "So will you come? Maggie has discovered some new techniques during our trip and wants to show them to you."

Guilt pressed on Quint's chest. "I will certainly try."

Canis chose that moment to approach Sophie's

chair and distract the group. She plucked a piece of chicken off her plate and held it down to the puppy.

"You know, Olivia has been asking for a dog," Colton began. "Maybe I'll get her one while I'm here. From whom did you buy Canis, Sophia?"

"The owner of a little tea shop over in—" Her jaw snapped shut, realizing to what she'd just admitted. Quint nearly groaned.

Winchester and Colton exchanged a look. Sophie recovered quickly, however. "I bought him for myself, but Papa won't allow a dog in the house. So I gave him to Quint."

"Of course," Colton drawled. "Because Quint—"

"—is such an infamous animal lover," Winchester finished.

"Right." The duke chuckled.

Anger burned the back of Quint's throat. He slapped a hand on the table, rattling silver and glass. "Enough. Both of you, apologize now or I shall throw you out."

Winchester dabbed at the corners of his mouth with his napkin. Quint had the annoying impression his friend hid a smile behind the cloth. "I beg your pardon, Lady Sophia."

"And I as well," the duke told her, not bothering to hide his smile. "We are being unforgivably rude."

She waved a hand. "I know it seems strange. However, oftentimes you don't know what you want until someone beats you about the head with it. Would you both not agree?"

The other two men shifted uncomfortably, and it was Quint's turn to suppress a smile. Leave it to Sophie to turn it around, commenting on Colton and Winchester's tempestuous courtships with their wives. From then on, his two friends behaved themselves (mostly) and Sophie departed (via the front door) not long after.

When he returned from seeing her out the door, Colton and Winchester were waiting. No one spoke for a long moment. Colton finally cleared his throat, rubbed his jaw. "Quint, I am the very last man who would ever question the wisdom of with whomever you choose to . . ."

"Dally," Winchester supplied when the duke paused.

"Exactly. But I feel, for the sake of my wife, that I must ask, have you lost your ever-loving mind?"

No, not quite yet. "I am not dallying with her."

Winchester made a choking sound. "Really? You do realize whom you're speaking with? Not only would we spot a lie from a league away, the two of you returned from your tête-à-tête with swollen lips. Just what is going on?"

"She is an innocent, Quint," Colton said when Quint did not answer. "The daughter of a marquess. You cannot think to escape any repercussions from whatever is happening."

They both stared at him as if he were a stranger, which seemed appropriate since Quint hardly knew himself these days. The shame and regret over what he'd done to Sophie spread like a fungus in his chest, but a part of him wanted to dig in his heels. He hadn't forced her—she'd even enjoyed it—and he did not want to give her up. Even if never seeing her again was the right thing to do, for reasons that Colton and Winchester couldn't know, Quint needed Sophie more than he'd ever admit.

Yet he knew it would soon be over.

Both men would tell their wives and the women would immediately intervene on Sophie's behalf against him, the man they perceived as taking advantage of Sophie's virtue. Never mind that she had instigated—even asked for—every single one of their physical encounters.

He felt as if the ground were being yanked out from under him, just when he was starting to regain his footing.

Heat suffused his body, a swift and fierce fury that set his temples throbbing. "Never once," he said through clenched teeth, "in all the time we've known one another have I interfered in your relationships. Demanded answers to questions that were none of my business. Tried to make you feel guilty for the incredibly *asinine* way both of you have acted over the years." As his heart pounded in anger, his breath grew shallow and darkness crept into the edges of his vision. "Nothing gives you the right to interfere in my life. To insult her"—he dragged in air—"and make jokes."

A cold sweat broke out on his skin, and Quint knew he had to get out of there. If he had a fit in front of these men, he'd never be able to face himself. He rose abruptly.

"Are you all right?" Winchester asked, brows lowered in concern.

"Fine. Indigestion." Quint waved a hand. "Leave Sophie alone. We're friends. That's"—a wheeze—"all we shall ever be." He hurried from the room, disappearing into the safety of the house.

Nick stared at the door after Quint disappeared. "That was . . ."

"Odd."

He looked at Winchester. "In a word. I never would've believed it, if I hadn't seen it with my own two eyes."

Winchester nodded. "He's fallen hard."

"Like a rock."

"It happens to the best of us, Colt. But he's right. We shouldn't have given him a hard time."

Nick cocked a brow. "When have we *not* given each other a hard time? Hell, you and I scuffled a few times when I returned from Venice. Quint is well aware of that, so why is he so touchy all of a sudden?"

"I couldn't say. What was with the breathing at the end? He looked ready to faint."

Nick leaned back in his chair. "He was furious, I suppose."

"That wasn't fury. That was something else," Winchester said, absently twirling a spoon on the table. "I've only been back for a few days, but I've heard rumors."

"Rumors of what?"

"About Quint. That he's a recluse."

Nick made a dismissive sound and rolled his eyes. "Please. His staff is always making up fantastic tales."

"This isn't from the staff. He hasn't been at the clubs. Or his scientific gatherings. Begged off on the opening speech at the Royal Society. They say he never leaves the house, and no visitors—ever."

"Except Lady Sophia." Nick thought about this. Something had definitely been off earlier, when he'd met Quint on the terrace. The butler had tried his damnedest to bar him—a duke as well as a lifelong friend—from the house. If Nick weren't so cheerfully impolite, he never would've made it inside at all. And it also explained why Quint had been reluctant to go out to any of the clubs. "Is he ill?"

Winchester shrugged. "I couldn't say. Looked fine, other than that bit at the end. Kind of nice to see him stick up for a woman, didn't you think? Can't say I've ever seen him so worked up."

"I know," Nick agreed with a grin. "I never would have put the two of them together. Why, after all this time, do you suppose?"

"It's not exactly new," Winchester said. "Something happened between the two of them right before his betrothal. I never told Julia, but I came across Quint and Sophia, alone, at a ball. Kissing quite vigorously, as I recall."

Nick blinked at this news. "But the betrothal?"

"A mistake. Quint didn't care a whit about the Pepperton girl."

"Yet he was prepared to marry her."

"Indeed, though I believe he only proposed to her because things with Sophia never progressed. Like he was trying to get her attention by courting another woman. Interesting, is it not?"

Neither spoke for a moment. Nick realized, with no small amount of regret, that he would not be able to return to Norfolk tomorrow as he'd hoped. Damn.

"What are you going to do about this?" Winchester asked. "About Quint and Sophia, I mean."

"I haven't decided. Julia will have a fit if I keep it from her. She'll also demand to come to London, and the doctor doesn't want her traveling for another few weeks."

"Maggie will also want to know. We promised each other no more lies, so I cannot very well keep this from her."

"Nothing says you have to tell her right away," Nick suggested.

The two men sat silent, contemplating their wives. Julia's anger did not bother Nick one bit. When she was angry, her face flushed and her breasts heaved in the most enticing . . . He shifted in his chair, not wanting to dwell on that thought here. He'd been trying to keep his hands off her since the birth, to give her time to recover, but it had been damned difficult.

"You know the old saying, what is the best thing about an angry wife?" Winchester asked.

"No, what?"

He grinned. "Seducing her into forgiving you."

Nick chuckled. "So true. Fine. I'll give them two weeks. Then I'll tell Julia."

"Two weeks," Winchester agreed. "Surely he knows he must marry her."

"If Sophia agrees. She's always been prickly on the subject."

"Hardly matters if this were to get out. She'd be ruined. No woman wants that."

Winchester would know. His wife had been embroiled in a scandal during her debut, banished to the country for years. "Quint must have a plan in mind. He never does anything without thinking it through a hundred different ways."

"True. So what about Quint and this business about not leaving his house?"

"Ridiculous. Quint is too logical to become a recluse. Most likely he's on to another one of his puzzles. Let's give him a few days."

"And then what?"

"We ambush."

Chapter Fourteen

Sir Stephen stifled a yawn as he—she—bounced in the carriage on the way home.

Too many late nights, Sophie thought with a smile. But they had been worth it. Her investigation was moving along quite nicely. Based on Pamela's disappearance from Madame Hartley's, she he had three solid suspects: Comte de Saxe, Weston, and Tolbert.

She had tried to approach it logically, as Quint would, and not jump on the idea of Tolbert as the person responsible merely because she did not like him. So she'd investigated them all equally.

The *comte* was the easiest to rule out. He'd arrived in London only a week ago, having been in Vienna for the last year, and the first girl had been found over four months ago.

Lord Weston had been trickier. He lived in London most of the year, and Sophie confirmed he frequented both The Kitty and Madame Hartley's. She had needed to find out if he'd ever been to The Black Queen, because, thanks to the tattoos on the victims, the man she hunted was definitely familiar with all three establishments.

Tonight, she had learned he had never been to The Black Queen. He'd told Sir Stephen he had no knowledge of that particular brothel and asked if the girls were talented. Sophie had shrugged and alluded to a wild night with a particular brunette named Molly. Perhaps Molly would be more inclined to talk if she thought Sir Stephen was sending business her way.

Which left her with Tolbert as her last suspect. Now she just had to prove it—because one did not make accusations against a peer of the realm without proof.

The thrill of the discovery threatened to burst out of her chest. She couldn't wait to tell Quint. In fact . . .

She rapped on the ceiling with her walking stick. Jenkins opened the small partition. "Yes, sir."

"Jenkins, take me to Lord Quint's."

"Very good, sir. I'll go around the back."

She tried to ignore the fluttering of anticipation in her belly. She hadn't seen Quint since the day of the luncheon with Winchester and Colton. That had been awkward enough, and she hadn't wanted to add to Quint's troubles by returning so soon. It had been stupid to show up during the middle of the day anyway.

And now that his friends were back, she had to be more careful. Popping over to Quint's whenever she wanted was no longer possible. Even now, at this late hour, she'd need to ensure he was alone.

You just want him to kiss you there *again.*

Well, yes. No denying that, she thought even as her face went up in flames. It had been . . . indeed, no word she knew would do the experience justice. And yet, as satisfying as it had been, she wanted to drive him to the same heights of pleasure. Each time he had satisfied her, he'd hurried her out the door. Never giving her the chance to reciprocate.

The idea of touching him, making him shudder and shake with need, had taken root in her brain. She longed for Quint to take her as a man takes a woman, the two of them naked and writhing in ecstasy together. Moisture pooled between her legs just thinking on it.

A voice, one that had been appearing more often of late, whispered that she was in too deep. That her feelings for Quint had long surpassed friendship and had developed into something *more*. Sophie pointedly ignored that annoying warning.

She needed him to help with the investigation, and he needed her to help him recover. That was it. Once the investigation had concluded, they would return to their usual lives.

Or, at least he would return to his normal life. Sophie had no idea what constituted *normal* for her any longer.

By the time she crept through Quint's gardens, the moon was well past the midpoint in the sky. It shone brightly on the leaves and flowers just starting to bloom, with the moist, earthy smell of nighttime enveloping her. When she came up the steps, a familiar figure stood on the terrace.

"I am impressed," she told Quint. "You are outside, and without any assistance this time."

His teeth flashed white in the darkness. "I am. And I have you to thank for it."

"No, you did this. You deserve the credit. Have you tried to go farther?"

He shook his head. "Not yet. I'm not sure I'm—"

Ready. She heard the word as clear as if he'd said it. "Well, then it's a good thing I'm here."

"Yes, I noticed you've been staying away. Was that to punish me for the luncheon?"

"Punish you?" She felt herself frown. "Why would I want to punish you?"

"For allowing Colton and Winchester to treat you so horribly. If it makes you feel any better, I took them to task after you left."

"I was not upset with you, Quint. I had no one to blame but myself. I never should have come unannounced during the day. They were right to point out my foolishness."

He drew closer and her heart started pounding. She'd become so weak where he was concerned. The mere memory of his hands and mouth could make her dizzy with wanting. His palm cupped her cheek, thumb rubbing softly over her jaw as his ruggedly handsome face stared down at her. "I worried they'd scared you away for good. And there would be little I could do about it, trapped as I am."

Trapped for now, she wanted to tell him. Because he would get better. She would see to it.

She wrapped her hands around his wrists. "You could always ask me to return."

His brown eyes glittered in the moonlight. "And you would do it?"

"Yes," she whispered. "I cannot stay away, it seems."

"And thank God for that," he murmured before bending to kiss her.

This was a gentler kiss than the ones they usually shared, a kiss of familiarity. Of welcome. To reacquaint themselves. He tasted of peppermint tea, she noted as his tongue twined lazily with hers. He kept hold of her face, her hands clasping his wrists, and she let his calm, steady presence wash over her.

"I'm glad you returned," he said against her mouth

when they paused for breath. "Did you want to discuss your investigations?"

Her mind properly muddled by his kisses, she clung to him. "Investigations?"

He chuckled. "Come inside, Sir Stephen. Let us see what you've learned."

She was dressed as a man, smelled of hair pomade, and Quint did not find it deterring in the least. He didn't bother leading her to his study. Instead, he took her through the house and led her up to his chambers. No way could he keep his hands off her, and she deserved privacy for what he had in mind.

Her cheeks were flushed when he closed them in. Was she considering what would happen as well?

He watched as she removed her light brown greatcoat, placing it on the bed. Her deep-blue wool topcoat had been padded in the shoulders, but otherwise molded to her lithe frame. She had the hips of a woman, but the cut of the coat helped to hide them a bit. Her long, lean legs were clearly visible in the trousers, though the brown fabric had been gathered generously about the waist, obviously to hide her more womanly curves.

Focus, he reminded himself.

"So your three men, the Comte de Saxe, Weston, and Tolbert," he began. "What have you learned?"

Sophie's gaze sparkled as she told him about eliminating both the *comte* and Weston. "Which means it must be Tolbert," she finished excitedly.

"No, it means it *may* be Tolbert. Just because he was the last person to see Pamela alive does not mean he killed her. In fact, Mulrooney saw Tolbert leave that night. Alone."

"You read my notes," she said, seemingly surprised.

He walked to the bed and sat on the edge of the mattress. "Of course I did. You left them here. I assumed you wanted me to read them."

"I did. So did anything occur to you?" Sophie leaned against the bedpost. "For example, what about the man who got rough with Pamela, the one Madame would not name?"

"Not unusual in those places. Men will often seek out what they cannot find at home. So the Pamelas of the world see things most other women do not."

She nibbled on her lip, and he felt his blood stir. It was becoming increasingly difficult to restrain himself around her. She was a fever in his system, and he lost all sense of reason around her. And seeing her dressed as a man tonight did little to abate his fascination.

"So you don't think the man is worth investigating?"

"Possibly. It's hard to say. Pamela was predisposed not to like that sort of thing, so she may have overreacted. My sense is that Madame would have confessed a name if she truly believed him to be a threat."

"I suppose that is true."

"Did they find any letters or keepsakes in her things?"

"No," Sophie answered. "None at all. Left behind her money, clothes, and a small amount of jewelry."

"So not running away. Which means she snuck out to meet someone, not knowing he was dangerous. Did you check with the constable, to see if her body has turned up?"

"Madame did. And no, they've not found anyone fitting Pamela's description."

"You could try her family, see if she wrote to any of them and mentioned a man."

"She wasn't close with her family, but I could try. I still plan to watch Tolbert, to see if he's involved."

An uncomfortable weight settled on his chest. "I don't like the idea of you trailing Tolbert all over town by yourself. What do you hope to see him do, kidnap a girl, strangle her, cut off her hand, and dump her in the Thames?"

"He won't notice me." She smirked. "And I don't know what I hope to see him do. But if he is the one hurting these girls, I want to see him stopped."

"Sophie," he sighed. "This is extraordinarily unsafe. I cannot allow you to put yourself—"

"Allow me?" she snapped. "Are we back to that again?"

He clenched his jaw. "It is one thing for you to ask questions and collect evidence. It is another thing altogether to track a potential killer in the hopes of catching him in the act."

"I need to observe him. I need to gather proof. Surely you can understand that."

Yes, he could understand it. But that did not mean he had to like it. Anything that put her in harm's way did not sit well with him. "Maybe I will come with you."

Now where had that idea come from?

Her eyes widened. "Could you?"

He thought about it. She'd already worked one miracle with the terrace. Perhaps it was unfair to expect another. "I am not sure. Perhaps if I stay in the carriage . . . But I might very well suffer a fit—"

"Which I've already said is not a problem. And I'll be there the entire time."

He swallowed, nodded, and reached for her hand, seeking the connection. She was like his own personal talisman against the madness in his future. "It will likely only get worse, you know. We should not be encouraged by what happened on the terrace."

"Balderdash. I do not believe that." She stepped between his legs and smoothed his hair off his forehead. "You are getting better. I know it."

He didn't have the heart to disappoint her. Didn't mention the two failed experiments he'd conducted on himself since the last time he saw her. First a salt bath, which had left him dehydrated and weaker than when he'd started. The other a poultice of bruised garlic applied to his armpits, backs of knees, and ankles. In addition to making him feel ridiculous, he'd smelled terrible. In the end, neither remedy had lessened his anxiety when he'd tried to go outside.

He pulled Sophie closer, more than ready to distract her from this conversation. She came willingly, met his mouth in a soft, determined kiss. Her hands fell on his shoulders, while his fingers clasped about her hips. She ran the tip of her tongue along his bottom lip, then bit him gently. Pleasure and pain combined to spark in his groin. He tightened his grip, deepened the kiss, his own tongue diving inside her mouth to stroke hers.

Before he knew it, he'd slid her topcoat off. It took little effort to divest her of the waistcoat and cravat as well. Then her hands were at his throat, untying his cravat while she continued to kiss him, her mouth wicked and warm. His erection pulsed in anticipation of tasting her again, of having Sophie naked in his bed.

When she went to work on his waistcoat, he broke away from her mouth. "Sophie, stop." He needed as many barriers as he could get between himself and her soon-to-be-naked body.

"Why?" Her half-lidded eyes looked down at him. "Let me touch you, Quint."

God, the mere thought caused a shiver to work its way down his spine, hardening him further. "No," he told her. "You cannot."

Her mouth hitched into the impish, sexy half-smile that frequently preceded deviltry on her part. "Oh, I can. And I think you want me to." She gestured to the very obvious erection in his trousers.

"If you touch me, I won't be able to control myself."

"Perhaps I want you to lose control. The way you make me lose control."

"You're nearly naked, in my bed. One of us needs to keep a level head."

"No, one of us does not." Her hands reached out and slipped a few buttons on his waistcoat before he could stop her.

He moved her back and stood. There needed to be distance between them. He'd never wanted a woman this badly. But he wanted Sophie, wanted to take her—hard. Like an animal in heat, just pure instinct and drive, where nothing mattered but desire and pleasure. The risks, however, were far too great. For one thing, he could not chance impregnating a woman with a Beecham child. To do so would be impossibly cruel.

"You do not know what you're asking for. But I do, and it cannot happen."

Then Sophie pulled her shirt over her head—and he forgot to breathe. All that luscious, creamy skin, the white bandage around her bosom. Slim arms, small shoulders, the delicate column of her throat. "I know precisely what I am asking for, Quint. And it's you."

His breath coming short and fast, Quint's gaze raked over her body, fingers flexing at his sides as if he itched to touch her. "Are you certain?" he asked, eyes gone dark with lust. His member strained under the cloth at his groin, and Sophie longed to run her hands over him, to feel him twitch in her palm. To drag her tongue down his body, to take him in her mouth.

"Yes." She'd thought of little else for three days. He'd already shown her more pleasure than she'd ever dreamed, and she trusted him.

Which meant she had to tell him.

It was such a humiliating thing to admit, the stupidity of her debut. Especially to the ever-logical Quint, who thought before he acted, weighed the possibilities, and kept himself in control. Sophie had run headlong into one scrape after another all her life, and owning up to them was never easy.

He closed his eyes and pinched the bridge of his nose. She knew he was thinking intently, which he did entirely too often. Certain times required little or no thought. *This* was one of those times.

She came forward and finished unfastening his godawful puce-colored waistcoat. Shoved it off his shoulders. He looked down at her, brows drawn in confusion, but did not stop her. She took that as encouragement.

Gathering fistfuls of his shirt, she pulled the cloth from his trousers and began pushing it up his chest. He took over, bringing his shirt over his head in one swift motion. Stepping back, she took it all in. Wide shoulders, dark brown hair dusting his chest, and flat abdomen leading down to narrow hips . . . so deliciously *male*. He had muscles she did not expect and yearned to explore. The scar on his neck had mostly healed over, the skin now puckered and pink. She traced it with her fingertip, and he gave a tiny shiver.

"I am very glad you did not die."

He bent to kiss her in response, his tongue sweeping into her mouth, stroking over hers. She loved the way he kissed. So possessively. A woman could drown in his kisses.

When his fingers hit the fall of her trousers, she broke off from his mouth. "Quint, I must tell you something."

He paused and pushed the hair off of her forehead. "Did you want to stop?"

"Definitely not." She took a deep breath. "You should know . . . I am not a maiden."

"Good." He went back to work on her trouser buttons.

Sophie struggled to breathe. *Good.* Was that all he had to say? And he said it so matter-of-factly, as if it were of no consequence at all. The relief and shock made her dizzy. This event, this *mistake*, had haunted her entire adult life. Wasn't he disgusted? Outraged? Disappointed? She stepped back and sagged onto the bed.

He froze, head cocked as he watched her. "You thought I would hold such a fact against you."

She should've expected him to have an unconventional view of virginity. But she'd kept this secret for so long, had let it determine the course of most of her adult life. How could he not care?

"Most men would."

He came over and pulled her to her feet. His gaze burned, the golden-brown irises bright and hot, intent on her face. She'd never had a man look at her the way Quint did, as if he were studying and memorizing every detail. As if she were the only woman on earth. As if she *mattered*.

His hands cupped her face, his thumbs brushing over her cheekbones. "The right man would not bemoan the loss of your innocence. The right man would want to ensure you had been handled carefully the first time, with respect and affection. The right man would get down on his knees and thank the heavens you were in his bed—maidenhead or no. *I* am that man."

Before she could respond, before she could breathe after such a declaration, he bent, wrapped his arms under her bottom, and lifted her straight up off the floor. He placed her on the coverlet and stretched out beside her. He stroked the tip of his finger over the cloth covering her breasts. "Did you love him, the man who took your maidenhead?"

"Yes."

He seemed to absorb that. "Taking your innocence was only a small part of why I did not want to bed you, Sophie. There are more important things at risk than your hymen. Like the fact that I cannot marry you."

She ignored the pang of disappointment that settled behind her heart at those words. "Who said anything about marriage? I have no intention of forcing you into marrying me. But you said 'things,' so what else is there?"

"We must take precautions to prevent you from conceiving. Each time. No exceptions."

That sounded reasonable. She did not want the responsibility of a bastard. "Any other reason you do not want to take me to your bed?"

"Yes." He rolled onto his back, bringing her with him so she was on top. "Because once I have you, I'll not want to let you go."

He angled her mouth toward his and took her lips in a blistering kiss. She melted against him, his large body easily bearing her weight. Deliberate, rhythmic licks of his wicked tongue made her dizzy as his hands slid to cup her backside. He rocked his pelvis into hers, the hard length of him dragging sweetly against the spot that ached most. "Damien," she gasped.

"God, Sophie," he growled against her mouth. "How was I ever supposed to resist you?"

She understood what he meant because she hadn't been able to resist him, not from the moment she'd met him. He kissed her again—ardently, desperately—and she could scarcely form a thought in the onslaught.

Hands on her shoulders, he pushed her upright. "Here," he said, "let's get you out of this." Fingers working quickly, he divested her of the bandage, freeing her breasts. Her nipples puckered further in the cool air, the small mounds already aching with need. He made no move to touch her, just stared at her chest for a long moment. "You are so lovely."

One fingertip came up to trace the right breast. She closed her eyes, the light touch streaking through her bloodstream like fire. Heavens, she hated to think what would happen when he—

Warm, tight heat enveloped her nipple and her lids flew open. Quint had risen up to suck on her breast. Then, using his lips, teeth, and tongue, he proceeded to drive her out of her mind. With her knees on either side of his hips, her groin lined up perfectly with his, and each tug of his lips had her grinding into his erection.

He fell back with a groan, face flushed, lids screwed tight. "You have to stop," he panted, clasping her hips to keep her still. "I want to make this last."

Instead of listening, she bent to kiss his throat, his chest, reveling in the unique taste and texture that made up this fascinating man. Her lips brushed his nipple and he started, so she did it again.

In an instant, he flipped their positions. "Minx." Sitting up, he unbuttoned her trousers and lowered them down her legs. Drawers were next, then stockings. Leaving her completely naked. "*Ty prekrasna*," he whispered in a rough language she didn't understand. "You are beautiful."

"Except for my scar."

He traced the outline of the healing wound on her thigh. It no longer hurt, but Sophie hated the way it looked. "We match," Quint said, lifting her hand and placing it on his scarred throat. She felt the rough, uneven skin as his hand continued up her thigh, dipped between her legs. He hummed when he found the wetness there. "Oh, God, Sophie. You're so wet. It makes a man think he's died and gone to heaven."

She reached for his waist, for the buttons on the trousers he still wore. "Damien, please." She slipped two free before he twisted away. He got up from the bed and went to his dresser. Opening the drawer, he soon returned with two long strips of . . . cloth? They were limp and had a tiny ribbon at one end. He tossed one onto the side table and carried the other as he climbed back onto the bed.

"What is that?"

"A condom," he said. "A French letter. It will protect you from conceiving."

In very little time, he stripped off his boots and trousers, and then affixed the sheath. She had a momentary flash of concern over the size of him before he settled between her thighs. He used a finger, then two, to stretch her, and then she felt the blunt head of his erection working its way inside. He was much larger than Lord Robert, if memory served. And that had been a struggle. She tensed.

"Relax," he told her. "I can fit." He slid forward a half inch and then hissed through his teeth. "You were made to fit me."

Bracing himself on the bed with his hands, he pushed forward steadily in a slow invasion of her body, one she had not experienced in a long time. He gave no quarter, no chance for escape, even if Sophie had wanted to. But she didn't, because finally he was fully seated inside her, their hips locked, and it was the most exquisite feeling in the world. He was a part of her in a way Robert hadn't even come close.

"You are so tight. Tell me I can move, Sophie."

Her body had adjusted, so she told him, "Move, Damien."

He dropped onto his elbows, bracing his knees on the bed and giving her more of his weight, before withdrawing slightly and pushing back in. The fire licked through her veins and she clutched his shoulders. When he remained still, she said breathlessly, "Tell me you're going to do that again."

"Oh, *kotyonok*," he chuckled. "I promise I will do that again." He snapped his hips and she gasped. "I'll do it again and again until you come apart."

He began thrusting in earnest, setting a relentless rhythm. The rest of the room fell away until it was only the two of them, panting and sweating as they climbed higher and higher. "Move your hips to meet mine," he told her, and she did, amazed at how the simple change in angle increased the ache of pleasure.

Everything was building inside her, a coiling of sensation, when he reached down and stroked a finger over the nub between her legs. On the third stroke, she exploded, her body flung apart into a million pieces, and she shouted and shuddered beneath him. Dimly, she realized his movements had become uncoordinated as he stiffened, a hoarse cry torn from his throat.

When she floated back down, he collapsed beside her. He rolled away for a moment and then came back, pulling her against him. His hand cupped her breast possessively. "How do you feel?"

"Astounded," she answered, the only coherent word that came to mind.

He smiled. "Then I cannot wait to show you what else we are capable of."

Chapter Fifteen

Quint dragged his hand over Sophie's hip, content to lie next to her while they recovered. There would be time enough for regrets tomorrow. But for now, he intended to bask in the aftermath of their love-making. Contemplate all the things he'd like to do to her. He would have her at least once more before she went home.

"Tell me what you like," he urged.

"About you?" Her face tilted up at him. "Feeling insecure, Damien?"

He reached around and pinched her buttock playfully, which drew a yelp out of her. "No, I mean in bed. Do you like to be on top? The man on top? On your knees? Tell me your preferences because I'm not done with you yet."

She blinked in confusion. Her mouth turned down at the edges, and he realized his mistake. "Wait, I assumed—"

"That I've had many partners. I understand." She sighed, her breath rushing over his skin. "Really, what else could you think? I should have told you all of it.

There was only one other man before you, and it was a long, long time ago."

That would explain her tightness, he supposed. "But why did this one man not marry you?"

A dry chuckle escaped her lips. "You would get right to the heart of it. He did promise he would marry me. It was the year I debuted and I'd fallen for him, you see. He said that many couples anticipate the wedding night and we would soon be betrothed, so what was the harm?"

He cursed inwardly. She was not the first innocent to fall for such a pack of lies from a scoundrel. Quint had been traveling at the time of her debut, away for several years, yet he wished he had been here. Perhaps if he'd met her instead . . .

"Anyway," she continued, "we did. Anticipate the wedding night, that is. And I kept waiting for him to seek out my father, to ask for my hand."

Quint stroked her stomach, calming her, while a storm gathered in his chest. He did not like where this story was headed. Not one bit.

"*Aaaaaand* I waited some more. Finally I cornered him at an event, alone. I asked when he would speak with Papa and he told me never. That there hadn't been any blood, and innocent maidens don't enjoy it as much as I had."

His hands curled into fists, the pressure in his head building and making it throb. "He told you that you *enjoyed* it too much?"

"Yes," she answered easily as if Quint weren't ready to explode at any minute. "And what could I do but slink away in shame? I couldn't tell my father, not about that, and by then I certainly wouldn't have married Rob—"

She bit it off, but Quint had to know. "Rob? Robbie? Robert?"

She stiffened slightly on the last one, giving him his answer.

"Robert who? Was he a gentleman? He must have been if you thought he was good enough to speak with your father." Now on his back, he folded his hands behind his head. Her debut would have been eight years ago. Rapidly, he ran the names of all the titled Roberts he knew through his mind. There were quite a number, as it was a common name amongst the *ton*. Who would have been about her age, unmarried—?

"Stop it," Sophie said. "I know what you're trying to do. Stop. It was over a long time ago."

"I cannot help it. I want to rip his head off. After I pummel him for a week."

Propping up on an elbow, she swung a leg over his thigh. Her fingers trailed down his chest, through the sparse hair on his stomach. "I had no idea you were so bloodthirsty. Quite a different side to such a man of science."

"You're attempting to distract me."

She chuckled, her touch tracing his inner thigh. "Is it working?" His shaft came to life, blood rushing to fill the *corpora cavernosa* within to produce an erection, and she laughed harder. "I'd say that is a yes."

"We are not done talking about it, Sophie. I want a name."

She slid between his thighs, raining kisses along his hip bone. "You shan't get one, Damien. Let it go." With her mouth poised over his growing arousal, her moist, hot breath teased his skin. He shivered as she said, "It's in the past."

No, it was very much *not* in the past. But Quint decided to let her think she'd won for now.

Especially when her tongue flicked the glans of his penis. He nearly jumped out of his skin. "*Yes.* God, do that again."

He watched as the tip of her pink tongue emerged to slide around the sensitive head, and fire raced through his shaft to his bollocks. "Tell me what to do," she said. "I want to please you, but I don't know how."

"There isn't much to do wrong," he said with a short laugh. "Except use too much teeth." She was staring at his genitalia with confusion, so he explained, "You know your clitoris? The tiny nub you rub to bring yourself—"

"Yes," she said quickly, her cheeks turning pink.

"Well, this"—he gestured to his erection—"is the very same thing, only a bit larger. Yet the same principles apply."

"Meaning licking?"

"And sucking," he added, his voice rough with the very idea of her mouth wrapped around him.

She moistened her lips and reached for him. He tried to keep very still, to let her explore, but it was excruciating. She started with light kisses, then tiny flutters of her tongue, to learn the taste and shape of him. He was panting by the time she took him in her wet, warm mouth, her lips stretching completely over the head and sucking him inside. His eyes nearly rolled back in his head, and he let out a long groan.

"You're killing me, *kotyonok.*"

Emboldened, she drew him in deeper. Slick, tight suction as she slid back up. He wanted to watch, but it felt too exquisite to keep his lids open. Figured Sophie would be a quick study. She kept up the motion, bobbing up and down, and his breath grew labored. If she kept this up . . .

He reached and snatched her shoulders, bringing her on top of him for an open-mouthed kiss. She straddled him and he thought about how easily he could slide into her, naked, unprotected. But he would not risk impregnating her. His family line was cursed, and he would not wish a Beecham child on any woman.

"Sophie, hand me the condom on the table."

She reached over, putting her breast in his face. He took full advantage, tonguing her nipple and drawing it into his mouth. He spent some time on her breasts, showering them with attention, while she gasped and writhed over him. When she started begging, he affixed the new condom and grasped her hips, lowering her down onto his shaft.

"What do I do?" she panted, her brown eyes glittering with arousal.

"Ride me. Rock your hips like this." He clasped her hips and rolled her pelvis. Her eyes went wide. "Feels good, doesn't it? This position provides more direct stimulation to your—"

She did it again, harder this time, and he couldn't finish his sentence. The woman didn't need to be told twice, apparently.

After that, it was all sensation. Sophie ground down on top of him while her breasts bounced and the mattress protested. She curled her fingers on his stomach, nails digging into his skin, and he started to meet her, thrusting up into her warmth, their hips slapping together. Sweat rolled off his forehead and into his hair. The sizzle soon built in the base of his spine, and he knew he wouldn't be able to hold back much longer.

"Come on, Sophie. God, let me feel you." He reached

and pressed his thumb on her clitoris and her walls instantly clamped down on his erection. She threw her head back, shouted, and spasmed around him, which triggered his own explosion. It went on forever, the thick, ropy strands of ejaculate expelling from his body and into the protective barrier while he shuddered beneath her.

She fell onto his chest, boneless and sweaty. He felt precisely the same way, utterly relaxed and completely satiated. In fact, he could not remember the last time he'd felt this at ease. Probably never, now that he thought about it.

"I do not think I can move," she mumbled against his sternum.

"Then don't." He wrapped his arms about her, kissed the top of her head. "I like you precisely where you are."

Sophie had no idea how long this light, all-relaxing state would last, but she meant to enjoy it. Quint seemed in no hurry, either. She rested half on top of him, tucked into his side, with her foot dragging over his lower leg. Her fingers twined in his crisp chest hair while he drew lazy circles on her naked back with his palm.

"I cannot recall the last time I felt this good," he murmured.

She smiled against his shoulder. "Good, how?"

"Feeling insecure, Sophia?" he teased, throwing her earlier words back at her.

"Maybe. I do not have as much practice at this as you do."

"A good thing. If you'd had more practice, you might have killed me."

She swatted his shoulder. "Be serious."

"*Kotyonok,* I am nearly always serious."

The foreign word made her tingle, especially the way he said it, with hard, guttural consonants. "You keep calling me that. What does it mean?"

"Kitten. It's Russian."

"I like the way it sounds."

"I noticed," he said, wryly. "And it fits." He indicated his stomach, so she sat up slightly and saw red scratches on the taut skin of his abdomen.

"Did I do that?" She covered her mouth, horrified. "God, Quint, I am so—"

"Do not apologize," he said sharply. "You marked me because you were enjoying yourself, enjoying me. Which means, when I see these marks tomorrow, I can remember the look on your face when you found your pleasure atop me. Sophie, any man who does not appreciate that is a fool."

He drew her down and leaned over her. "I want you to like what I do to you, as well as what you do to me. You should enjoy it, and there's no way you can tell or show me often enough. Women should like physical pleasure as much as men do."

"But ladies—"

"Are still women. I know you are taught it's not proper to like intercourse, and the man who had you first scared you into believing it, but nothing we do together that brings us both pleasure is wrong. If you never believe me about anything else, believe that."

It sounded logical, but she couldn't help but think there was something wrong with her. She'd scratched him like a lion. "I'll try," she replied.

"Good. What time did you need to leave? It's nearly four."

She sighed. She hated to leave, but staying was out

of the question. "I should leave now, before the servants are awake."

He kissed her, a tender, soft, lingering kiss that made her toes curl. "Thank you for tonight."

"My pleasure. Literally."

He chuckled. "And mine as well. Now let's get you dressed and in a carriage."

Rising, the two of them found their various articles of clothing on the floor and began putting them back on. His eyes darkened when she slid the drawers up over her hips. "I never thought I would find men's undergarments so appealing," he said.

She tied them at the waist. "No time for that again, at least not tonight."

"Good thing I know where to find Sir Stephen in the future, then."

"Does that mean you only want me to return when I'm dressed in my male clothing?" She stepped into the trousers.

He was already tucking his shirt in, obviously more used to donning his own clothes than she. "Indeed, no. I like you in whatever you're wearing. Most especially, however, when you're wearing nothing."

"And I you. You are certainly hiding a fair bit of muscle for a man who never leaves his desk."

"Now that I know you like it, I'll be certain to show it off more." He picked up her bandage. "It seems a shame to put this back on."

"No need. My breasts aren't so large and they'll be hidden by my coat on the way home."

He came up behind her and cupped the bare mounds in his palms, causing them to swell. She swallowed a moan.

"That means they'll be bouncing and swaying on

the ride home," he growled. He ground his hips into her backside. "It's enough to make me hard again."

She remembered their earlier conversation about him accompanying her to investigate. Perhaps now, when he was relaxed and satiated, would be the best time to push him past his fears. She rocked back into his hips. "Then I think you should ride with me, so you can see them for yourself."

His hands fell and he tried to step away. She spun and grabbed hold of his shirt. "You can do it, Damien. I know you can."

He frowned, ready to admit defeat before even trying. She stood her ground. "I will be with you. Only me. No one else. And I promise you may fondle my breasts the whole time."

A reluctant laugh escaped before he could stop it. "A tempting offer, to be sure. But why are you so determined to see me embarrass myself?"

"Because I do not see your weaknesses as embarrassing. I see them as human. You're afraid, Damien. And I understand that, probably better than you realize. I've let fear and shame rule my life for so long, and you've set me free from all that. Let me help you this time."

He crushed her against his chest, holding her so tight she could scarcely breathe. "I will only disappoint you in the end," he said into her hair.

"You do not know that, not for certain." He started to shake his head, and she said, "You're all about evidence and proof. So prove me wrong, Quint. Let's go outside and see the worst that can happen."

Quint stared out at the gardens, his heart racing. The base of his skull had already begun to ache. "You will regret this," he told Sophie, who stood at his side. "When you're scraping me off the ground and carrying me back into the house. Do not say I didn't warn you."

"We shall see," was the stubborn woman's response. "The carriage is in the mews. I asked Jenkins to keep facing forward no matter what happens and not to intervene. When we are finally inside he'll take us once around the block. Then you may return to your house."

He blew out a breath, wiped damp palms on his trousers. "Why does it matter to you?"

After a moment, she said, "Because I love hearing your lectures. Seeing you standing up in front of a room full of scholars and learned men, your ideas bursting forth. Every pair of eyes on you, waiting to soak up the knowledge you readily impart. It's . . . humbling."

"I—I had no idea. You never came up to me afterwards. Why did you never tell me?" He hadn't ever seen her in any of the crowds, not that he gave all that many lectures. It was never more than one or two a year. But he would have liked knowing she was there.

"I never told anyone. Not even Julia. It was silly, really. Like I am some sort of zealot, one of your devoted followers. Lurking in the back row, hiding just to hear you."

The words were a punch in the solar plexus. Everything in him softened, a warmth blossoming through his veins. "Sophie," he said and reached for her.

"No, none of that," she eluded his grasp. "Stay focused. Besides, you know the definition of a phobia. It's an *irrational* fear—and you are a rational, logical man. You can do this. You *will* do this."

He exhaled and scrubbed a hand through his hair. "Fine. Let's get this over with."

"Just keep your eyes on me." Sophie stood in front of him and clasped his hands. "I'll lead you down. All right?"

He nodded, and she began walking backward, keeping hold of him the entire time. His feet shuffled forward, but he focused on her face. The small, pert nose. The heart-shaped bow of her upper lip, resting atop the full, lush bottom lip. The big, round brown eyes that held such confidence, such depth of feeling that he almost believed he could do anything.

Now at the bottom of the stairs, he knew they were in the gardens. His lungs began to work harder as the urge to return to the house hit him full force. His heart hammered as if he were in a race. "Keep looking at me, Damien," Sophie urged. "Think about what you're going to do to me when we reach the carriage."

That was interesting. He thought about her breasts, now bare beneath the waistcoat and shirt, bouncing in the carriage as they had when he'd been driving into her body. She bit her lip, almost as if she knew what he was remembering. Sweet cadmium, she was lovely. And her mouth . . .

He continued running a series of lurid images in his mind, all the things he'd like to do to Sophie if only he had enough time. Arousal, fueled by panic and excitement, hummed through his veins, as if he hadn't just spent himself twice in the last hour. He wanted her again. Dimly, he realized she'd reached back to open the gate. He kept his gaze trained on her face, even when she glanced away briefly.

Then they were inside the carriage, with him nearly pushing her up the last remaining steps. She fell back against the squabs and he pounced, covering her as best he could in the cramped, dark space as the wheels began to move.

He swooped down to claim her mouth, ravenous for her, delirious with it, as if he'd never had her. She clung to him, returning the kiss and running her hands over his back. He threw her greatcoat open, unbuttoned her topcoat, and jerked her shirt and waistcoat out of the way, shoving the fabric higher until he could get to her bare skin. Sliding down, he drew her nipple into his mouth, sucking deep.

Her fingers tunneled into his hair. "Oh, God. *Quint.*"

He released her breast and returned to her mouth, kissing her feverishly. "If we were not in a carriage, I'd be inside you already," he whispered darkly with a roll of his hard shaft along her core.

"Oh, yes," she whimpered, clutching his buttocks with both hands.

"I cannot get enough of you." He ground against her once more. "If only you had on skirts."

She was panting now, writhing under him. "Next time," she promised.

Lust roared through him, his erection nearly painful. "Touch me, Sophie. Please." She moved her hand to stroke his cock through his trousers. "More. God, Sophie. I need you."

Together, they worked the buttons free with due haste, and he groaned when her hand found bare flesh. "Yes. Harder. Stroke me. Faster. *Yes. Like that.*"

Her hand pumped him and he thrust into her grip. So good. So tight. "God, yes. Keep going." He couldn't think, couldn't breathe, and everything inside him wound taut. Sophie was there, talking to him with sweet, low words of encouragement, and he kept rocking into her fist. Then it rushed over him, his back bowing, body clenching, as he spilled his seed in hot pulses all over Sophie's silk waistcoat. He shuddered, gasping her name as the spasms continued to echo throughout his limbs.

When it finally ended, he noticed that the carriage had stopped. "We're back," Sophie said softly.

He blinked. *Oh, God.* He straightened, sitting up and giving her space while he tried to collect himself. Once again, he'd completely lost his sense of control around her. Exhaling, he rubbed his eyes. He'd never treated a woman so disrespectfully. And Sophie certainly deserved better of him. He'd debased her, ejaculated all over her. Christ, what must she think of him? He didn't carry a handkerchief, so he whipped off his loosely tied cravat and cleaned her up the best he could.

"Well, that's one stain Alice won't be expecting," she said, dryly.

"Better take it off and let me have it. I'll have my valet clean it."

Woodenly, he helped her remove the topcoat and the soiled waistcoat. Then he slipped her topcoat back over her arms. He couldn't even look at her as he buttoned up his trousers. "I'm sorry."

"Damien." She laid her palm on his cheek, bringing his gaze to hers. "Remember, nothing we do together that brings us both pleasure is wrong."

"I doubt that was pleasurable for you, me using you like that."

"You would be wrong. Did you enjoy pleasuring me out on your terrace?"

"Of course," he answered quickly.

"Well, it is the same for me. I enjoy giving you

pleasure, you stubborn man. Now get inside so that I may return home. Do you need me to help you?"

"No. I'll be fine," he said, even though he wasn't sure. But she'd done enough. He did not want to burden her further. So he picked up her hand and pressed a kiss to her fingers. "Sweet dreams, *kotyonok.*"

Chapter Sixteen

Sophie surveyed the ballroom from her spot in the back corner. For two days, she'd been searching for Lord Tolbert, but she hadn't been able to locate him. Until tonight. With help from Alice's network of servants, they'd learned Tolbert planned to attend the Earl of Portland's ball. The marchioness had been thrilled when Sophie requested to come along.

Good thing her stepmama did not know why.

She was not here to dance or engage in polite conversation. No, she attended merely to watch Tolbert, to see where he went when he left here.

Because Pamela had been found yesterday, dead. Strangled, raped, her right hand severed. Struck in the back of the head. Thrown into the river. Sir Stephen had returned to the Thames Police Office last night to see the body. Despite being bloated from the water, the girl had fit Madame Hartley's description.

And Sophie was convinced the blame for her death lay squarely at Tolbert's feet.

Unfortunately, Tolbert had not yet arrived. When he did, however, she would be waiting.

"Lady Sophia." The Duke of Colton bowed in front of her. In his impeccably turned-out black evening clothes, it was easy to see why Julia had fallen so hard for her husband.

"Colton." She curtsied. "I hadn't expected to see you here. Isn't this event a tad on the respectable side for you?"

"Yes, but respectability is a nice change of scenery every now and then."

"The benefit of being a duke, I suppose."

"Indeed." He grinned.

Sophie nearly rolled her eyes. "You are fortunate that Julia puts up with you."

"I'm well aware of that, which is why I would do anything for my wife. Including leave my newborn son and daughter to come to London in order to see you."

"Me? Julia sent you to see me?"

"Yes," he said with a nod, then folded his arms over his chest. His gray gaze studied her face. "She is worried about you. Said your letters are infrequent and vague. And you refused to come and visit Harry."

Sophie shifted in her slippers and clasped her gloved hands. "I plan to visit in a few weeks." *After I prove that Tolbert is guilty.* "I hardly see why my absence is a matter of grave concern."

"I doubted it as well, until the other day. Now I happen to agree with her."

"Do not be ridiculous. I'm perfectly well." *Other than nearly dueling, getting stabbed, tracking a killer, and having a torrid affair, of course.*

"Sophia," he said tersely. "You and I do not know one another well, but I do know Quint. And I suspect he is the reason you are avoiding my wife."

She tried very hard not to react. "What did Quint tell you?"

"Nothing, but he is one of my oldest friends. And the way he is acting has me concerned for the both of you."

Did he know of Quint's fits? She couldn't imagine Quint would readily share that information. "There is no reason for concern. We are friends."

"Yes, that is what he says as well." He sighed. "Sophia, most men are foolish, vain creatures. We tend to run shallow. Quint is . . . deep. He is unlike other men. Whatever he feels, he feels it all the way through, with no exceptions. And he is exceedingly loyal."

Was this a warning? Sophie wasn't sure how to respond. Not to mention that no one need tell her of Quint's nature. She'd seen him at both his best and his worst. "And you mention this because?"

"Because I can see how he feels about you. I've never seen it before in the twenty-odd years I've known him. And he is not a man to dally with an innocent woman."

"So, you're asking me what my intentions are?"

"Yes, in a manner of speaking. He is acting strangely, refusing to leave the house. You are clearly visiting him whenever you feel like it, unchaperoned. Do you plan to marry him?"

"He has not asked, if you must know."

"I'm . . . surprised." Colton rubbed his jaw. "I assumed . . ."

"That he asked and I turned him down?" An unnecessary question, considering the shock on the duke's face.

Taking your innocence was only a small part of why I did

not want to bed you, Sophie. Like the fact that I cannot marry you.

That had stung. Quint hadn't explained why, exactly, but she could not blame him. Not really. She was the ruined daughter of a marquess who spent her evenings skulking about gaming hells dressed as a man. Not exactly proper wife material.

She'd avoided examining her feelings for him. Pointedly refused to worry over the future. And she would not allow Colton—or Julia—to force her to face up to it now.

"I will not hurt him, if that is what you are concerned about," she told Colton. "And Quint is much stronger than you think."

A man suddenly stepped into their small circle, a man she had not seen in eight years.

A man she'd hoped never to encounter again.

"Lady Sophia, it has been a long time, has it not?" Lord Robert, now the Earl of Reddington, wore a knowing smirk as he bowed. How had she ever thought him handsome, with his neatly styled brown hair and elegantly tailored clothes? All that perfection hid an underbelly of dishonesty and cruelty.

Blood rushed in her ears. She dragged air into her lungs and made no effort to curtsy. "My lord."

"Colton, never thought to see you back in England." Robert nodded toward the duke. "Heard you're a respectable family man now."

Colton, clearly unhappy at the interruption, inclined his chin politely. Painful small talk ensued until the host appeared to ask Colton for a word. The duke bowed to Sophie. "We'll continue our conversation later, my lady."

Sophie wanted to beg him to stay, but that could attract undue attention. So she found herself alone with Robert. God above, she must remain calm and end this conversation as quickly as possible.

"Sophie—" She stiffened, and Robert grinned. "Oh, come now. You don't mind if I call you Sophie, do you? After all we're such *old friends.*" The last two words were said with such barely veiled innuendo that revulsion skated down Sophie's spine.

"I do mind, if you must know." Her voice sounded hollow to her ears. "And I hardly think we are friends."

"Of course we are." He leaned in closer and she took a step back, only to press against the wall. His breath smelled of brandy. "We were very good friends once."

Had she truly thought herself in love with this man? "Once, but that was quite a long time ago. Tell me, how is your *wife?*" she hissed.

"Dull. I thought that's what I wanted at the time, but I was a fool."

Yes, you were, she wanted to say. Instead, she tried to step around him, but he quickly blocked her path. "Let me pass."

"You cannot leave now, not when I've finally returned. You know, I've thought about you often over the years." He moved in and she planted her feet. She would not cower. "You've never married," he continued. "I wonder why that is."

"It has nothing to do with you, if that's what you're thinking," she snapped.

"You needn't lie to me, Sophie. You forget, I know you." One finger stroked the bare skin of her arm, above her glove, and she jerked her arm away.

"You know nothing about me, sir."

He smirked at her. "Come now. We enjoyed one

another once. I was thinking we could renew our acquaint—"

Lifting her foot, she rammed her heel down on the top of his dress shoe. He gave a satisfying yelp, and she skirted him, escape the only thing on her mind. The French doors leading to the terrace were not far and she hurried toward them.

Quint had not seen Sophie for the past two evenings, and he knew precisely why. She was quietly busy watching Lord Tolbert. The idea turned his blood cold. Not because Tolbert was a murderer. The man may or may not be responsible for the killings. No one could know for sure, not without more proof.

And Quint hated the idea of Sophie wading through the underbelly of London, risking herself, to find said proof. Especially when he could do nothing to protect her. He'd hired Jenkins, of course, who drove Sir Stephen about Town, but it wasn't the same as being there himself.

Not to mention, if he had to sit through one more of Jenkins's glowing reports of Sir Stephen's derring-do, he'd lose his mind even sooner.

So he decided to discover answers, even from the confines of his own house.

Tolbert had unfinished business with Sir Stephen, who was supposedly Quint's cousin. Quint assumed that a vaguely worded note to Tolbert, requesting an audience regarding the argument with Sir Stephen, might be enough to get Tolbert's attention.

The note worked, and Tolbert agreed to come by before he went out for the evening.

Quint had everything arranged the way he wanted when Taylor announced Lord Tolbert. Dressed for the evening, Tolbert's dark eyes were wary as he stepped inside the room. "Evening, Quint."

"Excellent," Quint said, coming around the desk. "Welcome, Tolbert. Brandy?"

The earl sat in the chair Quint indicated. Quint took the seat opposite and did a rapid examination. Tolbert was short for a man, four or five inches short of six feet. The heels on his dress shoes were unusually high—clearly to increase his stature—as well as worn. Plain cravat pin. No watch fob. The glove on his right hand was missing a button.

They were positioned close to the fire, which was stoked higher than usual on a spring night. He poured Tolbert a generous portion of brandy, handed it over. Repeated the exercise for himself. The two of them sat back with their spirits. Quint pretended to drink his while they made polite conversation. Tolbert, on the other hand, made short work of the first glass, quickly proceeding to the second.

Quint poured just as much this round.

"I daresay this is the best brandy I've had in ages. From where did you get it?"

"A tiny village in France. They only produce twenty bottles a year. Costs a fortune, but it's worth it." When Tolbert was distracted, Quint poured the brandy from his glass into a plant by his chair.

"Indeed. What are the chances you'd sell me a bottle?"

"No need. I'll be happy to give you one." He got up, rang for Taylor. When the butler appeared, Quint requested a bottle for Tolbert.

"Very good. There are only three bottles left, my lord."

"Never mind that, Taylor. I'm happy for Tolbert to have one of them."

Taylor bowed, retreated, and Quint turned to Tolbert, who looked more at ease. Excellent.

"Appreciate it, Quint. I've never believed what they say about you, you know."

"That is good to hear. I was sorry to learn of your problems with my young cousin."

"A trifle impertinent, the lad."

"Yes. He gets it from his mother, unfortunately." Quint rolled his eyes, as if mothers were the obvious root of the world's problems. "You can understand, I'm sure."

"I suppose."

"My mother wasn't much better," Quint lied, refilling Tolbert's glass once more. "Some days I wished I had the sort of parents who ignored their children."

Tolbert made a noise. "My father was worse than my mother. Strict disciplinarian, he was. I couldn't wait to get to Eton."

To pick on other boys, no doubt.

"I heard you and Stephen were in The Pretty Kitty. Haven't been there myself. What did the lad do?" Surreptitiously, he dumped more brandy into the plant. Refilled his glass.

"I had a girl all lined up. Bought her for the night, just wanted to finish my cards first. Then I see Sir Stephen leading her to the stairs. I waited until they came back down and laid into the boy."

"Understandable. So did you get what you paid for that night?"

"Indeed." He grinned. "She more than made up for the trouble."

"Ah. Work her over, did you? Sometimes the girls like it when you get a bit rough, I've found." Quint watched every one of Tolbert's features carefully.

His brow pinched ever so slightly before it was gone, and he shifted in the chair. Confusion, but Tolbert did not want to show it.

"Not really. I've other ways of getting my money's worth." Eyes clear, he never blinked or looked away. It was the truth.

Quint put his glass down with a decisive thunk. He rose and went to the door to call for Taylor. Throwing the wood open, he nearly ran into the butler. Taylor leapt backward, his face turning red, and Quint eyed him carefully. Had the servant been eavesdropping? "Taylor, show Lord Tolbert out, won't you?"

"Wait, what—?" Tolbert said behind him.

Quint spun and strode toward the desk. "Thank you, Tolbert. I have all that I need," he said, dropping into his chair. He reached for a letter he'd been writing before Tolbert arrived. Picked up his pen. "Taylor will see you out."

Tolbert grumbled and departed, likely off to spread tales of Quint's idiosyncrasies. Now alone, Quint wondered again over his butler. Had the lad been listening at the door? True, Taylor had obviously never been a butler before, but that didn't equate to something sinister. Nevertheless, someone in the house was keeping Hudson and the rest of the Home Office well informed, and Quint didn't like it.

Not one bit.

The brisk spring breeze cooled Sophie's over-heated skin as she moved to the edge of the terrace, away from the house. Away from Robert. The unbelievable *nerve* of that man. She would've kicked him square in the bollocks if she hadn't been in these blasted skirts.

Robert was no longer repulsed by her, she guessed. Well, she was certainly repulsed by *him*. Buttoned-up, stuffy, aristocratic snob. And she'd wanted to marry him?

I would never dishonor my family by marrying you. After all these years, that still hurt. Even though she did not want him, the idea that she was not good enough stung.

Deep lungfuls of the crisp evening air soon calmed her. She needed to get back inside and continue to watch for Lord Tolbert. Then follow him, though she would need to do it from her carriage. No chance of donning Sir Stephen's garments in time.

A door farther down the terrace opened and she froze. Expecting to find Robert, she whirled—then sagged in relief. A man she did not recognize had emerged from one of the lower rooms to take some air. "Excuse me," she said and made to return to the ballroom.

"A moment, if you please, Lady Sophia."

His cultured, smooth voice stopped her. "Have we met?"

"We have not, so forgive my impertinence. But since we are alone and you are the person I've been waiting to see, I think it prudent to step over one of Society's little ridiculous boundaries." He bowed. "I am Lord Hudson." He had very dark hair, cut close to the skull. A walking stick in his left hand, he came forward with a noticeable limp.

"You were looking for me? Why?"

He cocked his head to study her. "Does a man need

a reason to seek out an attractive young woman on a beautiful night such as this?"

"I suppose not, but I really should be—"

"Yes, I know. You are anxious to return to the ballroom. Busy, always so very busy. Just like your father. But I wonder if anyone knows how truly busy you are, Lady Sophia."

That gave her pause. She felt at a distinct disadvantage in this conversation. "What do you mean, sir?"

"I am a man who makes it my business to know things. After all, that is the real power in the world. Knowledge—and the ability to wield it."

Her heart began a steady thumping in her chest. He was talking in riddles. If he knew something, she wished he'd just spit it out. "Blackmail, you mean."

His head fell back as he laughed. "God, you are bold. I admire that. Little wonder he's so enamored of you." He drew closer. "I do not blackmail people, dear girl. It's . . ." He waved his hand, as if searching to find the right word. "Common."

"So what do you want with me?"

"We have a mutual friend, Lady Sophia. One who does a good deal of sensitive work for me. Right now he is completing a project that will do some people I know quite a lot of good. But we're on a bit of a schedule. And you're . . . distracting him."

So this was about Quint? It must be the cipher he had told her about a few evenings ago. The papers he hid in his bedpost. Did this man work for the government? She relaxed a little. For a minute or two, she'd been worried he might be dangerous.

"You want me to stay away from Quint."

"There are many things I want." He clasped his

hands behind his back. "And I suspect there are things you want. Am I correct?"

Her annoyance grew and she opened her mouth to speak, but he cut her off. "For example, I know you are building a reputation for yourself with your investigations. Quite clever, dressing as a man."

Her stomach plummeted. "How did you . . . ?"

One corner of his mouth lifted. "I told you, it is my business to know things. And I must admit, I did not expect you to succeed. But you did, over and over again. Clever, clever girl."

Her stays dug into her skin as her ribs rapidly expanded, her breath quickening.

"Those who help me are rewarded handsomely," he continued. "There are things I can provide. Wealth, power . . . respectability. Even for a woman investigator. The Home Office, in fact, has many uses for clever women. I am a very good friend to have. Very good indeed."

Sophie's head was spinning. Would he not say it already? What did he want from her? The Home Office. Why on earth were they watching *her*? And what would Hudson do with the information he'd learned? She did not want to embarrass her family. If anyone found out she and Sir Stephen were one in the same, she would be ruined. "I do not need a position."

"But we haven't talked about what happens to those who do not help me."

Mouth dry, she tried to swallow. "Are you threatening me, sir?"

"My dear, I never threaten. I present facts and allow you to choose your own path. But I think I have taken up enough of your time this evening. In truth, I merely wanted to introduce myself." He bowed. "I just hadn't counted on how charming I would find you. Good evening, Lady Sophia."

Hands trembling, she did not wait for him to disappear, merely spun on her heel and fled to the ballroom. Once inside, she rubbed her arms, chilled to the bone. Though it had not been freezing on the terrace, she could not seem to get warm. A glass of brandy would not go amiss at this point.

"My dear, I've been looking for you." Her father, brows drawn in concern, appeared in front of her. He glanced at the terrace and then back at her. "Were you outside? Alone?"

She straightened her shoulders, determined not to worry him. "Only for the briefest of moments. Never fear, no one else was about."

"Too bad," he muttered. "If you were compromised, at least I would have a grandchild soon."

"Papa! You do not mean that."

He bent and kissed her forehead. "Of course I do not mean it. But I am anxious for a grandchild. Your stepmama as well. Furthermore, marriage would allow you a greater amount of freedom, Sophie."

God help the citizens of London in such a case, she thought wryly. "I suppose that is true, though I am quite happy with my life."

"Are you?" He cocked his head, his gaze shrewd. "I'm not so certain. It's been quite some time since you've been the carefree girl I used to know. Three or four years, I'd say."

She struggled not to react, though she knew precisely the period to which he referred. The first time she and Quint had kissed and his request to court her. Her refusal. His betrothal. That had been a very dark time, yet she'd recovered. Hadn't she?

"I am fine, Papa. Shall I slide down the banister tomorrow to prove it to you?"

He chuckled. "I would love to see your stepmama's face if you did."

Sophie grinned at the mental picture. The marchioness would never approve. "I can scarcely believe she married you all those years ago, knowing you had such a hoyden for a daughter."

"Love trumps many things, Sophie. We are willing to overlook much in those to whom we lose our hearts."

She threaded her arm through his, locked their elbows, and rested her head on his shoulder. "How did you get to be so wise?"

"Nearly twenty-eight years of fatherhood to the smartest, bravest girl in all of England, I suppose." He patted her hand. "Which is how I know you think I'll change my mind about your marrying this Season."

She stiffened and tried to pull away, but he held her tight. "No, do not run away. You do that each time I try to discuss it. You need to face whatever fears you're harboring about marriage and get beyond them."

"And you believe giving me a time limit will accomplish that?"

"Yes, I do." He gestured to the crowd of well-dressed lords moving about. "You can have your pick of all the eligible men here. So choose one and be done with it, my dear. Then you may get on with your life."

The parade of overly starched, perfectly coiffed men in the room did nothing for her, however. There was only one man she wanted—a rumpled, distracted, intelligent, handsome man.

The one man who'd already said he would never marry her.

Chapter Seventeen

Colton and Winchester arrived before ten the next morning.

Quint was in his study, drinking tea and working, Canis curled up at his feet, when his two friends strode in. They carried épées—the long, thin, heavier blades used for fencing. Quint put down his pen and rubbed his forehead. Could he not get a minute's peace?

"Ready to lose?" Winchester asked, he and Colton staring down at Quint expectantly.

"What is this all about?" he asked.

"Exercise, Quint. Remember?" Winchester lifted the épée and lunged at a nonexistent opponent.

"Yes, I know what exercise means. But why now? Why here?"

"Would you rather meet at Angelo's?" Colton asked. "I could make some time this afternoon."

"As could I," Winchester added. "Perhaps that would be better because—"

"I do not want to go to Angelo's," Quint snapped. "And I do not require exercise. Not today."

"Everyone requires exercise. Even stubborn polymaths. Come along, Quint," Colton chided.

Quint sighed and rubbed the back of his neck. The two men had a clear purpose and Quint hated to disappoint them. But he was beyond fixing. "I do not know what you hope to accomplish, but you are both wasting your time."

Colton elbowed Winchester. "I like to waste my time. You?"

"Bloody love it. Cannot think of anything else I'd rather do today." Then the two of them grinned, the idiots.

Quint dropped his head against the chair back. "You are both children."

"True. And don't forget what happens when children don't get their way."

"Are you going to throw a tantrum, Colton?"

The duke shrugged. "I might. God knows I've seen Olivia do it often enough. Now get up, you lazy viscount. We're going to the ballroom."

"It's closed up," Quint sighed. "It hasn't been used—"

"Since Lady Sophia challenged you to a fencing match?" Winchester raised his brows. "Your staff talk, Quint. Now let's go."

Quint had no choice but to lock up his work and follow the two men up the stairs to the ballroom. Taylor had opened the curtains to let in the morning light and a few of the windows had even been cracked to allow for fresh air. All three of them began stripping off topcoats, waistcoats, and cravats, until they wore only shirtsleeves. Quint rolled the shirt cuffs up to his forearms.

Colton handed Quint an épée and dropped into one of the chairs that had been brought in. Quint stretched out his shoulders and knees, thinking. The three of them had fenced so often over the years that Quint knew exactly how the match would go. Winchester had nearly four inches on him in height, but the earl lost patience easily. Quint merely needed to remain calm and wear him down.

Winchester lunged first and a steady stream of parries and thrusts began. Quint defended him easily, barely breathing hard. Which was precisely his plan, to reserve his strength.

"How was the Portland event last evening, Colt?" Winchester asked, slashing downward with his blade.

"Uneventful. I did chat with Lady Sophia for a few moments."

Quint's feet faltered a bit, throwing him off balance, and he had to shift to keep Winchester's weapon from landing a blow.

"Indeed?" Winchester continued. "Did she have anything of interest to say?"

"No. We were interrupted, and then she left with MacLean and his aunt not long after."

Quint felt himself frown. Why would Sophie let MacLean escort her home? Did she care nothing for her reputation?

As he tried to process this, Winchester said, "She left the ball with MacLean? Are you certain?"

"Saw it myself. What, do you suppose, is that about?"

Quint grit his teeth. Drove forward. First she went riding with MacLean, now he escorted her home. The Scot was obviously courting her. So the question was, had Sophie encouraged him?

"I could not say," Winchester answered. "Quint, you and Sophia are friends. Has she set her cap on MacLean, then?"

"No," he snarled. He feinted left and then charged

right. Winchester countered with a parry, so Quint returned with a riposte his friend was not expecting.

"Jesus, Quint," Winchester muttered, dropping back a step as he countered.

"I hope she knows what she's about," Colton said. "MacLean has a string of innocents trailing behind him if the rumors are to be believed."

Sweat rolled off Quint's forehead. He continued to change up his attack to keep Winchester guessing. "She is not interested in MacLean," he said, though no one had asked.

"Most likely you're right, though I'm still confused why he did not take her directly home."

Quint froze and Winchester's blade nearly nicked his shoulder. Quint spun to pin Colton with a hard stare. "Where, precisely, did MacLean take her?"

"Odd, that." Colton's face revealed nothing. "They drove to The Pretty Kitty. MacLean went inside for a few moments, leaving Sophia and his aunt in the carriage."

Heat suffused Quint's entire body, as if he'd swallowed a flame. Rage burned his belly, up his throat, to the roots of his hair. "Left her in the carriage? Outside The Pretty Kitty?"

"I thought it was strange as well. I mean, what errand would MacLean have at one of O'Shea's gaming hells that a proper lady would ride along for?"

Growling, Quint whirled and renewed his attack on Winchester. He was more furious than he'd ever been in his life. They'd had this discussion. He'd told her no more recklessness. That she was to come to him for whatever help she required—not MacLean. No one else but *him*, damn it.

Both men grunted, dripping with perspiration, as the blades clashed and clanged. Quint could not stop. He felt possessed, as if his body and mind had completely separated.

It was one thing to follow Tolbert, with Jenkins keeping watch. But to cavort about Town with MacLean? And what had she told MacLean about her reasons for visiting The Pretty Kitty?

The next time he saw her . . . he had no idea what he might do, but she best be prepared for anything.

"Quint!"

He paused, the shout registering in his brain. When the fog cleared, he saw that he had backed Winchester up against the wall and Colton had grabbed Quint's arm. Panting, he lowered his weapon.

"For God's sake, man," Winchester breathed, leaning over to put his hands on his knees. "What are you trying to do, kill me?"

Colton gently, yet forcibly, removed the épée from Quint's fist. "That is quite enough exercise for today."

The moon had just disappeared behind a group of clouds when Sophie entered Quint's gardens.

She'd had a frustrating few days. Losing Tolbert last evening at The Pretty Kitty had been a disaster. The earl had entered and snuck out the back, apparently. Which made him appear ever guiltier, in Sophie's estimation. Had he known he was being followed? She and MacLean had kept hidden, well out of sight, so it seemed unlikely.

She planned to follow Tolbert again tonight but wanted to see Quint first. He always made her feel better. She wouldn't stay long, just long enough to shake some of the gloom hanging over her.

Canis lumbered from around a bush, happy to see her. She reached down and scratched behind his scruffy ears. "Have you been taking care of him?" she whispered as he licked her hand. "That's a good boy."

No light shone through any window of the house. If it were not for the dog's appearance outside, she might worry Quint was abed. An image flashed in her brain, of Quint, naked on his crisp white bed linens, and warmth spread from her belly up to the tips of her breasts. She'd thought about their last evening together many times. It had been . . . incredible. But it always was, every time he kissed her.

When she reached the terrace steps, she nearly tripped. Quint was there, arms folded and sitting on the balustrade, his eyes boring into her. His expression was shadowed, and the hard angle of his jaw did not move or twitch. She could feel the weight of his gaze as she climbed toward him.

"Good evening," she said tentatively. He sat unmoving, silent. Was he upset? Angry? Ill? "Shall I come back? Tomorrow, perhaps?"

"No, you should stay," he said, his voice oddly tight. "So we may catch up on your investigation. I want to hear every last detail of what you've been doing to prove Tolbert's guilt."

"That should not take but a minute. Finding him has proven more difficult than I imagined."

"Really? Even when you have so much *help*?" He stressed the last word, and she frowned.

"I learned last evening that he would be at Portland's affair. I followed him from there to The Pretty Kitty, but lost him. He went out the back door."

"Just you followed him?"

"No. Lord MacLean accompanied me."

The silence was deafening, and it suddenly dawned on Sophie. "My God, you are jealous of MacLean."

"Do not be absurd. What I am is *furious* you took

such a risk. Letting MacLean take you to The Pretty Kitty, staying in the carriage while he went inside. Why would that seem a good idea?"

"I had to follow Tolbert, and yet MacLean insisted on seeing me home. I had no choice but to ask MacLean to help me. And did you not say that it was unwise for me to travel into these parts of Town alone? I finally have an escort along and now you're upset over that. Make a decision, Quint."

"Did MacLean try anything?"

She blinked and it took a second to follow the jump in logic. "Try—oh." She put her hands on her hips. "No, he did not try anything. We had a chaperone, you ridiculous man."

Quint sneered. "Oh, yes. His aunt, who no doubt is elderly, quite deaf, and likely remained asleep through the entire endeavor. A superb choice."

How had he known? Nevertheless, she had no intention of admitting it. "It hardly matters because he is not interested in me. In fact, he tells me I remind him of his sisters."

"You do not honestly believe that drivel, do you?"

"I do happen to believe it, yes. Though it hardly matters because I am not interested in *him*." She strode to the terrace steps, ready to leave and put this entire conversation behind her. "I'll return after you've calmed down." *Like next month, perhaps.*

When she reached the gardens, a hand on her arm spun her around. Quint's face, hard and unyielding, glared down at her. "Do not walk away, Sophie. Not this time. You want an escort on your nighttime errands? Fine, let us go." He gestured to the rear of the property.

"You will accompany me? In the carriage?"

"Yes," he gritted out.

She could feel Quint vibrating, see his pulse racing at the base of his neck. He was breathing rapidly, but she wasn't sure if that was from anger or trepidation over being out of the house. Perhaps both.

Part of her wanted to force his hand, to get him in the carriage to see what happened. But was he ready? Was she pushing him too far, too fast?

"Does the idea of me riding with Lord MacLean upset you so much?"

Instead of answering, he took a brown bottle from his waistcoat pocket. He removed the cork, brought the bottle to his lips, and swallowed the contents. As he replaced the vial to his pocket, she asked, "What was that?"

"A tincture of valerian root. I sent a footman out to procure some this afternoon."

"I had an aunt use it once for sleeplessness. It would put her right under. Are you certain that's wise?"

"I'm certain. Let's go."

Quint kept his eyes closed, his head resting on the seat back, as the carriage bounced through London. He felt little, if any, anxiety—at least not yet. Heart rate appeared to be normal. His breathing regular. He felt muddled, however, as if there were a tangle of spiderwebs in his brain.

"Are you feeling ill?"

"No," he answered. "The tincture is working."

"Or perhaps you do not need it."

"We shall see." He had wanted to ride without ingesting the herb first. It was imperative to find a long-term solution that did not rely on valerian root, orange water, laudanum, alcohol, or anything else that would dull his senses over time. He needed to find a way to calm his mind without herbs or spirits.

He'd just been . . . desperate. The idea of her and MacLean out about Town had been more than he could handle. So he'd latched on to a temporary cure in order to accompany her. He just hoped he wouldn't be required to do any calculations or answer deep philosophical questions along the way.

Sophie, in Sir Stephen's attire, shifted in her seat, the sound of her clothing whispering over Quint's skin. Fortunate he had his eyes closed; the sight of her in trousers—showing off her long legs and taut buttocks—never failed to stir his blood. He was anxiously awaiting the ride home. The effects of the tincture would wear off by then, he hoped.

"Why are we going to Covent Garden?" he asked her. Though he couldn't see, he'd been tracking the turns. By his estimation, they had just left Piccadilly.

"Word from Tolbert's valet is the man planned to visit White's, then Madame Hartley's. I plan to get to Madame's first and wait inside. That way, I'll not lose him again."

"You are wasting your time. As I said, based on my observation of him, I cannot see how Tolbert is your killer."

"I believe you are wrong," she said. He could imagine her lifting her chin as she continued. "He was the last person to see Pamela alive. Did he force her to sneak out and meet him? Did he drug her and slip her out the back, then walk out the front door as if nothing happened?"

Quint snorted. "The latter would require a heavy dose of luck. The upper floor at Madame's is well-trafficked and there is a guard at the back door. The chance that Tolbert could accomplish a kidnapping and not be seen is extraordinary."

"I did not realize you were so well acquainted with the inner workings of Madame's establishment."

The ire in her voice had him smirking. "Jealous, Lady Sophia?"

She said nothing.

He disliked her silences. She was rarely quiet, which was one of the things he appreciated most about her. It was as if she brought life wherever she went. "To be clear," he said, pushing for a reaction, "I paid for services twice, once at the age of eighteen and again at the age of twenty. The first was a brunette named Beth, who had a trick she did with her tongue where—"

"Quint!"

Though his eyes remained firmly shut, he pictured Sophie's indignant embarrassment. He grinned. "I did pull both Colton and Winchester out of there a time or two over the years as well. But tonight I think I'll stay in the carriage."

"Are you certain? I do not know how long you'll be waiting. You should return home—"

"No, it's not safe for you to be here on your own."

"You forget that I've been doing this for a year. I can take care of myself."

"And you forget that I have recently sewn a rather large gash in your leg. I'd rather not repeat that exercise any time soon. If you need me, have Mulrooney fetch me."

"You are just worried I'll ask MacLean for help again," she said, amusement in her voice, as the carriage slowed. "We're nearly there. I'll return when I can. Then we'll follow Tolbert and see where he goes."

Chapter Eighteen

"That's another two shillings, Sir Stephen."

Sophie grimaced. She'd been playing whist for over an hour, her partner an older viscount who had trouble keeping track of the cards. As a result, Sir Stephen had already lost five pounds to their opponents. Good thing she had a sizable amount of pin money saved up. Sir Stephen's habits were deuced expensive.

She'd chatted briefly with Madame for a few moments when she'd first arrived. Madame was deeply concerned over Pamela's death. The idea that one of her girls had been killed so brutally did not sit well with the proprietress. Sophie assured her the man responsible would be held accountable.

Just as soon as she could prove it.

Sophie was studying the cards in her hand when she heard a voice say, "Can we get in a game?"

No, it couldn't be. Her head snapped up. Robert and another man were standing by her table, expectant expressions on their faces. Her hands clenched in her lap, her body frozen. Before she could move or decide what to do, two of the men at her table agreed to get up, including her partner. *Hellfire.*

Robert sat across from her, his friend to her left. "The Earl of Reddington," Robert said by way of introduction. "I do not believe we've met before."

"Sir Stephen Radcliff," she mumbled, trying to keep her face averted. The spectacles would fool most people, but Robert knew her intimately. Very intimately. It would be unwise to let him get a good, close look at her.

The cards were dealt and the bidding began. Sophie kept her cards in front of her face. Robert seemed more interested in drinking than the play, which suited Sophie just fine. His friend was not unknown to her, but only as a casual acquaintance, and the two newcomers chatted as the play progressed.

The years had been kinder to Robert than she'd hoped. He was still fairly attractive, with his smoky blue eyes and dimpled chin. A lock of his short, dark hair fell over his forehead as if by accident, though she knew it had been deliberately styled to appear that way.

When the talk turned to women, Sophie ground her teeth.

"Reddington, who've you got in mind for tonight? That pretty blonde last week was a right handful. You should try her."

"I haven't decided." He finished his brandy and waved his empty glass at a footman for more. "Perhaps I ought to take two tonight."

Two women at once?

"In the mood for something a bit spirited, eh?"

"Always." Sophie saw Robert grin out of the corner of her eye. "I have to make the most of London while

I'm here. God knows there's no fun to be had in Wales." The two men droned on, both clearly soused, and Sophie tuned them out. She did not care to hear Robert bemoan the realities of the life he'd specifically chosen.

Ladies should not enjoy it so much.

A perverse satisfaction coursed through her at learning Robert's marriage was not a happy one. Not to mention a healthy dose of relief that she hadn't ended up tethered to him for life. They were clearly mismatched in every way.

The right man would get down on his knees and thank the heavens you were in his bed. A lump of emotion formed in her throat. Quint preferred her enthusiasm. He encouraged her not to hold back, not to try and pretend.

And he'd been as desperate for her as she for him. She liked knowing she could make him lose control. By the look in his eyes earlier when she'd arrived dressed as Sir Stephen, no doubt this evening would be a spirited one as well.

". . . a virgin's hardly worth the time," she heard Robert's friend say, catching her attention.

"Not true," Robert said, his voice a trifle too loud. "You just have to know how to handle them."

"You make the girl sound like a horse."

"Precisely."

Sophie's blood began to boil, her ears turning hot. Trying to stay calm, she played her card and then took a sip of her watered-down whisky.

"All women," Robert went on, "need a man's firm hand to guide them. To show them how to express their passion. One must slip the bridle on carefully in order to ride her."

"And what bridle would that be, your pump handle?" Both of them snickered, and Sophie curled her fingernails into her thighs. She'd heard bawdy talk before, but this was different. This was hateful. And it made her want to smack the drunken smirk off Robert's face.

"If need be," Robert answered. "Women leave my bed wearing grins, that's for sure."

"If that's the case, then why did I see the fair Lady Sophia give your foot a good stomping the other night?"

Sophie's ears started ringing, her body vibrating with fear and anger. If he so much as dared . . .

"She'll take a bit more coaxing, is all. But I know how to handle that one. She'll be begging for it before too long. After all, I've had her—"

With a cry, Sophie launched herself across the table at Robert, knocking him and his chair to the floor. There had been no plan or forethought, merely blinding, maddening rage. Drinks and cards spilled onto the floor. She'd never attacked anyone in her life, would've never even contemplated it, if he hadn't said anything. But now, bursting with fury, she pulled back her fist—and punched him directly in the eye.

Strong hands lifted her off Robert, who wore an expression of absolute bewilderment. Sophie struggled for a moment, then stilled as Mulrooney, Madame's doorman, dragged her across the room. "Come on. Anyone who starts a fight gets tossed."

Robert's face twisted into surprised, ugly fury. "You'll be hearing from my seconds!" he yelled.

"Perfect!" she shouted back. "I look forward to putting a bullet into your heart, you maggot-eating swine!"

* * *

The carriage door suddenly opened. "Is this one yours, my lord?"

Quint opened his eyes to blink at Mulrooney, who held a sullen Sir Stephen up by the collar. "Yes, he is."

Mulrooney hefted Sir Stephen inside. Sophie, disheveled and flushed, scrambled onto the seat. She avoided Quint's eye, her chin lifted defiantly.

"What happened?" he asked Mulrooney.

The doorman looked to be fighting a smile. "Started a fight, your lordship. Launched himself across the card table and corked the Earl of Reddington right in the eye." He winked at Sophie. "That be a right fine hook you have, sir."

Sophie nodded tersely, saying nothing. "Thank you, Mulrooney," Quint said, pressing a coin into Mulrooney's palm. "I'll see the lad home."

"Very good, your lordship." Mulrooney shut the door and strode through the lamplight back toward the brothel.

Quint turned to Sophie, who was sitting with her arms crossed. Her leg bounced impatiently. "You started a fight with Reddington? Why?"

"It doesn't matter. Shall we go?" She pounded her fist on the roof.

Jenkins opened the small partition. "Where to, sir?"

"My house," Quint answered and the carriage started off.

Her gaze fixed on the darkness outside, Sophie seemed in no mood for explanations. He gave her a minute to calm down. Finally, when her breathing returned to normal, he asked, "Tell me why you hit Reddington, Sophie."

"He's a pig."

"So is Colton, yet you've never planted a facer on

him. Tell me what Reddington said or did to upset you."

She shook her head vehemently, lips pressed firmly together.

"It will take me less than an hour to learn it for myself, you know. You might as well tell me, *kotyonok*," he said softly.

"He's a disgusting, dung-headed horse's arse."

He blinked a few times, surprised, and guesses as to what had happened began floating through his head. What had he been thinking, letting her go in alone? Tamping down the anger directed at himself, he reached out and pulled her over to his lap. She resisted at first, but he was stronger. He wrapped his arms around her, removed her spectacles, and cradled her against his chest. He hated that he hadn't been inside to protect her from whatever had happened.

Eventually she relaxed and dropped her head into the curve of his neck. He kissed her forehead. "Did he touch you?"

She gasped. "No. Quint, no. Not that. He—" She exhaled a shuddering breath. "He said naught but lies."

"About Lady Sophia?"

Her silence was his answer. So who was Reddington to her? Because Sophie would not attack a stranger in a public setting—especially while dressed in disguise. Then it hit him. The Earl of Reddington had taken the title four or so years ago when his older brother unexpectedly died. Before that, he'd been known in Society as Lord Robert Langley.

The pieces fell into place.

The man who had taken Sophie's maidenhead. The man she'd loved, whom she'd wanted to marry.

Reddington was the man who'd rejected her, shamed her, during her debut. *Hurt* her.

A tempest gathered in Quint's chest, a storm of fury and protectiveness he'd never experienced before. Sophie had not deserved Reddington's cruelty. She was honest and passionate, and much too good for the likes of Reddington. The man had broken her heart, and now he was speaking ill of her in public.

Unacceptable. Infuriating.

He soothed her—and himself—by stroking her back. "I am proud of you, *psihi mou.* You are the strongest, bravest woman I know. Reddington is a fool."

She surprised him by bursting into tears.

He held her tighter, hating her tears, hating Reddington, and hating himself for not being a man worthy of marrying her. He should've been inside, handing Reddington a beating the likes of which he'd never seen. Instead, he'd been cowering in a carriage like a doddering old man.

Sophie cried great, gulping, unladylike sobs that tore at Quint's insides. She obviously still had feelings for Reddington. That's why she'd never married; she'd spent years pining away for the man who'd stolen her heart. And now that Reddington had returned, he'd hurt her again.

Quint knew what he would do. Reddington's fate was sealed.

When she quieted, she whispered, "I've ruined your shirt."

"Ruin them all you like, if it makes you feel better. I never pay attention to my clothing anyway."

"I cannot believe I cried. I never cry."

"Everyone cries, Sophie. Lacrimation is a perfectly

normal, necessary function. And I know you're not a woman prone to weeping and falling apart."

She drew in an unsteady breath. "Thank you."

"Me? I've done nothing." Less than nothing, if such a thing were possible outside of mathematics.

"Just sitting here," she said, laying her palm on his jaw. "Hearing your voice utter words such as *lacrimation* . . . it calms me."

"Shall I detail the lacrimal apparatus for you, explain how tears work?"

"Yes," she sighed, relaxing against him. "I love listening to you talk."

Quint was more than happy to oblige her.

When they arrived at Quint's house, he insisted on carrying her inside. She tried to walk, but he would not be dissuaded—and after the tender way he'd indulged her on the ride home she was loath to argue. So she pressed her face into his throat and held on, the familiar smell of him stealing into her lungs to calm her.

He'd made so much progress in the last two weeks. From being terrified to step foot outside his house, to now taking carriage rides and walking through the gardens. Before long he'd be riding his horse down Rotten Row at the fashionable hour.

"We never found Tolbert," she said as he easily climbed the terrace steps.

"Forget Tolbert. He is not the man you're after."

How was Quint so certain? Something about Tolbert bothered her. Was it merely because she did not like him, or was it more?

"Quint, I owe it to the women—"

"And you will. But not tonight." He strode inside, kicked the door shut with his boot. "Tonight you're mine."

His staff abed, the house was utterly still as he took the stairs. Seconds later they were in his chambers, where he laid her on top of the bed linens. He sat to remove his boots, then went to the dresser for a condom, which he placed on the small table by the bed. She was content to watch him, on her side with her hands folded beneath her cheek, as he removed his waistcoat and cravat. He pulled his shirt over his head, then peeled down his trousers. He was strong and big, his half-hard arousal bobbing between muscled thighs, and the sight of him took her breath away.

He started with her boots, then set to work on the rest of her clothing, saying nothing, his expression serious and determined. When she was completely naked, he stretched out on top of her, bare skin to bare skin. He felt delicious.

His mouth found hers, and he kissed her, softly, with reassurance. She wished she knew what he was thinking—not that she planned to stop what he was doing in order to ask. They both seemed to realize this was not a time for words, that actions were more important at the moment. His lips coaxed hers for what seemed like hours, and he soon nibbled and teased all the hurt and anger right out of her.

There was no hurry this time. Quint was careful in his handling of her—stroking her hair and staring down at her with tender, kind eyes—and all the feelings she normally kept buried threatened to overwhelm her. She forced those notions away. This was not the time to act a lovesick schoolgirl. He'd already made his wishes quite clear on their future, and she hardly wanted a husband. No, what they had now suited her perfectly.

And it obviously suited him, as the erection near her thigh proved. She bit her lip, amused at the direction of her thoughts.

"Are you laughing?"

"Of course I am laughing." She giggled, unable to prevent the tide of mirth from bursting free. "I am naked, you are naked. You are about to stick things in me. It is ridiculous when you think about it."

His brow furrowed. "It's a penis, Sophie. Not a 'thing.'"

That caused her to laugh harder.

"Stop wriggling," he said huskily, his shaft hardening further. "I want to make this good for you."

She sobered instantly. Her fingers grasped his erection and stroked him slowly, swiping her thumb over the tip. She felt him shiver. "You will. You always do."

"Sweet mercury," he breathed when she did it again. "I love when you touch me."

"Then I won't stop." She pressed light kisses to the hard curve of his jaw.

"Ah, God, Sophie." He thrust into her grip. "You completely undo me."

Fire licked through her, arousal building in her loins, as she worked his erection in her fist. He gave little gasps and grunts, eyes closed, muscles shuddering. She loved the unbidden sounds of pleasure, seeing how she could affect him. There was a heady power in pleasuring a man—especially when that man was the ever-controlled Quint.

He threaded their fingers together, stopping her, and pressed their joined hands to the bed. He kissed her long and slow, his tongue showing no urgency despite the hard shaft against her thigh. She loved the way he kissed, with absolute focus and determination, and her body responded, melting under his. Since she hadn't the use of her hands, she rubbed her foot over the back of his leg to hurry him along.

"Damien," she said against his mouth, "stop teasing me."

"Never," he murmured. "I want you begging."

He didn't release her hands, just continued to lick inside her mouth until she squirmed under him. Keeping hold of her hands, he slid down to her breast, where he laved the nipple with his tongue. When he drew a tip deep inside his mouth, pleasure pulsed between her legs. She was panting, desperate for him, needy for some kind of relief to the wicked burn.

"Now, Damien," she breathed.

With a shiver-inducing scrape of his teeth, he freed her breast. "Not yet. You're not quite ready."

She shook her head, though he couldn't see it. She was indeed quite, quite *ready*.

He moved down between her legs and released her hands. Her fingers wound through his thick locks, holding on as he dropped kisses on her inner thighs. "So beautiful. Do you get this wet when you pleasure yourself?"

It was asked so matter-of-factly, as if he were truly interested and not attempting to embarrass or shock her. So she answered honestly. "I have no idea."

He captured her right wrist and brought her hand down to the moisture gathered in her channel. "Feel," he said. "Let me see you touch yourself. Show me, Sophie."

Levering up on one elbow, she saw him between

her legs, his dark eyes glittering and rapt with genuine curiosity. The sight of her obviously aroused him. The realization obliterated any shame or reservations she held. When she hesitated, however, his gaze flicked to her. "There is no right or wrong between us, *kotyonok*. I'll never judge you or make you feel tawdry for what happens in this bed. I need you to enjoy yourself. Moreover, I like to *see* you enjoy yourself."

She knew he was challenging her, that he wanted her to accept that Robert had been wrong. The reasoning was so simple, so straightforward, yet it could only be the result of one man's logical mind. And since Sophie never backed down from a challenge, she fell onto her back, closed her eyes, and began an exploration of the soft, slippery folds. Dragged her fingertips through the wetness. Quint growled, a low sound of male approval, and she grew confident, dipping a finger inside.

He snatched her wrist and sucked the same finger past his lips and into the moist warmth of his mouth. His tongue swirled around the digit, making her gasp as he licked the arousal off her skin. "I love the way you taste," he said and placed her hand back on top of her core. "Keep going," he urged and shifted to reach for the French letter.

Pulse pounding, she rolled the pad of her finger over the nub at the apex of her cleft. Ripples of excitement stole through her, her back arching off the bed, and she couldn't hold back a moan. Quint was on his knees, affixing the condom while never taking his gaze off her. When he was ready, he hefted her legs up, the backs of her knees in the crooks of his elbows, and spread her wide. "Put me inside you, Sophie."

She did not hesitate, reaching down between them

and positioning him at her entrance. He rocked forward and began a deliberate and careful invasion of her body. "Ah, God. Yes," he said. "Oh, hell. I cannot wait." He snapped his hips and pulled her toward him at the same time, seating himself inside, stretching her.

"Did I hurt you?"

"No. You feel so good, Damien. Do not stop."

He set a punishing rhythm, arm muscles flexing and bulging as he held her up and brought their hips together. She could only clutch the coverlet, feel the exquisite sensations as he withdrew and filled her once more.

"Touch yourself again," he ordered, his voice husky and low. "Bring yourself pleasure while I watch."

She obeyed and it only took mere seconds before she exploded around him, her walls convulsing through the fierce orgasm. She shouted his name, and felt him stiffen as her body continued to ride out the incredible bliss. His hips jerked, movements unsteady, and he threw his head back, groaned, with his shaft pulsing inside her.

When the world stopped spinning, Quint withdrew and quickly dealt with the sheath. He dropped onto the bed next to her, still breathing hard. "My God, Sophie. You are . . . really, there are no words."

"None? Not even from a man as eloquent as you?" she teased.

He was all seriousness as he rolled to face her. "For the first time in my life, I have a hard time explaining it. You make me feel as if I'm out of control yet grounded at the same time. It's terrifying and exhilarating."

"If it eases your mind, I feel the same way."

A beat passed before he blurted, "I cannot marry you."

"I know. I am not asking you for that, Damien. Nor do I expect it."

He'd already made his position on the matter clear. In many ways, it was precisely what Robert had believed: She was good enough to bed but not the type of woman one married.

She was surprised how much that hurt.

"Did you love the Pepperton girl?" she heard herself ask.

"No," he answered quickly. "I only asked her to marry me because she was the most sought after girl that year and I have a fortune large enough that her father could not refuse me."

Sophie felt a little relief at that. He hadn't loved the Perfect Pepperton, but he'd still planned to marry her. Because that was the kind of wife he wanted.

"But you left after she eloped. You were gone for months. I assumed . . ." Sounded silly to say it now, but she'd assumed the Pepperton girl had broken his heart.

"The reason I left England had little to do with Elizabeth. My betrothed running off with a groom was embarrassing, yes, but I've survived far worse. There were other reasons I went away."

She waited for him to continue, to tell her about the other reasons, but he surprised her by switching topics. "Tell me what Reddington said tonight," he said in a gentle tone.

"Mere bragging, is all. He approached me at the Portland ball, said he'd been thinking of me over the years and wanted to renew our acquaintance. But he meant—"

"I know what he meant."

She cleared her throat. "He kept pressing and would not let me get away. So I stomped on his foot and escaped outside." Quint stiffened next to her, so she said, "I was unharmed. He's a bother but not dangerous."

"And tonight?"

"His friend was ribbing him, saying how Lady Sophia had clearly turned him down. Robert said I just needed more coaxing, that he'd had me already and knew how to get me to respond. That was when I leaped across the table to hit him."

"Am I to understand that he admitted, in public, to bedding you?" he asked, his jaw tight.

"He might not have gotten the words out completely before I punched him, but he certainly implied it."

Quint shot to his feet and began pacing with no care for his nakedness whatsoever. Sophie was mesmerized. The light from the fire cast shadows over the taut skin and hard angles as he shifted angrily. She loved watching him. Loved listening to him, too. Then there was the way he'd held her in the carriage while she cried. Something had shifted between them tonight, something monumental. She just couldn't quite—

Oh. Oh, *hell*.

She knew precisely what it was, this near-to-bursting giddiness in her chest. It was her stupid heart swelling with love for Quint. She closed her eyes. She *loved* him. Oh, heavens.

"He should not even dare imply it. I'll have his hide for that," he snapped, gaining her attention.

She forced any foolish thoughts of love and hearts from her mind. Notions of weddings, shared memories, and rumpled children must be firmly dismissed.

"You needn't worry," she said quietly. "He challenged Sir Stephen and I accepted."

"You did?" He stopped and faced her.

"Yes, I did. And now, thanks to you, I know how to handle a pistol."

"I'll stand as your second."

She eyed him carefully. "You will? Are you certain?" When he nodded, she asked, "How will you—?"

"Never you mind. Allow me to worry about that."

Chapter Nineteen

"Lords Reddington and Pryce," Taylor announced.

Quint said nothing as the earl and another man strode into his ballroom. Taylor bowed and withdrew.

Reddington was handsome. Easy to see how all that masculine beauty would have turned a young girl's eye. He had the classic aristocratic profile, chiseled jaw. Close-cropped, neat hair. Elegantly attired. He was, in short, everything Quint was not.

The realization did not help Quint's mood. The man had held Sophie's heart in the palm of his hand and had thrown it away. The unbelievable *fool*.

"Not sure why I'm here. Your note made little sense, Quint." Reddington crossed his arms over his chest.

"I am performing my duties as Sir Stephen's second."

A crease formed on Reddington's forehead. "Well, then you should speak to Pryce, here. Arrange it all."

Quint had no intention of fighting Reddington anywhere else. He may be well enough for closed carriage rides at night with Sophie, but a field at dawn was another matter altogether. "It's arranged. Our side chooses swords. And we'll be fighting now."

"Now?" he asked, brows shooting up.

"Yes. Right now. Right here. With me."

That flustered the other man a bit. "This is highly irregular. It's not the way it's done."

"It is the way *I* do it, Reddington. I mean to have satisfaction and you'll give it to me."

Reddington gave an uncomfortable chuckle. "We have no quarrel, Quint. I was attacked last evening without provocation. Sir Stephen accosted me for absolutely no reason. This should be handled on a field of honor."

"Let us consider this the ballroom of honor, then. And I mean to handle it now." Quint got up and stalked to the table where two foils were positioned. He hefted one.

"In place of Sir Stephen?"

"Yes. I am acting in his stead."

"And what are those two doing here?" He pointed to Winchester and Colton, who hadn't yet said a word.

Quint took his weapon and walked to the middle of the floor. He held Reddington's stare. "They are here to ensure I do not kill you."

Reddington drew himself up, squared his shoulders. "If you believe I'm afraid of you, you are wrong. Everyone is talking about you. They say you're cracked."

"Then you shouldn't have any problem besting me."

Reddington glanced at Pryce, jerked his head toward the table. "Who is Sir Stephen to you?" he asked Quint as his second went to examine the foil. The caps had been removed, making the swords deadly.

"My cousin," Quint answered.

"The lad needs a strong hand, if you don't mind my saying."

"I do mind, actually. Accept your weapon and I'll prove how much."

Pryce brought the foil to Reddington, who then checked it over as well. "If you hoped I'd have a difficult time with swords," he said, "I hate to disappoint you. I've been studying with a French master for years."

"Good. Perhaps I'll break a sweat before I beat you."

Reddington's eyes narrowed at that, a slight flush stealing over his cheeks. He thrust the foil at Pryce and stripped down to his shirt. Quint had already removed his outerwear, so he merely waited for Reddington to prepare.

Colton stepped forward and marked off the starting distance. Quint and Reddington both took their spots, arms raised in position. "*Allez!*" Colton shouted and both men charged.

When facing a new opponent, Quint assumed the defensive position to start. He liked to learn his opponent's habits first, then counter them in order to win. Reddington had not lied about the training, but his movements were dramatic, wasteful. Smaller movements were always better, and Reddington's style was too bold, his attacks handled with the grace of an elephant. He also did not try and change up his moves, as if unable to extrapolate from the ones he'd practiced. Quint soon spotted the patterns, knew what Reddington planned before the man executed it.

After a few moments, Reddington grew impatient in the face of Quint's calm. He lunged, aiming for Quint's shoulder. But Reddington landed off balance, and when Quint flicked his blade, it caught

Reddington on the forearm. The man hissed as blood streaked across his skin.

That triggered Reddington's anger and his movements turned even clumsier. Another flick and Quint slashed the top of Reddington's thigh. Sensing he needed to reposition, Reddington fell back and that was when Quint attacked. The earl grunted, blood running from the two wounds, as he tried to defend himself.

Within seconds, Quint slashed Reddington's left pectoral, then the right. Twin spots of red bloomed on the man's chest. Reddington retreated once more, but Quint followed. He didn't let up, didn't give Reddington a chance to recover, and with one twist of his wrist, Reddington's foil slipped and clattered to the ground. Quint aimed the tip of his weapon at Reddington's heart.

"Quint, that's enough," Winchester said, now on his feet. Pryce and Colton were there as well. But Quint didn't move. He leaned in. "Lady Sophia is friend to both my cousin and myself. Do not disrespect her again or you'll suffer the consequences."

"Lady Sophia? This is all over a woman?" Confusion cleared and he smirked at Quint. "Oh, I see. Your cousin overheard how the lady and I are old friends, and he must be jealous. Well there's more than enough to share—"

With a sharp flick, Quint cut Reddington's cheek. The man let out a howl of pain. "I am unarmed, you bloody whoreson!" he yelled, hand to his face.

"Leave her alone," Quint growled. "Do not breathe her name. If you do, I will"—he dropped the end of the foil to Reddington's crotch—"turn you into a eunuch. Do we understand one another?"

"You're cracked," Reddington whispered. "Everything they said is true."

"Do we understand one another?" Quint repeated, his voice a deep snarl, the tip of his foil pressing into the other man's scrotum.

"Yes! Yes. Fine. I shall stay away from her." Reddington glanced wildly at the men surrounding them. "Get him off me before he goes even madder."

Colton pulled Quint away while Winchester removed the blade from his hand. Pryce had already gathered Reddington's things and the two men scurried from the ballroom without a second glance.

Still angry, Quint flung himself into a chair and proceeded to wipe his brow with his shirttail.

Colton cleared his throat. "I feel as if I'm missing a crucial piece of this story. Who, precisely, is Sir Stephen? You've no cousin in London, Quint. You've no cousin anywhere that I know of."

"And what does this have to do with Lady Sophia?" Winchester asked.

"Reddington was overheard besmirching Lady Sophia's reputation last evening."

Silence descended as the two men absorbed this. "When are you just going to marry the girl?" Colton finally asked. "She said you haven't yet asked her."

"I cannot marry her. I cannot marry anyone." Not until he recovered, if ever.

His two friends exchanged a look. "You were prepared to marry the Pepperton girl. And she was a nitwit," Colton pointed out.

"That was before." Before the shooting. Before the fits. And he'd only proposed to Pepperton's daughter to prove someone would want him, even if that someone wasn't Sophie. Fortunately, the betrothal had ended in disaster. *Alone. Better to be alone,* he reminded himself.

"Are you prepared to ruin Sophia, then?" Winchester frowned. "I won't allow you to do it, Quint, and neither will Maggie. A lady's reputation is absurdly fragile and you're risking her ability to hold up her head in public. For what? To remain a bachelor?"

He knew Winchester's outrage stemmed from the way society had treated his wife after her scandal. And yet . . . "You do not understand," he muttered.

"You are correct. I don't," Winchester snapped. "So make me understand, Quint. Because the second Julia and Maggie catch wind of what's going on, you'll likely find yourself in front of a parson—whether you want to be married or not."

"It's obvious you care for her, Quint," Colton said reasonably. "You've never dueled in your life—been staunchly against it, as long as I can recall—and here you are defending her honor at the risk of your own life. Not to mention Sophia would not proceed in this unless those feelings were reciprocated. So why not marry her?"

Quint refused to tell them. He knew he should, that they would likely sympathize about his illness. But the words would not come. He'd rather they think him a blackguard than a bedlamite. "Sophie knows my position on the matter. We've come to an understanding of sorts."

A stunned silence descended, the air thick with disapproval.

Finally, Winchester blew out a heavy sigh and shook his blond head. "I never thought I would say this, but you are a bloody disappointment, Quint. I expect better from you."

Quint struggled not to show how much that hurt

as Winchester turned to Colton. "I'll not wait any longer," the earl said. "You and your wife can do what you must, but I'll not stand by and watch both Sophie and Quint come to harm." He tossed the foil to the ground in a furious crash and marched out of the ballroom.

Sophie strolled about The Black Queen, trying to appear interested in the play when what she was really doing was waiting for a chance to speak with another one of the house girls. She'd already cornered one girl but she'd been too scared to talk to Sophie. Scared of what O'Shea might do if he found out. The same reaction that Molly had had the last time Sophie was here.

She would not give up. All she needed to learn was whether Tolbert frequented this establishment, since at least one of the killer's victims had worked here. Red, the errand boy she paid for information, thought he'd seen a man fitting Tolbert's description last week but couldn't be certain.

Smoke, sweat, and desperation hung heavily in the air while sounds of gaming filled the room. Sophie hadn't asked Quint to come with her tonight. He was improving, but she did not want to push him too much. After her run-in with Reddington last evening, he no doubt needed a break from the strain of these outings.

And your heart needs a break as well.

That little voice inside her head was starting to annoy her. She did not want to love Quint. It was foolish. Their affair was temporary, and he'd repeated his desire never to marry her. Was that what she deserved? A man who bedded her nightly but did not want to take her as a wife?

Swallowing the sudden lump in her throat, she sat down at a pharo table. All the girls were busy, so she'd amuse herself with—

"You. Come with me." A beefy hand landed on her left shoulder.

Though her insides quivered, she tried to think what a privileged gentleman might say. "No, thank you. I've got my eye on this table here for a spot of—"

"I think you misunderstood," the man said. "Boss wants t' see you."

Damn and hell. She really hoped that meant the floor boss and not the *boss* boss. Because the *boss* boss would be James O'Shea, would it not?

"Excuse me," she murmured to the men at the table, who all watched Sir Stephen with a mix of fascination and horror.

The man waiting for her was huge, a solid mound of muscle. A brick wall with legs. His face was scarred and showing evidence of too many brawls. She could try to outrun him, but she doubted she'd get very far. "Lead on, then," she said with a bravado she definitely did not feel.

They traveled the floor, weaving through patrons, tables, dealers, and croupiers. Sophie's dread grew with each step. Where were they going? Who wanted to see her and, more importantly, why? Quint had told her not to return to The Black Queen and she hadn't listened. Heavens, if they killed her, Quint was going to relish telling her *I told you so.*

Oh, excellent. Now she wasn't making any sense at all.

Another man stepped aside, allowing them to enter a door in the back. There was a set of stairs and

Sophie had little choice but continue up. Her heart pounded, mouth as dry as a desert, as they wound through a series of corridors. Finally, he stopped and threw the latch, pushed open a door.

A group of men sat inside. Some were playing cards at a round table on one side of the room and a few more were leaning against the wall, watching. A large, rough-looking man sat behind a large desk. He waved her in. "Come, have a seat, Sir Stephen." A few snickers at that and a rough hand at her shoulder pushed her farther into the room. "I am O'Shea, but I suspect you already knew that. Won't you sit?"

Clearing her throat, she sank into the chair. "While we have not had the pleasure of being introduced, I certainly know your name."

"Do ya not love how fine the quality speaks, boys?" he said with a chuckle, his brogue thick. "We don't stand on ceremony here, sir. You can drop the act."

Sophie blinked. What act, exactly, was he referring to? Sweat trickled between her shoulder blades. "I'll try and remember, Mr. O'Shea."

"Just O'Shea'll do. Would you care for a drink, Sir Stephen?"

Her eyes darted about the room. They all watched her carefully, as if this were some sort of test. But she'd been drinking spirits regularly since she began her charade as Sir Stephen. She could handle a drink or two. "Yes. Thank you."

More snickers from the men in the room, but she paid them no attention as O'Shea pulled a bottle of light brown liquid from a drawer. Sophie relaxed. Whisky would not be a problem.

"Tell me," O'Shea said, pouring two small glasses. "What were you speaking with my girl about earlier?"

"Procuring her services for the evening," she lied easily. "Is that not what the girls are for?"

"Usually. Yet you didn't take her to a room, I noticed." He handed her a glass of spirits. "*Sláinte.*"

He threw his back and waited for Sir Stephen to do the same. Sophie tossed a good portion of the spirits in her mouth and then instantly regretted her haste. It tasted . . . terrible. But she was afraid to spit it out. She forced it down her throat, shuddering as the fire hit her stomach. "Gah," she exhaled when her lungs were able to function.

O'Shea and the other men all broke out into guffaws. "That's how I reacted when I first had it, too. You'll get used to it." He motioned at her hand, commanding her to finish the glass.

Bracing herself, Sophie threw the rest down her throat, swallowing quickly. She couldn't breathe for a long moment. O'Shea was smiling at her. "More?"

"No, thank you," she wheezed.

"I insist," he said, his smile all crooked teeth as he poured another.

With a shaking hand, she accepted the glass and tossed it back. This one went down easier, though it made her eyes water.

"Now," O'Shea said, "tell me what you were really wantin' with my girls."

Her head started to swim. She felt relaxed. Loose. "I am looking for a man named Lord Tolbert. Does he frequent here?"

He rocked back in his chair, his piercing dark gaze trying to see through her. "You're askin' a lot of questions of my girls. I don't like it, especially when I don't know the reasons. And when you're talkin' to 'em, it's clear you're not fuckin' 'em. Which means they aren't makin' me money."

The room had taken on a fuzzy glow. "How did you know?" She nearly bit her tongue. Why had she asked a ridiculous question?

"Because I know you're not who you say you are." He threw back the rest of his whisky, saluted her with the empty glass. "Lady Sophia."

Sophie froze, her breath catching.

"I know everything that happens in my clubs, your ladyship. Now, if you were really wantin' to find Lord Tolbert, you'd put on one of your fine silk dresses and call on him in your fancy part of town. Which makes me wonder why you're in my part of town, dressed in trousers, askin' questions."

No doubt it was due to the spirits, but Sophie wasn't nearly as worried as she should have been. "He might've hurt a friend of mine. I wanted to see if he's hurt anyone else."

"Is that so? And who might this friend be?"

"You do not know her."

He pursed his lips and scratched his jaw. "Does this have anything to do with the girls pulled out of the river?"

Shock registered before she had a chance to hide it. "No," she lied.

His look said he'd read her fib easily. He sat forward, his expression harder than rock. She could see the ruthless killer just beneath the surface. "You need to understand, your ladyship," he started, "that bad things happen to people who stick their noses where it don't belong. If you want to stay safe, you'll not return. Otherwise, I'll hand you to the boys over there." He nodded toward the group of men on the other side of the room. "Have you ever been passed around to seven or eight men in one night?"

The lump in her throat made it impossible to speak.

She shook her head. He was capable of such cruelty, she had no doubt.

"I'm thinkin' you would not like it, my lady. Now, why don't you return home?" He jerked his head at the man who'd brought her here. "Make sure our friend gets in a carriage, won't you, Tommy?"

She followed Tommy to the door, one last glance over her shoulder at O'Shea. She expected to find him gloating but instead, he was pulling pen, ink, and paper from his desk. That was odd, she thought. Who'd've guessed he knew how to write?

"Tommy," O'Shea called. "Bring up Red when you're done."

Sophie rested against the squabs, determined to stay awake. The carriage tilted and whirled around her, as if it were already moving, only it was perfectly still. They were still in front of The Black Queen. The night had not gone well, but she needed to learn one thing before returning home.

"There he is, my lord," Jenkins said from the driver's seat.

Sophie jerked, realizing she'd nodded off. Shaking herself, she flung open the carriage door and stepped out. A boy with a shock of red hair ran by. She called, "Red!"

The boy halted. "Evenin', guv. You still 'ere?"

"I'm . . . leaving now." Her tongue felt thick, unco-ordinated. "What've you got there?" She pointed to the paper in his hand.

"A note."

"From O'Shea?"

He glanced around nervously. "It might be."

"Where're you taking it to?" Her words were slurring. And she was so tired.

"Whitehall."

Sophie blinked. Whitehall? Why would O'Shea be sending a note up to someone in Whitehall?

"Thanks, Red." She thrust a handful of coins at him. "You ever need t' find me, 'member, ask for Alice at the Marquess of Ardington's house in Berkeley Share—I mean, Square. She'll know how t' get me. Be off with you, now."

The boy pocketed the coins and took off at a run. Sophie hoisted herself back into the carriage—but slipped on the step, nearly hitting the ground. She tried again. The second time proved a success and she fell onto the seat with a sigh. Closing her eyes, she decided to nap on the way home.

Quint could scarcely believe it. Inside the carriage, Sir Stephen was sprawled on the seat, asleep, and reeking of whisky. "Damnation," he muttered.

"Came out of The Black Queen half seas over, my lord," Jenkins said. "I thought you might want to help me get him inside. Not sure I could handle it myself."

Annoyance and anger rushed through Quint's veins, so much so that his hands were shaking. Why had she gone out without him? And to The Black Queen, of all places. The last time she'd been there, she'd nearly been stabbed on the street, for God's sake. What was wrong with her?

"Thank you, Jenkins. I'll help you get him inside the marquess's town house. Let's go." *Before I change my mind.*

He folded himself into the carriage, too furious

with Sophie to be bothered at the idea of taking a short trip. Besides, he'd wanted to try a ride without ingesting the tincture; well, here was his opportunity. He sat and lifted Sophie into his arms, settling her in his lap. The smell of spirits was strong, and he wondered why she would've allowed herself to get soused in a gaming hell. Did she care nothing for her safety?

His teeth were clenched, but it had nothing to do with the ride. Sophie was the most stubborn, irritating, headstrong—

She stirred, curling into his chest and pressing her face against his throat. "Damien," she breathed, then made a purring noise. "I knew I'd find you."

"Did you?" he asked, dryly. "Had the entire evening all planned out?"

"No," she answered, serious. "Nothing ever goes as planned. Never expected to see O'Shea."

Quint stiffened. O'Shea. She'd seen James O'Shea. Cold, icy fear slid through him, his heart thumping hard. "What did O'Shea want, Sophie?"

"He made me drink. God, that stuff tastes terrible."

"Yes, it does," he agreed, though he'd never shared a drink with O'Shea. He had enough sense never to find himself in such a predicament. Reining in the emotion churning in his gut, he forced himself to remain calm. "What else did he want, Sophie?"

"Told me to stay out of his part of town." She started kissing his neck. He hadn't worn a cravat and she was able to cover a lot of ground in a short amount of time.

"Stop that. Why did O'Shea tell you to stay out of his clubs?"

She bit him gently and sucked hard, no doubt leaving a mark on his skin. The sensation went straight to his shaft, which had already perked up the moment she'd sat on his lap. But he needed to talk to her. He tried to shift her away from him. "Sophie, concentrate."

"I cannot, not when you're here. You smell divine." She dragged her nose along his jaw. "I want to lick you."

A shiver slid down his spine and settled in his bollocks. His voice sounding strangled, he said, "Later, *kotyonok.* Tell me what happened with O'Shea."

"Russian is my favorite," she said on a sigh.

"Sophie," he snapped. "O'Shea."

She waved a drunken hand as if the revelation was of no concern. "He said I was talking to the girls instead of fucking them. Such a rude word. *Fuck.*"

Quint closed his eyes, struggled for control. He was fully erect beneath her bottom. It would take some doing, but he could strip off her trousers and—

He shook himself. *Get a hold of yourself, man.* She was intoxicated, and he had no business making love to a woman in such a condition.

"O'Shea knew you were asking questions of his girls?"

"Indeed, he did. Knows all, that one." She shifted, throwing a knee on either side of him, straddling his waist, her core now resting on top of his cock. He groaned. "Told me to stop looking for Tolbert, too. Said if I didn't, he'd hand me over to his boys."

Quint sucked in a breath. That meant . . . "He knew you were a woman?"

"Yes," she hissed, dragging out the word as she rocked her hips over him. "Mmm, you feel so good, Damien. You're hard where I'm soft."

Horror and desire warred inside his body. He wanted to lock her away to keep her safe. And he wanted to bend her over the opposite seat and make her scream his name.

She leaned forward and kissed him, her tongue lapping and nipping at his lips. "Kiss me, Damien."

He turned his head. If he started, they'd never stop. Not to mention the carriage had slowed. "We're here," he told her. "I need to help you inside."

"No, I need to help *you* inside." She dragged her hips over him once again, leaving no doubt to her meaning. Her fingers started for his trouser buttons, but he grabbed her hands, stilling them.

"Not here." He took a few deep breaths, trying to control the inferno raging inside him. How did she manage it so quickly?

"We've arrived, my lord," Jenkins called from outside.

Quint shifted Sophie so he could carry her. Jenkins opened the door and Quint slowly stepped to the ground. His heart kicked hard, a ringing beginning in his ears. Could he do this? Then Sophie wrapped her arms about his neck and started nibbling on his earlobe, which made him forget all about his unfamiliar surroundings. His legs wobbled as he entered the gardens behind the Barnes town house.

"Quit that," he whispered. "Someone will see you."

"I don't care," she said but then stopped, putting her head on his shoulder. "*I love you.*"

Quint nearly dropped her, his body going slack in surprise. Had—had he heard her correctly? She loved him? As in, *loved* him? Panic of an altogether different sort clogged his throat. He'd never expected it. Never thought . . . Didn't she have more sense than to fall in love with a man half-cracked?

He thought back to his mother, standing over his

father's bedside, weeping, as the viscount screamed during one of his many bloodletting treatments. Quint had watched from the corridor, terrified. She'd come out to hug him, saying, *We must do everything we can to help your father, Damien.*

That will not be me, he had vowed. And definitely not Sophie. He would not allow it to happen. When he finally tumbled over the cliffs of madness, he would do it without hesitation—and completely alone.

Winchester had been right; Quint was a disappointment. Sophie had given him something precious, something he had absolutely no right to accept, and he'd taken it without thought to the consequences. Now their . . . friendship had gone too far, and he had no choice but to do the honorable thing. She might not understand at first, but eventually she would come to see reason. No woman should be tethered to a lunatic.

He glanced down and saw she'd fallen asleep. Or lost consciousness, to be precise. Alice, Sophie's maid, hurried out from the servants' door. "Here, my lord," she called softly. "Bring her this way."

He followed the maid through the dark kitchens and up the narrow set of servants' stairs. Once they were indoors, his anxiety lessened somewhat. There were no other servants about as they continued up the two flights and began the long walk to Sophie's bedchamber. He just hoped they did not run into any member of the family.

Alice opened the door and he slipped inside. Sophie's chamber was . . . unexpected. Decorated in pink and white, there were ruffles and bows each way you turned. The femininity seemed incongruous with her personality, especially considering her current garb.

He placed her on top of the bed and stepped back. "Thank you, my lord," Alice said. "Is she hurt?"

"No. Merely soused. She'll have a terrible headache in the morning. I have a remedy—"

"As do I, my lord," the maid said, lifting her chin. He'd momentarily forgotten how proprietary Sophie's maid was toward her charge. "Now if your lordship will excuse us."

"Of course." With one last glance at Sophie, he walked out, his heart feeling much heavier than an adult man's usual eleven ounces.

Chapter Twenty

Sophie squinted against the gray midday light filtering through the carriage window. It even hurt to blink. God, her head ached, a constant throb behind her temples. Never, ever would she ingest spirits again.

Parts of last night were fuzzy, but she remembered most of her conversation with O'Shea. He'd warned her away from his establishments, said he knew she was Lady Sophia, and sent a missive to Whitehall. The last was indeed interesting. Whom did O'Shea know in Whitehall? It made little sense that the king of London's underworld should correspond with anyone in the government.

She also recalled a bit of Quint on the ride home. He'd appeared out of nowhere, holding her close and letting her kiss him. She had a vague recollection of telling him she wanted to lick him. The tips of her ears grew hot. He must think her completely wanton.

Not that Quint hadn't encouraged such behavior in the past. He seemed to like her aggressiveness, if memory served.

No time to think on that. She and Alice were waiting to trail Lord Tolbert. Since Sophie would not be able to return to O'Shea's establishments any time soon, she decided to watch Tolbert during the day. Which meant dressing as herself and dragging her maid along. Propriety was nothing but a nuisance.

Currently they were in a hackney down the street from Tolbert's lodgings. She did not expect to see him yet; gentlemen were hardly seen before the early evening. But she could not risk missing him again.

She'd just closed her eyes to rest a moment when Alice shook her arm. "My lady! There he is!"

Lids flying open, Sophie watched as Tolbert strode down his steps and into a waiting carriage. She instructed their driver to follow, promising double his fare if they did not lose the other vehicle. They set off and it became clear that Tolbert was headed toward the docks. Sophie's heart began pounding with anticipation.

Finally, Tolbert's carriage pulled to a halt outside a small row of shops. She lost sight of him for a brief moment in some traffic, but then caught the top of his beaver hat as he entered a pawnbroker's shop.

"What do you suppose he's doing in there?" she wondered aloud.

"Likely selling off the family silver, if his lordship's debts are to be believed, my lady," Alice answered.

Sophie remembered the ring Pamela had owned, the silver ring with paste emeralds. If Tolbert had killed those girls, it would stand to reason he would sell off whatever meager possessions the women had worn at the time, if any. Did the jewelry have anything to do with severing the right hand of the victims?

Excitement swelled in her chest. She was close to catching him, she could feel it.

Tolbert returned to his carriage ten minutes later. "Shall we follow, miss?" her driver asked.

"No," she called back. "Wait here." She reached for the handle.

"Where do you think you're going, my lady?" Alice said sharply behind her. "Your ladyship cannot step inside a shop such as that."

Sophie waved a hand. "And who will know in this part of town? No one will see me."

"It is highly improper."

"Alice, if we wrote a list of everything improper that I've done in the last year, this would not even qualify for the first ten." She quirked an eyebrow, and Alice sighed.

"I'll accompany you," the maid said, and the two of them stepped out of the carriage.

The bell over the door of the shop clanged when they entered. There were glass cases lining nearly every wall, each filled with bric-a-brac that had been either stolen and fenced or sold in desperation. It proved a depressing atmosphere, in Sophie's opinion.

A short, older man with thin hair and spectacles stepped out of a back room. "Good morning, ladies. How may I be of assistance?"

Sophie lowered the hood of her cloak and stepped to the nearest case, placing her reticule on top. With her expensive clothing and cultured voice, no doubt he would pin her as a lady of quality. She hoped that did not influence his willingness to impart information. Very few men took women seriously, which was why she'd started dressing as Sir Stephen in the first place. "Good morning, Mr. . . . ?"

"Benjamin, my lady. I am Mr. Benjamin, the owner. How may we help your ladyship?"

"I am looking for a ring, Mr. Benjamin. A very specific ring that a friend of mine has lost recently. It's a silver band with green stones set in the shape of a shamrock. Have you seen one like it?"

"Not recently, no, my lady. But perhaps your ladyship'd be interested in this amethyst ring in the shape of a heart." He reached toward a case and began to unlock it.

"No, thank you, Mr. Benjamin. I am quite interested in finding my friend's ring. Are you certain no one has brought it in recently?"

His prodigious forehead wrinkled. "No, I am certain, your ladyship. Everything passes through my hands and I have not seen such a ring."

If he was lying, she could not tell. She opened her reticule and pulled out a shilling and slid it across the counter, keeping her finger on it. Avarice lit his gaze as he reached for the coin. She did not release it, however. "I will gladly remove my finger if you give me one more piece of information. That man who just left, what was his business here?"

"His lordship?" His expression turned calculating. "It'll cost your ladyship more than a shilling."

"Now, see here—" Alice started, but Sophie put a hand on her arm. "How many?" she asked the pawnbroker.

"Three shillings."

Alice sputtered, but Sophie returned to her reticule. She pulled out the two additional coins, holding them in her palm. "Fine. Three shillings."

"His lordship sold a necklace. Ruby. Quite lovely."

"May I see it?"

"Beg your ladyship's pardon, but I'm not sure that's good business. If all my customers—"

Sophie reached once again into her reticule and found another coin. "Four shillings. And I will hand them over when I see the necklace."

He paused, then hurried to the back. When he reappeared, he held a small velvet case, which he presented to her. It was a thin gold necklace with one large ruby surrounded by smaller stones. "That is nearly two carats worth of rubies, your ladyship."

"Thank you, sir—"

The bell over the door chimed. "Benjamin, I forgot—"

Sophie spun and blinked at Tolbert, who had stopped just inside the door, his expression reflecting his surprise at her presence. He removed his beaver hat and bowed while she searched for something to say.

"Lady Sophia." He drew closer. "I wouldn't expect to find you in a shop such as this, especially in this part of town. Were you buying today?" He leaned a hip against the glass case, watching her speculatively.

"Merely browsing. I lost a bracelet not far from here last week and thought Mr. Benjamin might have seen it." She was relieved to see that the pawnbroker had removed any evidence of the ruby necklace.

"Is that so?" Tolbert looked to the other man, then back to her, his expression wary. "Any luck in locating it?"

"No. Sadly, I fear my bracelet is lost forever."

"Pity."

A tense silence descended. No one moved, and the situation rapidly turned awkward. Sophie got the distinct impression that Tolbert would not go first. With no other choice, she said to Mr. Benjamin, "If the bracelet turns up, contact me at once."

"Of course, my lady," the pawnbroker replied, wiping his brow with a scrap of cloth.

"Lady Sophia," Tolbert said with a nod.

"Good afternoon, Lord Tolbert."

Legs shaking, Sophie breezed out of the shop, Alice behind her, and hurried to the hired carriage.

A knock sounded and Canis rose abruptly from the floor at Quint's side. Quint's hand shot out to stroke the dog's head, reassuring the animal, while his eyes remained on his section of code. "Yes, Taylor?"

Taylor and Vander, the valet, entered the study. Quint's eyes narrowed. Hadn't he specifically told Taylor that he did not want to see—

"Pardon the interruption, my lord, but we would like a moment of your time."

Was the valet here to complain about the nonexistent demands of his schedule? As far as Quint knew, all the man did was remain below stairs and polish boots. Taylor had been adamant about hiring a valet, and Quint had reluctantly given in—but it did not mean he needed a nursemaid hovering about at all hours. "Yes?"

Taylor cleared his throat—a nervous gesture, Quint knew from observation—and stepped into the room. "Vander has shared with me a theory that I believe your lordship might find interesting."

"Is that so?" He couldn't keep the sarcasm out of his voice.

Vander followed, staying behind Taylor, and Quint studied him. The man was big. At least two inches over six feet and about sixteen stone. He had black hair, clipped short, no facial hair, and the darker skin of those of Indian descent. First step taken with his left foot, so left-handed, then.

"Yes, my lord. Vander is from India. Bombay, specifically. And—"

"And he is able to speak for himself, I'm assuming."

The tips of Taylor's ears turned red, but he bowed and moved aside. Vander straightened and held Quint's gaze. "As Mr. Taylor said, I spent most of my life in Bombay. I am a practicing Hindu, my lord. Is your lordship familiar with our teachings?"

"A faith based on fate, purity, self-restraint, among other things."

"Indeed, that is so, my lord. We also believe in the concept of *samadhi*."

"Sanskrit, loosely translated as 'to acquire wholeness,'" Quint said, and Vander's eyebrows rose. "I am not completely ignorant of those cultures outside our shores."

"Then your lordship is aware of how some meditate to achieve this wholeness."

"Yes, though I fail to see how that should interest me. I do not ascribe to any religion, Vander. If you are thinking to convert me, you are wasting your time."

The valet's eyes flicked to Taylor, and the butler stepped forward. "We are not trying to convert your lordship. Merely make a suggestion."

"The meditation. You think I should try it."

Both men visibly relaxed at Quint's understanding, happy they need not explain it to him. He sat back, considering. Indeed, the idea had merit. Quint had been thinking of European methods, such as herbs and other remedies, but meditation had been favored by Eastern cultures for centuries. The practice was considered an exercise of the mind—and wasn't that precisely what he needed?

He couldn't prevent his skepticism, however. How could it help him? Sitting under a tree with his eyes closed for a protracted amount of time . . . how did that equate to getting better?

"My lord, I understand your hesitation. But meditation is about breathing and centering one's self," Vander said. "We use it to get to the place beyond thought, where peace and tranquility remain."

Quint sighed. The words meant little. What Vander spoke of wasn't quantifiable in Quint's world. One couldn't measure it or present it to a room full of people. And his initial reaction was that it would be a waste of time.

I love you.

There were those words again, resurfacing. He'd recalled them often in the last twelve hours. It seemed so improbable, so unlikely that a vibrant, intelligent woman such as Sophie would fall in love with him. And no doubt if you gave her the choice, she probably would wish she hadn't. He was not an easy person to love under ideal conditions, let alone now. What could she possibly see in him that would foster such a depth of profound emotion?

It didn't matter what he felt, or that there would never be another woman for him. He could not be what Sophie needed or what Sophie deserved.

He had lived his life searching for answers in books and experiments. He'd always believed that science and reason could explain everything. To date, however, he hadn't found answers on his own condition. Perhaps there were no answers. But didn't he owe it to Sophie to keep trying? He wanted to be the man she thought she knew, the one she believed herself in love with. Because until he was that man, he had to stay away from her.

You are a disappointment. I expect better from you, Quint.

Winchester had been right, damn it.

"I have seen Vander after his meditations, your lordship, and I must say that he appears very calm." Taylor turned red once again, almost as if he had said too much.

"Fine, Taylor. I can see this is the dog all over again. You'll not be happy until you get your way." He said to Vander, "I should like to separate the spiritualism from the practice. Is that possible?"

"Of course, my lord. You need not chant or pray, though if you do not, your lordship may not achieve *moksha*."

"I require freedom, Vander, but not of the kind you speak. Will you show me what to do?"

That evening, long after dark, Sophie was nearly bursting with excitement as she let herself in to Quint's gardens. The ring was the key. She had visited four pawnbrokers' shops this afternoon after seeing Tolbert in order to locate Pamela's shamrock ring. If she could find it and get the pawnbroker to describe the man who'd sold it, Tolbert would be facing a noose.

She couldn't wait to share the news with Quint.

His house was dark. No lights were visible through the windows, and the unusual stillness made the back of her neck prickle. Silly, really. Perhaps he'd gone to bed earlier than . . . ever. Well, the man did sleep at some point, didn't he?

She tried the terrace door and found it locked. Withdrawing a pin from her hair, she bent the metal into the necessary shape to work the tumbler. It took but a minute to spring the catch and then she was inside. Odd to be locked out. With a laugh, she realized she'd come to think of Quint's home like her second residence.

The space familiar and deserted, she slipped into his study and was surprised to discover it empty as well. Not that she'd expected to find him sitting in the dark, but the grate had gone cold. Was he in his chambers? So as to not be caught wandering the halls, she went to the bookcase next to the hidden stairs and triggered the latch. The door popped open and Sophie stepped into the corridor. Perhaps she'd find Quint in bed. Naked.

The image nearly had her licking her lips. The last time, the night she'd been thrown out of Madame Hartley's, seemed like ages ago. She ached for him—ached to feel his skin against hers, his weight pressing her into the mattress. No doubt about it, he'd turned her into a wanton.

At the top of the stairs, she felt for the latch in the dark. Finally, she had it and the door sprung open with a whisper of sound. A fire burned low in the grate, casting shadows about the dim room, and she immediately saw Quint on his bed. Fully clothed, he was stretched out with his eyes closed, Canis resting by his side. Was he asleep?

"I'm awake," he said as if he read her mind.

"Oh, good. I need to talk to you." Smiling, she nearly skipped to the bed in her excitement.

"I need to speak with you as well." There was something in his voice, a note of somberness not usually present. He still hadn't opened his eyes to look at her.

Did he not want her here? She stood by the side of

the bed, suddenly unsure of herself. "Is something wrong?"

He exhaled, long and deep, then lifted his lids. "You should not be here, Sophie."

Oh, that again? She waved her hand. "I'd never let a little thing like a locked door keep me away. Now, you must hear my news—"

"The door was locked for a reason."

She felt her face pull into a frown. "What do you mean? You wanted to keep me out?"

"This has gone too far." He sat up, sliding back until he rested against the head of the bed. "It's time for us both to put a stop to it."

"A stop to what, exactly?" Did he mean her investigations? Because he couldn't mean to try and prevent her from helping people, even after O'Shea's warnings.

"To our . . . whatever this is. You being here."

A strange, twisty sensation knotted her stomach and continued up her throat, like a vine strangling her insides. She searched his face, but his expression remained somber and serious. Resolved. It didn't make sense. What had changed?

"I don't understand. You don't want me to come here again? Is that what you're saying?"

"Yes. We've let this get out of hand. I had no right to do the things I've been doing. I knew it was wrong, and I let my common sense get away from me."

It was wrong. She struggled not to dwell on those words. "It wasn't as if I didn't agree, Quint," she said, astonished at the steadiness of her voice. "There's no need to take this squarely on your shoulders." In fact, she was far more responsible than he.

"I do take it on. It's entirely my responsibility." He dragged a hand down his face. "I never thought it would develop into something more."

Had he . . . ? No, impossible. He couldn't have learned of her feelings for him. So was this about him? "What do you mean, more?"

"You told me the other night, Sophie." She couldn't react, frozen with dread. He mistook it for confusion because he went on to explain. "When you were intoxicated. You told me you loved me."

Oh, no. Humiliation washed over her, her body heating with mortification. She had no memory of it, just bits and pieces of kissing him in the carriage. Yet she'd confessed that she loved him. God above, why would she have let that information slip? Though it was true, she'd known full well that Quint didn't want love from her. He'd repeatedly stated that he would not marry her. He wanted to bed her, yes, but bedding and loving someone were entirely different—at least for him, apparently.

She swallowed her anguish, tried to shrug. "I say that to everyone when I'm soused."

"I doubt it. And I cannot allow you to get hurt."

She was already hurt, but pride would not allow her to admit it. "So what of the investigations? You'll no longer help me, I suppose."

"We can correspond by letter, which is what we should've been doing all along." He grit his jaw and shifted his gaze away from her, and she realized it was not nearly as easy for him as she'd assumed. Perhaps he felt more than lust for her.

"And this is what you want, never to see me again?"

"It's not what I *want*, Sophie, but it is what has to be. We do not live in a world where we are free to play loose with the rules. You are risking everything, coming here and climbing into my bed night after night. Do you not want a future for yourself?"

"Forget my future. Forget the rules. I'm asking what you want, Quint."

"What I want does not matter. I am unable to choose."

"Why?"

"You know why!" he exploded and shot off the bed, his long legs traveling the room. "And until I am, this all must stop."

He was saving her from him, clearly. Yet he was the very thing she wanted above all else—ill or not. She wanted to point out the strides he'd made in his recovery, the carriage rides and walks in the garden, but knew he would argue those small actions had not been enough. "And what if you are never able to choose?"

"Then you'll be better off, believe me."

She stared at the taut line of his shoulders, the rigidity of his back, and her heart broke. Quint was exceedingly stubborn when he believed he was right. Still, she had to try and change his mind. "I won't, and you deserve to be happy. Let us try to be happy together."

"No. We will both end up miserable. This was a mistake. I never should have allowed it."

"*Allowed it?*" Anger bloomed and she welcomed it. Stoked it. "You allowed it? Really, Quint, that was quite generous of you. I am ever so grateful you gifted me with the opportunity to share your bed."

"Pettiness does not become you. You know what I meant."

"No, I don't know what you meant. You think to say what happened between us was a mistake and that I'll not argue with you? Slink away meekly? No, I won't. You are wrong. Just as you are wrong about your illness. You act as if you're the first person that's been shot and survived. Yes, you had a fever and you almost died, Quint, but you *survived*. And—"

"That is the second time you've said as much. How did you know of the fever?" He focused on her intently, his piercing gaze burning into her. Then recognition dawned. "My God, it was you." He rubbed his forehead, grimaced. "I thought I imagined a strange man in my room at night. Convinced myself it had to be a member of the staff, yet it was you. *Bloody hell.*"

The foul words out of his mouth infuriated her further. "Yes, I saved your life. Nursed you back from the undertaker's clutches. I bathed you, changed your sheets, fed you . . . and I would do it again, if necessary. It only proves that, even if you are going mad—which I do not believe—you should embrace what time you have left, instead of feeling sorry for yourself."

"You have no idea what you're talking about. I saw my father descend into madness and you did not. I witnessed what it did to my mother." He shoved his fingers into his hair. "I will not put anyone through that."

"You are not your father," she said in a gentler tone. "And I am not your mother. No one knows what the future holds, and loving someone means you're willing to face an uncertain future together. That you're better together than apart."

He shook his head. "I won't do it, Sophie. I won't drag you down with me."

She knew he cared for her, but he hadn't said the words. She needed to ask, no matter the answer, because it was better to know where things stood. She braced herself. "Do you love me?"

"No." His gaze never wavered and he almost looked sorry, like he knew how painful the admission would be.

"And even if I did, it would not matter. I cannot marry you. I had no right to let things even progress—"

She held up a hand, stopping him. A lump had wedged in her throat and threatened to choke her. She dragged in a breath, her stays poking into her ribs, and dug deep for composure. Really, what more could be said? Escape became paramount, but not before she regained a bit of dignity. "You're right, then. I do deserve better. I deserve someone who loves me and wants not only to bed me, but to marry me as well. I'll not make that mistake again."

She spun on her heel and disappeared into the welcoming darkness of the secret passage. Back into the night, alone, where she belonged.

Chapter Twenty-One

The small square across from Sophie's house stood empty this late morning, only the birds unfashionable enough to rise so early. Sophie took a seat across from Julia and Maggie, then opened her parasol to keep the rare morning sunshine off her face. Her two friends had arrived suddenly—likely because their husbands had informed them of the luncheon at Quint's—and demanded to see her. Knowing the direction this conversation was likely to take, Sophie had suggested they quit the house and its ever-present army of vigilant ears.

"How is Harry?" she asked of Julia.

"Demanding. He's very much Colton's child," Julia answered, her beautiful face softening for a moment. "But he's a dear—and Olivia is thrilled at having a baby brother."

She smiled, happy for her friend, and turned to Maggie. "And your wedding trip? How was it?"

The Countess of Winchester, stunning with her black hair and green eyes, beamed. "Lovely. I swear, we went to nearly every collection and museum on the Continent. Simon was very patient."

"I have no doubt you made it worth his effort," Julia said with a smirk.

"I did, yes." Maggie grinned.

A heavy silence descended and Sophie knew what was coming next. Her friends had not come to gossip or share stories about the recent events in their lives; they'd come to get answers from her. And the wait was excruciating.

"Quint and I were lovers, but that's all over now," she blurted.

Julia's mouth tightened, her lips white. "Lovers?" she repeated. "You and Quint. He . . . he actually bedded you?"

"Yes. Why is that so surprising? I may be a spinster, but—"

"You're no spinster," Maggie interrupted, reaching out to clasp her knee. "You're beautiful and vivacious, Sophie. What man wouldn't want you? I think what Julia means—"

"What I mean is, why hasn't he procured a special license?" Julia snapped, her blue eyes flashing fire. "If he took your innocence, he should marry you. Did your father refuse him?"

"He hasn't spoken to my father. But all of this is irrelevant because we won't be seeing any more of one another."

Maggie blinked while Julia's jaw fell open. "He . . . broke it off with you after taking your innocence?" The duchess shot to her feet. "I'll have Colton call him out! That is . . . it is despicable! I never would have guessed Quint for such a reprobate."

"You cannot have Colton call him out. And how do you know that I didn't break it off?" She took a deep breath. "I know you want to help, but this is between Quint and myself." At least it *had* been. "And Quint did not take my innocence. That was"—she waved a hand—"quite some time ago."

Julia dropped heavily back into her seat, her face registering confusion and surprise. "*What?* When? You never told me. Who was it?"

"It was during my debut, and it was a mistake. He—" She chuckled dryly. "He convinced me that he planned to offer for me, that we were only anticipating the wedding night. But there was no blood and I enjoyed it, so . . ."

"So he assumed you'd been taken before," Maggie whispered, sympathy swimming in her eyes. "Oh, you poor dear."

Of course Maggie would understand, having endured a scandal during her come-out that resulted in being married off to someone double her age, though it hadn't been her fault. Sophie gave them a wan smile. "He married someone else and moved away. In the end, it was a fortunate miss."

"I cannot believe you never told me," Julia said quietly. "That was why you were so opposed to marriage, because you didn't want anyone to find out."

"Yes." She could see how much this revelation hurt her closest friend, the knowledge that Sophie had been keeping secrets from her.

"Who was it?"

"I am not going to tell you. Knowing you, you'll march up to his front door and cosh him over the head with a skillet." She didn't mention that she'd punched Robert and would likely be facing him on a field at dawn. "He's inconsequential."

Maggie shook her head. "That's all very well, but you're no widow or demirep, Sophie. Quint is aware of Society's rules. If he bedded you, he should marry you."

A bird trilled nearby, and Sophie tried to decide how much to tell them. Had Quint informed Colton or Winchester of his illness? She could not reveal something so personal, not when Quint was struggling to keep anyone from learning of it. Her friends would not let up, however, without answers. So she gave them the only one she could. "He asked and I have refused."

Julia rocked back in her seat. "He asked you to marry him and you said no?"

"Yes," Sophie forced out, the lie burning in her chest.

Both women seemed to struggle with this. They exchanged a worried glance, so Sophie said, "I am not sure we would suit. I've been unmarried for so long that it seems foolish to rush into something at my age."

"You told Colton that Quint hadn't asked."

"I lied."

"If that is true," Julia said, "then why do you look so terrible? You look as if you haven't slept all night."

Because I didn't.

Julia didn't give her a chance to answer, saying, "Colton told me of the luncheon and how you and Quint behaved around one another. He said he's never seen Quint this way over a woman. He actually *dueled* for you. And I know you. You would not enter into something like this, not with a man like Quint, if you did not have feelings for him."

"He *dueled*?" Sophie's stomach dropped. "When? And against whom?"

"You didn't know?" Maggie asked.

"No," Sophie breathed. My God, he could have

been killed. Why on earth would he duel when he
believed the practice barbaric?

"He bested the Earl of Reddington. In his ballroom—
with swords. Nearly killed the man, from what I understand. Colton and Winchester stood as his seconds."

Shock robbed Sophie of words. He'd fought Redding-
ton for her—for Sir Stephen, actually—and had won.
How had he explained Sir Stephen to Colton and
Winchester?

She thought back to last evening.

Do you love me?

No.

She knew now he had lied. Quint would not
engage in a duel over her honor unless he loved her.
A tiny portion of the unhappiness weighing on her
heart lifted. She wished she could've been there, to
see Quint best Reddington, the swine.

Not that this information changed anything between
them. She meant what she had said—she deserved
someone who wanted more than a quick tumble.
While Quint believed he was saving her from a terrible fate, she needed a man who couldn't live without
her. A man who would rather stand together against
life's ups and downs.

A man who wouldn't give her up so easily.

"Quint and Simon have been close the last few
years, Sophie," Maggie said gently. "And my husband
is concerned. And upset. Quint has said he cannot
marry you, that he cannot marry anyone, and Simon
believes it is related to why Quint is a recluse these
days. Do you know anything about it?"

She should've known the issue would not go away
so easily. However, she would not allow everyone to
turn Quint into a rake, seducing women at every turn,
nor did she want to be the cause of tension between

Quint and his two closest friends. Better they think worse of her. "To be clear, he asked and I have refused. And I do not know what Winchester is talking about. In fact, Quint took a carriage ride with me only a few days ago. He has most assuredly left the house."

Julia blew out a heavy sigh and Maggie frowned. Guilt pressed heavily on Sophie, both for the lie and for the other secrets she was keeping about Sir Stephen. It made her even more miserable.

"And you say it's done?" Julia finally asked, though she still appeared dubious.

"Yes. Without doubt. We both came to our senses."

"Well, that's something," Maggie said. "I suppose it'll all blow over in a few weeks' time. I wish you would reconsider, however. Quint is a fine man. He'd make an excellent husband. You'd never be bored and he'd never take a mistress."

"My wishes hardly matter because my father has decided on a husband for me."

"Who?" Julia screeched. "Has the betrothal been announced?"

"No, not until the end of the Season. And he refuses to tell me the man's name. Papa's convinced I'll find a way to scare him off."

"Wait, allow me to understand," Maggie said. "Your father is forcing you to marry someone you don't know when you could instead marry Quint? That makes no sense, Sophie."

Indeed, it did not—unless one considered Quint's feelings on the subject. "I hope to convince my father otherwise. I don't seriously think he'll go through with it." But really, what did it matter now? She could not have Quint and anyone else was a poor substitution. Perhaps she should just give in and be done with it.

Which only proved she'd truly gone and lost her mind.

Maggie and Julia exchanged a concerned look. Then Julia glanced away, crossed her arms, and thrust up her chin—a move Sophie recognized from their years of friendship. Julia was hurt.

And that silent censure wounded Sophie like nothing else. She and Julia had become fast friends all those years ago, sort of a secret club of imperfect women who were different from the rest: Julia, abandoned by her husband but a virgin, and Sophie, not innocent but unfit for marriage. She'd never contemplated a world without her closest friend. "I apologize," she blurted. "I know this is a lot to take in."

"It is," Julia admitted, never one to prevaricate. "And that's not even the whole of it. Maggie saw Pearl Kelly recently as well. So maybe you'd care to explain what you and she are involved in now?"

Quint finished the deep breathing, his body relaxed, his mind peaceful. His heart rate had slowed considerably until it became a steady, pleasant tap in his chest. After he rose and stretched he had to admit there were tangible benefits following even a few meditation sessions. He felt . . . calmer. Every joint and muscle loose, as if he'd just spent himself inside Sophie.

And didn't that reminder depress the hell out of him.

He walked along the garden path toward the house. The night was crisp and quiet. Canis trotted near his feet, even his dog strangely subdued. Quint half-hoped Sophie would disregard last evening's speech and come barreling through the gate. Yell at him. Tell him he was wrong. Kiss him.

Do you love me?

No.

What an unequivocal lie that had been. He'd loved her almost from the first moment he'd seen her seven years ago, in a white and pink gown at a ball. She'd watched him from under thick, brown lashes, studying him, and he'd felt her assessment down to the marrow in his bones. Nevertheless, better not to tell her. He could not marry her and prolonging this . . . dalliance between the two of them only hurt her further.

As he came up the terrace steps, he noticed the faint glow of a candle along the main corridor, near his study. One of the servants? He had strict rules about the study since the break-in. No one was allowed in it without him present. He watched as the light faded. Odd, that. Hurrying forward, he glanced around for the source of the light.

His eyes were well adjusted to the darkness so he had no trouble seeing in the shadows. The study door remained locked. The entry was empty, the stairs clear. He checked the small closet used for coats. Nothing.

From where had the light come, then?

He rubbed his forehead. This made no sense. He'd seen a light . . . hadn't he? But no one was here, that was a certainty. Was his mind playing tricks on him?

And here he thought he'd been getting better.

"Damn it," he muttered to absolutely no one.

The knocker on the front door sounded, startling him. It was nearly midnight. Who in the world . . . ? His heart picked up in rhythm, hopeful. Without thinking, he went over and jerked open the door.

The Earl and Countess of Winchester stood on the stoop. Winchester's jaw was tight, while Maggie's forehead was creased in concern. Quint sighed inwardly.

"Good evening, Quint. May I come in?" Maggie asked.

Quint took a step backward. "Of course." He held the door, allowing them entrance. Both his friends stepped in, but Winchester turned to his wife. "I'll be in the carriage, darling." He pressed a kiss to her forehead and threw a glare full of warning Quint's way. Quint nodded in understanding. He would listen to Maggie and take care not to hurt or offend her in any way, *et cetera*.

Winchester spun and went out the front, closing the door behind him. "Shall we sit?" Quint asked the countess, retrieving the study key from his pocket. He unlocked the door and opened it for her. "I'd offer you a drink, but I don't have any spirits handy."

"That's fine. I had enough champagne at the boring political dinner we attended tonight." She removed her cloak and threw it over the arm of the sofa, revealing a dark emerald evening dress. "It was the only way I could get through it."

"Sadly, I'm afraid you've loads more of those in your future." He dropped into an armchair after she settled on the cushions.

"I know, but I drag him to art exhibits and lectures, so I cannot complain. Speaking of, have you seen the Guardi exhibit?"

"No." He shifted uncomfortably. How much had Winchester told his wife? "I've been occupied with a project these days."

She folded her hands in her lap, looking incredibly prim for a woman the *ton* had dubbed the Half-Irish Harlot. Fitting that it should be her to come and see him, as she'd had a number of tribulations in her short life. He liked Maggie. She was intelligent and honorable, not to mention she kept Winchester humble. Hard to hate a woman who could do that.

"I don't quite know why I'm here, Quint. I'm certainly not going to take you to task." She chuckled and raised her hands in surrender. "God knows, I am the last person who would ever throw stones at impropriety. But I do feel as if I'm able to see the situation a bit more objectively. My husband is . . . well, I've rarely seen him so angry and frustrated. And Julia is equally hot-tempered about it. They're of a mind to lock you and Sophie in a room with a parson and not let you out until you're good and married."

Quint exhaled, shook his head. He would not put it past the duchess. Or Winchester. "I cannot marry her."

Maggie nodded. "Interesting. She said you asked and she refused."

His chest constricted, lungs burning for one interminable second. Sophie had tried to protect him, to cast the blame on herself rather than him. While the gesture touched him, he could not allow her to lie for his sake. "She is attempting to keep Colton and Winchester from throttling me. I have not asked her, nor will I."

"Why not?"

She asked it calmly, reasonably, her green eyes full of curiosity rather than fury. He suddenly had the urge to share the truth rather than hide behind more lies.

"My father went mad. Did you know?"

"No, but he died when you were . . ."

"Six."

"A bit before my time. And my sympathies, Quint.

That must have been traumatic for a small child to see."

"It was," he admitted. "It tore my mother to pieces. They loved each other very much. And for me, well, I had always hoped that if I worked at it, remained focused and studied, I would avoid the same fate as my father. But I was wrong."

"What do you mean?"

He told her of the fever after the shooting, nearly dying, the fits, the terror, and the desire to remain inside his house. Now that he'd started, he couldn't hold it all back.

"Oh, that's terrible," she breathed when he finished. "I am so sorry. I had no idea. We assumed you had recovered and we did not think . . . We wanted you at the wedding, of course, but Simon rushed for a special license and knew you were—"

"Do not worry," he interrupted. "You and Simon were happy, deservedly so. I do not begrudge you for focusing on that, after so many years apart."

"And Sophie," she urged. "Where does she fit?"

He hesitated, and Maggie continued, "I know of Sir Stephen and her investigations into the river killings. I understand she's come to you for help. Tell me what I am missing."

He opened his mouth to lie, to pretend Sophie meant nothing to him—and he couldn't do it.

"I see," Maggie said, the lines of her face softening. "I thought as much. You do realize you've bungled the whole business, don't you? Her father plans to marry her off at the end of the Season. She'll be marrying a stranger when instead she could be marrying *you*."

He didn't want to think about Sophie marrying someone else. Couldn't begin to contemplate another man between her thighs, bringing her pleasure . . .

giving her children. A pomegranate-sized lump settled in his chest. She deserved to be happy; he just didn't want to have any knowledge of her marriage.

"I cannot—"

The door burst open and Taylor rushed inside. His eyes were wide with fear. "My lord, I apologize, but I thought I should fetch you straight away. Lady Sophia's maid is at the back door. Sir Stephen's been taken."

Alice stood wringing her hands, her face pale. "The boy, the one from The Black Queen, she pays him for information. He saw them take her tonight, my lord."

Quint's stomach plummeted. "You spoke with the boy?"

She nodded. "Not even fifteen minutes ago. He came straight to me after it happened."

"She was at The Black Queen?"

"Yes. Right outside. Said he dragged her into an alley—" Her voice hitched on a sob and she pressed her fist to her mouth.

"Quint, bring her inside," Maggie said from behind him. "Alice, do come in and sit down."

Quint led her to the kitchens and helped her onto a stool. Winchester had now joined them, along with Taylor, but Quint didn't pay attention to anyone but Sophie's maid. "Did he say what happened then?" Different scenarios acted out in his head, none of them good.

"They tied her up, sack over her head. He said she fought but they got her into a carriage. Headed toward Bishop's Gate. That's all he saw before he came to me."

"Who are 'they'? O'Shea's men?"

"A man he did not recognize and Lord Tolbert."

"Oh, my God," Maggie said quietly.

"What am I missing?" Winchester asked.

Quint could only rub his brow. He'd been so certain that Tolbert was not responsible for the killings. He'd obviously been wrong. Tolbert had taken her. But where?

He forced down the panic at her abduction, forced down the anger at not being able to protect her. No time for that now, not until Sophie was found. *Think*, he ordered himself.

Alice said, "I asked her ladyship not to go back there. Too dangerous, I said. But she got a note, you see. Told her that another girl would be taken tonight. My lady was all too eager to return there after the last time, though."

"The last time?" Winchester asked, his voice rising.

"Yes, my lord. The other night, her ladyship learned O'Shea's been sending notes to Whitehall. She thought it was odd. More like dangerous to me."

"Nothing happens in or around his clubs that O'Shea doesn't know about," Winchester said to Quint.

It was as good a place to start as any, Quint supposed. "Then let's go. We'll take your carriage." He hurried toward the stairs.

"I'm coming," he heard Maggie say to Winchester.

"Absolutely not," Winchester returned sharply, then softened his voice, murmuring to his wife. Quint didn't hear what else was said because he dashed up the stairs and into the front entry.

He jerked open the door. Winchester's carriage waited, the driver atop.

"My lord!"

Spinning, he saw Taylor coming forward with a

pistol in each hand. "Here. Your lordship may need these." The butler held the weapons out—weapons Quint had never seen before.

Quint glanced up at Taylor. "Why does a butler have loaded pistols at the ready?"

A flush rose on the young man's cheeks. "For protection, my lord."

That didn't quite satisfy the questions piling up in his brain, but Quint filed it away to deal with later. "Give those to Lord Winchester, will you?"

"Give what to me?" Winchester asked, coming alongside.

"The pistols." Quint tilted his chin toward the weapons, which Winchester accepted. He took a deep breath at the threshold, bracing himself. "Let's go."

Seconds later, the two of them set off for East London. Quint kept his eyes closed, his breathing even and deep. Focused on Sophie. Brown eyes with hints of gold. Long lashes. Her quick smile. The way she laughed. The taste of her. How she shivered when he stroked her.

"I sent Maggie to fetch Colton. He'll meet us there."

Quint nodded, lids shut tight. He had to find Sophie before anything terrible happened. This was all his fault.

If it were possible in her current position to kick herself, Sophie would readily do it. She'd been so, so stupid.

An unsigned note had arrived via Alice earlier, informing Sir Stephen that Tolbert planned to take another girl this evening. So when Tolbert had ventured to The Black Queen tonight, Sir Stephen— armed with both a pistol and a knife—had followed.

No way would she lose him again tonight. The note could have been a lie, but in case it was not, she meant to see what he did.

Tolbert had spent the evening at the roulette table, losing steadily, until a large man she recognized as one of O'Shea's gang arrived to whisper in Tolbert's ear. After a nod, Tolbert had gathered his things and left. Sophie hurried after, only to discover Tolbert hadn't returned to his carriage. Instead, he strode purposely along the walk, swinging his cane and whistling. She'd followed him at a distance, waiting to see where he went next. Why hadn't he taken his carriage?

A scuffling noise behind her had been her only warning before a hand clasped roughly over her mouth. Beefy arms enveloped her, the smell of tobacco and sweat so strong it nearly made her gag. She went limp, hoping he'd drop her—and he did, but only for a half second. She screamed, praying Jenkins would hear her, but the man swore and quickly scooped her back up, tighter this time. "Nice try," he said, squeezing her and cutting off her air. She tried to slide her hand into her pocket to get her knife as he dragged her into a nearby alley.

When he reached for a length of rope, she had fought. Had used her legs to kick at anything she could reach. Bit his hand. Wrenched, twisted, yelled, and did whatever she could think of . . . but another man she couldn't see joined in behind her and she was quickly subdued. Stomach plummeting, she watched as he tossed away both her pistol and her knife.

After that, it had gone quickly. They tied her hands, gagged her, and dropped a cloth sack over her head. A cuff to the jaw had caught her off guard, though it likely shouldn't have, and she fell to the hard, wet brick of the alley. They'd tied her legs and lifted her up roughly.

She was tossed in a carriage, in which she'd now been riding for some time. She had no idea where she was, unfortunately, when it finally stopped. The sack over her head hampered not only her sight, but her sense of hearing and smell as well. Foreboding bubbled in her chest as she was lifted and carried through a door. Then there were stairs.

She attempted to stave off the rising hysteria. *Oh, God. I'm going to die here.* She was going to die and she'd never get to see Quint again. She'd never see her father or stepmama—or Julia. Why had she ventured out alone tonight?

She hoped Jenkins had followed whoever had kidnapped her, but she could not count on it. She could not count on anyone other than herself. She had to remain calm and keep her wits. That was her best chance to stay alive.

A door opened. The air inside the sack was hot and steamy, making breathing uncomfortable.

"Excellent. Put her there, if you will."

The cultured, deep voice was slightly muffled by the cloth, but recognition flitted on the edges of her mind. She'd heard it somewhere. Who was it?

Then she was falling, helpless, until she hit the floor with a smack. Pain exploded on her right side, robbing her of breath for a few seconds. *Damnation.*

The cloth slid off her head. Sophie's eyes burned, even in the low lamplight, and she had no choice but to screw her lids shut. After a few seconds, she blinked, letting her eyes adjust as quickly as she could. She was in a bedchamber. A crude bed rested on one wall, while a long table stood on the opposite side of the room. A few chairs were scattered about, but nothing else.

Two men stared down at her. Lord Tolbert, wearing a smug expression, and Lord Hudson . . . the man from the Home Office. The one who'd approached her at Portland's ball. He was smiling congenially at her while leaning on the cane in his left hand. "Lady Sophia. I am indeed grateful that you could join our little party."

Chapter Twenty-Two

Quint would never know how Winchester and Colton accomplished it, yet the two men somehow managed to convince O'Shea to come down to the carriage at Quint's request. No matter the progress Quint had made recently, the thought of entering a crowded gaming hell had terrified him. There was every chance he would be fine once inside . . . and there was every chance he would not. Suffering a fit now, when he needed to remain sharp and in control to help Sophie, was not a risk he could take.

"And what makes your lordships think I know what happened to her ladyship?" O'Shea asked from the opposite seat. Winchester sat inside the carriage, next to Quint, while Colton and Fitzpatrick, the duke's manservant, stood guard outside.

Quint stated the obvious. "Because you knew she and Tolbert were here, inside The Queen. Did you pay him to kidnap her?"

O'Shea laughed at that. "I wouldn't give Tolbert money if he promised me a pot of gold that shits sapphires."

"But you saw her here earlier."

"Indeed, we did, your lordship. And after I told her not to return." He made a sound of disappointment. "Really, I thought she was smarter'n that."

"Who took her?" he ground out.

O'Shea reached into his coat and pulled out a metal flask. "Shall we have a drink? I might be persuaded to answer if you show a bit more respect, my lord."

"Not a chance. Even if I did drink, which I do not, I wouldn't drink with a man who allows his own employees to be murdered and doesn't do a damn thing about it."

Winchester tensed, but O'Shea just smirked and uncapped the flask. He lifted it to his mouth, swallowed. "And what makes you think I have not been doing something, your lordship? Perhaps I have been handling the situation in my own way."

"I do not believe that," Quint said. "If so, the man would be swinging from London Bridge by his innards."

"It's not always about violence, my lord. There are other ways to use information."

"Meaning you were blackmailing the killer?"

The edges of his mouth kicked up. "Your lordship is a quick one. Nice to see some rumors are true."

Quint ignored that. "Which means it isn't Tolbert." Tolbert could never afford to meet anyone's blackmail demands. Quint had been right in the first place. But if not Tolbert, then who?

"Which means it isn't Tolbert," O'Shea confirmed with another swallow. "Lord Winchester?" He gestured with the flask. "Want to give it another go?"

"No," Winchester said emphatically. Unsurprising, since Winchester had to be carried out of O'Shea's office the last time the two drank together. "So who was it? Who took Lady Sophia?"

"Tolbert has to be involved," Quint murmured, his mind working this over. "You wouldn't allow him to enter the club if he were not. What were you using him for?" He closed his eyes. "You were blackmailing the killer, so you needed Tolbert . . . because Tolbert was bringing you information. Tolbert was playing both sides."

"What do you mean, both sides?" Winchester asked.

"It would be too risky for the killer to be seen with each girl himself," Quint continued. "Tolbert frequented the brothels, so he would speak to the girls and make arrangements for the killer. Which explains why Tolbert was the last to see Pamela, the most recent victim, alive."

"He got three of my girls before I wised up," O'Shea said. "That's why Tolbert moved on to Hartley's girls. I threatened to feed his bollocks to the pigs if he took any more of my property. But in all fairness, Tolbert didn't know the girls were to be killed. He thought they were bein' hired for a bit of rough sport."

"What about when the girls began washing up? When the newspapers began reporting it?"

"He finally believed me after this last one. None too bright, our Lord Tolbert."

Quint's heart sped up. Tolbert's involvement meant that he could have delivered Sophie into the hands of the killer. His chest constricted, a weight pressing down on his sternum. "Who was Tolbert working for, then?"

O'Shea scratched his jaw. "Seems I have something you want, my lord. I think it's only fair—"

"A thousand pounds."

"Two."

"Done."

O'Shea put the spirits away and leaned back in the seat. "He was working for Lord Hudson. Do you know him?"

Quint froze, his mind reeling. Dear God. Hudson. The Home Office. He pinched the bridge of his nose. "*La Gauche.* Of course."

"'The left'? What are you talking about?" Winchester's blue eyes were narrowed in confusion and concern.

"One of the girls," Quint explained, "the third victim, had a regular. She called him *La Gauche.* The roommate assumed the nickname to mean the direction of his erection, but she really meant the way he leaned. Hudson uses a cane in his left hand."

"Good God," Winchester murmured. "Hudson is ruthless. Everyone in Parliament is scared to death of him."

Quint knew precisely how ruthless Hudson could be. They had to find Sophie. He narrowed his gaze on O'Shea. "Where does he take the girls?"

O'Shea held up his hands. "All I know is it's near Blackfriars Bridge."

That made sense. All the bodies had washed up downriver of there. He nodded toward the door, and Winchester threw open the latch.

O'Shea unfolded from the seat and started out. "My lord." O'Shea put a foot on the step, stopped, and glanced over his shoulder. "He won't have killed her yet. He likes to play with them first, make sure they're good and scared."

* * *

Sophie tried to swallow around the gag, her mouth gone dry from fear. Or was it terror? Or fear-like terror? *Oh, God.* She was nearly hysterical.

Her hands had gone numb, the rope cutting painfully into her skin. She'd tried to loosen the knots enough to slide her hands free but had been unsuccessful. If only she'd been able to hold on to her knife.

"This"—Hudson waved in the direction of her legs—"is a decidedly appealing look for you. I hadn't thought a woman in men's clothing could be so arresting. Well done, Sophia."

Tolbert inspected her in a way that made her skin crawl. "No wonder you did not want to duel." He rubbed his crotch through his trousers. "If I'd have known earlier that you were Sir Stephen, this all would have had a very different outcome. Too bad for you."

"But fortunate for me." Hudson's dark eyes glittered, and a shiver slid from the base of her skull all the way down her spine.

"I'll leave you to it, then." Tolbert turned and took a few steps to the door. "I'll expect double the usual payment tomorrow—"

Hudson moved in a blur, removing the end of his cane to reveal a long, thin sword. In a flash, he wrapped himself around Tolbert's back, and all Sophie saw was the motion of Hudson's arm and a splatter of red spray onto the opposite wall. Tolbert flailed and then crumpled to the ground, a pool of blood forming beneath him.

Had he . . . ? Sophie stared in horror. She'd never seen anyone killed before. Had certainly never seen so much blood. *Oh, dear Lord.* Bile rose up in her throat and she forced it back down. Took several deep breaths through her nose. Then a strange metallic smell assaulted her and dizziness set in. *Do not faint. Stay alert.*

She looked away, tried to gather her strength. While Hudson's attention was elsewhere, she began working at the knots around her hands once more. She needed to get out of here. The ropes were tight, and each twist and pull rubbed off more skin. The agony made her want to weep.

"You can stop trying to get out of your ropes," Hudson told her as he came around to stand behind her. She couldn't see him and had no idea what he planned but assumed it was unpleasant. She braced herself. "You're only hurting yourself unnecessarily. We're going to have fun together, you and I."

He reached down and untied her gag with one hand. The cloth fell away and she worked the stiffness out of her jaw.

"No screams, Sophia?" He chuckled. "Though it wouldn't matter if you did. This area is quite deserted."

"Why am I here?" she croaked.

"I thought it was time to meet like this. You're beginning to be a nuisance. Poor Tolbert. You made him quite jumpy over the past few days."

Poor Tolbert, indeed. Sophie avoided glancing over at the body. "But now that he's dead, you can let me go. I don't know anything, not for certain."

"Come now. You thought Tolbert was killing those girls. Do you not want a chance to learn what really happened?"

The more she knew, the more of a risk it was for him to keep her alive. She shook her head vehemently. "No. It can be Tolbert, for all I care. I don't need the truth."

"It's much too late for that. Our time to be together has arrived." He crossed to the long table and set his sword stick on it. She hadn't noticed before, but as she struggled to sit up, she could see metal instruments resting on top as well. Clamps and knives. A medicine bottle. God, was that a bone saw?

"The door is locked," he told her, noticing her movements. "There is no window. If you think to escape, you won't."

A bone saw. The bile rose once more and she gagged. She struggled not to cry. He appeared before her, now holding the medicine bottle. "I have a few questions before I give you this." He held up the brown container.

"What is that?"

"My own special blend. I have it nearly perfected. It should keep you lucid enough for our fun but docile enough that I may untie your hands."

Sweat prickled between her shoulder blades. *Keep him talking until you can distract him.* "What questions?"

"Where does Quint keep his work? I know it's not in his desk."

"You were the intruder!"

He grimaced, affronted, as if she'd asked him to polish his own boots. "My dear woman, other people do that sort of thing for me. Though had it been me, I certainly would have found what I needed."

Doubtful. "Why are you so desperate for Quint's work?"

"One of my contacts, an important Russian diplomat, discovered my . . ." He waved a hand, searching for the word. "He discovered my work with these girls, the work you so doggedly pursued these last few months. He's disappeared, unfortunately, but relayed a message that he'd not expose me if I could turn over something of value to the Russian government. Your lover's cipher solution will serve my purpose, if only he would finish it."

Sophie tried not to react to the word "lover." "So ask Quint to turn over what he has so far."

"I did. He refused, which I understand. Men such as Quint and I, we strive for perfection. We don't care to leave things half-finished."

She understood the threat, that he would control whatever was to happen in this room. That she would not get away. Blood pounded in her ears. "Nevertheless, I do not know what he is working on or where he keeps it."

The focus with which he stared unnerved her. It was as if he could see every thought in her head. "You are lying," he finally said. "Good. You'll tell me soon enough."

He pulled the stopper out of the bottle and came forward, limping slightly without his cane. "Wait." She tried to scoot back, but it was impossible with bound hands and feet. "You do not want to do this. My father—"

"Your father may be powerful, my dear, but not nearly as powerful as I. And I've learned to cover my mistakes." He gestured to where Tolbert's body lay on the ground, then started forward.

"I must know something first," she blurted before he could reach her. "Did you kill Rose, the girl from The Pretty Kitty?"

She could tell the question caught him off guard by the way he faltered. "Yes, though I wasn't able to do what I wanted with her. She caused me no end of trouble. I had to use my walking stick on her and nearly broke the thing in two."

Sophie nearly winced. Poor Rose. "Was her body thrown in the river?"

"Yes, but I weighted her down better than the others. She deserved not to be found after what she put me through."

That logic hardly made sense, so Sophie ignored it. "Why did you cut off their right hands?"

His lips curved into a chilling smile that was equal parts sinister and proud. "Right hands were their most lucrative asset, wouldn't you say? It's the greatest source of pleasure for both the woman and her customer. And each one is unique. They're quite pretty to look at, actually. Too bad I cannot show them to you."

Her stomach roiled and she took a deep breath. "Why . . . why are you killing these poor girls?"

He sneered. "'Poor' girls? They are nothing more than whores. I've been doing this work for years, and no one gives a damn about these girls."

Years? "The bodies only started washing up in the last four months."

"Because my other disposal methods were becoming tedious. Surprisingly, pigs cannot eat as much as one would assume. And to answer your other question, I do this because it amuses me. Power is"—he inhaled, his chest expanding—"arousing. When you hold a person's very life in your hands . . . well, there is nothing quite like it."

He uncorked the bottle. "Now." He started forward once more. "Open up like a good girl."

"It would be near the water," Quint said. His fingers tapped rapidly on the carriage seat, a staccato symphony of barely restrained panic, as he, Colton, and

Winchester rode toward Blackfriars Bridge. "Likely an abandoned building so he wouldn't be concerned about the noise."

Colton and Winchester exchanged a look. Quint ignored them. He had to think like Hudson, not get bogged down in emotion. If he let himself feel, then the fear and anger would take over. He'd never find Sophie in that case.

"He wouldn't trust servants or a hackney, so he'd drive himself there in an unmarked conveyance. With his knee, he'd have trouble navigating too many stairs while carrying a dead body, even a small woman, so first or second floor. No windows, not if he could avoid it. He'll—"

"Quint," Colton said gently. "Take a breath. We'll locate her."

He closed his eyes, dragged in deep pulls of air.

"Why weren't you with her when she went out as Sir Stephen?" Stood to reason that Winchester would ask, since he tended toward the overprotective when it came to women. "Surely you had to know this was a possibility?"

The censure was quite clear in his friend's voice, and it was nothing Quint hadn't asked himself a hundred times. *How could you let this happen to her?*

"And why did we have to pay O'Shea a bloody fortune to bring him to you tonight, instead of the other way around?" Colton asked.

There was no way to keep it from them now. He couldn't. He would need their help again in saving Sophie, not to mention he owed them answers after all this time. He deliberately kept his lids closed. "I am unwell. I started having fits after the shooting."

"Your father?" Colton asked. Both men knew details

of the Beecham family legacy, so there was no need to explain it.

"Yes, precisely. I never know what will induce an attack and found it's best to remain in my home. Or in a carriage."

"Goddammit, why did you not tell us?" Winchester's voice cracked like a whip.

"I am managing. While there may not be a cure, I've been attempting experiments on myself. A few have been somewhat successful."

"Such as?"

Vigorous lovemaking with Sophie. "Exercise. And meditation."

The carriage took a corner quickly, causing knees to jostle against one another in the cramped space. When they righted, Colton said, "Still, you should've told us. Sophia obviously knew."

Quint didn't answer. Yes, he supposed he should have told them, but he did not need anyone worrying over him. Bad enough Sophie had learned of it.

"You father's fate will not be yours, Quint. I'll not allow it." Winchester's tone was hard, determined. "Whatever resources you need, personally or politically, they're yours."

"Thank you," Quint returned somberly. The smell of the river grew even stronger, the distinctive musty rank odor that emanated from the Thames. They were almost there.

"Have you left the house at all before this?" Colton asked.

"Only recently. A few short trips with Sophie." His gut clenched at her name on his lips, churned with the fear of what was happening to her at this very moment. If Hudson hurt her, Quint would tear him apart.

"How close are we to the bridge?" he asked, now looking to the window.

"Five blocks. Maybe six."

"We should get out and walk. Hudson may hear the carriage."

"Will you be able to get out?" Winchester asked him.

Quint had his doubts. His heart already pounded with anxiety over whether or not he would find her. One thing he knew, he would not prevent anyone from reaching her. God forbid Winchester or Colton stopped to baby him instead of saving Sophie.

At the next corner, they passed a stopped carriage—a brougham that Quint recognized. "Hold up, there's Jenkins's carriage. He must've followed Sophie here."

Winchester ordered his driver to pull over. Within seconds, the three of them were on the walk, with Fitzpatrick jumping down from the box. Quint blinked rapidly as his vision began to blur. *No,* damn it. He fought against the rising panic with a few deep breaths.

A hand clapped his shoulder. "All right?"

He nodded at Winchester as Colton said, "The carriage is empty. Think Jenkins went inside?"

"Very likely, if he's not out here." Quint pointed at a building two down from where they stood, a large structure with no windows on the second floor. A curricle was posted in front, one Quint bet belonged to Tolbert. "Start there. Your only hope is to surprise him, but you must get in quickly and quietly." His heart was beating too hard, too fast. A ringing started in his ears. They stared at him, unsure what to do. But it was Sophie who mattered—not him. "Go!"

The three men had four guns between them and they hurried down the street. Quint started after, hating himself, hating his inability to help her. *She needs you, you worthless bedlamite.*

He forced his feet to continue on as the buildings around him tilted and swayed. It felt like being tossed at sea while standing on dry land. Sweat broke out on his forehead. *I cannot do this.* He needed Sophie, needed to touch her and have her anchor him. Needed to hear her voice. Needed her reassurance that he wasn't broken.

He put a hand to the brick building on his right in order to hold it up. Sucked more air into his lungs. It hardly seemed enough, however, and he could feel his chest constricting. He tried to reassure himself that they would find her. Sophie was smart. If there had been a way for her to leave a clue, a trail, a *hint* to where she'd been taken, she would do it.

A thought suddenly occurred as he crossed the narrow street before Hudson's building. Where was Hudson's conveyance? Or had he arrived with Tolbert? For some reason, he doubted Hudson would travel about with Tolbert. And the bodies were always dumped in the water. Easier to do from a punt or small boat than the shore or a dock. Less chance of someone observing you.

He squinted down the narrow, brick passage to where the Thames churned and swirled, a low hum from this distance. The sky was fairly clear, with the moon casting a dim glow over the city. Enough to see that the back of the building was close to the bank.

Then he saw movement along the edge of the water. He strained his eyes. A watchman? Thief? Smuggler?

No, it appeared to be someone . . . carrying a body.

Chapter Twenty-Three

Quint did not hesitate. He sprinted along the alley as quietly as he could manage. If those figures were indeed Hudson and Sophie—and if he stopped to calculate the probability, they most certainly were—then surprise would be essential to Sophie's remaining unharmed. There would be nothing keeping Hudson from killing her if he thought himself trapped.

If she wasn't already dead, of course.

Fear knotted in his chest as he pressed deeper into the shadows. She was alive. She had to be. He would not lose her now, not after all these years.

I love you.

Had she any idea what those words meant to him? They were . . . everything. They were solving an impossible equation, discovering a new planet, proving a theorem, and eradicating illness all combined—and he would damn well hear her say them again.

He kept breathing, continued moving forward, his focus entirely on the figures down by the bank. As he drew close, he saw a man moving stiffly, his weight heavily on the right side, toward a punt near the bank. Definitely Hudson. The bundle in his arms was well covered, however, so Quint couldn't yet tell if it was Sophie.

Winchester appeared at the rear door of the building, now at Quint's left. "Stop!" the earl shouted, and Hudson gave a start, turned, and then hurried toward the punt.

Quint sprinted for the water, but Winchester got there first. Hudson had dropped the bundle onto the bank and was stepping into the punt when Winchester grabbed him and threw him down on the ground. The rest happened quickly. Hudson reached into the bundle and withdrew his cane. "It's a sword!" Quint yelled as he ran forward.

Too late. Hudson threw off the end, revealing the blade, and silver glinted in the moonlight as he lunged for Winchester, who barely avoided being run through. The edge sliced across his side, however, and Winchester staggered back.

Quint was now on the soft ground of the river's edge. Hudson's eyes were glazed and bright when they locked on to Quint's, and Quint knew this was what true insanity looked liked. It sent a shiver down his spine. Without waiting to see what Quint would do, Hudson dashed as best he could along the bank, then up toward the next block of buildings.

"Go get him, Quint!" Winchester said, his voice tight with pain.

Winchester was unwrapping Sophie's blanket, still holding his side. "She's alive," he announced. "Drugged, but alive. I'll stay with her. Go, Quint! You've got to catch him."

When he heard the word "alive," relief nearly drove Quint to his knees. Hudson would suffer for this. "Take care of her," he said to Winchester and bolted after Hudson, who had disappeared into one of the dark corridors between buildings. Unless Quint suffered a fit, Hudson could not outrun him. The best Hudson could hope for would be to dodge into a building, and Quint was determined not to give him such an opportunity.

Once on the street, he saw Hudson round a corner ahead. He gave chase, boots slapping on the wet brick as he ran. He tried to control his breathing and not look at anything other than Hudson's back. The area was largely deserted at this time of day, but the side streets did contain the occasional tavern or brothel. Would Hudson try to escape through one? If so, what was Quint going to do?

Hudson crossed to a large door on the opposite side of the street, disappeared behind it. The monstrous building had no markings, no windows, but a number of horses were posted outside. A gathering of some kind? Had Hudson entered here for a reason, or was it coincidence driven by desperation?

Since he was only a few steps behind, Quint had no choice but to follow.

He threw open the door, unsure what to expect. Roars and cheers erupted from within the bowels of the building, sounding like the crowd at a horse race. The interior was well lit, and he could see no sign of Hudson near the entryway. There was only one way to go, a door that led deeper into the enormous space. Quint paused, rubbed his temples. *Maybe it's not as bad as you fear,* he told himself. Perhaps the walls were magnifying the sound.

Forcing himself forward, he immediately saw that it was *worse* than he'd feared. It was a pugilist match. A makeshift ring had been set up on a dais in the middle of the cavernous room, and inside it were two bare-chested fighters circling one another while men stood around to watch. Magistrates frowned on boxing matches, so they were held in secret—or outside the city—and they were popular. The crowd tonight easily contained over a hundred men, shouting and clapping.

You can turn around. Go back to Sophie. Tell them all you lost him. Allow another girl, perhaps even Sophie, to be hurt in the coming weeks.

Under no circumstances would he let that happen, not if he could prevent it. Hudson was here somewhere. Quint merely needed to remain standing long enough to find him. And staring at the dais, he came to a conclusion.

He forced himself forward, to take the steps deeper into the space. The room was hot, made worse by the strong smell of spirits, tobacco, and unwashed bodies. Edging closer to the ring, his vision sparkled as his shoulders brushed against other men in the crowd. His head ached, every beat of his racing heart echoing in his skull, while he twisted and turned through the throng of people observing the fight. *They're not paying attention to you,* he kept repeating. *They're watching the fight. No one cares that you're sweating or about to collapse onto the floor.*

His lungs constricted and he struggled for air. He never stopped, however. Reaching the ring was paramount, no matter what happened to him after this. They could drag him off to Bedlam as soon as this was all over, just as soon as he'd prevented any future threats to Sophie's life. It was taking forever to reach the dais in this crowd, unfortunately. Hopefully Hudson was encountering the same problem in his escape.

Quint was no more than ten feet from the ring when a hand landed on his shoulder. He started, then looked up to find Lord MacLean staring down at him. "Quint, never thought I'd see you here. Are you trying to get closer?"

"The ring," Quint told the gigantic Scot as loudly as possible. "I need to get onto the dais."

MacLean blinked. "Why?"

"Lord Hudson. He hurt Lady Sophia," was all Quint needed to say before MacLean was shoving and pushing his way down front, Quint alongside him.

"Move over, gents," MacLean yelled. No one dared to stop him, not even in this rough neighborhood, and they reached the ring in seconds.

Quint hoisted himself up using the ropes around the ring. MacLean did the same. "Look in the crowd," he shouted to MacLean. "Short dark hair, close to the scalp. He'll be limping."

"'Ere now," said one of the fighters, his lip swollen and bloody from his opponent's fists. A pair of umpires followed. "You can't be comin' up 'ere."

The crowd started to turn as well, screaming for the swells to get out of the ring, to allow the fight go on. No doubt money had been wagered on the outcome, and Quint and MacLean's presence was preventing the conclusion. Quint did not care in the least, leaving MacLean to deal with the angry mob, as his gaze swept over the room. A sea of disgruntled faces stared back at him—all except one.

He saw it then, the back of Hudson's head as he picked his way through the horde to the back of the room. "Stop him!" he shouted, pointing at Hudson. "He's the banker and he's taking off with the money!" Revealing Hudson as a murderer in this group might not raise eyebrows, but the threat of losing money certainly got their attention.

The men by the ropes quieted, turned, and spread

the word to those behind them. The shouting turned to murmurs that rippled along each row. Hudson sensed something was wrong and tried to hurry, but the crowd had turned against him, sentenced him without knowing all the facts.

"Dinna let him get away, lads," MacLean boomed. "Dinna let him take your money!"

The murmurs grew louder and hands began reaching for Hudson. He slapped them away, pushed forward, to no avail. Reminiscent of the Place de la Révolution years earlier, the situation quickly grew out of hand as the masses converged on their quarry. All hope for a bloodthirsty brawl had now shifted to the back of the room, where a well-dressed gent had been trying to escape. Quint could see Hudson struggle, fighting back, screaming at the attackers.

"We best get down there before they rip him apart," Quint told MacLean. The two jumped down from the elevated platform. Quint let MacLean lead, the big Scot handily moving anyone in their path. Strange to be in a position where he needed to rescue Hudson, but Quint would much rather see the man tried in front of a magistrate than pummeled to death at a boxing match.

MacLean moved quickly, so it was mere moments before he and Quint reached the middle of the chaos. Men had already started drifting back, some cheers breaking out. When Quint could finally see, he learned why. Hudson had been stabbed repeatedly, his body beaten, lifeless eyes staring up at the rafters.

Now in the closed carriage, Quint relaxed as best he could. Deep, focused breathing. Clear, uncluttered mind. Sophie had been squired home by Colton. He hadn't seen her but had been assured she was merely drugged and would be fine once she slept it off.

Winchester was still about, dealing with the authorities. Hudson had been a prominent figure in His Majesty's government, and several top-level officials had arrived to take control of the situation. As long as no one questioned Sophie or discovered her involvement in this mess, Quint was content to sit back and let others handle the affair.

The carriage door opened. A man stepped inside, a hat concealing his face. When he glanced up, Quint could only stare.

The Marquess of Ardington. Sophie's *father*.

Quint experienced a rare moment of speechlessness.

"I see you were not expecting me." The marquess sat and removed his hat. He looked so much like Sophie, with his light brown hair and easy smile. "How are you feeling, Quint?"

"Fine, sir," Quint answered by rote, straightening. "Why are you here?" Did he know of Quint's dalliance with his daughter? Did he know of Sir Stephen and the investigations? Several more questions leapt to Quint's mind, but he held them back until he knew what the marquess was about.

"It seems I owe you a great deal of gratitude," Ardington said.

Quint's throat nearly closed with the anxiety choking him. Gratitude? "For?"

"Discovering Hudson's secret. No one else had, you know. Not many cared about the women murdered and tossed into the water. But for some reason, you were looking into it."

It was on the tip of Quint's tongue to correct the

man, to herald this as Sophie's achievement. She'd been the one to gather clues along the way and talk to those affected, eventually ferreting Hudson out. Quint never would've even bothered to involve himself if it hadn't been for her.

But he couldn't tell her father as much.

"I had help," was all he could manage.

"I heard. Some lad named Sir Stephen. Well done, the two of you." Ardington lifted his chin in acknowledgment. "His Majesty owes you both a great debt, as do I."

Ardington knew of Sir Stephen? Quint wanted to laugh at the absurdity of this conversation. Wait until he told Sophie. "Why?"

Ardington rested his hat on his lap and folded his arms. "Quint, Hudson was not the only person aware of what you were working on."

The cipher.

"Though I did not learn of it through Hudson," Ardington continued. "When I did become aware of what you were up to, I started to wonder, why hadn't Hudson told anyone about it? Cracking Vigenère's cipher would be a great help to His Majesty's efforts in many places, yet Hudson kept that information to himself."

"How did you learn of it?" Quint asked, unable to let that go before learning the rest.

"I put someone in your house. Someone to keep an eye out for you."

For half a second, Quint thought Ardington meant Sophie—but then it hit him. "Taylor."

Ardington smiled. "Indeed. I wanted him to protect you, incidentally. He may appear young and is a rather incompetent butler, but he's damned smart and a good agent."

Agent?

"Does that mean . . . ?"

"It does. I've worked for the Home Office for many years, though it's been in a reduced capacity for the last several. My second wife is not so fond of the dangers."

"Does Soph—Lady Sophia know?"

Ardington's mouth quirked. "No, she does not. I didn't want her to worry. I protected her the best I could—well, spoiled her, more like it. But I wanted her to have the normal life of a young girl."

Quint smothered a snort. Had Ardington any idea what transpired in his own household? He'd heard it said that a man too focused on external matters could miss the most obvious things under his nose. Fortunate for Sophie, he supposed.

"What had Hudson planned to do with the cipher solution, if not turn it over to the Home Office?"

"My guess is he'd already sold it to a foreign power, either France or Russia, which is why he put pressure on you to finish. I've long suspected he was selling secrets, and I've been trying to catch him in the act. That was where you came in." Ardington sat forward, his brows lowered. "Incidentally, they won't tell me the name of the girl Hudson kidnapped. Seems she was hurried to safety before anyone arrived. Do you know her identity?"

"No," Quint lied, looking Ardington dead in the eyes.

The marquess nodded. "Likely another girl from one of O'Shea's clubs. Well, I merely wanted to thank you and see if you were recovered. I'll leave you to get to your bed." He reached for the latch.

Was that it, then? Quint could only conclude that Taylor hadn't shared news of Sophie's late-night visits to Quint's town house. If he had, no doubt Sophie's father would be calling for the bans to be posted—or for Quint's head on a platter. Perhaps young Taylor had his uses after all.

"I want to keep Taylor," Quint blurted.

The marquess took that in stride. "If he so chooses, I'll allow it. You'll need to increase his wages, however. Your servants are grossly underpaid."

They were? Quint set that aside for later inspection. "The burn inside his wrist when he came for the interview?"

Ardington relaxed against the seat, an amused expression on his face. "Cosmetic only. That was my touch. I knew you would see it and take sympathy on the boy."

Clever. "Yes, I did."

The marquess scratched the side of his face. "Quint, are you aware that I knew your father?"

Quint's stomach dropped. No one ever spoke of his late father, at least not to Quint. "No, sir."

"I don't know if you've learned about his accident, but I feel it prudent to tell you, considering . . ." He cleared his throat.

Quint could feel his face heating. Clearly Taylor had been interested in more within Quint's household than just the cipher and laundry. "Accident?"

"He fell one day while riding his horse, hit his head badly. Suffered a nasty concussion. The doctors did not think he would live, but he pulled through. I swear to you, he was never the same after that accident. I think his brain never healed." He shook his head. "And it only grew worse in the next few years. You may believe otherwise if you wish, but I knew him before the fall. And he was not mad then, Quint. Far from it."

Quint sagged into the squabs, his mind racing. Was it true? Had what he perceived as madness all been the lingering effects from a concussion? The brain was mysterious, and physicians had yet to learn how head injuries could affect one years afterward.

The marquess reached over and patted his knee. "Get some sleep, boy. You look terrible." He turned the latch and began to step out of the carriage.

"One more thing," Quint said. "To whom are you planning to betroth Lady Sophia at the end of the Season?"

Ardington raised a brow. "Have you not figured it out yet?"

Sophie awoke slowly, something familiar—a touch, a smell—warming her from the inside, bringing her body alive. A heavy, gentle hand stroked her head. She hummed contentedly and nestled deeper into her bedding.

A male laugh rumbled above her. "Come now, *kotyonok*," she heard. "Wake up."

She knew that husky tone. Her lids flew open and she found Quint sitting on the edge of her bed. "Quint," she breathed. Relief flooded her—relief so profound that tears gathered in her eyes. At one point, when Hudson had held her down to force the liquid mixture in her mouth, she had despaired of seeing Quint or feeling his hands on her ever again.

"Shh," he murmured and stretched out next to her

on the bed, folding her in his strong arms. His body was warm and smelled like soap. She put her face into the crook of his neck and inhaled, fighting back the tears. No one liked a weepy woman.

"Go ahead and cry, if you like. I know you're struggling to hold it in. Are you worried I'll think less of you?" His hand cupped her jaw and tilted her head up. Serious brown eyes gazed down at her. "Because I will tell you now, I could never, ever think less of you, Sophie. You are *everything* to me."

She sucked in an unsteady breath right before he bent to press his lips to hers. Though she was half-covered by the bed linens, he pulled her tight, kissing her carefully, intently, as if to impress the truth behind his words. She melted into the mattress, grateful to be alive and to be kissing him once again. Her fingers curled into the fine fabric of his shirt to hold on to him, as if this all might be a dream.

Was she dreaming? How was he here, in her bed-chamber? She broke off from his mouth, and he shifted to press tiny kisses to the edges of her lips and jaw. "Are you really here? Or am I not awake yet?"

Pulling the coverlet down, he palmed her breast through the thin shift she wore to bed. "You feel perfectly awake to me," he murmured against her throat as he pinched her taut nipple, eliciting a gasp from her.

Ripples of pleasure stole through her body as slick heat gathered between her thighs. "If this is a dream, I don't ever want to wake up," she announced, kicking the coverlet completely off.

"Then keep your eyes closed," he said, continuing to taste and lick his way down her chest. Her breasts swelled under his lips and hands, and she bucked when he drew a cotton-covered nipple deep into his mouth.

He released her with a groan and returned to loom above her. "Sorceress. We need to talk and your body is far too tempting."

She threw a leg over his hip, the rough fabric of his trousers teasing her skin. "We can talk later. I need you, Quint." The admission did not embarrass her in the least. She'd been frightened and nearly killed, and she wanted him to make her forget. "Make me forget," she repeated, this time aloud.

A shudder went through his big body, and she knew he was remembering, too. How terrified he must have been. And yet he'd fought his fears to save her. When she'd come to during the ride home, Colton had answered all her questions patiently, filling in the missing bits on how they'd found her. She and Quint definitely needed to talk, but that could wait. Right now, she wanted to feel his bare skin alongside hers.

Rolling onto her back, she grasped the hem of her shift and brought it over her head. Tossed it to the ground. Quint's eyes grew dark, hot, as they traveled the length of her bare form. Then he picked up her hand to examine her wrist, where the ropes had abraded her skin. The wounds were ugly and sore, but she would heal. Quint pressed his lips to the inside, where the flesh had rubbed raw. "I am so sorry you were hurt. I should have been with you."

Sophie thought back to Tolbert, of seeing his throat sliced open. "In that case you may have been killed." Without waiting for a response, she pulled him down on top of her, brought his mouth to hers. He settled in the cradle of her hips as she nipped his full, enticing bottom lip and wrapped her legs around his lean waist.

Something sparked between them and the kiss turned desperate. Ravenous. He pressed her deeper into the bedding as he slanted his mouth over hers, again and again, his tongue demanding and fervent as it circled with hers. She was sweltering, writhing, and burning alive. Aching for more. "Please, Quint," she murmured, grinding her core over the hard ridge of his shaft.

He jerked and tried to pull away, but she tightened her limbs, holding him. Defeated, he closed his eyes. "Sophie, you've been hurt. Drugged. Scared out of—"

"I'm fine. Don't stop because you think I am too fragile for this. I'm begging you, *please.*"

He shifted quickly, sliding down and settling between her legs. "Hold your knees. Open yourself for me."

She grasped her knees and held them wide as he stared at her most intimate parts. "You are so beautiful," he whispered before dipping his head. She felt the flat of his tongue drag along her seam and she nearly exploded then. "So delicious," he murmured, then followed up with another lick. "I love how wet you get for me, *lyubov moya.*"

Her legs trembled when he moved to gently suck the tiny bud, drawing it into his mouth. Then he switched to long, slow strokes with his tongue. She was panting, delirious with sensation, when he returned to applying more pressure with his lips. He continued to alternate, never continuing long enough to push her over the edge. Consequently, he was driving her out of her skull.

"Quint!" she moaned when he blew on her swollen flesh and teased her further.

"Tell me, where do you ache most? Here?" He nipped at her inner thigh. "Or is it here?" He kissed her lower abdomen. "Or is it perhaps here?" He slid two fingers inside her and her eyes almost rolled back at the magnificent fullness. She brought her hips up to allow him deeper. *Yes, oh yes.*

The pleasure began building as he thrust his fingers a few times. Her head thrashed on the pillow, the need so overwhelming and sharp she could hardly stand it. Her body was strung impossibly tight, every muscle tensed. "Oh, God. *Please!*"

"Quiet. We wouldn't want to wake the house." He tossed her a small pillow, then returned his mouth to her. One swipe of his tongue was all that was needed, and she used the pillow to muffle her cries as she exploded, quivering and convulsing, the ecstasy ripping through her stronger than any she'd ever experienced. It went on and on, with Quint not letting up until he'd wrung every shake and shiver from her body.

When she finally floated back to herself, he stretched out beside her.

He kissed her forehead. "Better?"

"Oh, indeed," she muttered. "But don't stop yet, please." She reached between them, intent on disrobing him as quickly as possible.

His hand caught her. "Wait. Stop."

She looked up, noted his flushed skin, dark eyes, and the pulse throbbing at the base of his neck. Even if she couldn't feel the erection digging into her thigh, it was plain he wanted her. "Why?"

"I won't bed you tonight. Not until after."

She blinked up at him. "After what?"

He lifted her hand and pressed his lips to her knuckles. Then he twined their fingers together. "Will you do me the honor of becoming my wife, Lady Sophia?"

Her jaw fell open. This was not what she'd expected. She'd never thought . . . "What?"

"I cannot guarantee it will be easy, being married to a man like me. And I have no idea if I'll ever recover enough to be as I was before. But I do not want to spend another minute apart from you, without you by my side."

"But I thought . . . your father, the illness?"

"I'll explain later, but I have reason to believe it may have been related to an injury. So I may or may not be like him." His hand slid to cup her jaw, his expression serious. "Even so, if I have two minutes or two decades left on this earth, of sound mind or addled, I need you to share it with me. I cannot give you up, Sophie."

Emotion tightened in her chest. Still, she wanted the words. "Do you love me?"

He frowned slightly, his eyebrows lowering in concentration. "What I feel for you . . . it can be neither quantified nor defined. It is so profound, so revolutionary, that no methods to date are equipped to even measure it. A new word should be imagined just to express the depth and scope of it, because 'love' does not even come close."

She inhaled raggedly, both ready to laugh and cry at the same time. "Oh, Quint," she breathed, throwing her arms around his neck. "*I love you.*"

He held her close. "So does that mean you will marry me?"

"Yes, I will marry you."

His arms tightened and he kissed her temple. "Thank God," he exhaled.

"Will you finally take off your clothes now?"

"No."

She bent to see his face. "No? I just said I would marry you. That means—"

"That means," he interrupted, "that I shall not bed you until after the ceremony."

"That's ridiculous," she said. "It's not as if we haven't been intimate already, and I know you want to."

"You once said," he told her quietly, "that you needed a man who wanted more than just to bed you. I am that man, and I shall prove it to you."

"Quint," she said, both touched and confused. "That is a sweet but unnecessary gesture. You've just asked me to marry you, so there's no reason to prove anything to me."

He kissed her briefly, resolutely, then rolled away and stood up. "There is every reason. You are worth any amount of frustration or difficulty. I never want you to feel undeserving of a proper courtship. That"— he pointed at her bed—"was our last encounter until you are my wife."

She sighed, ready to take him to task, but then noticed his clenched hands, the muscle jumping in his jaw. His eyes were locked on her naked form. So she stretched languidly, putting her body on full display in the hopes he'd change his mind. Quint's quick intake of breath made her grin. "I hope, then, that you are planning to procure a special license."

"Yes," he rasped. "But only because I need the wedding to take place in my home. We'll still wait a month, however, so you'll have time to plan a day as perfect as you wish."

Her hands slid seductively over her skin, her palms cupping her breasts and plumping them. "I think I could convince you to change your mind." Muttering a curse in a strange language, Quint spun and strode to the door.

Sophie laughed. Then she thought of something. "Will you call on my father to ask for his approval?"

Quint glanced over his shoulder, hand paused on the latch. "I believe I already have it."

Chapter Twenty-Four

True to his word, Quint did not bed her again before their wedding. Sophie did her best to entice him, but he remained resolved. Most nights, under the cover of moonlight, she stole through the mews and snuck into his house. He always kissed her, every bit as passionately as before, but they spent their time talking while strolling through the gardens hand in hand. The weather had turned unseasonably warm, and he seemed to favor being outdoors. Sophie was more than happy to oblige him, pleased with how far he'd come.

Since the night he'd visited her chambers, he had remained at home, preferring to finish work on breaking the cipher. He said he wanted to wait until after their marriage, when she could accompany him, before venturing out. He had taken to hosting their small group of friends for dinner parties, however, and Sophie enjoyed seeing him laugh and joke with Colton and Winchester. Though he wasn't ready to attend a ball or stroll down Bond Street with her, he seemed lighter, happier. He would recover, she would ensure it.

This particular night, the scent of jasmine floated through the air as they sat together on a stone bench in his gardens. He'd just finished telling her the story of when Colton had punched Winchester in the middle of White's, making them both chuckle, when she lay her head on his shoulder. "You are in a rare mood tonight."

He kissed the top of her head. "I finished cracking the cipher today. Turned it over to your father."

She sat up. "You did? That's wonderful." It had been a shock to learn her father worked for the Home Office, that he had kept so much from her over the years. But the two of them had spent many hours talking lately and, though she had not revealed her identity as Sir Stephen to him, learning of his work had comforted her. It seemed a passion for investigation and spying truly was in her blood. "What did Papa say?"

"He was pleased, of course. I'll have to explain it again in a few weeks to the coding men at the Office, but for now it's done."

She rested against his broad shoulder once more. God, how she loved this man. Canis ambled over and sniffed Sophie's feet before settling by Quint's side. The dog placed his head on Quint's knee, and she was pleased to see Quint reach down and stroke the dog's neck. Considering he was a man who purported not to care for animals, man and beast had gotten on remarkably well. Still watching Canis, she asked, "How did my father know we would suit, do you think?"

"He saw us together."

"He did? When?"

"At the ball. The one where you followed me into the library and asked me to kiss you. He said he could tell by the way you looked at me that night."

Had she been so obvious? "But he couldn't have known it would be reciprocated, especially when you betrothed yourself to the Perfect Pepperton not even a month later." She couldn't keep the bitterness out of her tone.

He tilted her chin up and found her eyes. "I only asked her to marry me to gain your attention. I had foolishly hoped to make you jealous, enough so that you would see I was worthy of courting you properly."

Sophie nearly fell off the bench, her mind spinning. "Wait, it was all a ploy? Do you know how ridiculous that was? I was nearly heartbroken—" She sucked in a breath. "But what about when she ran off with the groom to Gretna Green? You were prepared to go through with the marriage."

He lifted a brow in what she recognized as a *Have you not figured it out yet?* gesture. "Sophie, who do you think provided them with the means and the carriage with which to elope?"

She pushed his shoulder. "Quint! I cannot believe you are just now telling me this. After all this time—"

"I never wanted you to know. The plan failed and drove you further away from me. I was an idiot. I thought I'd lost you for good, which is why I left and traveled the Continent."

"What if I had married someone else?"

"But you didn't," he pointed out, logically.

"But I might have," she snapped.

In a blink, he lifted her up and over onto his lap, strong arms holding her in place. "Then I would have found a way to stop it in time." The earnestness in his expression and his voice touched her heart. She believed him. Cupping his head, she brought him down for a bone-melting kiss.

He pulled back too soon, grinning in response to

the frustrated glare she gave him. "Six days, *kotyonok*. You can last."

"I still say no one will know."

"I will know. And so will you." He gently drew a hand over her short curls. "You are more than a willing bed partner to me. You are my life, Sophie."

Hard to complain when he put it so sweetly. She leaned into him, rested her hand on his chest above his steady heartbeat. "Stubborn man," she muttered, though it came out more like a breathy compliment.

"You've been strangely quiet on things other than plans for the wedding. What is next for Sir Stephen?"

She arched to see his face. "I hadn't thought . . . that is, you don't mind if after we're married . . . ?"

"Did you think I would stop you?" His gorgeous, full lips turned into a frown. "Why on earth would I do that?"

"But you said it was dangerous. I assumed you would want me safe at home."

"I do want you safe at home, but that would make you unhappy, I think. I want you to have a life of your own, Sophie. There may come a time when—"

"Do not say it," she said, sharply.

He sighed. "Stubborn woman," he returned.

"How do you feel?"

His wife crawled lazily up his body, her hand sweeping across his sweaty chest as Quint tried to catch his breath. "Amazing," he said, then opened his eyes. "Happy."

The wedding had gone smoothly this morning. A small number of friends and family had gathered at his town house for the ceremony and a lavish wedding breakfast had followed. Sophie had been beautiful in her elaborate yet simple rose-colored gown, and he'd hardly been able to take his eyes off her all day. As soon as he'd managed it, he'd dispatched their guests, snatched his new bride, and rushed her up to their chambers.

Night had fallen, but neither of them had noticed. Sophie was now giving him her impish half-smile, her lips red and swollen from the previous moment's activity. "Good. I plan to keep you happy."

"Indeed, I am a very fortunate man." He reached for her and took her mouth in a blazing, thorough kiss. "How do you feel?"

"Frustrated," she said, rubbing against him. "Like I want my new husband to pleasure me again."

"I'll need a few moments, then." Though likely not as long as usual. In addition to finally having Sophie back in his bed after nearly a month, she'd insisted on foregoing the condoms. He'd tried to argue, but she had been persuasive, reminding him that his father's condition had most likely been the result of an accident. It was the first time he'd ever slid into a woman without one, and the overwhelming, blissful sensation meant he hadn't lasted long. Twice.

She leaned in to nip his earlobe. "Tell me about my ring again," she whispered against the shell of his ear, causing him to shiver.

Satisfaction flooded him, pulling his chest tight. She had loved the ring, as evidenced by the tears in her eyes when he'd presented her with the gold band of multicolored stones. He'd worried that she wouldn't care for it, that it was too much for a practical woman like Sophie. Happily, he'd been proven wrong.

He lifted her hand, the one that now wore proof of their marriage. "It's an acrostic ring. Each stone is the first letter of the word." He pointed, starting at the far left. "Vermeil. Iris. Topaz. Amethyst. Then malachite. Emerald. Aquamarine." He kissed her hand. "*Vita mea.*"

My life, properly translated into Latin, but Romans had used it to mean *my everything.* Which was precisely how he felt about the woman lying next to him.

Sophie stared at it and bit her lip. "I do not think I shall ever tire of looking at it. Or hearing you explain it."

"I'm glad." He settled her into his side. "Before I forget, Julia brought a wedding gift for you and said I needed to give it to you tonight."

Sophie's head turned sharply. Quint knew Sophie's relationship with her closest friend had been strained after all the recent revelations. His wife had tried not to let it show, but Quint knew her better than anyone. Not being on level ground with the duchess had upset her. "What is it?"

"I haven't the faintest idea. It's in the drawer."

Sophie scrambled to the small table by the bed and withdrew a box from the drawer. Sitting up, she untied the silk ribbon and lifted the lid. Quint peeked over to see a stack of letters inside. On top was a piece of paper, which Sophie picked up to read.

After a moment, she began laughing.

"Well?" he asked.

Sophie wiped the corners of her eyes. "It's the advice Pearl Kelly gave Julia about men, from when she was trying to woo Colton as a courtesan. Ages ago, she promised to let me read Pearl's notes when I finally set my sights on a man."

"So why give them now, when you've already caught him?"

"She said just because I've married you doesn't

Joanna Shupe

mean I cannot teach you a thing or two. Julia claims there are tricks in here even Colton had not heard about."

"Good God," Quint exclaimed. "Now I am curious."

Sophie set the letters aside. "Not tonight, my dear husband. I plan to read those alone and surprise you whenever I can."

He clasped her wrist and tugged. She landed on top of him. "With you, my darling wife, I would expect nothing less."

Don't miss the other books in Joanna Shupe's
Wicked Deceptions series, now available!

The Courtesan Duchess

Can a bold-faced lie lead to everlasting love? One by one,
the impetuous heroines in the Wicked Deceptions series
intend to find out, each in her unique way . . .

How to seduce an estranged husband—and banish
debt!—in four wickedly improper, shockingly pleasurable steps . . .

1. Learn the most intimate secrets of London's
   leading courtesan.
2. Pretend to be a courtesan yourself, using the
   name Juliet Leighton.
3. Travel to Venice and locate said husband.
4. Seduce husband, conceive an heir, and *voila,*
   your future is secure!

For Julia, the Duchess of Colton, such a ruse promises
to be foolproof. After all, her husband has not bothered to lay eyes on her in eight years, since their hasty
wedding day when she was only sixteen. But what
begins as a tempestuous flirtation escalates into full-
blown passion—and the feeling is mutual. Could the
man the Courtesan Duchess married actually turn out
to be the love of her life?

"The powerful passion in this riveting tale of
betrayal and forgiveness will knock your socks off!"
—SABRINA JEFFRIES

The Harlot Countess

*Lady Maggie Hawkins's debut was something
she'd rather forget—along with her first marriage.
Today, the political cartoonist is a new woman.
A thoroughly* modern *woman.
So much so that her clamoring public
believes she's a man . . .*

FACT: Drawing under a male pseudonym, Maggie is
known as Lemarc. Her (his!) favorite object of
ridicule: Simon Barrett, Earl of Winchester. He's a
rising star in Parliament—and a former confidant and
love interest of Maggie's who believed a rumor that
vexes her to this day.

FICTION: Maggie is the Half-Irish Harlot who seduced
her best friend's husband on the eve of their wedding.
She is to be feared and loathed as she will lift her
skirts for anything in breeches.

Still crushed by Simon's betrayal, Maggie has no
intention of letting the *ton* crush her as well. In fact,
Lemarc's cartoons have made Simon a laughing-
stock . . . but now it appears that Maggie may have
been wrong about what happened years ago, and that
Simon has been secretly yearning for her since . . .
forever. Could it be that the heart is mightier than the
pen *and* the sword after all?

GREAT BOOKS,
GREAT SAVINGS!

When You Visit Our Website:
www.kensingtonbooks.com
You Can Save Money Off The Retail Price
Of Any Book You Purchase!

- All Your Favorite Kensington Authors
- New Releases & Timeless Classics
- Overnight Shipping Available
- eBooks Available For Many Titles
- All Major Credit Cards Accepted

Visit Us Today To Start Saving!
www.kensingtonbooks.com

All Orders Are Subject To Availability.
Shipping and Handling Charges Apply.
Offers and Prices Subject To Change Without Notice.

Romantic Suspense from
Lisa Jackson

Absolute Fear	0-8217-7936-2	$7.99US/$9.99CAN
Afraid to Die	1-4201-1850-1	$7.99US/$9.99CAN
Almost Dead	0-8217-7579-0	$7.99US/$10.99CAN
Born to Die	1-4201-0278-8	$7.99US/$9.99CAN
Chosen to Die	1-4201-0277-X	$7.99US/$10.99CAN
Cold Blooded	1-4201-2581-8	$7.99US/$8.99CAN
Deep Freeze	0-8217-7296-1	$7.99US/$10.99CAN
Devious	1-4201-0275-3	$7.99US/$9.99CAN
Fatal Burn	0-8217-7577-4	$7.99US/$10.99CAN
Final Scream	0-8217-7712-2	$7.99US/$10.99CAN
Hot Blooded	1-4201-0678-3	$7.99US/$9.49CAN
If She Only Knew	1-4201-3241-5	$7.99US/$9.99CAN
Left to Die	1-4201-0276-1	$7.99US/$10.99CAN
Lost Souls	0-8217-7938-9	$7.99US/$10.99CAN
Malice	0-8217-7940-0	$7.99US/$10.99CAN
The Morning After	1-4201-3370-5	$7.99US/$9.99CAN
The Night Before	1-4201-3371-3	$7.99US/$9.99CAN
Ready to Die	1-4201-1851-X	$7.99US/$9.99CAN
Running Scared	1-4201-0182-X	$7.99US/$10.99CAN
See How She Dies	1-4201-2584-2	$7.99US/$8.99CAN
Shiver	0-8217-7578-2	$7.99US/$10.99CAN
Tell Me	1-4201-1854-4	$7.99US/$9.99CAN
Twice Kissed	0-8217-7944-3	$7.99US/$9.99CAN
Unspoken	1-4201-0093-9	$7.99US/$9.99CAN
Whispers	1-4201-5158-4	$7.99US/$9.99CAN
Wicked Game	1-4201-0338-5	$7.99US/$9.99CAN
Wicked Lies	1-4201-0339-3	$7.99US/$9.99CAN
Without Mercy	1-4201-0274-5	$7.99US/$10.99CAN
You Don't Want to Know	1-4201-1853-6	$7.99US/$9.99CAN

Available Wherever Books Are Sold!
Visit our website at www.kensingtonbooks.com

Books by Bestselling Author
Fern Michaels

___The Jury	0-8217-7878-1	$6.99US/$9.99CAN
___Sweet Revenge	0-8217-7879-X	$6.99US/$9.99CAN
___Lethal Justice	0-8217-7880-3	$6.99US/$9.99CAN
___Free Fall	0-8217-7881-1	$6.99US/$9.99CAN
___Fool Me Once	0-8217-8071-9	$7.99US/$10.99CAN
___Vegas Rich	0-8217-8112-X	$7.99US/$10.99CAN
___Hide and Seek	1-4201-0184-6	$6.99US/$9.99CAN
___Hokus Pokus	1-4201-0185-4	$6.99US/$9.99CAN
___Fast Track	1-4201-0186-2	$6.99US/$9.99CAN
___Collateral Damage	1-4201-0187-0	$6.99US/$9.99CAN
___Final Justice	1-4201-0188-9	$6.99US/$9.99CAN
___Up Close and Personal	0-8217-7956-7	$7.99US/$9.99CAN
___Under the Radar	1-4201-0683-X	$6.99US/$9.99CAN
___Razor Sharp	1-4201-0684-8	$7.99US/$10.99CAN
___Yesterday	1-4201-1494-8	$5.99US/$6.99CAN
___Vanishing Act	1-4201-0685-6	$7.99US/$10.99CAN
___Sara's Song	1-4201-1493-X	$5.99US/$6.99CAN
___Deadly Deals	1-4201-0686-4	$7.99US/$10.99CAN
___Game Over	1-4201-0687-2	$7.99US/$10.99CAN
___Sins of Omission	1-4201-1153-1	$7.99US/$10.99CAN
___Sins of the Flesh	1-4201-1154-X	$7.99US/$10.99CAN
___Cross Roads	1-4201-1192-2	$7.99US/$10.99CAN

Available Wherever Books Are Sold!
Check out our website at **www.kensingtonbooks.com**